"The beauty of Hawkins's writing is that even when it moves into the magical—and rest assured that it does—the emotions of the characters are authentic. Every scene, no matter how far from daily reality, is rooted in kindness and friendship, the belief we can all be better, and the hope that starting over is possible. *A Cup of Silver Linings* is the perfect way to spend an afternoon, teacup in hand, dreaming about what could be."

—*Manhattan Book Review*

"The literary equivalent of warm custard or fuzzy socks.... For readers who enjoy the warmth and Southern authenticity of Fannie Flagg novels mixed with a dollop of Sarah Addison Allen–style magical realism."

—*The Augusta Chronicle*

THE BOOK CHARMER

A LibraryReads Pick
A SIBA Okra Pick
A *Woman's World* Book Club Pick

"Entrancing! Fans of *Practical Magic* and *Garden Spells* will love this book."

—*New York Times* bestselling author Susan Andersen

"Hawkins has created a delightfully quirky town.... Reminiscent of Sarah Addison Allen, Abbi Waxman, and Fannie Flagg, this is a great summer read for those who love small Southern towns filled with magic."

—*Booklist*

Also available from Karen Hawkins and Gallery Books

A Cup of Silver Linings

The Book Charmer

THE
SECRET
RECIPE

of

ELLA
DOVE

KAREN HAWKINS

G

GALLERY BOOKS

NEW YORK   LONDON   TORONTO   SYDNEY   NEW DELHI

G

Gallery Books
An Imprint of Simon & Schuster, Inc.
1230 Avenue of the Americas
New York, NY 10020

First Gallery Books trade paperback edition August 2023

GALLERY BOOKS and colophon are registered trademarks of Simon & Schuster, Inc.

For information about special discounts for bulk purchases, please contact Simon & Schuster Special Sales at 1-866-506-1949 or business@simonandschuster.com.

The Simon & Schuster Speakers Bureau can bring authors to your live event. For more information or to book an event, contact the Simon & Schuster Speakers Bureau at 1-866-248-3049 or visit our website at www.simonspeakers.com.

Interior design by Jaime Putorti

Manufactured in the United States of America

10 9 8 7 6 5 4 3 2 1

Library of Congress Cataloging-in-Publication Data

Names: Hawkins, Karen, author.
Title: The secret recipe of Ella Dove : a novel / Karen Hawkins.
Description: First Gallery Books trade paperback edition. | New York : Gallery Books, 2023
Identifiers: LCCN 2023001195 (print) | LCCN 2023001196 (ebook) | ISBN 9781982195939 | ISBN 9781982195922 (pbk) | ISBN 9781982195953 (ebook)
Subjects: LCGFT: Novels.
Classification: LCC PS3558.A8231647 S43 2023 (print) | LCC PS3558.A8231647 (ebook) | DDC 813/.6—dc23/eng/20230117
LC record available at https://lccn.loc.gov/2023001195
LC ebook record available at https://lccn.loc.gov/2023001196

ISBN 978-1-9821-9593-9
ISBN 978-1-9821-9592-2 (pbk)
ISBN 978-1-9821-9595-3 (ebook)

To Nate, a.k.a. Cap'n Hot Cop.
If I had a penny for each time you made me laugh,
that pile of pennies would dwarf Mt. Everest.
Thank you for being there. For being present.
And for all the hugs and laughs.
Thou and I, my love.

PROLOGUE

ELLA

Baking is love. Every carefully measured teaspoon,
every delicious dash of spice, every tantalizing aroma,
is a gift of pure sensory passion.

The Book of Cakes, p. 13
Written: 1792–2019

It's a sad fact of life that in very large, very noisy families filled with big personalities, it's possible for a quieter, more solitary child to get lost. During her seventh year, Ella Dove was that child. It was the year after her father died, and Ella was deeply, deeply unhappy. So unhappy that one day, she decided to run away from home.

Ella loved her momma and, yes, all six of her usually annoying sisters. But before she was born, her four older sisters had paired up—Madison and Alexandra, Taylor and Cara. They were each other's closest, best friends. Then Ella was born. And as patterns had already formed, she became the leftover child.

A few years later, Ella had gotten super excited when Momma and Daddy announced there was another baby on the way. Ella had hoped that her new sister would become her best friend, but it didn't happen. Ava hated being indoors and was flower-crazy from the time she could crawl. Meanwhile, Ella preferred the coziness of the kitchen, where she and Dad made the meals for their growing family.

Of all the Dove girls, Ella was closest to their father, who'd made her his "special assistant" in the kitchen. Ella knew that in some families, mothers did the cooking, but Dad used to say that Momma had her hands full raising so many children and that the least he could do was cook. He was really, *really* good at it too, and created the most amazing meals for them. The hours Ella spent with her dad in the kitchen were some of the happiest of her life.

Which was why, after he died, Ella was left with a void in her heart that was so big, she feared she might fall into it and be lost forever. Loneliness, by itself, is a horrible, wretched state of affairs. But loneliness in the middle of a crowd is a million times worse. And Ella felt every inch of its brutal weight. It was only made harder a few months later by the arrival of baby Sarah. Although Ella and the rest of the family doted on Sarah, her arrival made Ella all the more aware of their dad's absence.

One day in late January, after a particularly difficult day at the end of an especially horrible week, Ella dumped her textbooks and school papers out of her bright orange backpack and refilled it with clothes, a toothbrush, her dad's favorite cookbook, and what little allowance she'd managed to save.

She had a plan, of a sort. She'd walk to the bus stop at the edge of town and use the $12.50 she'd saved from her weekly allowance to buy a ticket to take her as far away as possible. She loved her family, but a new place would give her a fresh start.

So, with her book bag slung across her shoulders, she headed down Elm Street and then turned onto Main, her breath puffing white as the skies turned gray. To her irritation, her book bag seemed to grow heavier with every step. Worse, by the time she reached Pickens Bridge Road, it had started to snow, the icy wetness freezing her chin and nose.

Ella lowered her head and set her jaw. *If I can just make it onto the bus, I can—*

"Ella Dove! What are you *doing*?" Aunt Jo leaned out the window of her old Chevy. Snow fell inside, melting as it landed on her round black cheeks and bright red coat. "It's *snowing*!"

Ella's heart sank. "Aunt Jo" wasn't Ella's real aunt. That was just what everyone in town called her. Since Dad's death, Aunt Jo and Momma—who'd always been close—had gotten even closer. Momma said Aunt Jo made an art out of being where she was most needed. "Momma sent you."

"Of course she sent me! She can't leave your sisters alone just to come looking for you, especially now that she has the baby. You know that."

Ella fisted her hands around her backpack straps. "You can't make me go back."

Aunt Jo's expression softened. "Ella girl, it's been a tough year for you and your family. I know that. But running away won't make things better."

"You don't know that."

"I do know that." When Ella didn't move, Aunt Jo sighed. "At least do it when the weather's better."

Ella had to admit she was cold and tired, and her pack felt as if it were filled with rocks.

Aunt Jo hit the unlock button and jerked her head toward the passenger side. "Get in. Your poor momma has enough on her plate right now without this."

Ella's lips quivered. "She'll be better off without me."

"You don't believe that, and neither do I. Come on, Ella. The Moonlight Café just called in an order, so I need to get home and start baking, and I'm not leaving until you come with me."

Momma had always said that if Aunt Jo had enough bakery orders, she could get out of the housekeeping business that was so hard on her aging back and knees, so Ella knew how important this order was. Defeated, her eyes burning from both the snow and the weight of her own sadness, Ella trudged around to the other side of Aunt Jo's car and got in. They were soon on their way, creeping along the slick streets.

"So." Aunt Jo slanted Ella a direct look. "What's going on? Did you have a fight with one of your sisters?"

"No."

Aunt Jo didn't look convinced. "Did your momma say something that upset you? You know she hasn't been herself of late."

Ella knew Momma was having a rough time. Everyone in town was talking about how sad it was that now that Dad was gone, Momma'd had to have baby Sarah alone. But Momma hadn't been alone. Ella and her sisters were there, and they were all helping with the new baby. "It wasn't that."

"Then what was it? What sent you out into this horrible weather?"

There were so many reasons. She felt alone and lost, which seemed easy enough to say, but whenever she tried to explain herself, her words seemed to tangle up.

Aunt Jo's gaze flickered over Ella's face. Ella didn't know what Aunt Jo saw there, but she suddenly said, "You miss your daddy."

Ella could handle anything but sympathy. Her eyes burned even more, and she feared that if she let herself cry, she might never stop.

Aunt Jo turned her attention back to the road, although it was obvious the older woman was thinking. Finally, she slowed the car to a stop, the wheels sliding a little in the snow. "Tell you what. *If* your mom says it's okay, how about spending the night at my house?"

It was tempting. Outside, the snow pelted the car, the frosty ice flakes hitting the window. Why not go to Aunt Jo's house? It was better than going home, where Ella would just feel miserable all over again. "I would like that."

"Good. Let's go before these roads get worse." Aunt Jo put the car back into gear and slowly turned it around.

They reached Aunt Jo's soon enough, a larger-than-it-seemed butter-yellow clapboard house, frosted with snow, that sat beside a huge oak tree at the edge of town. Aunt Jo pulled two shopping bags out of the back seat and then bumped the car door closed with one of her generous hips. Ella collected her book bag and followed Aunt Jo inside.

"Stay on that mat," Aunt Jo ordered as she shrugged out of her red coat. "You're wetter than a cat dunked in a pond. I'll get you a towel."

Ella dropped her book bag beside the door, hung her soggy coat on the hook next to it, and took off her boots. Madison always said Aunt Jo's house was as colorful as a box of crayons. She wasn't kidding; every room was a different color. The living room was a bright, warm shade of peach, the hall yellow, and the dining room green. Added in was a colorful assortment of chairs, pillows, and rugs. *It really is like a box of crayons.*

But as pretty as it was, the best part of Aunt Jo's house was that it smelled like vanilla pound cake. Ella closed her eyes and took a deep breath, soaking in the delicious scent.

Aunt Jo came back downstairs and handed Ella a towel. "Dry your hair. It's gone rat's nest on you." She chuckled, her warm brown eyes twinkling. "Your oldest sister would be horrified."

Even before Dad died, Madison had started getting weird about her appearance, which had turned her into a harsh critic of her less interested sisters. Ella dried her hair with the towel. "She's always cranky."

"It's been a tough year for all of you, especially your poor momma. She's raising you and your sisters by herself, and doing it while they're finding out about their—" Aunt Jo clamped her mouth closed and cast a wary glance at Ella.

Ella had seen that cautious look all too often lately. The Doves weren't like other families. Everyone knew that whenever the Dove family had seven daughters, they developed abilities that would allow good things to happen to their little town. Dad had told stories about their ancestors doing just that, which had delighted Ella and her sisters.

Her favorite was about the great wheat shortage of 1872, which had been caused by an invasion of cutworms, dark and hungry insects. At the time, the Dove family had had seven daughters and one of them, Emily Anne, had had the ability to draw songbirds to her like moths to a flame. Everywhere she went, birds fluttered nearby, singing their songs from the trees overhead and trilling their secrets outside her bedroom window.

At the request of the town, Emily Anne was sent out to skip through the fields of wheat, and her songbird friends fluttered after her, snacking on cutworms as they went. The rest of the South might have been devastated by the wheat shortage, but not Dove Pond.

Dad had dozens of stories like that, and Ella and her sisters used to beg him to repeat them. Now that he'd passed, Momma had taken on that job, sharing the history of the Dove family as if she'd been born into it. Aunt Jo had helped. She was one of the biggest believers in the Dove family lore, and she often said she hadn't been a bit surprised when, directly after Sarah's birth, all four of Ella's older sisters had discovered their special abilities.

Madison could tell how a person felt with a single touch. Alex could calm a wild animal simply by humming, while Tay could tell all sorts of things about a person just by holding something they'd written. Then, just last week, Cara had realized she could read people's romantic futures, prompting Aunt Jo to call her a "love guru."

Meanwhile, nothing unusual had happened for Ella, which was agonizing. Momma didn't seem worried and had pointed out that neither of Ella's younger sisters had yet found their special abilities either. They all would, Momma had said—it just took time. Still, Ella couldn't help but wonder. She wasn't like her sisters. Not even a little. What if she wasn't special and they were?

Suddenly tired, Ella sighed and half-heartedly continued to dry her hair with the towel.

"When you're done, come to the kitchen." Aunt Jo retrieved her shopping bags and headed for a red swinging door. "I'll call your momma and let her know you're here."

The door hadn't yet stopped swinging when Ella heard the older woman on the phone. Ella tossed the damp towel over a chair and went into the kitchen just as Aunt Jo set her phone aside and started unpacking her shopping bags. The kitchen was even more colorful than the other rooms. The walls were a light turquoise, the cabinets green, and the linoleum a dull gold, while the counter was a breath-taking ocean blue. Here and there sat colorful crockery and glassware. The whole room made Ella think of peacocks.

She slid onto an empty stool at the counter. "What are we making?"

"Two kinds of scones—cranberry-and-pecan, and vanilla with vanilla bean icing—a buttermilk pie, and ten pieces of apple cake with caramel drizzle." Aunt Jo pulled out some mixing bowls. "You always helped your dad in the kitchen, so you can help me."

"He taught me how to follow a recipe."

"Then you're an expert." Aunt Jo dragged a stool to the counter. "Let's get to work."

The next hour flew by. Aunt Jo's kitchen was warm, organized, and purposeful, much like the woman herself. Ella found herself sinking gratefully into that organized warmth, which was accompanied by the delicious scents and tastes of cinnamon, sugar, and toasted pecans.

"This caramel needs watching." Aunt Jo gave the scones in the oven a last look before she slid the stool beside the stove for Ella. "When the thermometer reaches 345 degrees, call me. I have to take it off the eye at 345 'cause it'll cook a little longer before we cool it with the vanilla mixture." She reached into the refrigerator, poured some cream into a measuring cup, and then added a pinch of salt and a strong dash of vanilla from a mason jar. "We'll add this when it's ready. While you watch the caramel, I'll peel the apples for the cake."

Aunt Jo left Ella at the stove, chatting over her shoulder as she worked, rambling about how proud she was of her homemade, moonshine-based vanilla. Every minute or so, she'd come to the stove, pick up the pan, and slowly swirl the caramel. "You have to swirl it low and slow, see? If you get the caramel on the cooler sides of the pan, it'll crystalize and—" A beeper sounded, and she replaced the pan on the burner and pulled the scones from the oven, which caused the room to flood with the scent of vanilla. Still chatting, Aunt Jo went to slide the scones onto a cooling rack while Ella turned her attention back to her task.

The caramel, a beautiful golden pool in the silver pan, sent up faint curls of steam that tickled Ella's nose. Somehow, she found herself drawn to the spices in the rack beside the stove. She reached over and trailed her fingers over the jars, the glass cool under her fingertips. As she touched the final jar, a tingle zapped her fingers. She yanked her hand back and stared at her fingers, and then looked back at the jar. *What was that?*

She slowly reached up again. The second her fingers touched the smooth glass, her fingers zapped again, and her heart started racing. She didn't pull her hand away but picked up the jar and read the label. *Cardamom*, it said. She twisted off the lid and sniffed cautiously.

Instantly, a sweep of elation ran through her, and she knew without question that the caramel needed this spice. Not much. But enough.

She glanced over her shoulder at Aunt Jo and wondered if she should ask permission first, but Aunt Jo was balanced rather precariously on a stepladder as she slid her jar of vanilla back into a cabinet. She was talking to herself, too, planning the next steps for the apple cake.

Ella turned back to the stove and, without giving herself time to question it further, sprinkled a pinch of cardamom over the caramel.

Instantly, the aroma changed, the delicious scent deepening. Ella's smile widened as she replaced the cardamom in the rack, a deep peace settling over her like a warm blanket. For one blissful moment, she knew without a doubt that everything was exactly how it should be.

Smiling, she glanced at the thermometer. "This is ready."

Aunt Jo was there in a second. She turned off the heat and slid the pan to a trivet. With a smooth, practiced move, she added the waiting cup of cream, vanilla, and salt she'd readied earlier. She stirred it all together and then poured the entire mixture into a waiting bowl to cool.

Ella cut a stealthy glance at Aunt Jo. *She didn't notice—*

Aunt Jo frowned. She bent down and sniffed the caramel. Her eyes narrowed. "Ella Dove, what have you done?"

Oh no. Swallowing hard, Ella reluctantly pointed to the cardamom jar.

Aunt Jo's eyebrows lowered. "You don't add things without asking."

"I know, but—" Ella gave a helpless shrug. "It was needed."

Grumbling loudly, Aunt Jo fished a spoon out of a drawer. She took a small scoop of the caramel and blew on it, muttering, "I should have been watching," between breaths. After the caramel had cooled enough, she slid the spoon between her lips.

Her eyebrows knitted as her gaze returned to Ella. "How much did you add?"

Ella mimicked a pinch.

"Well, I'll be. It's good." Aunt Jo licked the spoon as she shook her head in wonder. "Perfect, even. You have a gift for flavors. I—" She chuckled, her gaze suddenly soft. "My momma used to make chocolate-covered caramels when I was a tiny thing. She made them every Easter and the whole house would smell like this. Like happiness."

As Aunt Jo smiled, Ella's heart eased even more. Somehow, she knew the gentle memory was because of the cardamom.

"I declare, but I haven't thought of that in years." Aunt Jo gave a final chuckle and dropped the spoon onto the counter. "I remember those days so well now. The memories are so vivid, so real. It almost feels like I'm really there, like I'm hearing her voice and smelling that—" Her gaze fell on Ella, and she stopped, her eyes widening. "Ella! We may have found your special ability."

Ella blinked, her mind jangling with a thousand thoughts. Maybe, just maybe, she was special after all.

One of Aunt Jo's timers rang and they were pulled back into the rhythm of their baking. They spent the next hour finishing up, every moment busy and peaceful. Afterward, Aunt Jo made them grilled cheese sandwiches from homemade sourdough bread and thick slices of cheddar. While they ate, Ella thought about all the things she might be able to do with her gift, and wondered what it might mean for her future.

Later that night, after the Moonlight's order had been wrapped and the kitchen cleaned, Ella put on the big T-shirt Aunt Jo had lent her to use for pajamas. Too excited to sleep, Ella had leaned against the guest room window. She pressed her cheek to the cold glass, her breath making a perfect circle of fog. Something had changed. She still missed Dad, but the emptiness had lessened. In its place was the promise of something new, a beginning of a sort. In Aunt Jo's kitchen, Ella had found her place.

When she grew up, she would bake things in ways no one ever had, and people would pay her hundreds of dollars just to taste her desserts. Then she'd be free to travel and find real happiness somewhere out there in the world. Somewhere away from the memories that weighed her down here in Dove Pond.

But she had a lot to learn before that time came. Stifling a yawn, Ella turned from the window and climbed into the soft, creaky bed. She snuggled into the pile of pillows and pulled the blankets up to her chin. For now, she'd enjoy being here, in Aunt Jo's house, which was filled with warmth, a jumble of bright colors, and the delicious smell of caramel apple cake.

CHAPTER 1

ELLA

*Food brings people together, warms the heart,
and feeds the soul.*

The Book of Cakes, p. 21
Written: 1792–2019

Ella Dove came home on a lazy, scorching, bee-buzzed evening. As she turned her rental car off Interstate 40, her phone rang. Sighing, she hit the answer button on her car screen. "Hi, Tiff. What's up?"

Tiffany Harper, a fresh-faced social media whiz, had been Ella's assistant for five years now. Tiff and her team of production experts were worth every penny of the hefty amount Ella paid them too. "Are you home yet?" Tiff asked in her way-too-perky voice. No matter the circumstances, she always sounded as if she were about to announce she'd just won the lottery.

"Almost." Ella turned onto a small country road and rolled her aching shoulders. The last eighteen hours had been brutal. Just this morning, she'd stuffed as much as she could into her two largest suitcases, handed the keys to her Paris patisserie with its adorable apartment upstairs to its new owner, jumped into a cab, and headed for the airport. From there, she'd flown for ten long and bumpy hours to Atlanta, where she'd picked up the rental car Tiff had reserved, a feisty red Lexus. Now, after five hours of driving, Ella was almost home, jet-lagged to the bone, and already jonesing to leave. "I need a nap."

"I bet," Tiff said with sympathy. "But I thought you'd want to know that Matt from Ferndale Farms called. They're worried about your content now that you've moved stateside."

Ella grimaced. She would be so glad when her contractual obligation to Ferndale Farms was over. The name "Ferndale Farms" might make people think of cozy little farms set in the sunny countryside, but it was actually a huge multinational food syndicate. When Ferndale had bought her small Ella Dove Pie Company for a price she couldn't refuse, they'd offered a huge bonus if she agreed to do a brand partnership with them for two years. In the beginning, the extra social posts had seemed harmless enough—especially because she already had Tiff and her team to help produce content for her growing accounts—but sheesh, Matt was a pain. "How much longer are we obligated to them?"

"Let's see. This is August fifth, so . . . six months, one week, and two days."

Ella smiled. "You knew I was going to ask."

"Who wouldn't? I told Matt his target audience—your over two million followers on the Gram and four million plus on TikTok—would love the new content. Small towns are 'in' right now."

"It *is* a pretty town," Ella admitted grudgingly.

"Charming. Speaking of content, what do you have planned? We need something fresh."

"Content. Right. I'll make a cake first thing tomorrow." Just the thought of baking eased the tension in Ella's shoulders. Tired as she was, her soul itched to get back into the kitchen. "Maybe a lemon pound cake."

"And?" When Ella didn't answer, Tiff sighed. "What do I always say about content?"

Ella tried not to roll her eyes and failed. "'Cakes alone won't do it. You have to share bits of your life, too.'" She hated that, but Tiff was right. The metrics didn't lie.

To be honest, Ella couldn't believe she could make so much money just by sharing videos of her making cakes mixed with casual glimpses of her so-called baking life. Ella had made a small fortune thanks to the sponsorships Tiff and her team had managed to line up, which had allowed her to develop her brand far more quickly than other bakers. "Maybe I could do a time lapse of me setting up the kitchen at my old house with my favorite kitchen tools." At this very moment, a large yellow suitcase in the trunk of her car held her favorite cookbooks, three special aprons, a crazy-expensive Japanese knife, her favorite rolling pin, some unique cookie cutters, and more.

"Ohhh, that could be fun. Paul could do something cool with that."

"Paul's video editing skills are sick. He can make dust look interesting." Ella would rather produce content at the old Dove home than wander around town anyway. Being a Dove in Dove Pond inspired the exact kind of expectations she hated. People watched her as if she might wave a wand and make all their dreams come true. Her magic was in her cooking, in making a cake that could allow a person to relive a prized, sometimes-forgotten memory. When compared to her sisters' abilities, her magic seemed pretty tame.

"Terrific!" Tiff said. "And get some vid of your sister Ava's Pink Magnolia Tearoom. I saw the website and it's perfection."

"Sure," Ella said. "I'll go down there tomorrow and—" There, right above her wrist, rested a vivid slash of pink strawberry frosting that hadn't been there a second before. Her heart sank. *Stupid frosting.* She swallowed. "I'll get that content to you ASAP."

"Great. We can't wait to see what you come up with."

Ella ended the call and reached for her tote bag from where it sat on the passenger seat. She pushed aside a wrinkled newspaper, pulled out a napkin, and cleaned the frosting from her wrist.

She'd told Tiff she was coming home to take care of some family matters, but that was a lie. Over the past four months, she'd been plagued by annoying dreams in which she was chased by a giant, silver-papered cupcake with strawberry frosting. In every dream, the huge cupcake chased her through the tree-lined streets of Dove Pond to the highest point of Hill Street. The dream always ended with her standing alone and terrified in front of the Stewart house.

She might have been able to ignore those dreams, but every time she had one, sometime after the dream had ended, strawberry frosting would appear somewhere on her arms or legs. Sometimes it showed up as a plump rose, perfectly made, as if ready for a wedding cake. Sometimes, like just now, it showed up in a long, delicate curlicue. The frosting was always pink, always smelled like strawberry, and was always annoying. And it was why she'd come back to Dove Pond. There was only one person who might understand what was going on.

She turned her car down Main Street and fell in behind a faded blue pickup truck. The sun shimmered on the hot asphalt as a faint breeze rippled through the stifling air and flapped the red awnings that adorned the storefronts, the smell of heat, hay, and summer diesel hanging in the air. The early-evening sun warmed the small American flags still on the light poles from the July Fourth parade a month ago, and glinted off the plate glass fronts of the small stores she knew all too well.

People who didn't know Dove Pond would see only the names of the businesses, but she'd grown up here. She knew Paw Printz was "Maggie and Ed Mayhew's pet store" and the Ace Hardware was "Stevens's hardware," while the Moonlight Café was "Jules's place" and had the best meatloaf on earth.

Ella slowed down as she passed her sister Ava's new tearoom.

The old brick building featured a beautiful wrought-iron bow window filled with colorful pastel canisters of Ava's specialty teas. Ella absently wondered when she, or any of the other town residents, would drop the "new" part of "Ava's new tearoom." Probably never. The people of Dove Pond weren't the sort to embrace change. That was one of the many reasons Ella had left. She loved change. It kept her from drowning in boredom.

Sadly, Ava and Sarah didn't understand Ella's aversion to sameness. Their unbridled enthusiasm for Dove Pond and everything in it was as irritating as their heavy-handed attempts to convince Ella and her other sisters to move back home. Together, the two were as subtle as a dump truck rolling downhill without brakes.

Ella reached the end of the street, but instead of turning onto Elm Street toward the Dove house, she headed in the other direction. At the edge of town, the houses were smaller, had less trim, and were much farther apart. Ella turned off a windy, narrow road and into the driveway of a familiar yellow house.

Aunt Jo sat on her front porch, her cane leaning against the windowsill near her chair, her chunky bulldog Moon Pie asleep at her feet. Her colorful dress of blue and pink flowers clashed with her fluffy purple slippers as she steadily snapped green beans from a brown paper bag into the yellow bowl in her lap.

Ella parked under the huge oak tree, grabbed her purse, and climbed out, the humidity stealing her breath. Whew. Paris got humid, but not southern US humid. She climbed up the stairs, loving that the porch floor was painted a deep aqua while the ceiling above was a familiar but welcome haint blue. "Good afternoon."

"You're late." Aunt Jo dropped some green beans into the bowl in her lap. "I expected you last week."

Ella dropped her bag beside a faded wicker chair and sat. "Sarah told you I was coming."

"She never said a word." Aunt Jo snapped a bean in half with a bit more force than necessary. Although she was sitting in the shade, she shone with dampness, the humidity dewy on her dark skin. "You Doves aren't the only ones who know things."

Ella nodded toward the two glasses of lemonade sitting on the side table. "I hope one of those is for me."

"One is. This heat is something else." Aunt Jo pulled a handkerchief from her pocket and wiped her shiny brow, her eyes twinkling. "They say the water's so hot in Lake Fontana that the fish are jumping into boats fully cooked."

Ella laughed and took a sip of the lemonade. The drink was the perfect combination of tart and sweet. No one knew flavors better than Aunt Jo. "Don't order lemonade in France. You'll get a nasty beverage called citronade."

"France." Aunt Jo made a face. "Why did you have to move there, anyway?"

"A lot of reasons. It's beautiful."

Aunt Jo's gaze moved past Ella to the large fields around them where yellow and purple flowers dotted the green rye grass. "It's beautiful here, too."

"I know, but—" Ella shrugged. "I just wanted more. Not money or fame, but more . . . happiness, I suppose."

"You can't move to happiness. You have to find it where you're at so you can take it with you everywhere you go."

Ella tamped down her impatience. As if it were that easy to "find happiness." She forced a smile. "Plus I wanted to learn patisserie from the best."

"I could have taught you everything you needed to know right here."

Ella couldn't argue with that. Aunt Jo had a remarkable understanding of pastry, which Ella hadn't truly appreciated until she'd gone to cooking school and realized that, thanks to Aunt Jo, she already knew most of the methods that were taught. Ella swirled the lemonade in her glass, an icy drop splashing onto her knee. "I wish I could have taken Momma to Paris. She would have loved it."

Aunt Jo's eyes grew shiny. Moon Pie lifted his head and looked at Aunt Jo, who bent down and gave him another pat. "I still miss your momma. We were as different as day and night but had a lot in common. That's the mark of true friends. You're different and yet the same."

Ella couldn't argue with that. Momma'd had a heart condition—which eventually took her—and it had made her quiet and slow-moving. Meanwhile, Aunt Jo was as loud and powerful as a freight train. When she laughed, her round belly shook like a TV Santa Claus, and she laughed often. But while the two women had been physical opposites, both had strong, determined spirits.

Aunt Jo took a deep drink of her lemonade, a trickle of water dripping off the bottom of the glass and landing perilously close to Moon Pie's nose. "Your momma would have had a cow if she'd known some of her girls would up and move away."

"Ava and Sarah are still here."

"The rest of you aren't." Aunt Jo's gaze narrowed. "Do you even keep in touch with your sisters? Enough to know what's going on in their lives?"

"I know Ava's new tearoom has been a huge success and that Sarah's moved back in after their little tiff." Which hadn't been that little, although Ella and her other sisters had wisely stayed clear of the whole thing. "I also know that Sarah is dating the local sheriff, Blake McIntyre. It's about time they finally admitted they liked each other." Ella wasn't sure what was going on with the rest of her sisters, which she didn't want to admit. *I should give them a call while I'm here.* "Oh! I also heard that you're judging the First Baptist Bake-Off this year. That surprised me. You've always said you haven't seen crazy until you've seen First Baptist Bake-Off crazy."

There were two churches in Dove Pond—the First Baptist Church and the First Methodist Church. Most people went to one or the other, and due to the limited citizenship of their small town, the competition between the two churches had grown into something fierce over the years. That had made the bake-off a rather contentious event. Ella shook her head. "How did they rope you into that? Besides, I didn't think Bev Turnbull would ever give up her judge's seat."

"They caught her accepting a bribe. Twenty pounds of premium bacon."

"Whoa! What a scandal."

Aunt Jo nodded. "After an especially pointed sermon from Preacher Thompson about the evils of succumbing to enticements, she confessed all and resigned. After that, the preacher asked me to take over and I couldn't say no."

"Couldn't pawn it off on someone else?"

"Who? You?" Aunt Jo pinned Ella with a stern look. "You being a celebrity chef and all might turn people's attention away from the Bacon Bribery Scandal and focus on the actual competition."

"If I was going to be in town, I'd do it. But you don't need me, anyway; you'll be a terrific judge." Ella reached over and grabbed some beans from Aunt Jo's paper bag and began snapping them, dropping them into the bowl as she finished. "Just look at you, saving the day, as usual. This town would be lost without you."

Aunt Jo made a face. "It's hard to say no to Preacher Thompson. He looks as if he might be Idris Elba and Halle Berry's secret manchild."

Ella raised her eyebrows. "Why haven't I seen this guy?"

"Because you never stay long enough to visit new people, much less go to church. We could rectify that omission if you're of a mind. Come with me this Sunday."

That was only six days away. *Hmm. If I stay an extra week, then I could legitimately miss my annual Thanksgiving visit and kill two birds with one stone.*

Why not? It wasn't as if she had anything else to do. She didn't have much of a plan once she finished her mission here in Dove Pond. That was how she liked to do things. Overplanning took the fun out of life. Ella dropped another handful of snapped beans into Aunt Jo's bowl. "Sunday is a date."

Aunt Jo cut her a skeptical look. "Really?"

"Really. By the way, I brought you something." Ella reached for her purse and pulled out a small package. She handed it to Aunt Jo.

"What's this?" Aunt Jo undid the ribbon and opened the present. Inside the small box was a shiny cookie cutter. "This—why, this looks like my house!"

Ella nodded, pleased to see Aunt Jo's smile. "We're developing a line of Ella Dove kitchen utensils. I sent the company making our cookie cutters a picture of your house, and we're going to include it in the line."

"Well, well. That's nice." Aunt Jo placed the cutter back into the box and set it on the table at her elbow. "I've always loved this house."

"Me too." Ella grabbed some more beans from the brown paper bag at Aunt Jo's feet and went back to snapping them. "I wanted to give you that present, but I had another reason for visiting. Aunt Jo, I need your advice."

"Ask away. I like giving advice. It doesn't cost much."

Ella had to smile. "It's weird, but I keep having this dream and it always leaves me feeling lost, somehow."

"Oh?" Aunt Jo's hands fell back into a steady rhythm as she scooped up beans, snapped them, and then dropped them into her bowl. "How often have you had this dream?"

"Dozens of times. And it's always the same. I dream I'm here, in

Dove Pond, and I'm being chased up Hill Street by a huge cupcake with strawberry frosting."

"Does it catch you?"

"I don't know. I always wake up before that happens. But every time I have the dream, I find strawberry frosting on me the next day when I'm wide awake."

Aunt Jo's hands froze in place, her eyes widening. "Ohhh, Ella. That's not good."

Oh no. That was not the reaction Ella'd been hoping for. "It's just a weird dream, right?"

Aunt Jo set her bowl of beans to one side and leaned forward. "Your dream has crossed."

An uneasy feeling clutched Ella's stomach. "What do you mean 'crossed'?"

"It's moved from the dream world into reality. It expects you to do something."

Great. Just great. "Do what?"

"The dream will tell you what. If you want your dream to go away and that frosting to stop showing up, then you have to do whatever the dream wants."

Ella grimaced. "I was afraid of that."

Aunt Jo's eyebrows rose. "You know what the dream wants you to do."

"Maybe. In the dream, I always end up in front of the Stewart house. Angela Stewart Harrington and I had a dustup a few years back. It must be that."

Aunt Jo looked surprised. "You know Angela Harrington well enough to have had an argument with her? She's almost as old as I am."

"I went to high school with her grandsons, and they both played baseball, so I saw her when she'd come to town for team games. That's why I recognized her when I ran into her a few years ago on Fifth Avenue, when I was in New York teaching for Le Cordon Bleu."

"That's a big city. That's a chance meeting if there ever was one."

"I know, right? Maybe she was homesick for Dove Pond or was just being kind, but she invited me to spend the weekend at her house in the Hamptons. We had such a great time that it became a ritual. I spent almost every weekend that summer at her house with her, her husband John, and her grandsons. Sometimes her daughter, Jules, was there too."

Aunt Jo's eyes narrowed. "I heard you dated Gray at some point. I think Sarah mentioned it, or maybe Ava."

Ella shrugged. "He was at Angela's house, which was how we started talking, but it was nothing serious. Angela's the one I need to settle things with."

"Why do you think that?"

"Because of this." Ella reached back into her purse and pulled out a wrinkled newspaper. She handed it to Aunt Jo, pointing to a picture.

Aunt Jo's brow instantly furrowed. "That's Angela's second husband, John. He died a month ago."

"It's his obituary. He worked at the New York branch of a French bank. The article says Angela would be moving home to be with friends and family following the funeral." Ella took the newspaper back and looked at the picture of the handsome white-haired man. "He was always kind to me when I visited." She sighed and dropped the paper back into her purse. "About a week after I started having those dreams, that newspaper blew down the street and fell open to that exact page right at my feet."

"Then you did the right thing, coming here. What did you and Angela argue about?"

"She accused me of stealing a family heirloom."

Aunt Jo stiffened. "As if you'd do such a thing!"

"It made me furious, too." Ella still got mad when she remembered that day. It had been late evening and she'd come downstairs with her suitcase, ready to go back to the city. Unlike her normal visits, it had been a less-than-fun Sunday, because that was the day she'd broken up with Gray.

Dating Gray had been a mistake, but at the time it had just seemed like a fun summer fling. Or at least, that was all it had been to her. She should have known better; he was more intense and emotional than the men she usually flirted with. But he'd had a smile that she couldn't resist, and no man had made her laugh more.

On that day, still feeling a little down after facing Gray's hurt expression when she'd ended things, she'd gone through the kitchen on her way out and had found Angela and Jules arguing, their faces red. On seeing Ella, Jules had given her a hard, cold look and then stormed away.

Ella had assumed Jules must have discovered that Ella had broken up with Gray, but then Angela, looking tired and dispirited, had asked, "Where is it?"

"Where is what?"

Angela's mouth thinned. "The Book of Cakes has gone missing, and Jules is certain you took it." Angela had nodded toward Ella's suitcase. "Is it in there?"

Ella struggled to absorb the words. The prized possession of the Stewart family was an old, cherished cookbook filled with handwritten recipes from across the decades. Since most of the recipes were desserts, someone along the way had started calling it "the Book of Cakes" and the name had stuck. "Angela, I didn't take your cookbook. How can you even say that?"

"Fine. Then prove it." Angela, her back stiff, tapped her finger on the kitchen table. "Put your suitcase here. I want to see what's in it."

Ella simmered, but she yanked up her suitcase and dropped it on the table. "When you're done, I expect an apology."

Angela opened the suitcase. Besides clothes, Ella's favorite rolling pin was there, as were copies of two recipes she'd brought for them to try, and her favorite apron, too. But there was nothing else. Angela shut the case, looking yet more weary. "It's not there."

"Of course it's not. I can't believe you'd think it would be." Fuming, Ella snapped her suitcase shut. That was when Jules had burst back into the room.

It was obvious she'd been listening in as she descended on Angela. "Make her give it back! If she leaves, we'll never see it again!"

"As if!" Ella yanked her suitcase off the counter. "I would never *ever* steal anything, much less a recipe book. Not from you, Jules, and definitely not from your mother, who is a close friend of mine." She sent an accusing look at Angela. "Or so I thought."

Angela turned red but didn't reply.

"Then who took it?" Jules demanded, her voice shrill. "It's gone and no one has been here but the family and you."

"It wasn't me! Angela, you know me. Tell her I would never do such a thing."

Angela wasn't able to look Ella in the eye. All she did was spread her hands on the empty counter in front of her as she slowly shook her head. "I'm sorry, Ella, but I have to agree with Jules. None of us would have taken it, which leaves you."

That was it for Ella. "I didn't, and wouldn't, steal a cookbook or even a recipe from anyone. I'm not that sort of person. And if you don't know that by now, then I'm done with all of you." She turned on her heel and, suitcase in hand, headed out the door. She was so mad that the drive home was nothing more than a blur.

A week passed, and then two. Ella kept expecting a phone call with an explanation, if not an apology, but it never came. She didn't make friends easily, and she'd felt an unusually close connection with Angela. The confrontation had left Ella surprisingly low.

So, after a series of slow days filled with teaching and even slower nights spent perfecting recipes, she was relieved when, three weeks later, she was offered a job in Paris at a world-renowned patisserie. The job wasn't supposed to start for six more weeks, but as soon as she finished her final class, Ella packed her things and headed for France, desperate to put some space between herself and the weight of her thoughts. *The whole thing was a mistake. How could anyone think that I—a pastry chef, no less—would steal a family cookbook? No one reveres a cookbook like a chef.*

Realizing Aunt Jo was watching her with a concerned gaze, Ella forced a smile. "It was an ugly time."

Aunt Jo scowled. "I hope you gave Angela a good what-for."

"I told her the truth. That's all I could do. After that, I left for Paris, and we never spoke again."

"Ah. You left and so the situation was never resolved." Aunt Jo clicked her tongue. "Still running away from your problems, are you? No wonder your dreams are pushing you around. You need some pushing."

That wasn't fair. Ella said stiffly, "It's not my fault Angela accused me of stealing that silly cookbook—"

"Cookbook?" Aunt Jo's eyed widened. "The Book of Cakes?"

"You know it?"

"Years ago, Jules made a buttermilk pie for the Ladies' Club, and the recipe was in that book—I saw it sitting open on the counter. I only got a glimpse of it before she realized she'd left it out and whisked it away. It looked old."

"The first recipe came from the seventeen hundreds. It's an amazing collection," Ella admitted grudgingly. "All of the Stewart women pick a page and add some words of advice along with their favorite recipe. Angela's was for her hummingbird cake."

"She makes a fine one." Aunt Jo picked up her bowl of green beans and placed it back in her lap. "So you think your dream wants you to settle things with Angela."

"That must be it. I've tried to call her, but the number I had is no longer in service. I called Jules too, but she hung up on me. Repeatedly." Ella shrugged. "So I came here."

"You were right to come here. Poor Jules has a full house nowadays. Mark still lives there and helps his momma run the Moonlight Café. He's turning into a fine line cook. But then all the Stewarts are good cooks."

Ella started to point out that Mark's last name was Phillips and not Stewart, but then decided not to bother. His mother had worked at the family café from the time she was in high school on. Despite getting married later in life, the locals refused to accept her married name and continued to call her Jules Stewart and referred to her sons as "the Stewart boys."

Aunt Jo shot Ella a look from under her lashes. "Grayson is back in town, too."

Ella dropped her gaze to where the early-evening sun was slanting across the toes of her shoes, hoping Aunt Jo hadn't seen how much that surprised her. One of the things she and Gray had had in common was a dislike for their tiny, smothering hometown, so she'd never expected to hear that he was in Dove Pond.

"He bought the old Morris farm off old Route 9," Aunt Jo continued, "cows, sheep, and all. Jules says he's doing some cutting-edge agricultural stuff out there, turning that farm into some sort of scientific food haven and growing things without soil. It sounds like a scam to me. He's gotten all sorts of attention for it, though. The Raleigh news station did a whole segment on him and his farm."

Ella shrugged. It didn't matter if Gray was around or not. She needed to speak to his grandmother, not him.

Aunt Jo offered a green bean to Moon Pie. The bulldog sniffed it and then turned away. "Picky eater." She placed the bean in front of him and then returned her attention to Ella. "It's a pity you and Gray didn't work out. I like him."

Ella finished breaking the beans still in her lap and dropped them into Aunt Jo's bowl. "You know I don't like being tied down. It's too much like work."

"Real love is work; it just doesn't feel like it. That's how you know it's real." Aunt Jo pulled some more beans from the paper bag beside her chair and handed them to Ella. "Where will you go after you're done here? Sarah says you sold your shop and apartment in Paris."

Ella had no idea, but she wasn't about to admit that to Aunt Jo. "I might write another cookbook. Or maybe I'll open a new patisserie somewhere exciting. I've never been to Japan."

Aunt Jo frowned. "What *are* you looking for, Ella? Adventure? Excitement? Love?"

Ella let her gaze wander from the porch to the fields shimmering in the breeze. The rye grass ran greenish-gold to the purple line of the mountains that encircled their little town. It was beautiful here. And safe, too. But safe wasn't enough. Frankly, she wasn't sure what was.

Suddenly restless, she finished the beans and dropped them into Aunt Jo's bowl. "I should get going. Sarah and Ava will be waiting." Ella collected her purse, then stood and kissed Aunt Jo's warm, round cheek. "I'll come back tomorrow."

Aunt Jo gave Ella a quick, fierce hug. "It's good to have you home." The older woman released Ella and then shooed her away. "Get on with yourself. Your sisters will be wondering where you are. Tell them I said hi. And don't forget about Sunday."

"I won't." Ella headed off the porch to her car. Waving goodbye, she was soon on her way to Elm Street, where her sisters waited. It would be good to see them . . . or it would be, until the hounding began.

First thing in the morning, Ella would head to the Stewart house to talk with Angela, which would hopefully end those annoying dreams and frosting attacks. Ella could only hope she wouldn't come face-to-face with Gray. *Ugh. Why is nothing ever as simple as it should be?*

CHAPTER 2

ANGELA

It all started two weeks ago when Angela Colewell Stewart Harrington took a tiny blue pill to help her sleep on a plane. She'd been mind-numbingly exhausted after months of tending to John, her second husband and first love. He'd been ill for more than a year, and when he'd died in his sleep, his hand entwined with hers, she'd been left emotionally whipped. But oh, how she'd loved him.

As tired and desolate as she'd been, the quiet hours she'd spent sitting at John's side had forced her to do something she usually avoided—face the realities and failures of her own life. For years John had said that she needed to find a way to fix the shambled mess of her relationship with her daughter from her first marriage, Jules. He'd always believed that it was Angela's duty as a parent to rebuild the bridges that time and old wounds had weakened.

After John's death—the estate set in order, the Fifth Avenue apartment put on the market, and a list of updates for her beloved Hamptons house delivered to a trusted contractor—an exhausted Angela had set out to do just what John had told her to. She'd purchased a first-class ticket to Asheville, thrown some clothes into a suitcase, and headed to the airport, a small bottle of blue pills tucked into her purse.

She hated flying and it made her anxious, so Dr. Hodges always prescribed her a little something to make traveling easier. But this time, aware of how emotionally thin Angela was after her months-long vigil at John's side, Dr. Hodges had initially refused to write the prescription. He'd suggested she wait a few more weeks before traveling, saying she would be in a better place after some rest. But Angela had refused, empowered by the thought of doing something that might make her dark-right-now future feel brighter and better. She'd been so adamant about visiting her daughter that the doctor had eventually relented. He'd written the prescription, warning her that the medication would make her sleep all the way to Asheville, and that she was not to drive for twelve hours. That wasn't an issue for Angela. She no longer had her driver's license, as she'd allowed it to expire when it became clear that she needed glasses, which was one prescription her vanity refused to allow her to fill.

As soon as she settled into her first-class seat on the plane, she took the pill, pulled down her silk eye mask, and tried to ignore the way the floor moved under her feet as they slowly rolled toward the runway. As usual, the pill's effects were profound and immediate. She was asleep before takeoff.

Angela remembered nothing of the flight. She had vague memories of being shaken awake by a flight attendant, of numbly moving out of the way for a loudly beeping cart in the terminal, and then of watching the luggage carousel moving around and around and around and around until, oddly enough, her Louis Vuitton suitcase was the only one left.

When she went to collect her suitcase, she realized she was the last person from her flight standing in the area. But . . . *had* there been other people on the plane? Or had she imagined them? Was it possible she'd been alone this whole time? The idea was too complex for her to wrap her mind around, so she simply stopped thinking about it.

Staggering under the weight of her huge suitcase and large tote bag, she made her way to where a few taxis waited outside the small airport. It took her several tries and the promise of an insane tip before she found a driver willing to take her to Dove Pond. As soon as she was on her way, she sank into the back seat and closed her eyes, trying to think of the words that would convince Jules once and for all that although her mother had made mistakes, Angela had always, *always* loved her, and had never meant to hurt her.

This wasn't going to be an easy task. Over the years, what had begun as a serious rift had grown into a distance that was canyon-wide in proportion. And Jules, bless her heart, had made things even more difficult by refusing to air her grievances, instead engaging with her mother in a blank, polite, and soulless way. Even though it was obvious Jules believed her mother had committed a lifetime's worth of transgressions, she still did the minimum of what propriety demanded. Jules sent cards and gifts on the appropriate occasions, visited for a week each summer, and had never once interfered with her sons having a relationship with their grandmother. Angela was grateful for all of that.

But that was where it stopped. If Angela attempted to discuss anything personal with Jules, she'd stiffen and change the topic. And if Angela attempted to revisit that topic at any time, Jules would simply stand and leave, her silence deafening.

Jules never confided in her mother, never asked her advice, never shared a thought or a fear. They were pleasant acquaintances and nothing more. Jules had made sure of that by refusing to discuss the big events in her life. She rarely spoke about her husband's death all those years ago, never shared her hopes for her children or her fears as an adult, and she'd never once mentioned her boyfriend of the past dozen years, a certain gentleman by the name of Joe Kavanaugh whom Angela had once run into as he was leaving the house. Gray and Mark laughed whenever Angela brought him up, saying everyone in town knew about their mother and Joe, but that Mom "liked her privacy." It seemed that, over the years, secrecy itself had become a habit for Jules. Angela wasn't sure how, but she was certain that was her fault, too.

Thus was her complicated relationship with her daughter. It was a testament to the strength of that tiny blue pill Angela had taken that she could convince herself that one long, honest conversation—just one, mind you—would permanently change the trajectory of her and Jules's tangled relationship. In fact, while sitting in the back of the taxi in a half doze, Angela worked up a brilliant, Churchill-level speech for her daughter. The moment demanded no less.

It was almost ten at night when Angela and her luggage finally arrived at the Stewart house. She didn't even try to lug her luggage up the stone stairs that led to the porch but instead left her suitcase with her tote at the side of the driveway and tottered up the stairs, swaying in place as she rang the bell.

She waited, but no one came. So she rang it again.

Then again.

And aga—

The door opened and there stood Jules, the light from the foyer making her brown hair gleam golden like an angel's.

Jules's eyes widened. "*Mom?*"

Angela nodded. She was the mom. That was correct.

Confusion flickered over Jules's face. "What are you doing here?"

Later on, Angela would wonder why that short sentence triggered her, but it did. Suddenly too tired to think, she felt her grand speech fly out of her befuddled mind with a resounding whoosh, leaving nothing behind but tears and regrets. Angela was left facing her daughter without a thing to say.

And so, she promptly burst into tears.

"Oh, Mom!" Looking both alarmed and confused, Jules pulled Angela inside and awkwardly helped her onto a plump, flowered sofa in the middle of the living room.

By now, Angela was sobbing hysterically. All she wanted was for her child to love her. Was that too much to ask?

"What's going on?" Jules pressed tissues into Angela's hands, worry in her voice. "Has something happened? When I saw you at John's funeral a few weeks ago, you seemed fine. I mean, you were sad, of course, but . . . Mom, what's happened?"

Hiccupping, Angela blew her nose, took a deep breath, and attempted to remember her brilliant speech.

It started out well enough. She explained that she was newly aware of her own mortality now in ways she never had been before. That death had made her more cognizant of her own responsibilities. She remembered thinking at that point, *So far so good*.

But as she spoke, it suddenly occurred to her that Jules didn't look the least convinced. Indeed, her touching concern seemed to be fading with each word that fell from Angela's lips, which made her falter.

Didn't Jules understand that her mother had come all this way to take the blame for their complicated relationship? That, after years of misunderstandings and hurt feelings and unspoken words, Angela wanted to make things *right*?

And yet Jules's expression grew more distant as Angela continued, and Angela, still fighting the lingering effects of pill-fog, forced herself to listen to her carefully thought-out speech. She was horrified when, instead of the brilliantly lucid sentences she'd thought she'd been uttering, she heard herself rambling incoherently, randomly spouting phrases like "life is too short" and "death awaits us all."

Embarrassed, she stumbled into silence, which she broke with an awkward laugh that was more of a sob. "This isn't going the way I wanted it to. I thought— My doctor didn't want me to travel right now, but I—" She stopped, realizing she'd wandered off her subject again, and tried to regain control once more.

While she struggled, she absently rubbed at the tightness in her chest caused by her overwhelming emotions. She just wanted to sink into a bed and sleep for days and days and—

Jules grabbed Angela's hand. "Mom? Why didn't Dr. Hodges want you to travel?"

The brittleness in Jules's voice had made Angela blink. *I wish I could think more clearly. Why did he not want me to travel?* "He said I should stay home and rest, but I couldn't. I had to see you. I had to tell you that in person since—" Emotion overcame Angela, and another sob choked her.

Jules sucked in her breath. "Mom, are you saying—" She gripped Angela's hand more tightly. "Are you ill?"

Having a broken heart qualified as being "ill," so she nodded.

"Oh, Mom," Jules breathed, looking stricken. "How long do you have? Did the doctor say?"

Angela blinked rapidly. How long did she have? What an odd thing to say. That made it sound as if she was— No, no, no! She wasn't sick like *that*. Where had Jules gotten that idea? Confused, Angela pulled free from Jules and pressed her hands over her eyes, struggling to remember her own words. It finally dawned on her that when she had mentioned death making her more aware of her responsibilities, she'd meant John's death, not her own.

Oh no. Angela dropped her hands from her face. "I didn't mean to tell you that!"

"I'm glad you did." Jules recaptured Angela's hand and held it between her own. "You shouldn't keep things like that a secret. Mom, I'm—I'm *here* for you."

Angela looked into her daughter's brown eyes and saw nothing but genuine concern, an emotion Jules hadn't shown her mother in years. Angela suddenly realized she didn't want this moment to pass. She *wanted* her daughter to care about her. Deeply.

And so, instead of explaining how Jules had misunderstood all Angela was trying to say, she had nodded slowly, absently rubbing her chest where her guilt pressed.

"It's your heart, isn't it? We have a family history of— Why didn't you tell me about this at the funeral?"

Goodness! Why hadn't she? "I . . . You . . . . There were a lot of things I wanted to say to you at the funeral, but . . . there were a lot of people there." Yes, that was true. And it made sense, too. There had been too many visitors to allow for a private talk. "John had a lot of friends. Too many, and they all wanted to talk and talk. Well, you were there. You know how it was." There. That was better. "Plus, you and the boys were only there for one night."

Jules flushed. "We should have stayed longer. Mom, I'm so sorry."

To Angela's astonishment, she was engulfed in a warm hug. It had been over twelve years since Jules had hugged her, so Angela leaned in, wrapped her arms around her daughter, and hugged her back.

This. This was what Angela had wanted for the longest time. *John, you were so right. I should have done this a long time ago.*

Finally, Jules released her and pulled away, her eyes shiny with tears. "Let's get you to bed. Tomorrow, when you're more rested, we'll figure things out. You'll stay here, of course. You can't be by yourself right now. I'll go get your things from the driveway, and in the morning I'll call your doctor—"

"No!"

Jules looked confused. "Don't call him? Why not?"

"I—I just hate to bother him. Besides, why do you need to talk to him?"

Jules frowned. "I'd like to transfer your medical records here so Doc Bolton can continue your care."

"Oh, no, no." Angela waved her hand and said vaguely, "Dr. Hodges already took care of that and— Please, Jules. I'm exhausted. Can we talk about all of that tomorrow?"

"Of course." Jules stood. "Come. Let's get you to bed."

A scant ten minutes later, Angela found herself in her pajamas and tucked into bed in the downstairs guest room. Mumbling good night to Jules, she let her heavy eyelids slide shut and immediately fell into a deep, deep sleep.

The next morning, she awoke and, while Angela was no longer under the confusing effects of that dratted pill, Jules was so gentle, so kind, and so understanding that Angela couldn't bring herself to utter the truth.

That was two weeks ago. Now, here she was, still snug in Jules's guest room, fully rested, and things were . . . well, not perfect, of course, but so much better than they had been.

So far, Angela's unplanned deception had proven remarkably easy. Whenever Jules asked questions about her health, Angela would just look sad until Jules changed the topic. Plus, it wasn't hard for her to seem less robust than her usual self. She'd lost a lot of weight during those final few weeks with John, whom she missed every minute of every day. And although there were still awkward moments, Jules was showering her mother with thoughtfulness. And Angela was reciprocating in kind.

So far, they'd had several pleasant conversations, and although they hadn't yet gathered the courage to address the many misunderstandings that had torn them asunder over the years, Angela thought it was just a matter of time before they would be able to do just that. *And find some peace at last.*

Or so she hoped.

As far as she could tell, the only problem was that their reconciliation was based on what many would consider a lie caused by exhaustion combined with medication. *Technically, it wasn't a lie*, Angela told herself. *I never said I was dying. Jules assumed that. I merely allowed her to do so.* Therefore, Angela was guilty of nothing more than caring too much and, perhaps, of committing the sin of omission. But no more than that.

Besides, she couldn't regret the questionable decisions on her part that had led to this moment, as she and Jules were growing closer by the day. And it was lovely that she got to spend time with her grandsons, too. Mark still lived here, while Gray was temporarily staying in the apartment over the garage. All in all, things were nice. Nicer than nice. Still, Angela was aware that all the goodness was overshadowed by a faint but growing fear of being found out.

If only she could tell Jules the truth—that she wasn't actually dying; not yet anyway—without losing some of the precious, hard-fought-for progress they were making. But how? Admitting her pill-induced deceit would just raise Jules's ire, and Angela was already too familiar with her daughter's deeply stubborn nature. *I can't lose Jules's goodwill. I just can't. Not until we've made some real progress. It will take time to heal the wounds of our past. But once we've reached that point, I'll confess everything.*

A soft morning breeze lifted the white curtains from where they draped beside the bedroom windows, sending the hems dancing across the golden pine floor. It was late summer, and the mornings were comfortably cool, just beginning to carry a hint of the coming fall. She looked forward to spending the season in the mountains, with its refreshing temperatures and bright leaves. *Oh John, you always loved this time of the year.*

Angela sighed. She used to think death was the worst thing that could happen to a person, but now she thought it was being left behind. She was deeply lonely, and had she stayed in New York, she was certain that loneliness would have killed her.

Voices from the kitchen caught her attention and she leaned a little in the direction of the open door, smiling when she heard Jules's laugh. That was the beauty of old houses: since they didn't have insulation in the walls, you could hear every word that was said from end to end. Right now, Mark and Jules were putting together a shopping list for the Moonlight Café.

Angela remembered when she and her ex-husband Don, Jules's father, had run the Moonlight together for all those years. Of course, the menu had been different then, although a few of her carefully curated recipes were still featured. She listened as Mark and Jules discussed the weekend specials, the organic spinach order, and whether they needed to make more bacon aioli. There was such a quiet understanding between them, such a casual closeness, that Angela was hit with an unexpected twinge of jealousy.

She turned away from the doorway, catching sight of herself in the gold-framed mirror over the antique mahogany secretary. She looked a fright. What she wouldn't give to be able to get her hair done, add a delicate waft of blush to her too-pallid cheeks, apply a careful swipe of lipstick—things she rarely went without and now missed.

"Good morning!" Jules came in carrying a breakfast tray. She was dressed in jeans and a pink button-down shirt, only a smidgen of gray in her brown hair. She looked far younger than her fifty-seven years.

Good genes, Angela thought approvingly. Her gaze moved past Jules to a wedding picture hanging on the wall beside the wardrobe. The portrait was of Jules and Liam on their wedding day all those years ago. They'd been such a cute couple and he'd been a devoted husband and father. It still made Angela sad to think of how suddenly he'd died when the boys were in middle school.

Jules's gaze followed Angela's. "Whoever thought perms were a good idea should be shot. An entire decade of photos ruined."

"You did love your perms. And you have curly hair, so you didn't even need them."

"I was young and dumb." Jules put the tray on a table next to the bed.

"You didn't need to bring this. I can eat with you and Mark in the kitchen."

"You could, but then you'd miss this." Jules looked out the window at the view. "I know how much you like it."

"You don't need to coddle me. I'd be just as happy eating with you two."

Jules smiled. "You can eat with us in the kitchen tomorrow if you'd like." She looked like Don when she smiled, but then, she'd always favored him, as did Mark. They both moved with steady purpose, and had brown hair and brown eyes.

That last was a pity. Gray had Angela's pale blue eyes and thick black lashes, which gave him an intense, striking air. *Like grandmother, like grandson*, Angela thought with satisfaction. That was the one thing Angela had inherited from her mother that she didn't hate: the Colewell women all had those same startlingly blue eyes.

She realized Jules was watching her, so Angela turned her attention to her tray. "What's this? This isn't my usual breakfast."

"I spoke to Doc Bolton yesterday when he came to the Moonlight for a hot tea and he sent me a list of heart-healthy foods." Jules frowned. "I wish you'd let me have your records sent to him. He's not a specialist, but—"

Angela threw up a hand. "We've been through this before. I saw all the doctors I'm willing to see in New York. I refuse to see another."

"That's very fatalistic of you. Doc Bolton's very good at—"

"No. Now I've said all I'm going to say about it. At least for today."

Jules looked stubbornly unconvinced, but after a stiff moment she shrugged. "Until you're ready to see a doctor, the least I can do is get you to eat healthier. But I'm afraid most of our usual breakfast items are on the 'heck no' list."

"So you made me porridge." Angela looked at the oatmeal, which was livened up with a small scattering of walnuts. *Not even a teaspoon of brown sugar.* "What did Doc Bolton suggest, other than tasteless brown porridge and"—she peered at the dish next to her oatmeal—"barely-call-them-eggs?"

"Less meat, salt, and sugar, and more fruits and vegetables, low-fat dairy, plant-based protein, whole grains—"

"No. I'm not giving up flavor. I'd rather die first." Angela instantly regretted her protest when Jules stiffened. "I'm sorry. I don't know why I'm so picky this morning. I didn't sleep well."

Jules frowned. "Is the mattress too firm? I can pick up a mattress topper while I'm out."

She loves me. Oh, Jules, that's all I want from you. I want you to love me as much as I love you. Angela was instantly glad she hadn't succumbed to the temptation to put on that hint of blush. "The bed is fine. And thank you for making me breakfast. It was very kind of you."

Jules's gaze softened.

Angela drank in the sight like she'd just crossed a brutally hot, dry desert and Jules's smile was the coolest, freshest water on the planet.

Jules nodded toward the eggs. "Try those. They're just egg whites, but I fixed them up."

Angela picked up her fork and took a bite. She closed her eyes as she chewed so the flavors lifted. "Chives, a dash of red pepper, and . . . thyme. You have a very talented hand with spices."

"I learned it from Dad. He always says that even simple dishes need flavor."

Angela glanced up at Jules. "How is Don? I haven't spoken to him since he and Lisa moved to Florida." Lisa was Don's second wife. He'd married her a good ten years ago, and from what little Mark and Gray had let slip to Angela, their step-grandmother was a talkative, cheerful sort who was always telling everyone how wonderful Don was. *I bet he loves that.*

"They like it there. He's thinking about opening a restaurant because he can't find anywhere that serves fish the way he likes it."

Angela snorted. "He's too old to open a new restaurant. That's a young person's game." But she wouldn't put it past him to try. By the time she had left Don, it had been clear that he'd loved the Moonlight far more than he'd loved her, which was one of a myriad of reasons their marriage had fallen apart. "I don't know why he'd put himself through that when he could be relaxing on a beach."

Jules turned away, straightening up the room as she said in a cool tone, "Dad would find a way to do it if he really wanted to."

Angela instantly regretted that she'd mentioned Don. Jules was very protective where her father was concerned. *Hopefully, one day soon, we'll be able to honestly discuss your dad.* "He was right to hand the Moonlight over to you when he retired. You've improved it immensely."

Which was a simple truth. Jules had an innate business sense when it came to the café, and her excellent cooking, as well as Mark's, had cemented the Moonlight Café as *the* place to eat out in Dove Pond. Angela wanted to tell Jules how proud she was of her, but Jules's expression was still cool and distant.

Angela sighed. They still had a ways to go. When Angela had divorced Don, Jules had taken it in the worst possible way, blaming her mother for everything. *I never meant to upset her so much. Maybe*

I was selfish to want happiness for myself. Guilt pressed in on Angela, making it hard to breathe.

"Mom?" Jules's gaze had dropped to Angela's chest.

Angela looked down and realized she was pressing her hand against her chest. She dropped it. *I have got to stop rubbing my chest when I think.* "It's nothing. I just need my morning coffee."

Jules slid the cup of coffee on the breakfast tray closer. "Mark just ground it. It's Colombian."

Angela lifted the cream pitcher and grimaced when the milk that poured out was so thin, she could see through it. "Skim milk?"

"Doc Bolton said—" Jules caught Angela's expression and held up her hands. "Fine. I'll quit repeating what he said. But skim milk and decaf it's going to be."

Decaf? What was the point, then? She started to demand regular coffee, but the hint of worry in Jules's gaze stopped her. *She's taking care of me. A month ago, I couldn't even get her to return a phone call.* Forcing a smile, Angela took a sip of the coffee. "Mm. Delicious."

"The decaf is in the pantry, so you can have a cup whenever—" Jules's gaze had wandered to the window and now locked on the driveway. She scowled. "Not today."

"What is it?" Angela lowered her coffee cup and leaned to one side, trying to see around Jules.

"I'll be right back." Jules spun on her heel and left.

The second the front door closed, Angela got out of bed to peek outside, standing at the edge of the window so she couldn't be seen. She instantly recognized the curvy woman standing in the driveway in a pretty pink dress, her dark blond hair hanging in a braid over one shoulder.

"Ella Dove," Angela muttered. "Go away." Several years ago, Angela had run into Ella in New York and invited her to spend the weekend, and then every weekend after, at the family house in the

Hamptons. To this day, Angela wasn't sure why she'd done it. Perhaps it was because Ella was about the same age as Angela's grandsons—a year older than Gray, and a year younger than Mark. Or maybe it had been because, for one split second, Ella had reminded Angela of herself, excited and ambitious and alone in a big city. Whatever it was, Angela never regretted an invitation more.

Angela watched Jules step outside and walk over to Ella, arms crossed tightly over her chest. She spoke, not giving Ella a chance to do more than open her mouth. Try as she would, Angela couldn't catch more than a word here and there. She wondered if she dared to open a window but knew that would draw unwanted attention. *Pity.*

Whatever Jules had to say, she didn't wait for an answer, but turned on her heel and headed back up the drive. Ella watched Jules go with obvious consternation before heading back to her car. A moment later, Jules closed the front door with a decided bang, which sent Angela hurrying back to bed.

Angela picked up her coffee cup and tried to keep her voice casual when Jules returned. "Who was it?"

Jules hesitated, and then said, "Ella Dove. She wanted to talk to you, but I told her you were busy." Jules's mouth thinned. "Just the sight of her makes me furious. Our family had that recipe book for over two hundred years and she just up and stole it. A guest in your own house! And not once has she apologized, either."

"I wonder why she wanted to see me. Do you think she was going to confess?"

"Ha! Fat chance. She is boldly unrepentant." Jules's face tightened into an all-too-familiar glare. "You should have let me report that theft to the police."

It had been two weeks since Angela had had to face that frown, and it made her stomach sink. "Jules, we've been over this. It would have just upset Gray. And we didn't have any proof."

"That's what the police do, isn't it? Find proof? But you wouldn't even let me call them."

"The police wouldn't have done anything. They would have said it was just an old, splatter-covered recipe book, hardly worth pursuing." The second Angela said the words, she wished she could take them back.

Jules had stiffened, her dark eyes flashing. "That book had value to our family. But then, you've never seen yourself as a true member of the Stewart family, have you?"

And there it was. Some of the ugliness that had exploded into existence the moment Jules had learned that her mother had filed for divorce all those years ago. Jules had always been a daddy's girl. When Angela, desperately unhappy, had initiated the divorce proceedings, it hadn't been Don who'd accused her of being selfish and horrible, but her own daughter. Which was pure poppycock.

Angela and Don had known their marriage was over years before then. Sadly, Don hated change more than he did unhappiness and so, as usual, it was left to Angela to make things happen. She'd agonized over it, and Jules's instant, pointed fury had turned Angela's worry into deep guilt. Between that guilt, Don's avoidance of anything he thought unpleasant, and Jules's rage as the years progressed, the situation went from bad to worse.

"We shouldn't have let Ella get away with it," Jules said flatly. "She stole our family cookbook and, what's worse, has made thousands of dollars off *our* recipes. She has no shame. But then, you knew that. We *all* knew that, especially after the way she treated Gray."

That was the sticking point for Angela. It had been bad enough to lose the Book of Cakes, but the way Ella had chewed up Gray and so callously spit him out still made Angela fume. She'd trusted Ella and had thought they'd grown close, but apparently not. And not once had Ella tried to contact Angela to explain herself or ask for forgiveness, either.

Angela still couldn't think about that weekend without getting angry. It appeared that Jules felt the same, although it was irksome that her anger seemed more directed at Angela. *Thanks, Ella. Still ruining things for me, even when you're not here.*

She shoved thoughts of Ella aside and refocused on Jules. Angela refused to give up the peaceful accord she and her daughter had finally, *finally*, established. "Of course what she did to Gray was terrible. And the Book of Cakes is priceless. I—" It took a moment, but Angela swallowed her pride. "You're right; I should have called the police. I was upset after—"

"Mom?" Mark appeared in the doorway. He must have realized he'd interrupted something, because he didn't step into the room but stayed where he was, looking uneasily from Angela to his mother and then back. "Sorry. I'll go—"

"Nonsense," Jules said. "We were just talking about the lost Book of Cakes."

His frown was instant. "What brought that up? It's been gone for years."

"Ella Dove stopped by and wanted to talk to your grandmother, but I refused to let her."

"None of us should speak to her," Mark agreed swiftly. "I didn't know she was back."

"I'm sure it's temporary. She doesn't come back often and when she does, she never stays for long."

Obviously anxious to change the subject, he turned his attention to Angela and managed a strained smile. "Good morning, Grandma. How are you today?"

"Better than yesterday, but not as good as tomorrow."

Her levity made him smile for real and he said to his mother, "I came to tell you Gray's meeting me at the café with a shipment from his farm. We're getting the family rate, of course."

Angela nodded her approval. "That's very kind of him."

"He owes us for all the years we put up with his scowling, mopey ways."

Jules cut Mark a hard glance. "Don't tease Gray. He was young when that happened."

Long ago, Gray had suffered from intense anxiety. Angela wasn't sure of all the details, as Jules wasn't one to share, but Angela knew that he'd gotten therapy and had even been on some medication that had helped him overcome it. Though he seemed okay now, they couldn't help but worry about him, although Angela suspected Jules worried a bit too much.

Mark snorted. "Mom, if I can't tease him, who can?"

"No one," Jules said shortly. "If you want to be a good brother, tell him he should rethink his friends. He doesn't need to get involved with a biker gang."

That caught Angela's attention. "Gray's in a biker gang?"

Mark laughed. "Hardly. Mom doesn't like that Gray's been hanging out with Trav Parker."

"Travis Parker isn't good for Gray." Jules's mouth had thinned.

"You just say that because he has long hair and tattoos, but he was in the military."

"I don't care. Gray doesn't need to be around high-stress individuals like that." Putting an end to the conversation, Jules added, "After you take the delivery, would you prep two more pans of meatloaf? I didn't get a chance to do it last night."

Angela eyed her grandson. "I hear you've become a top meatloaf maker."

"You should try it," Mark said smugly. "I have a secret ingredient."

"Parmesan cheese isn't a 'secret ingredient,'" Angela said smoothly.

His mouth dropped open. He shot a quick look at his mother. "Did you tell—"

"Of course not! I would never *ever* reveal a secret ingredient. However, I did bring some home for her dinner last night. She's always been good at guessing ingredients by taste."

Angela added, "It was delicious. You should be proud."

"I am." Mark bent to give Angela a swift kiss on the cheek. "I'm glad you're visiting."

"I'm glad to be here." And she meant it, too. She waved as he left and had to smile when she heard him whistling a tune as he went out to his car. There might have been a distance between her and Jules, but Angela had always been close to her grandsons. Secretly, though, she had to admit that Gray was her favorite. Mark never seemed to need anything or anyone, blithely going through life without much thought. But Gray had complexity and depth. She wondered if he paid for that depth with the anxiety he fought. *People are such complex characters, aren't we? Darned if we do, and darned if we don't.*

Jules fished her keys from her pocket. "I'd better get going. I just wish . . ." She pursed her lips, her expression pensive. "Maybe we should get one of those monitors that goes off if you fall—"

"Jules, no!" Angela picked up her spoon. "I'm just going to eat this wonderful oatmeal. After that, I'm going to watch TV and take a nap." *Like any other aging fossil.* Sitting alone all day wasn't her favorite thing. In fact, she hated it, and was growing to hate it more every day. She loved the bustle of doing things. When she'd lived in New York, she and John had attended programs at museums and art galleries, gone to every fundraising event possible, and, when they went to the Hamptons, held large house parties that were the talk of the town. She loved being surrounded by people and was discovering that the isolation her supposed illness had thrust upon her was deeply demoralizing.

Catching Jules's worried look, Angela waved her hand. "Don't worry about me. I'll be perfectly fine by myself."

"If you think so." It was obvious Jules wasn't convinced of that. "Mark and I will be busy at the Moonlight a lot this week, but maybe Gray can—"

"Jules, stop it!" Angela laughed. "I'm fine here alone. Really, I am."

"I just worry, that's all." Jules glanced at her wristwatch. "Oof! I have to go. I made some soup for your lunch. Just pop it in the microwave for—"

"I know how to warm up soup. I worked in a restaurant for over fifteen years, remember?"

Jules managed a wry smile. "Enjoy your breakfast, then, and call if you need anything." With a wave, she left.

The second her car pulled out of the driveway Angela hopped up and carried her tray to the kitchen. She dumped her breakfast into the trash and set about making herself a real pot of coffee, a large amount of perfectly cooked bacon, and a cheese-forward omelet.

Somehow, some way, she had to find a way to secretly break out of her sickroom prison, at least for an afternoon. If she didn't, she might pop a cork and blurt out something that would ruin the delicate foundations she and Jules were building for themselves. Moments later, Angela took a grateful sip of her coffee, which was just strong enough to ring a bell. "What I need is an escape plan," she said out loud. What it would be, she didn't know, but she was sure that with enough time, she'd figure one out. Her sanity demanded no less.

CHAPTER 3

ELLA

Spices should bring out the natural flavors of a dish, not cover them up. It's one of life's little secrets that only truly good cooks know—enhance, don't overwhelm.

The Book of Cakes, p. 38
Written: 1792–2019

Her phone held at arm's length, Ella flashed a huge smile and fell back on her bed, her free arm outspread. The too-soft mattress was old and the wrought-iron bed older still, so her fall was met with wild bouncing and squealing creaks.

"What are you doing?" Ava stood in the doorway, her gray-green eyes alight with laughter. Ava was the second-youngest Dove sister. Slender, blond, and prone to wearing coveralls with patches that read AVA DOVE'S LANDSCAPING AND GOURMET SPECIALTY TEAS, she had a special, uncanny way with plants. She instinctively knew what different flowers, trees, leaves, and roots could do for people. Which was why her specialty teas did amazing things, from easing arthritis pain to helping frantic people find their lost car keys.

Ella slid off the bed and adjusted her red-flowered sundress. "My video guy suggested the bed-bounce thing. I had to film it in slo-mo, too. Paul has some music he thinks will work great with it."

Ava scrunched her nose. "People actually *like* seeing you bounce on a creaky old bed?"

"I've slept in this bed since I was four. Childhood stuff is guaranteed clicks, which makes my sponsors happy."

"And you make money doing that?"

"More than you know. Lots, in fact."

Ava shook her head. "What a strange world we live in."

"Isn't it, though?" Strange and irritating, just like this town. To Ella's frustration, she was already starting to feel that she might be stuck here for the rest of her life. She'd been in Dove Pond almost a week now and—other than having been graced with seeing Preacher Thompson doing his magic from the pulpit, and having to agree with Aunt Jo that he did look like the love child of Idris Elba and Halle Berry—had nothing to show for her efforts. No matter what she tried, she hadn't been able to get close to Angela.

Ella had visited the Stewart house at least a half dozen times, and she hadn't gotten so much as a glimpse of the woman. Naturally, Ella hadn't stopped at the house if she caught sight of Gray's orange vintage pickup truck in the driveway. The last thing she wanted to do was kick over that particular hornet's nest. Between her regrettably active dream life and the growing abundance of strawberry frosting she kept finding (just this morning, a perfect, exceedingly large swirl had appeared just above her left knee), the last thing she wanted was additional drama.

On Ella's first visit to the Stewart house, Jules had caught her in the driveway and flatly told her she wasn't welcome, which had set the tone for the rest of her attempts. If Jules or Mark was home, they simply said Angela wasn't seeing visitors. Mark, of course, said it in a much nicer way, but the message was the same.

To save time (and her dignity), Ella decided to only stop by the house whenever she was sure no one was home but Angela. That should have done the trick, except that Angela refused to answer the door no matter how many times Ella rang the bell. The last time Ella was there, though, she'd had the undeniable feeling that Angela was standing on the other side of the door, laughing. Ella didn't have any proof of that, but she wouldn't put it past her.

"Hungry?" Ava asked. "I came to see if you'd like some breakfast. I've been up for a while. The coffee's made, and the oven's already preheated."

Ella smiled. "I never say no to breakfast. You know that."

As they headed for the kitchen, Ella nodded at Ava's bright yellow overalls. "Heading to your greenhouses this morning rather than your tearoom, I take it."

"We're finishing up the strawberries. We had a bumper crop this year."

They reached the kitchen and Ava went to pour some coffee while Ella slid onto a seat at the counter. She would never tell Ava or Sarah this, but while her baker's heart loved the high-quality Viking appliances and the shiny granite countertops, she missed their old kitchen with its timeworn but sufficient appliances, cheap countertops, and golden-yellow linoleum floor. Over the years, Ava and Sarah had overseen the work done in their house, renovating it from the foundation to the roof while staying true to the house's original aesthetic except for here in the kitchen. Ava declared it had already been "ruined" when it had been updated in the early '70s, and so they were free to change things at will without consideration given to any sort of historical preservation.

Ella had to give them credit for accomplishing so much. The rest of the house looked the way it used to when they were growing up, only better. The floors were newly refinished, the windows no longer let in the cold, the plumbing and electrical systems were updated, and the roof was new.

Ava handed a cup of coffee to Ella before pulling a package of bacon from the fridge and setting it beside a waiting baking sheet. "Two eggs over medium and a double helping of bacon?"

"You know me well." Ella poured some milk into her coffee and pulled the mug close. "Sarah said your tearoom is on its way to making record profits this year."

Ava used tongs to layer the baking sheet with bacon. "Sarah is the town librarian. What she knows about the tea business can be written on the back of a very, very small gas receipt."

Ella laughed. Ava was right. Sarah knew everything there was to know about books, but marketing was best left to Ava, who'd turned her landscaping, greenhouses, specialty teas, and now a tearoom into four very successful businesses. "Where is Sarah?"

"She had to go into work early today to train the new librarian." Ava slid the pan of bacon into the oven and then reached into the refrigerator for the eggs.

"She's needed help for a while now. I'm glad they found someone." Ella wondered what the house had felt like when Sarah hadn't lived here, but she decided not to ask. It was obviously still a sore point for Ava. A few months ago, after she and Sarah had had an argument, Sarah had moved out. Ella and her other sisters had decided to stay out of it, although they'd sympathized with them both. As Madison had said, "They made the mess, they'll have to clean it up." Which was true enough, although it had been hard to watch. Sarah and Ava had always been close, especially when Ava had moved home from college after Momma's death and had practically raised her sister. It was good the two of them had found a way around their disagreement. "How is Sarah doing?"

"Pretty good. She and Blake seem to be making things work."

That was good. "They're going to do fine."

Ava gave a short nod and said in a fervent tone, "I hope so."

The noise of someone running down the stairs made both Ava and Ella turn toward the front hall. Kristen Foster hurried past them to the dining room. The teenager was one of Ava's projects and was now living in one of the house's many guest rooms. She was dressed in jeans and a wrinkled T-shirt, her long, auburn, purple-streaked hair pulled back into a messy ponytail with a bright pink scrunchie. Kristen had worked for Ava for several years now, first in her greenhouses and now her tearoom. After Kristen's mother died, her grandmother Ellen, who lived in Charlotte and was a successful architect, had become her guardian. After much complaining and begging, she'd reluctantly allowed her granddaughter to live with Ava while finishing her last year and a half at Dove Pond High.

As Kristen liked to remind everyone, the arrangement was only temporary. Ella had to admit that it was nice having a young person in their old house. She was pretty sure the house liked it too, because the wood trim gleamed a little brighter whenever Kristen was around.

Kristen stooped down and groped under the dining room table, coming out with her tennis shoes. Hopping around on one foot, she slipped one on and then the other.

"Want some breakfast?" Ava asked as she set a frying pan on the stove.

"No, I'm late. I'm picking up Missy. We're meeting up with Josh and his dad to go fishing."

Ava lifted one eyebrow. "You like to fish?"

"I might. I'll let you know after this morning."

"Right. Before you go, have you called your grandmother lately?"

"Last night. By the way, I'll be going to her house after work Friday afternoon and staying until Sunday. She says she has a surprise f—"

"Hello?" came a man's voice from the front door.

Kristen grimaced and then yelled, "In here, Dylan!"

Dylan was Kristen's father. Until just a few months ago, neither he nor Kristen had been aware of that little fact, and both were still getting used to it.

"I wish he'd stop coming by every single morning," Kristen grumbled. "I see him all the time."

"Be nice." Ava expertly broke four eggs into the heated frying pan. "He's just stopping by to say hi. As he should."

When Ava turned to get the salt and pepper grinders, Ella and Kristen shared knowing looks. It seemed obvious to everyone except Ava that Dylan didn't stop by every morning just to see Kristen.

Dylan joined them in the kitchen. Tall, lean, and auburn-haired, with a tendency to favor plaid, he made Ella think of a handsome Hallmark movie lumberjack.

Kristen grabbed her keys off the counter. "I'm on my way out."

Dylan didn't blink at this obvious teenage brush-off. "I figured as much. I just thought I'd see if you'd like to have dinner tonight."

"I'm eating here." Kristen cast a sly glance at Ava, and then added, "Maybe you can eat here, too."

She and Dylan looked expectantly at Ava.

Ava's cheeks pinkened, but she shrugged. "Sure."

Dylan's smile exploded. "Great! That's—I'd love that."

"See you then." Looking smug, Kristen headed for the door. "Gotta go."

"Wait a second," Dylan said. "I'll walk you to the car."

Kristen was already headed for the door. Dylan followed, but his steps slowed as he walked past Ava. His gaze lingered on her as he stopped. "I finished that planter you wanted for the front of the tearoom. Want me to bring it by today?"

"Sure. I'll be there after three."

Ava's words were casual, her tone even more so, but Ella caught the undercurrent that lingered in every word.

So did Dylan. His smile widened. Obviously encouraged, he winked. "Great."

"Dylan?" Kristen called from the front door, her voice heavy with annoyance.

"Coming!" With a playful grimace, he left.

Ella noticed that Ava watched Dylan until the door closed behind him. "He looks as good going as he does coming, doesn't he?"

Ava flushed. "I wouldn't know," she said primly, adding a pinch of red pepper to the eggs before slipping some bread into the toaster and hitting the button. "It's been nice having Kristen here."

"How are her dogs doing at her grandma's?"

When she'd first moved in around six months ago, Kristen had brought her three dogs with her, but between school and work, she'd decided she wasn't spending enough time with them, so she'd asked her grandmother to keep them for her. To everyone's surprise, prim and controlled Ellen had agreed. There was no question that she now doted on those mutts. According to Kristen, her grandmother had ordered special doghouses for them, designed luxurious beds that matched her expensive couch, and bought them tons of matching sweaters and jackets.

"The dogs are doing well. Kristen gets to see them pretty often, too." Ava opened the oven and checked on the bacon. "She visits them every weekend at her grandmother's house in Charlotte."

"Having Kristen here has lots of benefits. She's pretty quiet, has her own car, and her dad is yummy."

Ava's face turned pink once more. "Stop that."

"Stop what?" Ella asked innocently. When Ava scowled, Ella laughed. "Don't you like him? He's easy on the eyes, that one."

"He's a great guy. I just—" Ava picked up a spatula and flipped the eggs. "I've been taking care of Sarah since I was nineteen and I never learned how to"—she waved the spatula in the air—"do all that."

"'That' as in 'dating.'"

Ava nodded. "He's asked me out a bunch of times, but I keep shutting him down. He's noticed, too. I think he's giving me some space, at least for now. I just . . . Ella, I don't know how to do the whole dating thing. I mean, look at me." She gestured to her overalls. "Who would want to date this?"

"Dylan, that's who. Ava, I know the signs. That guy likes you. Why not give him a chance?"

"Because I'm afraid it won't work, that's why." She eyed Ella with a touch of jealousy. "You've never felt like that, have you? You've dated more men than all the rest of us combined, and you never care how it ends, so long as it does."

For some reason, that stung a little. Ella didn't usually concern herself with other people's opinions, but hearing such a thing from her own sister felt . . . personal.

Shaking off her reaction, she shrugged. "I'm not dating anyone now, which I'm glad about. The last one was a bit clingy." They all eventually got that way, or so it seemed. Ella reached across the counter and refilled her coffee cup, then topped off Ava's.

Just past Ava was the shiny refrigerator, and Ella could see her and Ava's reflections in it. It was easy to see they were sisters: they were both blond, about the same height, and had the same Dove gray-green eyes. But that was where the similarities ended. Ella wore makeup, which Ava eschewed, and Ella was far curvier, a size twelve, the effect of years of tasting her own creations. She didn't trust rail-thin chefs. As Aunt Jo often said while patting her own belly, "They don't call it a baker's dozen for no reason. A hungry baker is a bad baker."

Ava placed the eggs, bacon, and toast onto the waiting plates and then set one in front of Ella. She slid the butter dish her way. "What are you going to do today?"

That was a good question. Ella hadn't told either of her sisters the real reason she'd come home because she hadn't wanted to face their disappointment that her visit wasn't just to see them. All she'd said was that she had a week or so off before she was due in New York. It had taken a lot of beguiling and a new peach scone recipe Ella had just developed to get Aunt Jo to not spill the tea.

Aware of Ava's sharp gaze, Ella buttered her toast. "Tiff needs more vids. Maybe I'll head downtown and see if I can find some good material there." Before that, Ella would try one more time to get Angela to answer the door. If that didn't work, then she might see if she could get some traction by talking to Mark. He'd always been kind to Ella, and she could see from his expression that he regretted not allowing her to speak to his grandmother. *Jules is the real problem. If I can't reach Angela today, then I'll see if I can get a few words with Mark when his mother isn't around, and get his help arranging a meeting.*

It was a long shot, but it was all she had. Hoping she didn't have to try that route, Ella picked up another piece of bacon. "So . . . what sort of meal are you going to cook for Kristen and Dylan this evening?"

"A pot roast." Ava shrugged, although there was a pleased look on her face. "After dinner, I think I'll suggest we play a board game. Maybe Scrabble."

"Ooh la la! The romance of a good game of Scrabble. Be still my heart!"

Ava laughed. "Yeah, it's so romantic. By the way, while you're downtown, stop by the tearoom. Aunt Jo is bringing us some cupcakes decorated like zoo animals. They'll photograph super well. People love cupcakes."

That held some promise. "I'll stop by later today."

"Sounds good." Ava nodded, then tucked into her breakfast.

They chatted for another ten minutes or so, and then, while Ella washed the dirty dishes, Ava left. The dishes done, Ella dried her hands and stopped by the large mirror in the front hallway to apply some lipstick and slip her feet into her red peep-toe kitten heels. She picked up her purse and headed out.

She drove past the Stewart house and was frustrated to see that both Mark's and Jules's vehicles were still in the driveway. Ella considered going home, but the thought of sitting in the house alone didn't appeal to her. Perhaps she'd kill some time and drive around while she waited for Mark and Jules to go to work.

Ella left and went through town, and then found herself driving down the windy county roads that she used to delight in as a teenager with her music blaring and her windows down. Golden and green fields framed by the blue-green mountains raced by. Aunt Jo was right about one thing: it was beautiful here.

She turned off County Road 9 and found herself passing the farm Gray had purchased. The old two-story Victorian farmhouse was set back from the road. It had large windows, a charming bow window in the front, and a wraparound porch. Two white vans and a large black work truck with a trailer sat in the drive, and there were so many men carrying wood, hammers, and saws streaming in and out of the house that it made her think of a kicked-over anthill.

She slowed, her gaze moving down the long drive to the large red barn that sat to one side of the house. Gray's bright orange '89 Ford pickup was parked there, although there was no sign of him, which was good. *I don't want to see him. Not even a little.*

And yet . . . she caught herself looking for him. It was funny, but she wished they were still friends, which was an odd thing to want from an ex-boyfriend. Certainly it was the first time she'd ever had such a thought about any of her exes, and there had been dozens. *It's because we were friends first.*

Although they'd been (and still were) polar opposites in just about every way, they'd been close in high school. She was outgoing and had tons of friends and lots of dates, while he'd been a quiet, silent sort who watched the world through a dark lens. He had a few close friends, but he rarely dated. It wasn't because he wasn't lusted after— because he was. Tall, lanky, with dark hair, sleepy eyes of pale blue, and a poet's angst about life, he was irresistible to most of the girls in their high school but never seemed to realize it.

Ella had known him better than anyone else, and knew he wasn't the romantic soul the cheerleading squad thought him to be. Instead, he was a boss-level worrier, intrinsically negative, unreasonably picky, and deeply shy. She'd teased him about it, too. Maybe more than she should have. It was no surprise that they'd drifted apart.

She glanced at the clock and realized it was almost eleven. Surely Mark and Jules would be heading to the Moonlight by now. She left Gray's farm in the rearview mirror and headed back to the Stewart house.

The driveway was blissfully empty, so Ella pulled into her now-regular parking spot. She stepped out into the late-morning warmth, headed up the walkway to the porch, and rang the bell. She could hear the dulcet tones of the bell echoing in the house as she waited. But no one came.

Rolling her eyes, she rang the bell again. This time, on impulse, she pressed her ear to the thick wooden door.

At first, she didn't hear anything, which she'd expected, anyway. Still, stubbornness made her stay where she was. She reached over and rang the bell again.

Nothing happened.

She grimaced. Maybe she'd just imagined Angela standing behind this door yesterday. Lack of sleep did weird things to people, and lack of sleep combined with random daubs of frosting did God only knows what. She sighed and started to remove her ear from the door, but just then, she heard the unmistakable sound of footsteps.

They came closer. And then closer. Finally, they stopped, so close Ella was sure that if the door disappeared, Angela would be only inches away. "Angela, I can hear you in there."

No answer.

Ella frowned. "Please, I just want to talk to you. It will only take a few minutes." Ella waited a second and then added, "It's about the lost Book of Cakes."

A muffled sound came from the other side of the door.

Ella took that as encouragement. "If you'll just open the door, I'll explain what—"

"Are you giving it back?" came a muffled reply.

At least she was talking. Ella put her hand flat on the door beside her face, the panel warm from the sun. "I would if I had it. I never took the book. That's what I came to—"

"If you're not giving it back, we have nothing to say."

"I didn't take it!"

"Yes you did. You also broke Gray's heart and I'll never forgive you for that, either." With that flat declaration, the footsteps retreated, slapping harder on the floor and so loud that Ella could have heard them even without her ear pressed to the door.

Soon, they faded away completely and Angela was gone.

"Great," Ella said loudly, hoping Angela could still hear. "Just great. All I need is a few minutes of your precious time to explain how I never *ever* took your recipe book!" There. She'd firmly and unapologetically told Angela the truth. That was all she had to do, wasn't it? *I'm done here. I'll just—* Her gaze fell on her left shoe. Two rosettes of strawberry icing rested on top of it, dangerously near the shoe's pretty bow. "Darn it!" She removed her shoe and hobbled down the steps to the yard. Muttering loudly, she grabbed a handful of grass and cleaned off the frosting. Apparently just telling Angela the truth wouldn't be enough. *I'll have to convince her of it, too.*

Ella slipped her shoe back on and returned to the porch. Scowling, she banged on the door. "Angela!" But there was no answer. Ella moved down the porch and, her hand arched over her eyes, looked into the windows.

Through the third window, between two long cream curtains, Ella could see into the living room. To one side sat a well-padded cream and green chair beside a large marble fireplace, with the top of Angela's blond head just visible over the back. On the table beside the chair was an open book, a piece of chocolate cake, a half-eaten bowl of what appeared to be ice cream, and a messy stack of empty Hershey's Kisses wrappers, some of them folded into some sort of tiny origami. Ella rapped on the window.

Angela didn't move.

"I just need one minute of your time!" Ella yelled. "Please!"

For a long moment, there was no movement. Then Angela reached over and picked up her bowl of ice cream and took a bite.

Ella cupped her mouth against the glass. "Angela, *please.* I never took the Book of Cakes. You have to know that! I—"

Angela put her bowl back on the table, stood, and walked toward the window. Ella noticed that she looked older than the last time they'd met. Angela had let her hair go, too, white roots in contrast to the soft golden blond.

Ella gestured toward the window and mimicked opening it. As

awkward as trying to have a serious conversation through an open window might be, at least they could finally talk.

Angela came to a stop on the other side of the glass. She stood there a long moment, her gaze locked with Ella's. Slowly, Angela reached toward the window.

Ella smiled. There. One conversation and—

The curtains swooshed closed, and Ella was left alone on the porch.

CHAPTER 4

GRAY

The next day, Gray grabbed the shopping bag from the passenger side of his pickup and headed toward his mom's house, walking past the steps leading to the apartment over the old carriage house. Gray had been staying in the little apartment with its lingering reminders of the 1920s while his farmhouse was being renovated. The apartment kitchen had been updated within the past twenty years, thank goodness, but the bathroom was still old-school with its pedestal sink, toilet with a wooden-handled cord, and quaint but deep claw-foot tub. It wasn't a horrible place by any means, but he couldn't wait to move out.

To be honest, the worst aspect of the little apartment was its proximity to his mother. He loved Mom—of course he did—but "helicopter mom" was too lightweight a description to apply to her, especially since Dad's death. She couldn't seem to accept that, yes, he and Mark were now grown up and didn't need her constant suggestions and worries. *She can't let anything go. Ever.*

Gray caught a glimpse of his grandmother peeking out the lace curtains of the sitting room of the old house. Before he could raise his hand to wave, she disappeared. Soon, the front door popped open.

"There you are!" she called as she walked briskly to him, her eyes locked on the paper bag in his hand.

He held it out to her. "Your order, madam."

"It wasn't an order. I just asked for a favor."

The tone of her text had been an order and they both knew it, but he just grinned.

"I hope you found the chocolates." She opened the bag and looked inside, her expression so like that of a child opening a Christmas present that he almost laughed.

"It's all there. Bacon, Dove chocolates, and ice cream. I had to go to two stores to get the Ben and Jerry's Mint Chocolate Chance."

"That's because it's so good. People know perfection when they see it." She closed the bag and hugged it. "Thank you. I'd have gone and gotten it myself, but you know how I dislike driving."

"I'm aware. Sadly, I can't make an ice cream run every day. I've got responsibilities."

She slanted him a side look. "But you could do an ice cream run every *three* days, couldn't you?"

He choked back a laugh. His grandma had never been like other people's grandmothers, who were sweet, gray-haired, and aproned. *His* grandmother was lean, sharp, purposefully blond, and boldly wore her makeup like a badge of honor. Or she usually did. For some reason, she'd stopped wearing her makeup this trip, although today he thought he could detect a tiny amount of blush and eyeliner.

He eyed his grandmother closely. Mom had told him in strict confidence that Grandma wasn't well, but to be honest, he hadn't seen a sign of it. She seemed plenty peppy whenever he was there, which wasn't often, but still.

She caught his look and put a hand to her cheek. "I know, I know. I look horrible."

"I wouldn't say that." He tilted his head to one side. "You look younger, in a way."

She sniffed her disbelief. "As if. I wish I could just—" She grimaced. "But I can't."

He narrowed his gaze. "Grandma, what's going on?"

She shrugged. "Are you hungry? I'm making grilled cheese sandwiches. Want one?"

He tried to remember if he'd had anything to eat today and couldn't. "I'd love one."

Chatting over her shoulder about why cheese should be its own food group, she led the way inside, heading for the kitchen. He followed, glancing at the clock near the stove and calculating how long he had until he needed to be back at his house. The electrical updates were getting underway this afternoon and he wanted to be there to make sure they didn't short him on the number of outlets.

Grandma put the ice cream and bacon away, tucking them into the very bottom of the freezer behind other frozen items, and then hid the chocolate behind the bread tin.

He slid a kitchen chair closer and sat down. "Hiding your groceries, eh? Afraid Mom and Mark might steal your goodies?"

Grandma made a face. "My daughter is trying to kill me with health food."

He grinned. "Mom is either at zero miles per hour or a hundred."

"She's at a hundred and fifty and I'm about to jump out of the car."

He laughed, leaning back as he watched her pull out a cast-iron pan and melt some butter for their grilled cheeses. Soon, the smell of browning butter filled the air, reminding him of the times, as a child and then as a teenager, he'd sat in this exact chair at this exact angle watching his grandmother cook whenever she came for a visit. How many times had they reenacted this scene? A hundred times? Or more? He wasn't sure. He only knew that when she came, she cooked, and he loved it. During his high school years, her visits had been the brightest spots.

He was sure he wasn't the only person who'd hated high school. Other than those poor slobs who'd peaked at age sixteen and then spent the rest of their lives reliving their high school days as school quarterback, head cheerleader, or some other now-dismal teenage milestone, most people wouldn't want to relive those awkward, less-than-fun years. For him, high school had been a painful, difficult time. He'd been swamped with the desolation of having lost his father and riddled with anxiety.

Anxiety. He mentally shook his head. It sounded like such an unassuming thing, when you thought about it. A feeling that something is wrong. Who doesn't feel that way on occasion? But for him, it had been heavier than that. It had felt as if something catastrophic waited on him every minute of every single day. He'd struggled mightily with it, and it had taken him years to find a way to handle it that worked for him. Now he kept his caffeine intake to a single cup of coffee a day, ran regularly to burn off his extra adrenaline, had learned some useful breathing practices, and worked hard to focus on the present. That worked most days. Once in a while, he had to lean on his prescribed medication, but not often. He'd managed his anxiety for years now and felt at peace with his ability to do so.

But when he'd been a teenager—whew, things had been different then. There was only one thing he'd liked—no, loved—about high school, and that was—

No. There was no use thinking about her. *She was a mirage. And that's that.*

"I'm glad you got here when you did," Grandma said. "I hate eating alone."

"I never say no to one of your grilled cheeses." Gray got up and pulled a glass from the cabinet to fill it with filtered water from the refrigerator door. "Would you like some water?"

"No, thank you." She pointed to her pan. "Real cheese and real butter, that's the secret. You should see the egg white things your mother keeps making me for breakfast." Grandma shuddered.

Gray nodded but wisely didn't say anything. When it came to his mother and grandmother, it was best not to get in the middle.

Grandma glanced over her shoulder at him. "How's your house coming?"

"Good." And bad, too, because it was taking an annoying amount of his time away from the new hydroponic system he was installing in the barn. He'd always had a fascination with growing things, which was why, when he'd gotten a sudden windfall of cash, residuals from a discovery he'd made while working as a food chemist, he'd decided to quit his nine-to-five job and buy his dream farm. Of course, it wouldn't be a "dream farm" until he finished setting it up, but he was getting there.

"Are you settled in your little apartment?"

He knew from the way she said "little apartment" that she didn't like that he was living separately from the rest of his family.

He waited and sure enough, after a moment, she flipped the grilled cheese sandwiches and said in a waspish tone, "I don't know why you just don't stay here in the house with your mother, brother, and me. We don't have cooties."

"I like my privacy. This way I can come and go as I choose, and Mom isn't giving me advice on the number of hours the CDC suggests we sleep."

Grandma's lips twitched. "She would do that."

"She would. I know because she's done it before. In fact, she did it just yesterday after seeing a light on in my apartment after midnight."

"Ridiculous." Grandma turned off the burner, slid the grilled cheese sandwiches onto two plates, and carried them to the table. She moved with the same assurance as his mom and was, in fact, similar in build and height. He wondered if they knew how much alike they really were. *Probably not. I, for one, would never tell either of them that.*

She went to fetch a mug. "I just made a pot of coffee. Want some?"

"No, thank you. I'm good with water for now." He scooted his chair closer to the table and waited for her to join him.

She filled her coffee mug and carried it to the table, eyeing her plate with an air of appreciation as she sat down. "There. Proper food."

"When have you had improper food?"

"You'd be surprised." She moved her plate closer. "So. I hear you're hanging out with a biker gang now."

Gray had to fight to keep from saying something off-color. "Is that what she said?"

Grandma nodded.

"Travis Parker isn't part of a biker gang. He rides a motorcycle, and that's it."

Grandma swallowed and then dabbed at the butter on her lip with her napkin. "That's not how I heard it. I heard that Parker boy is trouble."

"'That Parker boy' is nigh on thirty years old, owns his own garage, and is married to the town mayor."

Grandma's eyebrows rose. "Grace? I can't see her with a biker gang type. She's a sharp professional woman."

"Exactly. Trav is a great guy. He's adopted Daisy, the niece Grace has been raising. He's not wild or in a gang, and his bike is a regular motorcycle." Gray might have been stretching things a little about the bike. Trav's motorcycle was anything but "regular," but then what did you expect when Western North Carolina's best mechanic invested in a motorcycle? Of course it would be spectacular. *Trav is going to owe me a cold one for standing up for him.*

Grandma tsked. "Your mom is out on that situation, then." She finished half of her sandwich and started on the second half.

He eyed her plate. He'd had only a few bites so far. "Hungry?"

"I had gruel for breakfast. It doesn't stay with you."

"I bet." Gray pulled his plate closer and dug in.

They ate, enjoying their meal without talking more. He liked that about Grandma. She understood he didn't always like empty chatter. Mom had trouble understanding that, but Grandma not only understood it, but seemed to enjoy the quiet, too.

He watched her as he ate. She might look pale without her makeup, but her appetite was healthy, and her hands seemed steady, nor did she hesitate in any of her movements. *She doesn't look sick. Mom is probably being overly cautious, as usual.*

Gray tried to cut Mom some slack. He'd felt Dad's death deeply, and it had been even harder on Mom. But unlike her, he'd gotten help when he'd struggled, finding a good counselor and taking medication and even using some of Ava Dove's specialty tea to ease his more stressful days. But Mom wasn't the sort to even admit she needed help. *Stubborn and proud, that's what she is.*

Grandma pushed her plate away. "Now, that was a good lunch."

"A perfect lunch." Gray dropped his napkin on his empty plate, got up and collected Grandma's, and carried both dishes to the sink. He refilled his water glass, and then brought the coffeepot to the table. He poured coffee into Grandma's almost-empty mug. "Milk?"

"Lord, no. Cream, please. It's in the fridge."

He replaced the coffeepot and brought her the cream, glancing at the clock. "I've got to go. If I leave now, I'll have time to stop by the lumberyard."

She'd just poured cream into her coffee, but at this, her shoulders sagged. "You can't stay?"

"I wish I could, but I've got things to do. The electrician is coming, and I have to be at the house when he gets there."

She frowned. "Surely someone else could meet him."

The complaint he heard in her voice surprised him. He regarded her a long moment before he sat back down and crossed his arms over his chest. "What's going on?"

She pouted, turning her coffee mug this way and that. "It's stupid, and I know it, but I hate being alone all day."

"So don't be alone. Go somewhere. Go shopping or head to work with Mom and—"

"I can't." Sadness seemed to weigh down her thin shoulders. "I wish I could, though."

The wistfulness in her voice made him pause. "Why can't you?"

She rested her elbows on the table, her hands clasped around her mug. "It's about your mom and me."

Of course it was. "Grandma, you don't have to tell me anyth—"

"I want to," she said sharply. Her tone seemed to surprise her, because she winced, and then added in a calmer voice, "To be honest, I need someone to talk to and you're it."

He eyed her warily. "I refuse to get in the middle of a disagreement between you and Mom."

"I'm not going to involve you. I just want to tell you what's going on."

He supposed he couldn't fault her for that. Or stop her, for that matter. He sat back in resignation.

She stared into her mug for a moment. "A long time ago, I made a mistake that affected your mother in a way that . . ." Grandma sighed and pushed her mug away. "It was hard on her, and I knew it would be, but I never expected her to take it quite the way she did."

He took a drink of his water and waited.

"When you have children, they don't give you a how-to book, so you learn by making decisions. And sometimes by making mistakes. Most of those mistakes are little things, stuff they can forgive, if they even notice. But once in a while, you can make a doozy of a mistake, one that hurts everyone." She used one finger and absently turned her coffee mug in a circle, her expression pensive. "When I left your grandpa Don, I believed Jules would live with me. I never expected that she'd demand to stay with him. But she did." Grandma's lips tightened. "She didn't just refuse to live with me—she refused to talk to me, too."

Gray knew a little about this time in his mother's and grandmother's lives, but not enough to have an opinion. "I'm sure you both were doing your best during what must have been a difficult time."

She shot him a hard look. "Don't think I didn't fight for her, because I did."

He hadn't any such thought. To smooth the moment over, he murmured, "Of course you did."

It worked. Calmed, she returned her gaze to her mug. "Lord, how I fought for her. But she was adamant. Sat right there in court and told the judge she didn't want to live with me now or ever. Said I'd abandoned her and her dad, and she didn't want to leave him, her friends, or this house." Grandma blinked back tears. "I lost her, Gray. I didn't expect that. Maybe I was naïve. . . . I don't know."

He pulled a napkin from the holder and slid it across the table. Grandma wiped her eyes and muttered, "Thank you."

It was obvious to everyone who'd ever seen his mother and grandmother together that something was off between them. He and Mark knew it had to do with the fact that Grandma had divorced Grandpa, but until now, Gray hadn't truly gotten a sense of what had gone wrong. He could see them both—his mom too angry to be reasonable and stubbornly refusing to listen to her own mother, and his grandmother hurt and confounded by that anger, never quite adequately explaining her side of the situation. He loved his grandma, but she wasn't the best communicator when it came to her emotions—or other things, either.

Naturally Mom had never talked about any of this with either him or Mark. It was just like her to hide anything from them she thought might be "difficult."

His jaw tightened. She still acted as if he and Mark might fold at the first flash of a problem. *For the love of heaven, Mark practically runs the Moonlight, while I've already made a killing as a food chemist working in Atlanta.*

It hadn't been easy, but he'd worked long hours at an agricultural development company for seven years after college. The job had been grueling, but he'd gotten to work with some of the most distinguished and notable scientists in the world, and his research had received numerous awards. Best of all, he'd single-handedly led his team to a huge breakthrough that had contributed to the rise of healthier organic farming and left him wealthy from his portion of the patent. *And yet Mom worries I'm too fragile to hear about an ancient childhood disagreement with my grandma. Sheesh.*

Grandma pulled another napkin from the holder and dabbed at her eyes.

She looked so upset that his chest tightened in response. Recognizing the familiar feeling, he pushed his glass of water away, got up, went to the cabinet, and pulled out a canister of Ava's specialty tea. He poured some water into the teakettle that sat on the back burner and turned it on. "Go on, Grandma. I'm listening."

She sighed. "The last few months after John's stroke were difficult. For months, I sat by his bed, watching until he finally slipped away." She absently toyed with her paper napkin, folding it this way and that. "He was one of the strongest people I've ever known. Watching him made me realize how fragile life is. How swiftly it can disappear."

Gray had always liked Granddad John. To be honest, he'd liked him better than Grandpa Don, who cared only about a very few and specific things—the restaurant business, the Moonlight Café, and little else. But Granddad John made an effort to have things to talk about with both Mark and Gray. Once Gray began studying chemistry, Granddad John would email him articles he thought were interesting, many of them about new developments and regulations.

"After John died, I knew I had to fix things between Jules and me." Grandma cast him a guilty look. "I thought if we could have one very honest, very sincere discussion, we could get over our past and start healing."

"Just one?"

She scrunched her nose. "Silly of me, I know now. But at the time, it made sense. I flew here to do just that, but I'd taken this stupid pill to help with my flying anxiety and it made me wonky."

He raised his eyebrows. "Explain 'wonky.'"

She lifted a finger and made a circle at her temple. "I was out of it. I hadn't had more than two hours' sleep a night in the weeks before, which made it worse. Oh, and no lunch that day either, or breakfast. By the time I arrived on your mom's doorstep, I was exhausted and couldn't speak right and— Oh, Gray." Grandma propped her elbows on the table and pressed her hands over her eyes. "It was awful. I thought I was saying one thing, but apparently, I was saying something else. By the time it was over, your mother thought I came here to tell her I was dying."

Gray blinked. "Dying? She told me you were ill, not dying."

"Yes, well, she thinks I'm dying."

There was Mom, shielding him from bad news. *As usual, darn it.* The kettle began to whistle. He turned off the burner, poured the steaming water into a mug, and dropped in a tea bag from the canister. He carried the mug back to the table and sat back down. "Let me get this straight. You accidentally told Mom you were dying—"

"I never said it! She *thought* that was what I said."

"If she still thinks it, that means you never told her that she'd misunderstood you."

Grandma clapped both hands over her cheeks. "I know, I know," she groaned. "I was going to, but she was so *nice*."

"She was so nice," he repeated blankly.

Grandma leaned forward, her expression earnest and a little amazed. "Have you seen how she treats me now? She *talks* to me— really talks, and not just polite, chilly nonsense. And she's been sitting with me, fixing me dinner, acting as if she cares, sharing her thoughts and . . . it's been wonderful. It's the first time she's been that open with me."

Gray pulled his tea closer and tried not to roll his eyes. Now he really, *really* regretted letting his grandma confide in him. "So . . . Mom thinks you're dying, but you're not correcting her because you *like* that she thinks you're dying."

Grandma nodded, looking miserable. "I should tell her the truth."

"And soon."

"I know. But you don't know how wonderful it's been. I can't just give that up. We're getting close and . . . who knows? She may even tell me about her secret boyfriend."

Good Lord, what a mess. Gray took a slow drink of the tea and then put the mug back on the table in front of him. He didn't know what Ava put in the tea she made for him, but it always left him calmer, more peaceful. Heaven knew he needed it right now. "I hate to tell you this, but Mark and I think Mom broke up with Joe."

Grandma stiffened. "When?"

"I'm not sure. We think it happened after the July Fourth parade. She was in a bad mood that day." He thought about it. "Pretty much every day since, too. Whenever it was, he's stopped coming by the Moonlight. We rarely see him now."

Grandma couldn't have looked more disappointed. "Well, darn. I was looking forward to that discussion." She was quiet a minute, but suddenly brightened. "Maybe she'll tell me why they broke up."

"I doubt it. Mark tried to get her to talk about it, but she shut him down hard."

Grandma didn't look impressed.

Gray repeated, "*Hard.* As only Mom can do."

"But she's never told me about it. Not once."

"Or me or Mark either. Not that it matters, though. The only secret I wish I didn't know is yours."

"I had to tell someone." She reclaimed her coffee, eyeing him over the top of her mug. "To be honest, I'm sort of lonely. Jules thinks I'm sick, so I can't go anywhere. I'm trapped here, and now she's trying to get me to eat all of this horrible food. . . . Gray, I'm in prison. One I made for myself."

"You deserve to be in that prison and forced to eat nothing but whole wheat and low-fat dairy."

"I know it's my fault. I promise I'll tell her the truth . . . eventually. I'll have to." Her gaze met his, beseeching. "But for now, please keep this between us. I'm not yet ready to deal with it, and we're getting closer every day. I can't just let that go. Not yet, anyway."

He held up his hands. "I'm not getting involved. I can promise you that."

"Thank you," she said meekly.

As if. "Just tell me one thing. How do you see this ending? Because I can only think of one way, and it will be ugly."

"She'll be upset, but I'm hoping that by then she'll understand me better and know I'd never do anything to hurt her, not on purpose. Plus, I didn't lie to her. I'm just utilizing the outcome of a simple misunderstanding."

Gray didn't answer. He didn't have to, because Grandma knew her sauce was weak.

She fidgeted with her mug. "It hasn't been easy, Gray. Since I divorced her dad, she's looked at me as if I were the worst person in the world. No matter what I did, or how I did it, she has viewed it through that lens, and I was never again good enough. But this time, because she thinks our time is limited, that's all changed. So yes, I went with it. I've even tried to look sick, too. You probably didn't notice, but I've almost stopped wearing makeup."

Lord preserve him from women with large personalities. "You do look pale."

"Like a ghost." She pressed a hand to her cheek. "I feel naked without my Chanel Vitalumière foundation. And don't get me started about my lack of eyeliner or the mess my hair has become. Ugh! But I want it to look genuine, so . . . every once in a while, I pretend to be unsteady when I walk, and I've been keeping my voice weak when I talk so—"

He burst into laughter. When she glared at him, he raised a hand. "Sorry. That's a lot of pretending."

Humor lit her eyes unexpectedly. "You're not helping."

"I don't think anyone can," he said truthfully. He took a drink of his tea and considered everything she'd told him. "This won't end well. Any progress you and Mom make is going to disappear once she realizes what you've been doing."

"Yes, well, I might have a solution. It came to me this morning, so I haven't worked out the kinks yet, but . . ." Her gaze dropped to the table, and she traced a little circle on the surface with her finger. "I was thinking that maybe instead of telling Jules that she misunderstood what I was saying about death and whatnot . . . once we've grown closer as a family . . . I could just pretend I got better. Sort of . . . miraculously."

"Oh my God. You want to solve your lie with another lie."

"It could work," she said stiffly.

Gray couldn't disagree more, but he knew from years of experience that trying to tell either Grandma or Mom *not* to do something would just cement their decision to the contrary. "Good luck with that," he finally said. "You're playing with fire and—"

The sound of a car door closing made them both freeze.

Grandma stood so suddenly her chair almost tipped over. "That's your mom's car!" She dashed to the sink and dumped her coffee down the drain. She stuck her plate and mug and the cream pitcher into the dishwasher and then grabbed a bowl from the refrigerator and yanked off the plastic covering. "If she asks, tell her you made that grilled cheese for yourself. I'm supposed to be on this taste-free diet and I can't—"

"Hello?" Mom called from the front door. "I saw Gray's truck. What're you doing here?"

Grandma snatched up a spoon and hurried back to the table. She'd barely made it to her chair when Mom came into the kitchen, carrying several grocery bags.

Mom smiled at Gray. "How are things at the house?"

"Good. They're starting the electrical today. I stopped by to have lunch with Grandma."

"That was nice of you." Mom put the bags on the counter. "Mark was just saying you've been off on your own too much lately and we should make you come to dinner."

Gray shrugged. "I'm fine. Just busy, that's all." That sounded like Mark, though. Mom wasn't the only one who'd become overprotective when Dad died.

Mom came to give him a quick hug, and nodded toward the pan still on the stove and the open block of cheese nearby on the counter. "Made yourself a grilled cheese, did you?"

"You know how I love them." Gray glanced at Grandma to see if she appreciated his answer, which was both accurate and noncommittal, but she was too busy hunching over her bowl of cold soup, pretending she was dying, to notice.

Mom passed her mother and stopped to give her an awkward pat on the shoulder. "How's the soup?"

Gray had to admit he'd never heard his mother use such a soft tone with his grandmother.

"It's delicious." Grandma lifted her spoon with a hand that had just enough tremor in it to be noticeable. She blew on the spoon bowl as if the soup was scalding hot.

Gray raised his eyebrows. He'd never before realized what an accomplished actress his grandma was. The way she was sitting, the droop of her shoulders, the obvious heaviness of her head, made her look so much older and, yes, even a little ill. *Kudos, Grandma. You should go professional.*

Mom went to put away the groceries, pausing to point to the pan and cheese. "Gray, next time clean up after yourself, will you?"

"Did I leave that out? How thoughtless of me." He sent a glance at Grandma from under his lashes as he spoke. She sent him an amused look as she continued blowing on her cold soup.

Witch.

Mom emptied a grocery bag and turned to slide a loaf of bread into the breadbox. "You two haven't had any visitors today, have you?"

That was an odd question. Gray frowned. "No, but I've only been here a half hour or so."

"I've only seen Gray," Grandma said. "I wouldn't answer the door for anyone else."

"Good." As Mom put some apples into the basket on the counter, she sent Gray a quick, nervous look before she turned away.

What's going on? What visitor would make Mom so . . . Ah. "Ella Dove's in town."

Mom's mouth pinched into that flat, unhappy line as it always did whenever someone mentioned Ella. "You've already heard."

"Of course. She's big news in this small town." She'd always been big news, even before she'd gotten Insta-famous.

Mom's brow furrowed. "I hope you won't try to see her. You don't need the stress—"

"Mom, stop. I'm fine. I really am." Twice now, Gray had learned the cost of falling in love with Ella. When he'd been in high school, she was all he'd ever thought about. But she'd friend-zoned him so firmly that he'd never had the faintest hope. He'd eventually gotten over her, and after that he'd contented himself with watching her from a distance, admiring her accomplishments and wondering what would happen if he got back in touch with her. He never did, though, because he wasn't stupid. He'd dated other women, of course, but he'd never felt that same spark as he'd felt around Ella. And then, a few years ago, one fateful summer, he'd walked into Grandma's house in the Hamptons and there was Ella, looking more beautiful, charming, and effervescent than ever.

He knew that Ella and her artless charm, curvy body, and sensual personality had left an impressive trail of broken hearts in her wake. With that knowledge firmly in mind, Gray was determined that in no way would he join her sad herd of broken and discarded exes. But within a week, he was lost. He simply couldn't resist her. It was like going to the best, most outrageous, most extravagant party where champagne and laughter flowed like the ocean. You knew without a doubt that you were going to get swept out to sea, but you didn't care, because you knew you were going to love every second of it. And he did.

Truthfully, even as lost as he'd been in the throes of love, he'd known it wouldn't last. She'd made it obvious from the beginning that she just wanted their relationship to be fun and temporary. He'd tried to tell himself that he could do that, date her and then just walk away. That it wouldn't have lasted, no matter how much he might want it to. But once it was over, it had taken him a while to recover. Almost a year, in fact. He'd done it, though, immersing himself in his research and taking up running with a grim determination that had him competing in marathons by the end of the year. He still ran. Nothing helped him stay focused like a good ten-miler on the steep and winding roads around Dove Pond.

Grandma nudged his ankle under the table, and he realized his mother was staring at him with that worried expression he knew too well. "Stop it. I'm fine. I've been fine for years." Which was the simple truth, although he doubted she would—or could—accept it.

There were times when he saw a reflection in his mother of his own tendency to overthink every blinking thing. She had trouble letting go, and always had. Once something happened, like his struggle with anxiety while growing up, or the hurt she'd thought Grandma had caused, or Ella's supposed sins, those events were caught in Mom's steel-trap mind, never to leave or change. *Which is why Grandma is so willing to take such a huge risk, daring as her dishonesty is.*

Mom sent him a hard look. "Leave Ella be, Gray. She's stolen enough from this family."

"Stolen? What—" *Oh.* "The Book of Cakes. I'd almost forgotten about that."

Mom gasped. "How could you forget? That cookbook was a family heirloom."

Grandma nodded fervently. "It was priceless."

Gray shrugged. "She didn't take it. She wouldn't. You two were never fair to Ella."

Two sets of shocked, blazing gazes locked on him.

"You never saw Ella for what she really was," Mom said firmly, as though if she said it, it couldn't be questioned.

"I knew her better than either of you. And she didn't take that book."

"Then who did?" Mom ripped back, her mouth a flat line in her narrow face.

"I don't know, but it wasn't her. She said she didn't take it, and she's never lied. Not once."

"Ow!"

He and Mom looked at Grandma.

"Sorry." She pointed her spoon to her soup bowl. "I burned my tongue."

Mom cut her a hard look. "Stop trying to change the subject. You invited Ella to your house. You are responsible for that."

"I wouldn't have invited her if I'd have known she was a thief." Riled up, Grandma was forgetting to play ill. Her cheeks were now a healthy color, flushed pink by outrage.

Gray nudged her foot under the table.

Her gaze flew to his, surprised at the interruption.

He raised his eyebrows.

It took a moment, but she finally got the message. Instantly, she put a hand to her forehead. "Oh dear. My head is throbbing."

"Must be the weather," Gray answered, finishing his tea. "It's supposed to rain tonight." He pushed himself from the table. "Which is yet another reason I need to get going. I've got cows out in the field. I need to bring them in if there's going to be lightning."

"I can't imagine you having cows," Grandma said.

To be honest, he hadn't planned on it, but when the farmer who'd owned the farm mentioned he was going to "get rid" of them, Gray had impulsively asked that they be included in the purchase. "They're like puppies. They just want to eat, play, and sleep."

Grandma smiled her approval, but Mom looked as if she wasn't through talking about Ella. Thankfully, she thought better of it and, after a stilted moment, said, "The new line cook was impressed with the vegetables you brought the other day. He asked where we got them." But although her words seemed positive, she still sent him a measured look, as if searching for cracks in his armor.

Her nervousness spurred his anxiety once again and his throat tightened. *Stop that*, he told himself. If she kept this up, he'd have to run this afternoon just to regain his earlier calm. He carried his gym bag in his truck for just such times as this.

Grandma caught his gaze and winked.

That was it. Just a sly wink, and the touch of a smile too, but it was enough to make his shoulders return to the correct level. She understood him better than he did himself.

Gray stood. "I'd better go."

Mom folded the final shopping bag and added it to the pile on the counter. "Thank you for sitting with your grandma."

Grandma put down her spoon. "He was visiting, not babysitting."

"Hmm, wasn't I, though?" Gray asked, trying not to laugh. "In fact, I was just thinking that someone should put you down for a nap. You look tired."

Her eyes sparkled with irritation, and she bared her teeth at him. "Bless your heart. You're just the sweetest thing."

"He is. And a nap is a good idea." Mom picked up the shopping bags. "I'm going to take these out to the car. If I wait until later, I'll forget them."

The front door had barely closed before Grandma shoved her cold soup away. "Pure swill. I'm surprised Jules will even admit she made it."

Gray rubbed his shin. "I don't know why I'm even speaking to you after that kick."

"You deserved that kick. You owe me an apology for your nap suggestion, too. Fortunately, you can pay me back with a piece of coconut cake."

"Where on earth would I get that?"

"Stop by the Moonlight tomorrow on your way here for lunch and pick up a piece. If your mom is here when you arrive, sneak it upstairs and hide it in my nightstand drawer. I'll eat it after she's gone to bed."

He tsked. "I bet you were a horrible teenager."

"The worst. Which is how I got pregnant with your mom when I was only seventeen and then had to marry your grandpa Don."

"Oh geez. More family secrets I wish I didn't know. I assume Mom knows about that."

"She's been told. I'm not sure what she thinks about it, though."

"I have no idea. She's never mentioned it to me." He eyed his grandmother cautiously. "You're full of surprises today. I think you owe me cake rather than the other way around. My favorite, though, and not coconut."

"Everyone knows your favorite cake," Grandma said, looking unimpressed. "Coconut cake is better than strawberry. I've made a lifetime study of the subject."

Gray had to laugh. That was Grandma. As Mom was fond of saying, "No one thinks better of your grandma than your grandma." He grinned. "Fine. I'll get you your cake. Do you need anything else before Mom gets back from her car? I think I just heard the trunk close."

"Not now, but if you stand there long enough, I'm sure I'll think of something."

"Then I'd better go." But he didn't leave. "I hope this thing between you and Mom works out. It's going to be tricky when you get better all the sudden. She's not stupid."

Grandma sighed. "You're probably right. Maybe I'll just tell her the truth. I haven't decided yet. But that's for me to worry about, not you. Besides, don't you have cows to see to?"

"I do. I'd better get going." He gave her a quick hug and then headed out, passing Mom on the porch and saying a quick goodbye. But as he pulled out of the drive, he wasn't thinking about Mom, his cows, the electrical work, or even Grandma's odd situation. Instead, he found himself wondering what exactly had brought Ella back to town.

Whatever it was, he knew from experience he should stay away. Just seeing her would be the equivalent of playing Russian roulette with his own heart. "A sane man would avoid her," he muttered to himself.

And yet, even as he said the words, he knew that when it came to Ella, he was far, far from being sane.

CHAPTER 5

ELLA

If there is one thing cooking will teach you, it's how to plan. You have to be very creative to get four or five very different dishes to come off the stove and out of the oven at the same time.

The Book of Cakes, p. 47
Written: 1792–2019

The next morning, as Ella washed frosting from her hair in the shower, she realized it was time to move on to Plan B in her attempts to win a sit-down with Angela. *Mark, you'd better not let me down.*

He was the weak link. Every time he'd met her at the door at the Stewart house, there'd been a definite look of regret in his brown eyes. That was enough for Ella to head to the Moonlight long after lunch in the hope of catching him on a break. If she could gain his trust and, through that, his assistance in organizing a meeting with Angela, that would be a win. And right now, if Ella was ever going to sleep another night without waking up to find frosting rosettes in her hair, she needed all the wins she could get.

To her irritation, even though it was late in the day, she had to hunt for a parking space. When she finally parked and reached Main

Street, she noticed the newly redone and much wider sidewalks where she counted no fewer than thirty-seven people, the majority of them carrying shopping bags. That wasn't a crowd in New York or Paris, but in Dove Pond it was a bustling shopping scene.

Shaking her head in wonder, she made her way to Ava's tearoom, hoping to grab a bite while she was there, but darned if every seat wasn't taken. And no wonder, as the place was as charming as it was cozy. Wide-plank floor, whitewashed brick walls, a pressed-tin ceiling, and wrought-iron ice cream parlor–style seating might welcome people, but it was the long mahogany bar that ran the length of the room and held rows of delicious glass-cased pastries that captured everyone's attention. *Tiff is right. This place is gold.*

Kristen whizzed past with a tray of teas and coffees, smiling as she went. Ella returned the smile and then waved at Ava, who was too busy ringing up customers to do more than point to the last pastry case, where some adorable fairy-themed cupcakes sat in white lace cups. Knowing her fans would love them, Ella took a ton of pictures. Back in the day, she'd rarely seen people in Dove Pond she didn't know. It was rather startling to realize that of all the people in Ava's tearoom, Ella recognized only three, and two of those were Ava and Kristen.

Ella left the tearoom and wandered down the street, pausing to look into stores she used to know, but that were now drastically different. Christine DeVault's Antique Alley had once been a dark and dusty shop but had been freshened up with pale green paint and lovely brass lights to make it bright and adorable. Not only were there some surprisingly high-end antiques there now, but the store also offered local arts and crafts.

Next door to the antique shop was the Peek-A-Boo Boutique, owned by Christine's longtime partner and wife, Erma Tingle. In the old days, Ella and her sisters used to giggle at what Erma had called "fashion," but apparently Erma had taken a class in "quality clothing for the modern woman," as the stock was now excellent, both in quality and taste. Even Nate Stevens's Ace Hardware store had gotten in on the move to modernity, the entire sidewalk in front of the store lined with hydroponic planters, which Ella recognized as the same ones she had used to grow herbs in her apartment in Paris.

All in all, it was a bit of a revelation to realize how far Dove Pond had come since she'd lived there. Sure, her sisters had been saying as much for years, but it was one thing to hear it and another to see it in person. *Everything is the same, and yet is markedly different.*

Feeling a little out of place, she finally reached the Moonlight Café, wondering what changes she would find there. Inside, the air-conditioning felt deliciously cool. When Ella had been in high school, the Moonlight Café had been *the* place to hang out, and she was surprised to find that she was just as drawn to it all these years later. As she followed her waitress to her table, her business genes tingled. She'd missed the lunch rush, and the café wasn't busy, but judging by the number of tables that were in the process of being wiped down, it had been. As Ella walked past the kitchen, she glanced inside and saw Mark and another man, both working to set up for dinner, but no Jules. *Perfect.*

Ella took a seat at the counter and ordered an iced tea and the lunch special from her waitress, a fresh-faced, freckled girl with brown curly hair named "Missy," according to her name tag.

While waiting for her order, Ella admired the discreet updates Jules had done since taking over the diner after her dad retired. The café possessed the same comfort-kitsch of years past, and wisely, Jules hadn't veered too far into the modern. Just as there had been years ago, there were red tablecloths that echoed the shiny red vinyl seats of the booths, old white diner-style china with a simple blue ring, and a sparkly, linoleum-covered bar along one wall, reminiscent of a vintage ice cream parlor. Ella noted how a shelf of antique signs disguised the bulkhead needed for the new HVAC system, while a brand-new kitchen vent was just visible through the pass-through window. *Well done, Jules.*

"Here you go!" Missy set a chicken and avocado panini and fries in front of her.

"Thank you." Ella picked up her sandwich, but then realized that Missy was still standing there, beaming at her.

"Hi!" The girl waved awkwardly. "It's just cool to see you in person."

Ah. A fan. Ella regretfully put down her sandwich. "I come home at least once a year."

"Yeah, but you never come to town," Missy said matter-of-factly.

If Ella didn't feel judged before, she did now. "When I was in high school," she mused, eager to change the subject, "I used to come to this café just about every day."

"It's a great place, isn't it? Kristen and I love it." Missy glanced around and then said in a low, conspiratorial voice, "Although Ava's new tearoom is our favorite."

"Ah. You're one of Kristen's friends."

"Besties. I wanted to come by the house to meet you, but Kristen said it would be weird, so I didn't. And now, here you are!" Missy beamed as if she'd just found the Holy Grail. "I follow you on Tik-Tok and Insta. Love your food posts. I once made your double fudge brownies and my dad said they were the best he'd ever had."

Ella glanced around and realized that the few people within hearing distance were doing just that—listening. *Small towns. I forgot how they can be. Yet another reason to cut this stay as short as possible.* "I'm glad you enjoyed the brownie recipe."

Obviously unaware that Ella's response was less than enthusiastic, the girl shoved her hands into her apron pockets and said in a confidential voice, "I don't plan on being a waitress forever. One day, I want to be my own boss and own my own bakery the way you do. I can't cook yet, but I'm learning. Sort of."

Ella could have told the kid that it cost a phenomenal amount to start a small patisserie. To be honest, if it hadn't been for her social media funds and the huge check she'd gotten for selling her pie brand, she couldn't have afforded it, either. But she had no desire to kill the sparkle in the girl's eyes, so instead she merely said, "I bet you're a great cook."

Missy beamed. "I want to make those chocolate éclairs you made on your TikTok w—"

"Missy Robinson!" Marian Freely was the head waitress at the Moonlight and had worked there for decades. She had a wrinkled face at odds with the shiny, bright red hair piled high on her head and spray-starched into something remarkably like a beehive. "What are you still doing at this table?"

Missy flushed. "I was just seeing if Ella needed anything." She added with awe, "She has over two million followers on the Gram and three million on TikTok."

Marian made a sputtering, revolted noise. "I don't care if she has twenty million followers on her Grams, and thirty on her Ticker Tock. Get back to your tables, young lady!"

"You don't understand," Missy protested. "Ella's famous!"

"Ella Dove is Ella Dove," Marian said firmly. "And that's that."

Ella chuckled. "Marian's right. Besides, I can't take credit for those numbers. I have a social media specialist. My assistant, Tiff, and her team do all the work."

Missy's mouth dropped open. "You don't post yourself?"

Ella shrugged. "I take some of the photos and videos, but not all of them."

"Oh." Missy looked as if someone had popped her birthday balloons. "Do you do the cooking, at least?"

"I do all the cooking. But we have a video editor who adds music and special effects, adjusts the color, and . . . well, you know how it's done."

Mesmerized, Missy sank into the seat opposite Ella and leaned forward. "So when you post content, it's all edited and fixed up by, like, a whole team of people? While you just take an occasional picture or photo here and there?"

Ella nodded.

"And you make money off that?"

"A lot," Ella confessed.

"That's dope." Missy dropped her elbow on the table, rested her chin in her hand, and said dreamily, "I want your life."

"For the love of heaven!" Marian couldn't have sounded more disgusted. "Missy, get back to work. The silverware still needs rolling up, and Doc Bolton needs his coffee refilled. He's been trying to catch your eye for the last five minutes."

"I was just talking to Ella about—"

"Talking is not in your job description."

Missy cast a frustrated look at the older waitress but got to her feet and, with a reluctant wave to Ella, slowly went back to work.

"Kids these days." Marian shook her head. "They have the work ethic of a snail." She crossed her arms over her thin frame and eyed Ella up and down. "I'm glad you stopped by. I heard a rumor about you."

"Oh?"

"I heard you've been showing up at the Stewart house at all hours, asking to talk to poor Ms. Angela about how you stole you-know-what."

Ella could only stare at the waitress. *Oh my gosh. Jules is telling people I stole that book!* "I didn't steal it and I haven't been showing up at all hours, either. Most days, I've been stopping by between ten and two." Which was when Jules and Mark were both usually at the Moonlight. "And yes, I'd like to talk to Angela. We used to be friends."

"But not after—"

"*I didn't take it!*" Ella hadn't meant to speak so loudly, but the few people sitting in the Moonlight were now staring at her, including Missy. Ella's cheeks heated and she said in a quieter tone, "Marian, you've known me and my family forever. I would never do something like that."

"Jules is certain you took it."

"Well, I didn't!"

Marian flushed. Her gaze moved over Ella's face, and she shook her head. "You're right. You would never do something like that. She just seemed so certain."

"I didn't take it. I swear I didn't."

"Okay, okay. No need to get upset. Look, Jules hasn't been herself lately, what with her mother being so ill and all."

"Angela is sick?" *Oh dear.* Now that Ella thought about it, Angela *had* looked far less than her usual polished self when they'd seen each other through the window. *That isn't like her.*

"She's sick, all right. *Very* sick, from what I've heard. Heart issues, I think." Marian pursed her lips. "Maybe that's why Jules doesn't want you to see her. Maybe she's trying to keep Angela calm."

Ella didn't know what to say. "I only wanted to see Angela to tell her the truth about that book. I didn't come here to upset her."

Marian patted Ella's shoulder. "Don't look so worried. Maybe she'll pull out of it, although from what Jules has said . . . Well."

"I can't believe she's ill. I had no idea." Ella remembered Angela sitting in her living room, eating ice cream and chocolates, and how forcefully she'd yanked the curtains closed. "I saw her just briefly, but she seemed to have a lot of energy."

"She's a lot like her daughter. Jules refuses to admit she's ill, even when she is. When she had the flu last year, Mark had to threaten to tie her to a chair to get her to stay home." Marian shook her head. "I've worked here for a long time, first for Miss Jules's daddy, and then for her. I love that woman, I really do. She and I have always gotten along. But she can be a mite overfocused at times. I'll be honest with you, when she first told me her suspicions about the lost book, I told her you weren't a bad person. A little spoiled, maybe, by all the attention you've gotten since you left here, but that's to be expected."

That was faint praise indeed. Ella managed a wan smile. "Thanks."

"No problem. I—" Across the room, someone gestured to Marian that they needed their bill. "Look, we'll talk later. I need to get back to work. Missy's still in training and she can't handle more than two tables at a time."

"Sure. Thank you, Marian."

With a final smile, the waitress hurried off.

Still stunned, Ella looked at the open pass-through window behind the counter. If Jules was telling stories to Marian, it wouldn't be long before the whole town thought Ella had stolen the Book of Cakes. *And now Angela's ill. That must be why she came back to Dove Pond.* The information didn't deter Ella from wanting to make things right. If anything, it made the matter all the more pressing. *I need Mark's help even more now. Angela deserves to know the truth.*

Ella ate her sandwich slowly, waiting for him to take a break. As minutes passed, the café began to empty. She recognized a few of the customers, and found herself weirdly happy to exchange waves and small greetings with them. Mark looked up once from his place at the window, and catching Ella looking his way, gave a visible start before managing an uncertain smile.

She pointed to the seat opposite hers and then to her cup of iced tea, hoping he understood the invitation.

He looked hesitant, but after a few long seconds, he shrugged and nodded.

Good. She waved down Marian and ordered a piece of coconut cake and two forks. A few moments later, Mark walked out of his place in the kitchen, a mug of coffee in his hand. He still wore his apron, which was clean except for a drop of red sauce (ketchup?) on one pocket and a splash of flour in the center.

"You drink coffee at this time of day?"

"All day, every day." He slipped into the seat opposite hers and nodded toward the cake. "Aunt Jo makes a mean coconut cake."

"Perfection." Ella picked up a fork. "When we were in high school, I thought the Moonlight couldn't get any better. I was wrong."

Mark looked around the café, his pride obvious. "My dad used to say this place was better than Sofía Vergara. For him, that is the gold standard."

"That's a weird standard for a restaurant, but it sounds like your dad." She slid the other fork in his direction. "I'm glad you stopped by. I wanted to talk to you."

"If this is about Grandma, I'm not supposed to talk about her to you. In fact, I'm not supposed to talk to you at all."

"I figured as much." Ella decided that his sleepy brown eyes couldn't be more the opposite of Gray's intense blue ones. They were so different, these two brothers. "I'm glad you aren't letting your mom tell you what to do."

"She's not the boss when it comes to my personal life, although I avoid telling her about that as much as I possibly can." Mark eyed her with caution as he took a bite of the cake. "So . . . you're still in town and have been for, what, a week?"

"Longer. That's a record. I'd hoped to only be here a day or two at most."

"What happened? Car break down?"

"I haven't been able to do what I came to do, so . . ." She shrugged. "I'm sort of stuck."

"Ah. You have goals." He regarded her with a thoughtful expression, a question in his brown gaze. "I hope my brother isn't one of them."

"Goodness, no! That was years ago."

"Good. You messed him up pretty badly back then."

A flicker of regret hit her. This wasn't what she wanted to talk about. Not even a little. But she knew it was true. When she'd broken up with Gray, she'd seen the hurt in his eyes, and it had shocked her to the core. She'd told him all along that their relationship was temporary, but somewhere along the way, his feelings had gotten engaged. *I hate that I hurt him. We were friends once. I should never have started that relationship to begin with.* She realized that Mark was staring, and she sighed. "I just want to point out that I've been in town for a while now, and I haven't made any effort to see Gray. Not once. That's not going to change."

Mark put down his fork and picked up his mug. "Sorry if I was out of line saying that. But I care about him, and I wanted to be sure you weren't on the hunt."

On the hunt? Good Lord, how many insults must she endure today? "I didn't even know Gray would be here. I came to see your grandmother and no one else. Mark, I need to talk to her. I have to convince her I didn't take the Book of Cakes."

His expression, which had been cautious, instantly froze. "She won't believe you."

"I have to try." Ella hoped he didn't ask her why. She didn't feel like explaining her weird dreams and frosting episodes to him.

"She and Mom have decided you took that cookbook. There's nothing you could say to change their minds."

"Probably not. But until I say my piece, I'm staying in Dove Pond. That's a promise."

He stirred uneasily, tapping his fingers on the edge of his cup. Finally, he asked, "After you say 'your piece,' what then?"

"Then I'll go." And if Angela didn't believe her? *Will I be cursed with that annoying dream for the rest of my life? Spend eternity wiping strawberry frosting off my knees and elbows? Please, no.* "Mark, this is super imp—"

"Ella Dove? Is that you?"

Ella turned to find Zoe Bell walking toward their table. Zoe was the vice president of the town bank and dressed as if she were ready to walk down a 1960s Parisian runway. Today she wore a peach A-line dress with a thin gold belt and red pumps, her curly black hair worn short to emphasize her dark skin and large, light hazel eyes. Although glad to see her old friend, Ella couldn't help but wish it had been at a different time. Mark was already scooting his chair from the table as if ready to flee.

"Mark, sit." Zoe didn't spare him a look as she gave Ella a quick hug. "You look upset. Is Mark boring you?"

"Not at all."

Mark had sunk back into his chair at Zoe's order. Now he muttered a protest, but Zoe pinned him in place with a bright smile. "Be a darling and get me a chair." She didn't have to ask twice. He immediately hopped up and pulled out a chair for her.

"Thank you," Zoe said, sinking into the seat.

Flushed, Mark sat back down and reclaimed his mug. Still, the movement seemed to have loosened his tongue. "Avoiding work, are you?"

"No, I'm avoiding meetings. Those aren't 'work.'" Zoe hung her huge purse over the back of her chair. "What are you doing out in the dining area? Did your mom leave the cage open?"

"Nah. I climbed out a window in the office."

Zoe nodded as if that was exactly what she'd expected. "I saw your mom out and about a while ago. I should have known you'd escaped. That means you're the boss for, what, an hour? Maybe two?"

Mark grinned. "Two and a half. I may put the pie on sale in celebration."

"A capital idea." She noticed Ella's half-eaten piece of cake. "I didn't plan on eating, but that cake is calling." Zoe waved at Marian, pointed to the cake, and then turned back to the table. "Hey, I didn't interrupt anything, did I?"

Ella answered, "I was just going to ask Mark for a favor."

"Pray continue!" Zoe instantly leaned closer. "I love it when people ask Mark to do something other than make a sandwich. I— Oh! There's Sarah and Aunt Jo."

Ella's irritation rose as Zoe waved them to their table. *Darn it! At this rate, the entire town will be here.*

Mark got up and pulled two more chairs to the table. He helped Aunt Jo into her seat. "Were your ears burning? We were just talking about your coconut cake."

"Is that what it was?" Aunt Jo patted her ears. "I was afraid I might be catching the flu."

Mark laughed and sat back down.

From her seat, Sarah beamed at them as if she couldn't think of a better place to be. When Ella was a teenager, she used to hate Sarah's overly enthusiastic belief that "everything will turn out great!" For realists like Ella, Sarah's unabashed perkiness could be hard to take at times. But Ella had to admit that, of all her sisters, Sarah was the one whose special ability impacted the most people. When Sarah was with a book—any book—it would whisper its secrets to her, including who needed to read it. As Aunt Jo liked to say, "If Sarah Dove gives you a book, take it, or you'll miss something very, very important."

Sarah opened her tote bag. "Zoe, I have something for you." She dug around, her elbow perilously close to Ella. "It's here somewhere.

I— Ha!" She triumphantly pulled out a book and handed it to Zoe. "There!"

"*A Tree Grows in Brooklyn*." Zoe looked disappointed. "I read this in high school."

"It says you need to read it again."

"Again?" Zoe sighed, but she slipped the book into her purse. "Fine. I'll read it again."

Ella wished Sarah would give her a book to read. Maybe it would keep her bad dreams at bay. "I don't suppose any books have asked to visit me, have they?"

"Nope. Not lately."

Zoe returned her purse to where it had been hanging over the back of her chair. "Sarah, you and Aunt Jo got here just in time. Ella was going to ask Mark a favor."

Aunt Jo rubbed her hands together. "Do tell!"

Mark's smile faltered. "I . . . Ella and I should probably talk about this privately."

Ella hadn't expected this conversation to have so many observers, but the fact that Jules had already told Marian that Ella had stolen her cookbook made that a rather moot point. "I was going to ask Mark to get me in to see his grandmother. I have something important to talk to her about."

"*Very* important," Aunt Jo said.

Sarah looked puzzled. "Can't you just call her?"

"I've tried," Ella said. "But she's changed her number."

Mark nodded. "Grandma's horrible about signing up for things online. Because of that, she was getting at least fifteen spam calls a day and usually more. She couldn't block all of them, so she had to change her number. Not that it matters. If she knew Ella was trying to call, she wouldn't answer."

Zoe shrugged. "So the phone's out. Ella, I assume you've gone by the house and tried to see her there, too?"

"Multiple times. She won't answer the door."

Mark sighed. "I blame Mom for that. She's been protecting Grandma. In a way, we all have been."

"Why would Angela need protecting?" Zoe asked, obviously astonished. "She's fierce."

"And Ella wouldn't hurt a fly," Aunt Jo said in a no-nonsense tone.

Sarah added, "What is Jules afraid of? That Ella might bake them a cake?"

"No, no." Mark shifted uncomfortably in his seat. "It's not like that. Mom thinks . . ." He shot an embarrassed look at Ella. "Do you want to tell them?"

"Why not? It's not as if it's a secret. Angela and Jules believe I stole something from their family, a recipe book they've had for generations."

"It's called the Book of Cakes," Aunt Jo added.

Sarah looked stunned. "They think you *stole* it?"

Ella nodded.

"Baloney!" Sarah cast a furious look at Mark. "Ella would *never* steal anything, *especially* not a cookbook."

Zoe clicked her tongue. "That's the most ridiculous thing I've ever heard."

Mark flushed and cast a longing look toward the kitchen.

Before he could move, Ella reached over and placed her hand on his arm. "Mark, you've always been nice to me, and I really appreciate that. But I need to talk to Angela and explain things to her."

"I can't get involved," he said miserably. "You know that."

"Humph," Aunt Jo said. "*Someone* in your family owes Ella a visit with Angela. It's the least you could do after accusing her of something like that."

"The *very* least," Sarah added darkly. She slid a hurt look at Ella. "Ava and I figured you had a reason for coming home—we just didn't know what."

Ella's face grew warm. "I'm sorry. I was going to tell you. I just hadn't gotten around to it yet. But things have gotten complicated. Jules doesn't want me to see Angela, and she's ill, too."

Worry chased away Sarah's irritation. "Angela's sick? I'm sorry to hear that. I should bring her some soup—"

"No, no," Mark said in a hurry. "She's fine. Mom says Grandma just needs some quiet."

Ella leaned forward. "I promise I won't upset her. I just need five minutes. That's all."

His gaze searched hers. "And then?"

And then what? What can he want— Ah. He was worried about Gray. That left a bitter taste in her mouth, but she refused to acknowledge it. "After I see Angela, I'll leave town and never return."

Sarah made a distressed noise, so Ella added, "Except for Thanksgiving."

Sarah looked disappointed, but Aunt Jo's gaze was on Mark. "You have to do this."

"It's only fair," Zoe chimed in. "Angela will probably thank you afterward."

"I doubt it," he muttered. "Geez. This is—" He ran a hand through his hair in frustration, the curls now standing this way and that. "Fine," he said sullenly. "I'll help."

Ella couldn't keep an elated grin from her face. *Finally* something was going her way.

"When Mom finds out, though, she's going to be furious." He pulled a pen from his apron pocket, found a clean napkin, wrote down a phone number, and slid it across the table. "That's Grandma's new number."

Ella's excitement cooled. "Thank you, but she won't answer."

"Don't call her. Text her. She's big on texting. She sends out a few dozen a day, most of them orders." He stood. "Just promise you won't rile her up." He returned the pen to his pocket and claimed his empty cup. "I'd better get back to work. See you all later."

Zoe watched him amble across the dining room. "He's a nice guy, isn't he?"

Ella absently murmured a yes as she looked at the phone number. It wasn't the help she'd wanted. She'd been hoping he'd just set up a meeting for her, but this might work. Now she could reach Angela directly. Ella slipped the napkin into her purse.

"Now that that's over," Aunt Jo said loudly, "I have news."

Everyone looked her way.

"Something's happened. Something *bad*." Aunt Jo glanced over her shoulder to see if anyone was close enough to overhear before she scooted closer. "Someone sent me a present for the bake-off."

Zoe's eyes widened. "A *bribe*?"

"Shhhh!" Aunt Jo looked around, her eyes wide. Certain no one was paying attention, she added in a low voice, "A whole case of oranges."

Sarah didn't look convinced. "Are you sure that's a bribe? If I wanted you to do something for me, I'd send you apple pie moonshine, not oranges."

"Or a case of Fireball whiskey," Zoe said in a thoughtful tone. "That would do it."

"Probably," Aunt Jo admitted. "Whoever did this either doesn't know me well, or they weren't trying very hard." There was a hint of disappointment in her voice.

"Did they leave a note? Anything to let you know who sent it?" Sarah asked.

"There was a note, but it got wet during transport and you can't read a word of it. It's just a bunch of blue smudges."

"Whoever it is," Ella said, "I hope they can bake better than they bribe."

"Can't you just send the oranges back?" Sarah asked.

Aunt Jo shook her head. "The crate only says 'Florida.' I know just one person who lives there, my old friend Philamedra Phelps. I've already called her, and it wasn't her."

Zoe sighed. "I thought about entering the bake-off myself after Preacher Thompson said he expected fewer people to enter because of the big scandal, but then I remembered I can't bake."

"You're really, really bad at it," Sarah agreed.

Aunt Jo patted Zoe's hand. "But we admire your spirit."

"Thanks. I figured I would have as good of a chance as anyone else, unless Ella here decided to enter."

"Me? Lord, no. I won't be here for the bake-off."

Aunt Jo snorted. "Are you sure about that? You said you'd only be here a few days, and it's been more than a week already. The bake-off is part of the Apple Festival this year, which isn't that far away. In fact, at the last committee meeting, Grace said it would greatly benefit this town if you were a judge."

"She's right." Zoe's eyes shone with her enthusiasm. "Ella, you'd be a PR dream judge."

Ella felt the need to slam the brakes on this idea as fast as she could. "Sadly, I won't be here. Besides, this contest has already gotten way too complex."

"It's complicated," Sarah agreed. "Personally, I think Abby Lews is going to win."

Ella searched her memory. "Abby Lews?"

Zoe sent her a surprised look. "The dentist."

"She's sorta new," Aunt Jo said. "She's been here two years. Her office is in the same complex as Doc Bolton's."

"Abby's a good baker," Zoe said. "I've had her plum cake before. But I think the winner's going to be either Maggie Mayhew and her butter cake, or Haley Tilden from the Farmer's Depot and that spice cake she makes for the Methodist Ladies' Group. They say you'll think the angels came down and made it for her. It's *that* good."

Ella knew Maggie Mayhew, who co-owned Paw Printz with her husband, Ed, but she'd never heard of this Haley person at all. Sheesh, when had Dove Pond gotten so *big*?

The others continued talking about possible winners for the bake-off and Ella was disheartened to realize she knew only about half of them. Feeling a little left out, she sat quietly. *It doesn't matter. I need to focus on tomorrow.*

Her fingers itched to send a text to Angela this very second, but the memory of her face before she'd slammed the curtains closed made Ella realize she had to be cautious. If she didn't send just the right text message, Angela would simply block her. *I'll have one chance. Just one. I have to say exactly the right thing, whatever that is.*

Frowning, Ella considered all her options. One perfect text message followed by a few words with Angela, and Ella would be free to go to wherever her next adventure took her. She was ready for it, her restlessness growing by the second. She just hoped that wherever she went, it would be somewhere far, far away from this surprising and confusing little town where she'd grown up.

CHAPTER 6

ANGELA

Angela used to love breakfast. She loved thick slabs of crunchy toast slathered in real butter, over-easy eggs that exploded with flavor and warmth when she bit into them, and thick-cut bacon that sizzled as it hit the plate.

That was breakfast, not *this*.

She dug out a spoonful of gruel (she refused to call it anything else), considered it for a second, and then mournfully turned the spoon so that the mess plopped back into the bowl—gray, shapeless, and tasteless. Just like her life.

"Mom, stop playing with your food." Jules sat at the kitchen table across from Angela and pointed to her own bowl. "I'm eating the same thing." She took a bite, her expression flickering for just a second before she managed to swallow.

"Well?" Angela demanded.

"It could use a little seasoning. Some cinnamon, perhaps. But it's not bad."

That was a lie and they both knew it. Angela pushed her bowl away. "It's not bad. It's wretched, horrid, putrid—"

"Putrid?" Gray asked, his voice thick with suppressed laughter.

Angela looked over her shoulder to where Gray had just come into the kitchen from outside, his empty coffee tumbler in his hand. He was dressed in jeans and a faded, wrinkled T-shirt, his face unshaven, his dark hair a trifle too long.

He tsked. "Really, Grandma? Putrid?"

Angela cast a quick glance at Jules and, seeing her daughter laser-focused on her own bowl of gruel, stuck out her tongue at Gray.

He grinned and filled his tumbler with coffee, then reached into the fridge. He held up the cream so she could see it and, smiling widely, added a healthy dose to his coffee. "Mmm, I do love cream in my coffee." He took a sip and then sighed as if he'd just tasted heaven.

She looked at her own coffee, which was decaf and had water-thin skim milk in it instead of proper cream. *Darn it!* She glared at him.

He tasted his coffee again. "This is good, but you know what it needs? *More* cream."

Oh, if she were able to be herself, she'd rip her impudent grandson a new one. Alas, all she could do was say with an "I'll get you back for this" stare, "That cream will make you fat." *I hope.*

Jules looked up from her oatmeal. "Gray never has trouble with his weight, especially with all the running he does." She shot him a glance. "Did you run this morning?"

"Ten miles."

Angela sniffed loudly. "He may not get fat, but if he keeps drinking cream like that, he'll clog every artery he has and die before he's forty." That was harsh, but he'd been asking for it.

He grinned, leaned his hip against the counter, and took a noisy sip.

Wretch.

Jules glanced at the clock and, with an obvious flash of relief, put down her spoon. "I've got to go. Wish I had time to eat with you,

Mom, but you know how busy I am with the restaurant and all." She carried her bowl of oatmeal to the sink and dumped it down the disposal.

Right. It was work that had sent Jules to the sink to toss her oatmeal, not the painful blandness of it.

Jules rinsed her bowl and put it into the dishwasher. "Are you leaving now, Gray?"

He nodded and, as soon as his mother's back was turned, mouthed to Angela, "Lunch?"

She nodded fervently.

With a wink, he reclaimed his coffee tumbler and headed out, calling over his shoulder as he left, "See you guys later."

"Bye." Angela picked up her spoon and pulled her bowl closer. "Jules, before you go . . . Last night, after dinner, Mark was saying there are several new businesses downtown."

"There's now a tearoom, a flower shop, a photographer, a feed store, and a real estate office. Our new mayor, Grace, has been a lightning rod for bringing new businesses to our area."

"Interesting. I don't suppose Dove Pond now has, oh, a taxi or car service? Like Uber or something like that?" Angela waited hopefully. She knew the answer was no, but there had to be some other option, surely.

Jules's eyes narrowed with suspicion. "You're not planning on going somewh—"

"No, no! I just wondered because I've read that transportation options are the real sign of a town's growth."

"Oh. No, we don't have that yet, but I bet it won't be long."

Darn it. I was so hoping there was some way to get around.

Jules picked up her car keys. "Grace thinks we'll qualify for a state grant for local bus transportation within the next three years, but I'll believe that when I see it."

Great. *I'll be dead of boredom by then.* Realizing she was making herself depressed, she tried to think of something positive to say. "This housecoat you lent me is crazy comfortable. I may never dress again."

Jules looked pleased. "I should get you a caftan."

"I'd be tempted if I could avoid mirrors."

Jules laughed and came to the table. To Angela's surprise, she leaned down and gave her a kiss on the top of her head. It was a quick kiss, more of a peck than anything else, but the spontaneity of it made Angela's eyes misty. She tried to think of something engaging to say, but her emotions had clamped her throat closed, so all she could offer was a tremulous smile.

"It's nice having you here, Mom."

Angela blinked away yet more tears and took a gulp of her weak decaf coffee in an effort to clear her throat. "It's been nice, Jules. So, so nice." The moment was sweet, poignant, and worth every bit of boredom Angela had been living with.

Jules moved back to the counter and collected her purse. "I'd stay longer, but we're interviewing for a prep cook this morning. I need to get Mark off the line so he can do more of the management tasks."

"He's good at those."

"Yes. Yes, he is." Jules headed for the door. "See you this evening."

Angela waved. Moments later, she was standing at the front sitting room window, watching as her daughter pulled out of the driveway.

Well. Here she was, once again alone in the big, echoey house. Sighing, she returned to the kitchen and dumped her oatmeal and weak-ass coffee down the disposal and fixed herself some real coffee with extra cream. Holding the precious cup with both hands, she wandered through the house, restlessly wondering what she'd do today. Sheesh, but being at death's door was *boring*. She'd been here only a few weeks and here she was, slowly rotting away of ennui. *I'm a prisoner of . . .* She refused to call it a lie. Her story, then. *I'm a prisoner of my own story.*

There. That sounded much better.

Still restless, she wandered across the foyer into the sitting room. That was one of the beauties of these large old houses: because they had to heat one room at a time, they had all sorts of cozy rooms here and there, some for socializing, some for family, some for visitors. She liked that better than the "open concept" approach where one noisy TV set could keep everyone else from enjoying whatever they wanted to do.

Of course, right now, she yearned for something social. Wandering through these rooms reminded her of when she started working at the Moonlight. Some women thrived in the role of stay-at-home mom, which was a difficult, underrated job that required a depth of patience she'd never had. Don, sensing her restlessness and always struggling to find line cooks in their small town, had hesitantly suggested she work part-time at the café.

She'd agreed to a monthlong trial and, to her surprise, had loved it. She'd enjoyed getting to know the people of their town and found the pressure of keeping up with the fast pace in the kitchen both stimulating and challenging. Oddly enough, the job had also made her appreciate her time with Jules all the more.

Those were good days. Smiling, Angela wandered past the fireplace, where she caught a glimpse of her reflection in the mirror. Her smile disappeared and she raised a horrified hand to her hair. *I look like a Brillo pad! The gray is showing and—Lord help me, but I need a Botox appointment this instant!*

Closing her eyes, she turned away from the mirror. What she wouldn't give for a normal day out. First, she'd get her hair done, complete with a good blowout. Gray was not a color she welcomed, preferring instead the soft gold that said, "Yes, I color my hair but I pay a lot for it." Next, she'd get a mani-pedi, and maybe a chair massage just for that extra oomph. Everyone knew the benefits of stress relief.

And then, after a piece of pie and a latte from the Moonlight, she'd visit the Peek-A-Boo Boutique, the one and (sadly) only cute little clothing boutique in Dove Pond, where she'd spruce up her wardrobe. The robe was nice, but goodness, she could do with some new things. Although Angela had brought a huge suitcase—one big enough to hold a dead body if the need arose—she still somehow hadn't brought enough clothes. *Oh, to have a day out! I can almost taste it, I want it so badly.*

John used to laugh at her obsession with clothes, or he did until her things began to overtake his small part of their various closets. *He used to get so irked by that.* The memory made her smile and yet left her sad, too. She missed him so much that right now, she'd pay a million dollars just to have an argument with him.

A tear rolled down her face. She brushed it away and, horrified at the thought of weeping alone, clamped the lid on her sad thoughts and straightened her shoulders. *John would not approve of all these tears.* She swiped her arm over her eyes and went to her room to take a quick shower, ignoring her reflection as she dried her hair. She dressed in cream slacks and a pale blue shirt that went nicely with her eyes and, since she was alone, added a hint of eyeliner and just a touch of blush. She'd wipe it off before Jules came home.

That done, she went back to the kitchen and snuck the final bit of chocolate from her stash hidden behind the breadbox. *Gray needs to bring me more.* She found her phone and texted him. *I need more chocolate. And another piece of that coconut cake, too.*

A moment later, her phone pinged a *K*.

She snorted. "Can't even be bothered to write out the 'O.' I see where I stand." Feeling dismissed, she went to the study, found a book she hadn't yet read, and returned to the sitting room, where her coffee waited. There, she sat on the chaise and opened the book, hoping to kill time until lunch.

It seemed like twenty hours or more before she heard the welcome sound of Gray's truck pulling into the driveway. She tossed her unread book aside, ignoring it as it slid off her chair and hit the floor, and hurried to a mirror to smooth her hair.

She heard the kitchen door open and she went to join him, rubbing her hands together expectantly.

He set a large paper bag on the counter. She stepped forward eagerly but stopped when he pulled the bag closer to his side. "Don't shoot me, but they were out of coconut cake."

"What?" She couldn't keep the disappointment from her voice.

"I brought you bread pudding instead." He pulled out a small box and held it out.

She took it and tried to pretend it would be as good. After all, he had gone to a lot of trouble to bring it. "Did you see your mother at the café?"

"Just for a second. I told her this lunch was for my plumber and I hoped the bread pudding would convince him to give me a discount."

She eyed him with admiration. "That's pretty good."

Gray laughed. "It felt like I was back in high school trying to go to a party I knew she wouldn't want me to go to."

"Were there any parties she *did* want you to go to?"

"None. Not a one." He reached into the same bag and pulled out two boxes. "Ham and cheese on rye with extra mustard and chips."

"You've saved my life," Angela said fervently. She took her box and hurried to the table. "Have you been busy today?"

He joined her and pulled his sandwich from its box. "I haven't made it to the house yet. I went to the lumberyard to set up a delivery, and then to the appliance store in Swannanoa to order a new washer and dryer. After that, I stopped by the hardware store for some printer cables. I'm setting up a small office in the barn so I can chart the pH levels."

Like most small-town hardware stores, the inventory was vast and varied. In addition to providing the usual hardware items like gardening and plumbing supplies, as well as screws, paints, and tools, it also had pet supplies, lawn furniture, holiday decorations, and—in the spring—an adorable number of baby chicks for sale. "I haven't been to a hardware store in forever," Angela said wistfully.

"Whaaat? My fancy granddad John wasn't a fan of the paint aisle?"

"Sarcasm does not become you," she said loftily. "As you well know, he was a New Yorker through and through, so Fifth Avenue was more his style. As far as I know, he never got to experience the true delight of a well-stocked hardware store."

"That's a pity. I think he would have enjoyed it."

Angela sighed wistfully. "Maybe. He was a good man, but he wasn't what I'd call handy."

Gray's expression softened. "It won't be the same visiting the Hamptons without him."

She couldn't argue with that. Without John, the place was different—empty, even. They'd made so many wonderful memories in that house. And oh, how she'd loved it. When she'd first married John, he'd brought her to his expensive apartment in New York City on the Upper East Side. It had been grand and decorated to a T, and he'd expected her to be over the moon about it, but she'd never really felt at home there. But his far more modest house in the Hamptons, which had been in his family for decades, had won her heart. A delightful confection of a Dutch Colonial that was modest in size compared to its newer and more imposing neighbors, it had been built in 1821 and held all the charm of that period.

Angela had loved it the second she'd stepped over the threshold. The gray cedar–shingled house had golden pine floors and floor-to-ceiling arched windows that opened onto a slate terrace that led to a pool and overlooked the ocean. She never felt more at home than she did there.

She realized Gray was watching her and she forced a smile. "You're right: it's different now that John's gone. I'm happy I'm here, with you all."

His gaze moved past her to the kitchen. "Were you happy when you lived here?"

That was an interesting question. "I was, at first. But Don and I were very different people. We still are. Trust me, we make much better friends than husband and wife."

"That's sort of sad."

"It was, at one time. But not so much now. We're both happier, you know. To be honest, he wanted the divorce as much as I did, but he never liked change, even when it was for the better." She gestured to the kitchen. "It took me four years to convince him to let me update this. And it was horrible. The appliances were mixed and unmatched, the tile a lime green, and don't get me started on the warped cabinets. The stove was from the fifties and two of the burners didn't work, and he *still* complained when I replaced it."

"That sounds like Grandpa."

"It does." She thought for a moment and then chuckled. "We were sitting right here, at this very table, when we realized we'd run out of things to talk about. Oh, sure, we talked about Jules and the café, but nothing else. We never fought because we didn't talk enough to argue. We just slowly, one tiny step at a time, moved apart." She considered this as she took a bite of her sandwich. "I think that's why Jules resented me after her father and I split up—or one of the reasons, at least. She never heard us argue, which led her to think her father and I were happy, so it was a total shock for her when I filed for divorce."

"Mom never talks about it, but you can tell it was upsetting for her."

"It was upsetting for us all. But what else could I have done? There was no passion, no fire, nothing more than polite, distant companionship. When I met John six months later, I realized how right I'd been."

If Angela closed her eyes right now, she could still remember the first time she'd seen John. It had been during Asheville's Vintage Market Days and she'd been looking for things to put in her half-empty apartment. She'd filed for divorce months before that, but Don was dragging his feet, hoping she'd change her mind, which wasn't going to happen.

So there she was, wandering the booths and tents and trying not to drop the TV trays she'd just bought, when she turned a corner and came face-to-face with John. He was there on a business trip and was trying on a straw fedora. The second their eyes met it was as if lightning struck her through the heart. John claimed it was the same for him, which he proved just two months later when he asked her to marry him.

It had been so right, so perfect, that it had never dawned on her that her daughter would reject not just John, but Angela herself. Jules, who was already simmering with fury at the divorce, had taken the news of Angela's new romance in the worst possible way. And Angela, who'd already been imagining the three of them—her, John, and Jules—living in his gorgeous apartment and exploring New York City together, had been shattered by Jules's flat-out refusal to participate in any way.

Angela picked up a napkin and wiped a bit of mustard off the corner of her mouth. "Your mother refused to accept John. No matter how hard I tried."

Gray shook his head. "I'm sorry you two went through that. I love Mom, but once she gets an idea into her head, watch out."

"She's like her father that way. Neither of them takes to change very well."

Which was why the divorce, which should have been so simple, had become an endless array of court dates and heartbreak. Don, hating all the changes that were happening, had dragged his feet and hung his head, and Jules, interpreting that as hurt over Angela's new love, had stubbornly refused to leave Dove Pond no matter how much Angela begged. John had paid for the best lawyers available, but no lawyer could offset a child who defiantly stated to the judge that she hated her mother and wanted to live with her dad. The experience had broken Angela's heart and left her deeply conflicted, as she'd had no intentions of coming between Don and Jules to begin with. But as the divorce continued, she was horrified to realize that, while she'd found the love of her life, she'd lost her daughter.

"Grandma?" Gray's voice was deep with concern.

Angela shoved the unhappy memories away. "It was a difficult time, but this morning your mother kissed me." She smiled, some of the sadness lifting. "And without prompting, too."

He looked surprised. "She did?"

"Right here." Angela touched her forehead. "We're getting closer. I just need to stay the course. Although I still wish I could find a way to get my hair done." She picked up a potato chip, eyeing Gray thoughtfully. "I don't suppose you'd consider letting me stow away in a gym bag the next time you visit Swannanoa? I just need a root touch-up. It won't take long."

"Mom would notice. Besides, your hair doesn't look that bad."

"Ha! It's a mess." Oh, how she missed her regular hairdresser, Michelle, a quick-witted lady from a good Italian family. There were three things Italian and Southern women had in common: a firm grasp of the importance of family, a love for a really good homemade sauce, and the beauty of hair teased, sprayed, or tortured to just the right volume.

One day soon, Angela promised herself. She tucked a wayward strand behind one ear and focused back on Gray. "How are things at the house? When do you think it'll be ready for you to move in?"

He brightened and started telling her about the progress that had been made so far. It was obvious he loved his farmhouse and was excited about living there. *He's here in Dove Pond, where he belongs.* It was funny how relaxed he seemed now, when he'd been such a tightly wound mess in high school and even beyond. He'd been too quiet, too sensitive, too everything. A child tortured by his own fear and sensitivity. If she had to describe him now, the words *confident* and *calm* both came to mind.

It was wonderful and Angela wished Jules could see it, too. But Jules had a picture of Gray already stuck in her head, and she couldn't seem to let it go. Oh, she could blame Liam's death and Ella's alluring presence all she wanted for Gray's difficult teenage years, but Angela knew better. Sure, he'd suffered after his dad's death and, yes, he'd had a thing for Ella back in the day—he and about half of their high school—that never came to fruition. But it had been far more than those two issues that had caused his crushing anxiety.

Fortunately, he'd found a decent counselor and gotten a diagnosis that had led him on a path of self-care that had allowed him to thrive in a truly healthy and strong way. His only stumble after those painful high school years had been his brush with Ella in the Hamptons, but even then, despite Jules's and Mark's dark impressions of that time, Angela thought Gray had recovered well enough. Still, it was a pity he'd had to go through the pain of that breakup to begin with. *I blame Ella for that.*

Gray finished his sandwich and glanced at her empty plate. "You put that away like a pro."

"Pro-sandwich, that's me."

Gray collected their boxes and then emptied the trash and set it beside the back door. He winked at her as he slipped a new bag into the bin. "Now we'll hide the evidence."

"As one must."

"As one must," he agreed. "You didn't eat your bread pudding."

"I will," she lied.

He quirked an eyebrow.

She made a face. "I just had my mouth set for coconut cake. You know how that goes."

"When they have coconut cake, I'll bring you some."

"Thank you." She smiled.

"You're welcome." His phone beeped and he pulled it from his pocket. "The plumber is waiting for me. I'd better go." He picked up the trash bag, then shot her a curious glance. "What are you going to do for the rest of the afternoon?"

"I don't know. I guess I could read some more. Maybe dance on the kitchen table. If I get bored, I'll knock back some wine."

"Ah. The usual." He grinned as he spoke, his face softened by his smile.

He's handsome now, but he'll be simply devastating when he's older. He has good bone structure, just like John. The only real difference between the two was John's boldly positive outlook, which was in stark contrast to the flashes of worry that still shone in Gray's fine eyes, although only on occasion. *I wish Jules would give Gray credit for handling his anxiety as well as he does.*

When the boys were young, Angela had been aware that Jules was as committed to over-mothering her boys as she was to avoiding any sort of emotional connection with her own mother, which was ironic. Before this visit, Angela had assumed that, over the years, that unfortunate tendency had passed. But seeing Jules with Mark and

Gray over the past few weeks had proven that assumption wrong. She was just as bad now, if not worse. *Be careful, Jules, or you'll chase them away.*

Angela smiled at Gray. "I promise to call you if I fall off the kitchen table and bonk my head."

"Call 911 instead. I'll be out in the pastures and my cell coverage is weak out there. Besides, I know you've been wanting to get out of the house, so . . ." He shrugged, his eyes sparkling.

"Don't tempt me." She waved him away. "Off with you. And the next time they're out of coconut cake at the Moonlight, see what they have at Ava's new tearoom. I hear she keeps her cases filled with some serious desserts."

"Plan B for coconut cake is Ava's. Got it. See you later." With a wink, he left.

Angela went to the living room, held back the curtain, and watched until his truck disappeared down the road. As the sound faded, the house instantly became annoyingly quiet. But Mark was due home in a few hours. *That's not a long time*, she told herself, trying to find a silver lining.

Angela turned away from the window, letting the curtain swing back into place. Maybe, once she and Jules were on firmer ground, Jules might welcome a helpful tip from her mother about trusting her sons to find their own way in the world. Angela and her daughter were far, far from that scenario right now, of course, but it might be possible in a few months if things continued to improve between them. *I would be very circumspect, of course, so she wouldn't feel judged and—*

Her phone chimed, letting her know a text message had arrived. It was probably Jules checking in.

Angela pulled her phone from her robe pocket and read the text. *I made you a cake.*

She didn't recognize the number, but who other than Ella Dove would offer to make her a cake?

"The fool." As if Angela could be so easily won. Her thumbs flew over the keyboard. *Take your lousy cake and go away.* There. Short, sweet, and to the point.

Her thumb hovered over "send."

The cake wouldn't be lousy. Not one of Ella's cakes.

No, Ella's cakes were perfect. They were moist, rich, and filled with such delicious flavor that they sparked precious, delightful memories.

Angela's thumb moved a little farther away from "send." The last time she'd had one of Ella's cakes had been the day before the Book of Cakes went missing. Ella had arrived for their Hamptons weekend with a treat, as she sometimes did. This time it was a strawberry shortcake with homemade whipped cream. If Angela closed her eyes, she could still remember the fluffy perfection of the shortcake, the ripe flavor of the strawberries, the sweet thickness of the cream. But more than that, she remembered a summer day from her childhood that the cake made her recall. She'd been only seven years old, and on the hottest day of the summer, she and Daddy had gone down to Sweet Creek, which ran right through town, meandering behind houses and through the park, until it emptied into Dove Pond itself.

Daddy had loved creeks, and there was nothing he liked better than to roll up his pants and walk barefoot over rocks worn smooth by cool, shimmering water. She'd learned to love that same experience herself. That summer day, the heat of the late afternoon had dissipated as the coolness of the water washed over their feet. They'd held hands as they walked, and had laughed and talked as they splashed and scared off more fish than she could count.

Oh, how she relished that memory. And Ella's cake had made it so immediate, so real, that when Angela had finished swallowing the final bite, she'd had to wipe away happy tears. That had been one of the best days of her life.

But then that was the beauty of an Ella Dove cake. It wasn't just the flawlessness of the bake, or the richness of the flavors, although they were something to behold themselves. It was the unexpected memories those perfect combinations of flavor and texture stirred. The glimpses of special, exquisite moments from one's past were astoundingly real and, oh, so precious.

She looked at her phone. She wanted that cake. Wanted it badly. But she had no desire to see Ella. Angela refused to listen to a single lame word, hollow platitude, or pathetic excuse.

But Ella didn't need to know that, did she?

Smiling to herself, Angela deleted her text. In its place, she wrote two words. *Bring it.*

CHAPTER 7

ELLA

It's good to take chances. That's how all great discoveries are made. But do so armed with thought, caution, and an accurate measuring cup. Better to overprepare than to underwhelm.

The Book of Cakes, p. 63
Written: 1792–2019

Ella stood on the front porch of the Stewart house and stared at the doorbell.

This was it.

She was so close to ending her uncomfortable frosting-filled dreams. Finally, *finally*, her life could get back to normal. She would sleep through each night, dreamless, with no annoying frosting rosettes or curlicues on her thighs or elbows when she awoke. Better yet, she would be free to leave this town, her car windows down, singing a happy song as she drove to—well, she didn't know where she'd go, but wherever it was, it would be a far better and more fun place.

I just need to explain to Angela what happened, and that's it. Surely she'll believe me because it's the truth. The truth will win the day, as it always should. Right?

Right! Ella had been telling herself this all day, but it still felt as if a huge *maybe* sat right in the middle of it.

Grimacing at her own doubts, Ella shifted the cake box holding the peach-praline upside-down cake to her other hand and wondered if she was being naïve. Mark said Angela wouldn't believe Ella no matter what. *Was he right? Am I wasting my time?*

That was entirely possible. But what choice did she have?

Ugh. She straightened her shoulders. "I have to do this. I *have* to."

She reached for the bell once more. Before her finger could press the golden circle, the door opened, and there stood Angela.

"Hi!" Mark had said Angela was ill, so Ella eyed the woman cautiously. Angela did seem a little pale. Her hair was a mess, too, which would have never happened before. *Poor thing. No wonder Mark and his family are worried. I'll be sure not to upset her.* Ella forced a calm, sympathetic smile. "I came to—"

Bam! The door slammed closed, the lock clicking loudly into place.

Angela was gone.

Ella blinked and then, still dazed, looked down.

Her hands were empty. The cake box had disappeared.

What just happened?

Ella's mouth tightened. She knew what had happened—Angela had happened, that's what. All of Ella's good intentions disappeared. Fuming, she banged on the door. "Open up! I want to talk to you!"

No answer came.

Ella pounded on the door again. "Angela!" she yelled. "Open up! You have to talk to me before you eat that cake or I'll—" She stopped. Or she'd what? Yell some more? Bang on the door again? "You're cheating!"

Great. Just great. She'd been here less than a minute and her grand plan was already in shambles. What was she supposed to do now? Stage a sit-in on the porch? *Jules would love that.* Ella could already imagine Jules's furious expression when she came home and found Ella perched in one of her expensive rocking chairs.

I can't believe this. Ella glanced from the closed door to where her car sat in the driveway. *I can't just leave. There has to be another way. I can't let her get away with—*

The curtain of the sitting room flickered as if someone had just brushed past it.

Aha! Abandoning the door, Ella hurried to the window and, cupping her eyes to avoid the afternoon glare, peered inside.

Angela sat on a luxurious blue velvet chaise, the cake box in her lap, the lid open. A glass of milk sat on the table beside her, a fork in one hand as she admired the cake.

Ella must have made a noise, because Angela glanced up. For a startled moment, they locked gazes.

Slowly, without looking away, Angela stabbed her fork into the cake and lifted a bite to her mouth.

Ella had to fight the urge to bang on the window. "Stop that!" she ordered Angela. "You can't have that without talking to me f—"

Angela took another bite, her eyes sliding closed as she savored the cake.

"Darn it! I wouldn't have brought that cake if I'd known you were going to steal it!"

Angela shrugged, licked her fork, and continued eating the cake.

That was it.

Ella'd had it. She'd break this window, politeness be darned. No one stole an Ella Dove cake from Ella Dove. *No one.*

As she turned to look for a rock, the window moved under her hand. Startled, she looked back. *Was it open?*

She cast a wary glance at Angela but shouldn't have worried. The older woman's attention was locked on the cake.

Ella placed her hands flat on the window and pushed up.

The window slid open and, as quickly as she could, Ella climbed in.

"What— No!" Angela set the cake box to one side and jumped to her feet.

Ella lunged for the box, but Angela was quicker. She grabbed the box and awkwardly leapt over the chaise. She crouched behind it, clutching the box to her.

Over the cushions, they glared at each other.

Ella crossed her arms. "Well? Will you look at us? This is ridiculous!"

Angela seemed to suddenly realize that, in her zeal, she was crushing the cake box. She straightened and carefully set the box beside her glass of milk. "Get out."

"No."

"You're breaking and entering. I'll call the sheriff."

"Sheriff Blake McIntyre? The guy my sister Sarah is dating?"

Angela scowled. "I used to know his mother, but I suppose that can't compare."

"He's a stickler," Ella admitted. "To be honest, if you called him, he'd arrest me for breaking and entering, *but* he'd also arrest you for theft. You stole that cake and you know it."

Angela's eyebrows lowered. After a minute, she shrugged. "We're at a stalemate, then."

Ella couldn't argue with that. "You know why I came. I yelled it a dozen times outside on the porch."

"I don't want to talk to you. I thought I'd made that clear."

"Too bad." Ella sat down in the chair opposite the chaise and put her feet up on a footstool. "I'm not leaving until you hear me out."

Angela regarded Ella with a sullen gaze.

Ella waited. After a long, stilted moment, she added, "I need to talk to you because—well, it doesn't matter why. But it'll only take a few minutes. Five at most."

Angela's gaze narrowed.

"You might as well hear me out; I'm already here. Plus, if you'll listen to what I have to say, I'll leave you the cake."

Angela's gaze darted to the box and then back. "And if I don't listen?"

"Then I'll go, but I'm taking the cake with me."

Angela winced and gave the cake box a lingering, longing look. Finally, she gave a loud, exasperated sigh and plopped back down on the chaise. "You are a pain, Ella Dove!"

"Likewise."

"Fine." Angela picked up the cake box and settled it back into her lap. "Say what you have to say and leave."

Please let me find the right words. Ella splayed her hands over her knees. *Come on, Ella. This is your big chance.* She took a deep breath. "I'm not sure what happened to us that day in the Hamptons. We were so close, or I thought we were. And then the Book of Cakes disappeared and you accused me of stealing it. The whole thing happened so fast—at least it did for me. Angela, I was angry you thought I'd stolen your cookbook, but when you wouldn't listen to me and took Jules's side . . . that hurt."

Angela took a bite of cake. "Hmm. This is still warm. I do love warm cake."

Ella leaned forward. "I didn't take your cookbook."

Angela took a sip of her milk, her gaze on the cake and not Ella.

"After we had that argument, I shouldn't have stormed out. I should have stayed and faced you and Jules." Aunt Jo had been right about that, among other things.

"Interesting," Angela murmured, sliding a bite of cake into her mouth.

Angela was finally listening. That was encouraging, so Ella added, "To be honest, I was so insulted that you'd think I'd steal from you that I planned on never speaking to you again, but things have happened that made me realize that was wrong." Ella wasn't about to muddy her explanation by revealing her dream and frosting issues. That was her problem and not Angela's. "We left our argument unresolved, and so here I am."

Angela lowered her fork. "I have a question."

"Of course. Ask anything. I'm an open book. I—"

"Cinnamon, cloves, and . . ." Angela tilted her head to one side. "Ginger?"

Darn it. "You didn't listen to a word I said, did you?"

Using her fork, Angela pointed to the cake. "Fresh peaches too."

Ella sighed. "The Piggly Wiggly just got a shipment from Georgia. That's what made me decide to make that cake to begin with."

"It's delicious. This is the first upside-down cake I've had with pralines." Angela licked her fork, her expression softening. "John loved peaches, but I told him he didn't know good peaches until he'd had one right off the tree, made sweet by the heat. They should be soft, but not too much, and smell like . . ." Angela closed her eyes and took a deep breath as if she could smell those fresh peaches. "One summer, I had Jules bring tree-ripened peaches with her when she came to drop off the boys in the Hamptons for their vacation. You should have seen John's face when he bit into that first one. You'd have thought he'd seen a glimpse of heaven." Her eyes unfocused, Angela gave a soft little laugh, although there was a small catch at the end of it. "Later on, in the middle of the night, I heard a noise in the kitchen, and I found him eating another peach, and I—" She caught herself.

Her eyes widened. "My word, this is an Ella Dove cake." Accusation hardened her gaze as she looked at Ella. "That's what you wanted to happen, wasn't it? You wanted me to remember John so I'd be nicer to you and listen to your drivel about—"

"No!" Ella shook her head. "I can't control what memories people have. All I know is how to make desserts. After that . . ." She spread her hands wide. "I brought the cake as an offering of friendship. Nothing more."

Angela's gaze dropped back to the cake, and for a long moment she just sat there staring into the box.

Ella wasn't sure if she should say something or not. She was just getting ready to ask if Angela was okay, when the older woman whispered, "I miss him."

A single tear dripped down Angela's cheek.

Ella nodded, her throat tight. They'd been such a lovely, happy couple, the two of them. "I've never seen two people more in love." She reached over and tugged tissues from a box on the coffee table. She pressed them into Angela's hand. "Losing him must have been hard."

Angela set the cake to one side and dried her eyes. "It hasn't been easy."

Poor Angela. She'd loved someone wildly and madly, and he'd loved her back with the exact same passion and depth. *That's so, so rare, but look at the pain it's caused her.* As much as Ella appreciated the depth of Angela's love for her husband, she never wanted to feel that sort of pain. She hadn't lost a husband, but she'd lost a father, and knew the emptiness that could cause. *Never again.*

"It's been a difficult year." Angela dabbed her eyes one last time and tucked the tissue into her pocket. She took a cleansing breath and then turned a stern look at Ella. "Just so you know, one memory will not soften my feelings about your theft of the Book of Cakes. Jules was furious about that, and of course she blamed me, and I . . . well, I can't have that."

"Angela, I swear on my mother's grave I never took that silly thing."

Angela sniffed. "As Jules will tell you, that book was a *family heirloom.*"

"I didn't mean the book wasn't . . . Fine, it was a cool book, and it had some terrific homilies and recipes and whatnot in it. But why would I steal a book like that from anyone? The internet has millions of recipes. If I really need a recipe, I just have to do a search."

"The ones on the internet are not as good as ours." Angela stabbed the cake with more force than necessary. "Jules says you've made a killing off our family cookbook. She's shown me dozens of our special desserts on your social media accounts."

Ella had never heard anything sillier in her life. "Which desserts?"

"The hummingbird cake, the peanut brittle, the iced chiffon cookies, the—"

"That's preposterous! I am a pastry chef, Angela. I'm *famous* for the way I take common desserts and make them my own through my techniques and use of spices."

Angela sniffed. "All I know is that I see a lot of similarities between your recipes and the ones in our book. Sure, you've made tweaks here and there, but they're still the same."

"You . . ." Fuming, Ella stopped herself just in the nick of time. *Be calm. Don't let her get to you.* She took a deep breath. "I have a lot I'd like to say right now, but I promised Mark I wouldn't argue with you. I shouldn't cause you stress while you're ill."

A strange expression flickered across Angela's face.

It appeared for just a second, but Ella had seen that look before. She'd heard Angela tell John, "Ha, no, I didn't buy that ridiculously expensive Birkin purse," when Ella knew for a fact that at that very second that bag was resting in the trunk of Angela's car. "*Angela!* Oh my gosh. You're *pretending* to be sick."

"Nonsense," Angela said in a waspish tone.

But Ella knew better. "*Is* it nonsense?" She swept a critical gaze over Angela. "Yes, you're paler than usual, but then again, you're not wearing makeup. In fact, you don't look sick at all."

"It's . . . it's a heart condition. You can't just look at a person and tell if they have heart troubles."

"I just watched you jump over the chaise like a white-tailed deer, and you were breathing just fine. You weren't puffing a bit."

Angela shifted uncomfortably. "I have medication. That's why I wasn't out of breath."

Ella raised her eyebrows.

"I feel dizzy." Angela dropped her shoulders and tried to look tired.

Ella snorted. "Oh, honey, you are wasting your time. I've worked in too many kitchens not to recognize fakery when I see it. People are always trying to get off work for the flimsiest of reasons."

Angela scowled. "There are all kinds of 'sick.'"

"In this case, I think we're looking at the 'fake' kind. What are you up to?"

Angela tossed her fork into the cake box and said crossly, "That's none of your business."

"I wonder whose business it might be? Jules's? Your grandsons'? Mark thinks you're at death's door. He didn't exactly say that, but . . . Maybe he'd like to know how well you can vault over a chaise. I—"

"Stop it!" Angela spat out. "For the love of heaven, if you must know the truth, I came here to reconcile with Jules. Through a series of unfortunate events, none of which were my fault, she misinterpreted something I said and now she thinks I'm ill."

Ella leaned back in her chair. "She must be worried about you. I know Mark is."

Angela flushed. "I'm going to tell them the truth, of course. I'm just waiting for the right moment. In the meantime, the . . . misunderstanding has made Jules far more approachable. That's been nice. I'm hoping that this will give us some precious time to overcome some of our past."

Ella knew all about Angela's troubles with her daughter. That topic was the only one that used to bring tears to Angela's eyes whenever she and Ella talked. In fact, Ella had always wondered if Angela had been so welcoming to Ella because their relationship had, in some way, filled that void. *Angela used to say her estrangement from Jules was her one and only regret, and if her act is helping them to get closer, I can see why she'd be reluctant to give it up.*

"You aren't going to tell Jules, are you?" Angela spoke stiffly, but her gaze was pleading.

Ella thought about it for a moment. "For now, I'll keep my opinion on your fake illness to myself." It was tempting to use this information as a weapon, but she knew all too well how deeply Angela felt about it. *I can't do that.*

"Thank you. It's none of your business anyway. But in the meantime, what *is* your business is the fact that you owe me *and* my family for all the drama you've put us through."

Ella's mouth fell open. "*I* owe *you*? That's crazy."

Angela's gaze was piercing. "I'm not talking about the Book of Cakes. I'm talking about Gray."

Oh. Ella could tell that, for Angela, that was a much bigger faux pas than the loss of the family recipe book. "I don't want to talk about that."

"And I don't want to talk about the Book of Cakes. I guess that means our conversation is over." Angela waved toward the still-open window. "You can let yourself out."

God grant me patience, and if not that, then a glass of whiskey. "Look, I don't know what you've been told, but Gray knew from the first day how things were going to be. He knew I'd be leaving at some point. I didn't hide that."

"No, you didn't. What you did hide was that, before you left, you were going to rip out his heart and stomp on it. That's how you do things, isn't it? How many men have you left destroyed in your wake? Five? Ten? More?"

Ella flushed. "I don't like long-term commitments."

"You never have. What's sad is that you don't even know what you're missing. I knew I loved John from the first time I saw him, but those feelings were glitter compared to the gold we had once we got to know one another, faults and all." Angela shook her head, her disapproval evident. "You never stay long enough for anything to grow but crushed hopes."

Ella's face couldn't have gotten hotter. "Maybe I haven't yet met the right person."

"How would you know? You run away before you can find out. You waltz through the men you meet, leaving the second you feel something bigger than a flutter. Forget about the feelings of the other person, not that you ever pay attention to that. With you, it's all Ella, all the time."

That was harsh and Ella felt the sting of every word. "You don't know anything about my relationships."

"Don't I? You told me quite a bit back when we were friends, before I realized you'd practice your callous, selfish ways on my own grandson."

Ella winced. When she and Angela had been friends, they'd spent hours together in the kitchen trying various recipes, perfecting certain dishes, sipping wine, and yes, gossiping about their lives. Apparently, Ella had admitted far too much to her friend. It was the wine, Ella decided. She had a bad tendency to say too much after her second glass, and she'd often had more than that.

I shouldn't have to listen to this. The need to get away from here, far from Angela and this town and Ella's frosting-rich dreams, was growing by the second. Ella was so restless it was hard to stay in her chair. "I didn't come here to talk to you about Gray or anyone else. All I want is an acknowledgment that I didn't steal your family recipe book."

Angela leaned back, her gaze narrowed thoughtfully. "An acknowledgment. That's all you want."

Ella held up her hands. "Just that. Nothing more."

"I see." Angela pursed her lips. "If that's all you want, then maybe we could come to an agreement."

Relief flooded Ella, but it disappeared when Angela added with a smirk, "But it will cost you."

Great. Just great. Still, progress was progress. If Ella had to play Angela's games to be free of her troubling dreams, then she'd do it. "What do you want? More cakes?"

"That would be a nice start." Angela drummed her fingers where they rested on the top of the cake box. "Did you know this town doesn't have Uber?"

What? "No. I didn't know that, but I'm not surprised. What does that have to do with anything?"

"I don't have my driver's license anymore, but there are places I'd like to go. A hairdresser, perhaps. Maybe shopping now and then. That's where you would come in."

She wants me to . . . oh no. "You want *me* to chauffeur you around like I'm an Uber driver."

Angela nodded smugly.

"Why me? Why don't you ask—ohhh! You can't ask your family to drive you around because they think you're ill. If you went out shopping and having a good time, then they'd know you've been lying. So what you really need are *secret* rides."

"I prefer the word 'confidential.'" Unrepentant, Angela casually brushed a crumb from her lap. "Let's say one—no, make it two months of confidential rides and the occasional cake, and I'll acknowledge whatever you want me to."

Ella could almost hear Aunt Jo's glee at the news that Ella might still be in town when the bake-off came around. "I'm not staying here for an entire month."

Angela raised her eyebrows. "Why not? You have one of those work-from-home jobs, don't you?"

Ella frowned. "I won't do it. You want me to drive you all over the place for free—"

"Of course not!" Angela looked offended. "I'll pay for the gas, and who knows? I might spring for lunch now and then, too. But during these rides, which will be to places of my choosing, you may talk to me as much as you want, and on topics of your choosing, including the Book of Cakes."

It was a horrible, awful deal, at least for Ella. The urge to leave, to just get up and walk away, grew. She found herself looking at the open window where the summer breeze stirred the curtains and beckoned. *Surely the dreams will stop on their own. I just need to give them some time.*

Ella was standing before she realized it. "I can't do this." She turned on her heel and headed for the open window, her steps quickening the closer she got.

"Run away," Angela called after her. "That's what guilty people do when they've committed a crime."

Ella stopped, her hands fisted at her sides. *I am not running away!* But she knew that if Aunt Jo saw her right now, that's exactly what she'd say. *Darn it!* Ella spun on her heel to face Angela. "If I do this— and I'm not saying I will—then after that, we'll be good?"

Angela shrugged. "As far as I'm concerned, you'll be absolved of your sins—at least for taking the Book of Cakes."

I hate this. She's so darn smug. Ella scowled and absently rubbed her elbow where an itch had begun. Her fingers found a smudge of tiny stickiness, the scent of strawberries floating around her like perfume.

Who was she kidding? She didn't have a choice. "I'll do it, but only for one week and no more."

"Two months, and maybe longer."

Darn it! "One month, but that's it. That's all I'll promise."

Angela raised her eyebrows. "A *minimum* of a month. And then, at the end of that time, *if* I decide that you've done enough, I'll let you know."

Gah! Was nothing easy with this woman? Ella had to grit her teeth, but she managed to say, "Fine."

Angela's smile was bright and instant. "I'll see if I can get a hair appointment at the Stuff and Fluff tomorrow." Her eyes narrowed. "You know where that is, don't you?"

"Everyone knows the Stuff and Fluff." Ella and her sisters used to go to the Stuff and Fluff back in the day. The small beauty shop was located about twenty minutes away in the neighboring town of Glory. One side of the building housed a hair salon run by the very competent and locally famous hairdresser Teresa Caldwall, while the other side of the building served as a taxidermy service run by her husband, who was known for his adorable work with squirrels. It was said that one of his creations was in the Smithsonian National Museum of Natural History.

"I'll text you what time the appointment is once I call. Teresa knows I tip well, so I'm sure she'll work me in."

"Won't Jules notice if you show up with your hair suddenly perfect?"

"You leave that to me. I'm not without resources, you know."

Ella sighed. "All right. I'll see you tomorrow." She started to head back toward the window and then stopped. "I think I'll use the door."

Angela didn't look up. She'd already reclaimed the cake box and was pulling out her fork. "Use whichever you want, window or door. Just remember that no one can know about this. I want *confidential* rides."

"Right. I'm a secret chauffeur for a crazy woman who's pretending she's dying. Got it."

Seething, Ella left, closing the door behind her with a half slam. *Lord help me, what have I gotten myself into now?*

CHAPTER 8

ELLA

Patience isn't a virtue reserved only for the kitchen.

The Book of Cakes, p. 82
Written: 1792–2019

"I'm so glad you're staying in Dove Pond a while longer," Tiff announced two weeks later, her voice tinny from where Ella's cellphone sat on the counter propped against a cheese shredder. "It's social media gold."

"It's a pain in the rump, that's what it is." Ella pulled the scones from the oven and set them on the waiting trivets, the delicious scent of vanilla and cranberry wafting through the air. Beside the scones sat two dozen rose-water-and-vanilla-crème cupcakes, three dozen iced chocolate tea cakes, and a dozen blueberry scones drizzled with vanilla icing.

"Your fans are eating up the content from that town."

"Great." Ella tugged off her oven mitts and dropped them on the counter. The only reason she wasn't already on her way to New York was because of Tiff's coaxing . . . and, of course, Angela. And by gosh, Ella was going to see their agreement through even if it killed her. But that hadn't stopped her from venting to Tiff about feeling stuck. Every day made Ella feel as if she were sinking into Dove Pond quicksand, a thick and clinging mixture of relationships and expectations.

"By the way," Tiff said, "I extended your car rental. Right now, it's good for another month. We can extend it again if we need to."

"Thanks. I appreciate that." Ella leaned on her elbows so her face was level with her phone. "Look, Tiff, I know this place is charming and cute and adorable, but it's not perfect. If you stand in one place too long, it'll suck you in. People here know how to guilt you into doing all sorts of things."

"It's worth it just for the media numbers, which are lit. Have you seen them? The stats are in that email from Viv."

"No. I've been sort of busy." Which was an understatement. Had she realized that a half-crazy, supposedly too-sick-to-leave-her-house woman would demand to be chauffeured all over the place almost every single day, which she had been doing for the past two weeks, Ella wouldn't have accepted Angela's deal. And worse, Angela had to avoid Dove Pond all together, which meant extra driving. *That woman has more energy at eighty than I have now.*

"Dove Pond is fire," Tiff announced. "We've gotten calls from three of our biggest sponsors, asking for additional ad space. Three, Ella! Plus, two new major name brands came knocking just yesterday. Everyone is crazy about your 'Paris Metro to Country Cute' story."

"Paris to what?"

"'PM to CC.' That's what I'm calling it." Tiff's grin was ridiculously huge. "It's catchy."

"Terrific."

"The sponsors are loving the small-town vibe you're handing out, and they want in on it. Your videos from last week were dope. You got the assignment."

Whenever Ella wasn't toting Angela all over western North Carolina, she was making videos for her team. Ella had visited Ava's a number of times, plus Antique Alley and a half dozen other places in town. "I'm glad you liked them."

"Loooooved them! We're going to go big, Ella." Tiff leaned closer, her face filling the screen. "*Big!*"

Oh geez. "Yay!" Ella hoped her smile wasn't as wan as it felt and wondered what sort of toxic caffeine concoction was in the cup that sat beside Tiff's keyboard.

"The Pink Magnolia Tearoom has been a huge hit—almost a million point two likes and still counting. People are saying it's charming and 'looks like it's from a movie.' Wait until they see the videos from that odd little bookstore you sent me yesterday and—oh, the farmer's market from Saturday! I almost forgot that one. The crafts are to die for, and the flowers and produce are gorgeous. You even made me yearn for yams. Who yearns for *those*?"

Ella mutely struggled to contain a yawn. She was exhausted this morning. Ever since she'd started toting Angela around town, the dreams had changed. Aunt Jo said it was a promising development, which gave Ella hope, but the newest version of the dream was unsettling. Now every dream started with her leaving the house and walking down Elm Street. There she was, happily strolling along, admiring the architecture of the houses along the way and enjoying the warmth of the sun on her shoulders. But as she walked, she got the oddest feeling she was being followed.

Heart quickening, she'd stop and slowly turn around.

There, trying to hide behind a tree but sticking out on all sides, was the huge silver-papered cupcake, its top a swirled-up pile of strawberry frosting. It wasn't yet chasing her, but on seeing her stop, it hopped out of its hiding place and took a step in her direction.

Ell gasped and took a step back.

Which had made it step forward.

So she took another step back.

It did the same, only its step was larger and more threatening.

Heart thudding, she turned on her heel, ducked her head, and started walking away as fast as she dared.

But the faster she walked, the faster it came.

Soon, she was running, panting with the effort, a terrible stitch in her side. She could hear the cupcake running, too, its massive footsteps closing in. Gasping for breath, she'd realized she was now on Hill Street, running toward the Stewart house. Once she got close, she leapt up on the curb, planning to dive over the hedge into the yard. But just as she got there, her shoe caught the curb and threw her to the ground.

Behind her, she could hear the thunder of the cupcake as it bore down on her.

Terrified, she'd thrown her arms over her head and— *Bam!* She woke up.

Wide-awake and shaken, she'd lain in her creaky, old bed, trying to calm down her still-racing thoughts before getting up to get a glass of water. That was when she'd found a long streak of beautifully piped pink frosting swirling from her ring finger all the way up to her shoulder like an elaborate 3D henna tattoo.

The whole thing was disturbing. *Maybe next time, I should stop running and just eat that stupid cupcake. Maybe that's what'll put an end to this nonsense.*

"So, can you?" Tiff asked, a hopeful note in her voice. "At least a few. They'd make great vid ops."

Wait. What? Ella forced a smile and picked up the phone. "I'm sorry. Can you repeat that? I was thinking about something else."

Tiff's permanent smile flickered. "That's the second time you've zoned out. Why don't I just send you everything in an email so you'll have notes?"

"Yes, please. So sorry, Tiff. I didn't sleep well."

Tiff nodded in sympathy. "We all have those nights."

"Thanks for understanding. I'll get to those content requests as soon as I can. But in the meantime, you should be planning my exit strategy here. I'm not staying any longer than necessary."

"Sure." Tiff tapped her pen on her notepad. "We'll need a defining event for the grand finale of 'PM to CC.'"

"A finale?"

"Some sort of shindig, like a hoedown or a country fair. You know, something with that rich small-town flavor, and lots of photo ops. A 'Goodbye to Dove Pond' sort of event."

"I'd like that." Actually, she'd love it. Ella nodded. "Let's do it."

Tiff brightened and continued to talk about the perfect finale while Ella's gaze wandered to the large windows opening onto the backyard. Ava had planted purple, pink, and yellow flowers along the gray stone path that led to the back of their yard, where the fresh, bubbling blue water of Sugar Creek wound its way past. A huge weeping willow trailed its green leaves into the clear water, as graceful as the rushing creek under it.

Ava's plants gave her peace. Ella had seen her sister's expression go from outraged to completely calm as she walked through the long, decadently green rows of her greenhouses. *Kitchens make me feel the same way. Nothing calms my soul more.* For Ella, baking was like taking a deep breath. It let out all the bad and gave her room to see the good. Which was why she'd gotten up at the break of dawn this morning and started baking. It wasn't just because Angela wanted scones, although Ella would probably skim off a few and give her some. Instead, she was baking to lift her own spirits, which were dismally low this morning.

"I think that's it," Tiff said, interrupting Ella's train of thought. "The team and I will be looking online for events to use for that grand finale. Maybe you should ask your sisters for some ideas? They know that area well."

"Will do."

"Just one more thing. Once we pick this event, we should fly the team down to cover it. Would you be up for that? I mentioned it at our last staff meeting and they were psyched about it."

"Of course," Ella said. She'd be more than happy to pass the videography and interview chores to her people.

"Great! I'm going to offer our main sponsors a place at the table if we can find a big enough event to attract a crowd. What fun!" Tiff looked through her notes. "I think that's it. Check your email for those deets."

Ella managed a smile. "It all sounds great. Thanks, Tiff." Wiggling her fingers in a goodbye, she hung up. She wished she had Tiff's enthusiasm. Sighing heavily, she dropped the phone into her apron pocket just as Sarah came in.

"Scones, cupcakes, and chocolate tea cakes?" Sarah set a stack of books on the counter and went to get a plate. "What's gotten into you?"

Trust her sister to know she baked en masse like this only when she was upset. "A little of this and a lot of that."

Sarah pulled the butter crock from the counter and then slid a warm blueberry scone onto her plate. "You should take the extras to Ava's."

"I thought of that."

"I'm surprised Kristen and Ava haven't been here, stuffing their cakeholes. I could smell those scones all the way upstairs in my bedroom."

"Kristen left for school around seven, and Ava headed out about the same time. Said she had to meet a delivery truck."

"She's way too busy." Sarah sighed happily as she looked at the pastries. "I've had dreams that started like this. Just me and delicious desserts. Mm. Such good dreams."

"At least none of your desserts chased you."

Sarah's gaze flew to Ella. "Chased?"

Ella waved her hand. "It's nothing, really."

Sarah looked at the line of pastries. "Nothing?"

Ella had to laugh. "It's a little something, but that's all."

Sarah's eyebrows rose. "What's going on? You came home unexpectedly, then we found out Jules and her mother think you stole their family cookbook years ago, and now this. Even weirder, you're staying, even though it's obvious you'd rather be somewhere else."

Ella winced. "Is it that obvious?"

"We know you pretty well."

"Too well. To be honest, I've had a stressful few months." Ella got a plate and picked out a tea cake. "I didn't tell you this before because I don't understand it myself, but a while ago I started having these weird dreams where I'm being chased by a giant pink-frosted cupcake. I came back here to talk to Aunt Jo about it because when I wake up, I usually find strawberry frosting somewhere on me."

Sarah's eyes widened. "Wow! What did Aunt Jo say?"

"She said the dreams have crossed into the real world, which means I'm supposed to do something."

"Like what?"

"I'm not sure. The cupcake always chases me to the Stewart house, which is why I thought it had to do with the lost Book of Cakes. I've been hoping that if I can convince Angela I didn't take that silly cookbook, the dreams would stop."

"And?"

"She won't believe me. Meanwhile, Jules has done everything she could to keep me from even seeing her mother."

"That's not surprising. Jules has always been nice to me, but she seems strict, while Angela seems self-centered and—" Sarah made a face. "I'm being judgy, aren't I? Sorry. I hope you figure things out soon."

"Thanks. I hope so, too." Ella managed a smile, the chocolate tea cake on her plate helping. The light texture and chocolate flavor danced across her tongue and eased some of her frustrations.

Sarah took a bite of her scone and mumbled around it. "Oh my gosh. This is so good." She sighed happily and took another bite, her gaze wandering around the room. "Do you remember when Momma used to put cinnamon brooms in all the rooms every fall?"

"It made the house smell like happiness."

Sarah ran her finger over her plate to catch the crumbs. "That's what I think heaven will be like. Desserts and books and nothing else."

Ella had to laugh at her sister's serious expression. "Throw in a nice French press and some freshly ground coffee, and I'd join you." She went to stack the pans that needed washing beside the sink with the used mixing bowls, and then started loading the dishwasher.

She wondered if it was possible she'd made some progress with Angela, but just didn't know it. *Probably not.* Whenever Ella had imagined having her conversation with Angela about the lost Book of Cakes, she'd never thought Angela would listen to the truth with a bored expression, shrug, and say, "Whatever."

She's insufferable. Still, at some point in the past week, it had dawned on Ella that while their little drives hadn't exactly cleared her name, at some point she and Angela had slipped back into their old relationship. Just yesterday morning, while driving to a little boutique in nearby Swannanoa so Angela could buy a cardigan for the cooler weather, Ella had mentioned she was attempting to develop a brown butter cookie recipe that would meld the buttery taste with hints of ginger and lemon. She was having some difficulty finding the right balance, which had interested Angela immensely, and she'd offered several very good suggestions. It wasn't a conversation Ella could have had with many people.

Sarah looked up from where she was buttering her second scone. "That's about the fifth sigh I've heard in the past five minutes."

"Sorry. I'm just a little frustrated. I've been driving Angela Stewart around for the past two weeks."

Sarah's hand froze in place, the scone halfway to her mouth. She lowered the pastry. "Why?"

"To give me some time to convince her I had nothing to do with her cookbook disappearing."

"Driving her where?"

"Wherever she wants. I agreed to do it for a month." Ella had to fight off another heavy sigh. "I'm already regretting it. I didn't expect her to plan daily trips. One or two a week, great. But every day is a bit much."

"So that's where you've been. Ava and I thought you might have a secret boyfriend."

"More like a secret witch."

Sarah had to smile at that. "I take it driving Ms. Angela isn't working out well."

Ella slid another tea cake onto her plate. "It's not great. I'm still having the dream, so . . . I thought that once I'd told Angela I hadn't taken that book, she'd realize her error and the dreams would disappear."

"She's a dodgy old lady." Sarah started to add something, but then she tilted her head to one side, her eyebrows drawn. "Didn't Mark say Angela is too ill to leave her house?"

"She's not as ill as all that," Ella said cautiously. She shot a glance at her sister and wondered how much she should share. *It won't hurt her to know Angela's not a shut-in. I'll just skip the part about the lies she's been telling about her health. That's Angela's secret to tell, not mine.* "We've been running a few errands here and there, but nothing too physical. Jules and Mark don't know about it."

"Or Gray?"

"I haven't seen Gray since I came to town." Which had taken some doing, to be honest. More than once, she'd had to slip into any of a variety of stores, and once the post office, to avoid meeting him on the street. "I haven't told any of them I'm driving her around, and I doubt Angela has, either. Jules would hate knowing I'm spending time with anyone in her family. Angela is aware of that, and we've been visiting other towns so we don't run into her."

Sarah gave a silent whistle. "You're sort of stuck, aren't you? Between an Angela rock and a Jules hard place."

"Exactly. I'd appreciate it if you didn't tell anyone about this. Angela is determined to get out of the house, but Jules is super protective of her mom." Which was laughable. The last person who needed to be "protected" was Angela. *That woman is fearless. I sort of admire that, even while, on some level, it horrifies me.*

"Momma used to say Angela was both the strongest and the weakest person she'd ever met. Funny how often Momma was right about people." Sarah glanced at her phone. "Oops. I'm late. I'd better get to the library." She got up and carried her plate to the sink, then scooped up her stack of books. "If you get bored hanging with Angela, feel free to stop by the library. We have a really nice selection of cookbooks now."

"Thanks. I'll remember that." Ella waved goodbye to her sister and then finished the dishes. Afterward, she was just putting on her mascara when her phone started ringing with CeeLo Green's "Forget You." "The perfect ringtone for Angela," Ella said under her breath as she picked it up. "Good morning, this is your friendly courtesy shuttle. What will it be today? A foot massage? A dozen pink roses? Or maybe you've discovered a deep and endless yearning for a frozen yogurt shop four counties away?"

"You're so funny," Angela said. "Ever heard of a book called *The Forest of Vanishing Stars* by Kristin Harmel? I saw it on a list of best book club reads, and I'm a book club of one."

"I bet there's a copy in the library. Sarah would be more than happy to look."

"I want my own copy. That way, if I decide to underline something, no one fines me for it."

Of course Angela was an underliner. "Is there no rule you won't break?"

"Very few. Pick me up at noon. The bookstore in Swannanoa will have it. Oh, and on the way here, I need you to stop at the Piggly Wiggly and get me a few things."

Great. The grocery store. Ella was not only driving Ms. Dying all over the county, but now she'd become the old lady's personal shopper. Could this situation get any worse?

"Ella, get a pen and some paper. I don't want you to forget anything."

Grumbling, Ella dug into her purse for a notepad and a pen. As she expected, the list wasn't short, and it consisted mainly of various types of candies and cookies. "No ice cream?"

"I can't hide that in my nightstand."

That made sense. Ella was momentarily glad she wasn't living a secret life. It seemed very inconvenient. "If you're nice to me, I might bring you a scone. I just made some."

"Bring more than one and I'll give you the day off tomorrow."

She'll give *me a day off. How nice of her.* Ella thought of about twenty sharp, but not entirely polite, replies. *Don't do it*, she told herself. Instead, she hung up and got ready to leave.

Before she went to the Pig for Angela, Ella decided to take some of the cakes and scones she'd made to Ava's new tearoom. *Angela can wait. It won't kill her.*

The tearoom was busy, but not overly so. Ella was happy to see Ava behind the counter. She was making a latte, Dylan sitting close by, watching her. *As he always does.*

Ella held up the two pastry boxes. "I brought you a few things."

Ava brightened. "Gimme!" She took the boxes and opened them eagerly.

Ella slid onto a stool. "Hi, Dylan."

"Good morning!" He grinned, his teeth white against his auburn beard.

Ella didn't know many auburn-haired men, but Dylan's rugged good looks made her think of Jamie from *Outlander*. Ava was a lucky woman, whether she knew it or not.

He held up his mug of coffee. "Did you come to try Ava's Americano? It's divine."

"I haven't tried it yet, but I will." Ella looked around, admiring anew all the little touches Ava had implemented. "It's a lovely place." She glanced over at Dylan. "Ava says you're a terrific contractor."

He looked pleased as he turned to look around the room with her. "This was one of the most satisfying jobs I've ever done. Ava was determined to keep the historic details intact."

"She's got an eye for it."

His gaze returned to Ava, and he said in a wistful tone, "She's good at everything."

Wow. He's crazy about her. I hope she decides to give this relationship a chance. Ella thought Dylan was perfect for Ava—he was smart, kind, and as dedicated to this little town as she was. Ava's heart was here in Dove Pond, and it was here she'd stay. *It's different for me. I've never met a guy who made me want to stay in the same place for more than a month.*

Ava closed the door to the pastry case and rejoined them. "Those will come in handy this weekend. There's going to be a Labor Day parade and everything."

"A market-forward day," Dylan said with an understanding nod.

"Exactly!" Ava beamed at Ella. "How much do I owe you?"

"Nothing. I was bored this morning, so . . ." She waved at the full case.

"Can I at least fix you a caramel macchiato? I know how you love those."

Ella could never say no to caramel anything. "Oh yes! In a to-go cup, if you don't mind."

While Ava fixed her drink, Dylan said, "I heard you sold your pie company. Kristen loves the Ella Dove apple crumb pie. She gets one from the Piggly Wiggly about every other week."

"I should make her a real one while I'm here. It's much better than the manufactured ones." That predictable loss of quality had been her only reluctance in selling her company. The pies were still good and got rave reviews, but the corporate bakers didn't have the Dove family magic or Ella's deft use of spices.

Ava brought the macchiato and set it in front of Ella. "I'm excited I'll be able to offer my customers a genuine Ella Dove patisserie experience while you're here. I'm going to make a sign for the case so they know it."

Dylan grinned. "Charging extra?"

"Of course. I would never dishonor my sister by not doubling the prices for her bakery items."

Ella thought that was only fair. "I'm heading to the grocery store here in a few minutes. Do you need anything?"

"Yes! Three bottles of honey, the local kind. Oh, and a large thing of cinnamon."

Ella pulled her pen from her purse and added honey and cinnamon to her list. "Got it. I'll be back soon. Dylan, don't drink all of Ava's espresso while I'm gone. Save some for the customers."

He chuckled. "I'll try."

She was still smiling, her list in her hand, as she walked out of the door and turned down the sidewalk on her way to her car. Chuckling a little at the realization that getting both Angela's and Ava's sweets at the grocery store would make her look like a bingeing diabetic to the teenager at the cash register, Ella was just starting to take a sip of her drink when she ran into a wall.

It wasn't a real wall, but a person so tall and so broad shouldered that he seemed rock solid. She held her cup away from her, macchiato dripping over her hand. She muttered an annoyed "Great!" under her breath as she checked to be sure she hadn't gotten any on her coat.

"Ella?"

She knew that voice. Surprised, she looked up and had to shade her eyes against the late-morning sun that outlined the man in front of her. "Gray?"

He laughed and moved to the side so she wasn't staring directly into the sunlight. "How are you?"

Good Lord. He'd been in shape when they'd dated before, in a tall and lanky way that she'd found adorable. But he looked different now. He'd bulked up, grown some muscles, and had bulges in all the right places. In just a few short years, he'd gone from a light and refreshing lemonade to an expensive, smoky whiskey. And oh, how she loved a nice glass of whiskey on a cold night.

It was funny, but though they'd been good friends in high school, she'd never thought of him as dateable until they'd met up at Angela's house in the Hamptons a few years ago. As a teenager, he'd been a dark and gloomy sort of nerd, too smart for his own good and as tightly wound as a spring. They'd been instant friends, but little else.

Still, they'd grown close over the years, and she'd told him things she'd never told anyone else—about missing her dad, how she wished her Dove magic was something other than making really good cupcakes, and everything else she was going through. For her, Gray was a perfect friend. He listened, sympathized, and never judged. And she did the same for him.

She'd always liked him, although he experienced life far more intensely than she did. He was tortured by his own thoughts, caught in a well of anxiety brought on by his own father's death, something she could commiserate with in ways few other people around them could. Unlike his overly protective mother, Ella had accepted and understood his struggles, even though they were vastly different from her own.

But the whole "best but only friends" thing changed when Ella saw him in the Hamptons. As an adult, Gray was no longer shy or retiring or even nerdy. Sure, he was a chemist, but he exuded an air of confidence, which, combined with his smoldering good looks and quick sense of humor, had slayed her. They'd had an instant attraction they'd never had when they were younger.

But now? Lord help her, but he looked fine. Mighty, mighty *fine*.

Gray smiled, his eyes crinkling. "I heard you were in town."

"You . . ." She had to dampen her dry lips before she could continue. "Hi."

His smile broadened. "Hi."

She tore her gaze from his face and noticed that his red T-shirt was damp down the front and he wore running shoes. To her chagrin, she heard herself say pointlessly, "You've been running."

"There's a trail through the park. I was just on my way back to my truck."

She nodded, as if that was what she'd thought he'd say. "I'd heard you'd moved back, but I hadn't seen you around." Mainly because she'd been avoiding him. She'd thought this meeting would be awkward for him, but for some reason it seemed that she was the only one talking in a hopelessly breathless voice.

He shrugged. "I've been around. It's been a long time, hasn't it?"

Much too long, judging by how much she was tempted to touch his arm and see if it was as hard as it looked. *Stop it, Ella! Get a grip.* "It's been a while since we last spoke."

His eyebrows rose and he said softly, "Oh, I remember the last time we spoke."

Why, oh why, did I bring that up? She tried to think of something to say that would turn his thoughts away from the day she'd broken up with him. "I heard you bought a farm."

"I did. I'm staying in the carriage house apartment at Mom's while the house is being updated, but I hope to move there soon." As he spoke, his gaze moved over Ella's face, and she wished her summer freckles weren't in full bloom. They faded during the winter months, which she liked, but as soon as June hit, out they came, and no amount of sunscreen could stop them.

An amused gleam lit his blue eyes. "I see you're still baking."

Oh dear. I must have flour on me. She looked down at her dress, ready to brush it away.

"Not there." He slid the edge of his thumb across her cheek, leaving a trail of tingles on her bare skin.

Her heart raced like crazy. Whew, the chemistry between them was stronger than ever. "Sorry about that. I made pastries this morning and the flour is super clingy."

"It wasn't flour." He lowered his hand. A dash of pink frosting sat on his thumb.

She caught the scent of strawberry and hid a scowl. The frosting couldn't have been on her face a moment ago, because neither Dylan nor Ava had said anything. *It's getting worse. I hate that.* She dug a napkin out of her purse and handed it to him. Ever since she'd started having the frosting episodes, she'd had to keep napkins and tissues on hand. *Yet another way it's messing with my life.*

Gray wiped his hand on the napkin. "Thanks." He looked around and tossed the napkin into the trash can that sat beside a bench and then slanted her a curious look. "Word on the street is that you've sold your place in Paris and are moving back to the States."

"Yeah, I'm only in Dove Pond for another two or three weeks." Three weeks suddenly didn't seem like such a huge stretch of time. In fact, it seemed just about perfect.

"You're never anywhere long, are you?"

She shrugged. "I like adventures." She tilted her head to one side. "I heard you'd left your job in Atlanta. I thought you enjoyed being a food chemist."

"I did and do, but I disliked the corporate pressure we were under. So when my last project went well and I started getting some hefty residuals, I retired."

"Retired? You must have come up with something huge."

"Big enough. I developed a natural-ingredient-based fungicide that breaks down the most common mold that hinders organic strawberry production by—" He caught himself and gave a dry laugh. "Sorry. I was about to bore you to death with chemical theory."

"You've never bored me." That was true. But whatever the past had been, she was ridiculously thrilled to run into this new and obviously more relaxed version of Gray. "Maybe we could meet up for coffee. I'd love to catch up."

Something flickered behind his eyes, but to her surprise, he didn't jump at the offer. Instead, he merely said in a noncommittal tone, "Why not?"

His reaction was disappointing. What was going on here? He never used to hesitate where she was concerned. *Never*. "Call me. You still have my number, don't you?"

"I think so. Let me check." He tugged his phone out of his pocket to scroll through his contacts.

She had to smile. "You still have your flip phone."

He gave a lopsided grin. "It still works. I never give up on things until there's no hope."

She'd never thought she could be jealous of a flip phone, but here she was. "Send me a text when you're free. I—" Her phone pinged, and she pulled out her own phone to find a message from Angela. *WHERE ARE YOU?*

Sheesh, lady! Ella dropped the phone back into her purse and snapped it closed.

"Bad news?" he asked, his gaze scanning her face.

"Sort of." She forced a smile. "I wish we could chat more, but I have some errands."

"I've got to get to work, too. It was good seeing you, Ella." He lifted his hand and, before she could think of something witty to say, headed across the street to where his truck sat.

Ella was left standing alone on the sidewalk as she watched him leave. *Well. That was interesting.*

Maybe it wasn't such a bad thing she was stuck in Dove Pond for a few more weeks. Tiff said the sponsors were loving the content, and heaven knew Angela wasn't in a hurry to offer the absolution that Ella so desperately needed.

Ella absently slid a hand over her cheek, and then made a face when it came away sticky. *Darn it, more frosting! Will it never end?* Nothing was ever simple for a Dove, was it?

Still, she found herself smiling as she made her way back to her car. Despite the frosting, and Angela's annoying presence, it wasn't such a bad day after all.

CHAPTER 9

GRAY

"It's only been a week," Gray muttered under his breath as he untangled a length of water tubing from the pile on the barn floor. "Surely I can last longer than that."

"Last longer at what?"

Gray turned toward the voice. Trav Parker stood just inside the wide doors, his motorcycle helmet tucked under one arm. Gray grinned at his friend. They'd gone to the same high school but hadn't become friends until this last year, after Gray moved back to town.

He leaned to one side so he could look past Trav, but no motorcycle came into view. "Did you coast in? I can usually hear your bike a mile away."

"I parked down the drive. That bull of yours doesn't like my bike. I'm glad he's small; otherwise I might be intimidated."

"Pickles isn't done growing yet."

Trav snorted. "If I ever get a cow, you're not naming it."

"Hey, Pickles likes his name. And I'm not planning on getting any other cows, anyway. I'm just going to spoil the ones I got with the farm." Gray dropped the blue tubing he'd been trying to untangle.

"What are you doing here? You're usually busy this time of day running that garage of yours."

"I had to run to Asheville to get a part, so . . ." Trav shrugged and came farther into the barn. A talented mechanic, he'd inherited his garage from his father. Trav set his helmet on a barrel and slowly walked around the barn, eyeing Gray's work.

Trav wasn't a talker, but Gray didn't mind. "It's a hydroponic gardening system," he explained without prompting. "Instead of soil, plants grow in nutrition-laden water. I'm using grow lights, too. Solar-powered ones, so I can grow vegetables all year round. There's an array behind the barn."

"Impressive."

Coming from Trav, that was high praise, indeed. "Thanks. I'm using a vertical system in here, so I should be able to harvest an amazing amount in this space. The plants will mature up to fifty percent faster."

"Very efficient." Still wandering around, Trav absently rubbed his cheek, the noise of his hand against the stubble loud in the quiet. "What were you saying when I came in? About not lasting a week?" Trav came to a halt a few yards away, a question in his dark eyes. "Didn't have anything to do with Ella Dove, did it?"

Gray narrowed his gaze. "Who sent you? Sarah or Grace?" Ella's sister Sarah was close to both Trav and his wife Grace.

"Neither. Which is good, because if they had, I'd be sunk. What one thinks, the other says. It's annoying as all get-out."

It was weird that Sarah and Grace were even friends, as they were complete opposites. Of course, the same could be said of Trav and Grace. Trav was a quiet, muscled, tattooed, and scarred biker comfortable only in jeans and a T-shirt. Meanwhile, Grace was a perfectly put-together businesswoman who rarely wore anything other than designer suits and pumps. As mayor, she ran Dove Pond with the precision of a general. *Which is probably why Trav gets along with her so well. He was in the military for years.* "I hope neither Sarah nor Grace are asking about me and Ella, as it's not their business."

"Give them time." Trav sat down on a bale of hay. "If you don't want to explain what you were saying when I came in, then don't. I only asked because you sounded upset."

That was fair. Trav was always fair. Trav was the only person Gray ever talked to about his anxiety issues. That was because Trav had experienced his own, heavier version, as he'd suffered from PTSD after getting wounded in Afghanistan. Even now, when the sunlight from the open barn door slanted across Trav's face, Gray could see an angry red scar that ran up his neck and then disappeared under his beard stubble. "I was talking to myself. But yes, it was about Ella. We used to have a thing."

"And now?"

"I think . . ." Hoo boy, he hated saying it out loud. "I think I still like her." Who wouldn't? She was fascinating, funny, and endearing. He realized Trav was watching him and managed a shrug.

"That bad, hm?"

"Yes. No. To be honest, I don't know exactly what I'm doing. I mean, I do know. To a point." He blew out his breath in frustration. "We ran into each other last week. I knew not to act too interested, which is a death knell where Ella is concerned, so I played it cool."

"She plays hard to get?"

"She doesn't play. She *is* hard to get. She's as allergic to commitment as my cousin Steve is allergic to peanuts. If he gets even a whiff of one, even from a distance, he swells like a balloon."

"So you were playing it safe by not overreacting."

"It worked, too. She wanted to go for coffee, but I didn't take the bait."

"And?"

"I'm trying not to call her. But it's hard. She . . ." Gray shook his head. "I've got to keep my head on straight. To be honest, it was rough when she left last time."

Trav's eyebrows rose.

Gray picked up the line of tubing he'd been trying to untangle earlier. "I knew she'd leave, and I stupidly thought that knowing that in advance would make it easier." He found the end of the line and pulled it through the tangled loop. "I guess I had too much hope."

"Playing with fire, aren't you?"

"More like dynamite." He gave the knotted line a tug and it came undone. "But don't worry; I plan on keeping my feet on the ground this time."

Trav nodded. "I'm sure you will. I have to wonder, though. What do you want to happen here? What's your goal?"

Those were good questions. "Ella avoids long-term relationships. She'd prefer to stay at the too-hot-to-handle stage and then zip right past emotional involvement to the goodbye. This time, I'd like to keep things at a slow burn so that we don't rip through the important stages."

"You want to slow things down so the relationship has time to develop."

Gray nodded. "It's tough, though. She's— Whew. I'm going to have to fight my natural inclinations, and hers too. But I really want this to work."

"You'll do it. I can tell you're motivated."

Gray wished he could be even half as sure as Trav seemed to be. *I hope he's right.* He managed a smile. "Are you up for a run tomorrow morning?"

"You know it. Five a.m.?"

"Make it six. I'm not as young as you. I need time to wake up and stuff like that."

"Codger."

"Wasted youth."

"See you in the morning, old man." Chuckling, Trav picked up his helmet, his calm gaze meeting Gray's. "About Ella—I'm proud of you for giving it your best shot, despite your history with her. If this woman is worth the effort, then . . ." He shrugged. "You can handle whatever happens."

Gray knew that, but it still felt good to hear it. "I've got my head on straight." *So far.*

"We'll see how you do after our run tomorrow. I plan on leaving you in the dirt."

"Ha! We'll see about that. Watch yourself on the way out. If Pickles get motivated, he just might jump the fence."

"That I'd like to see." Trav chuckled, pulled on his helmet, and, with a final wave, left.

Gray neatly coiled the line of tubing and placed it on a hook before he left the barn. Outside, the morning sun slanted across the green field, casting long, early-morning shadows. He allowed his gaze to move from the fields to the oak trees along the drive to the faded blue farmhouse that sat across from the barn. The two-story house had been built in the early 1900s and had a large wraparound porch perfect for rocking chairs and perhaps even a swing. Across the yard, mingling with the moos from his cows, was the sound of hammering, and an occasional bit of conversation as workers swarmed in and out of the building.

Everything was coming together. When the renovation was completed, he'd have a home he'd be proud of, something warm and welcoming and far more his style than the soulless chrome-and-marble high-rise apartment he'd had in Atlanta. He wondered what Ella would think of the house and then cursed under his breath. *I have to stop thinking about her.* Darn, it was easy to say what needed to be done, but impossibly hard to do it.

Too restless to stay where he was, he headed for his truck. He'd fetch some more line from the hardware store in Swannanoa and finish the system later today. He'd already bought out the supply at the Ace in Dove Pond, or he'd have gone there. *Oh well, it's just an extra half an hour.*

He pulled out of the driveway and headed for the store. For weeks now, everyone in town had been talking about Ella. That wasn't surprising, as she was something of a celebrity—plus, if there was one thing people in Dove Pond knew how to do, it was talk. Gray had known it was only a matter of time before they ran into each other. Of course, that hadn't mitigated the shock he'd felt on seeing her. Just that one brief conversation had left him reeling, almost drunk with . . . darn, he didn't know what it was, but it had knocked him down.

She'd looked good. Her hair was longer and she was a bit curvier, which he liked. But as cute as Ella was, it was her personality that bowled a guy over. She was fun, playful, and naturally sexy.

Seeing her had reminded him of the summer he'd walked into the house in the Hamptons to find her and Grandma in the kitchen making a peach cobbler. Perhaps it was the surprise, or maybe it was just the latent crush he'd always had on her, but his feelings had exploded on seeing her standing there, a dash of flour on one cheek, her grin instant and welcoming. She'd seemed happy to see him, which had given him that most devastating of all emotions—hope.

That had been a huge mistake. He'd known Ella for a long time and knew her better than anyone. From some things she'd shared with him years ago, he suspected that her avoidance of any relationship past a quick, passionate fling was because she was attempting to avoid the pain she'd felt when her father died. Nothing hurt like being left behind. So the second she felt vulnerable, she ran away. He'd seen her do it time and again. And who could blame her for that? Gray certainly didn't.

That summer was no different. He might have been devastated when she broke up with him, but he didn't blame her. She'd warned him repeatedly that she was planning on leaving. *I should have believed her, but I kept thinking I could change her mind.*

Which had been stupid. It would take a lot to change Ella's mind. It would take patience, and effort, and maybe even a little conniving.

Which was why he'd decided that this time he would play her game better than she did. If she wanted to see him, then she had to be the one to make the move, not him. *Stay cool*, he told himself. *Keep it casual and slow, which will keep her from panicking.*

He'd just turned onto Highway 70 when his phone rang. He looked at the caller ID and cursed inwardly at the disappointment he felt when he saw his brother's name instead of Ella's. Scowling at his own weakness, he answered, "Hi, Mark."

"Consider this a warning," Mark said. "Mom's going to use Grandma's health to try to convince you to stay in the apartment here and not move into your house when it's ready."

"Grandma doesn't need a sitter."

"I know. That's why I'm warning you."

That was kind of Mark. "Thanks for looking out for me."

Mark snorted. "Yeah. That's what I'm here for."

Gray knew Mark believed he was just joking when he said that, but he had been doing that ever since Dad died. It had been really annoying, especially in middle school when Gray couldn't have a single argument with one of his friends without his brother butting in and threatening some sort of bodily harm. Now that they were adults, Mark's overprotectiveness—although expressed in different ways than Mom's—was just as frustrating.

"It sounds like you're in your truck," Mark said. "Where are you headed?"

"Swannanoa. I need to get some more line."

"Oh. By yourself?"

That was an odd question. "Yes. Why?"

"Nothing. Mom was just saying she hadn't seen much of you lately."

"I've been busy at the house."

"That's what I told her. But you know how she is. Maybe you could stop by for dinner tonight? Just to calm Mom's overactive imagination."

Gray frowned. As much as he hated to admit it, Mark was right. It had been well over a week since he'd seen his family. Even Grandma's requests for snacks seemed to have tapered off. "I'll be there. I should be back in time."

"Great. I'll let everyone know. Mom's making a roast with potatoes and carrots."

He did love a nice roast. He thought about the half sandwich sitting in his fridge at the farmhouse right now. It would be soggy by now, too. "What time?"

"Seven."

"Great. See you there." Gray closed his phone and dropped it into the passenger seat. A half hour later, he turned onto the main road through Swannanoa. He was just a few stores away from the hardware shop when he hit a red light beside a nondescript strip mall and slowed to a stop. While waiting for the light to change, he absently glanced toward the half-full parking lot.

There, walking into the Fancy Fixes nail salon, was Grandma.

Gray blinked and then leaned forward. Yup, that was her. *What in the heck is she doing here, in Swannanoa?* She didn't drive, so she couldn't be wandering around alone.

She was obviously on her way to get her nails done, which would be hard to hide from Mom. *Has she finally told Mom the truth? It's about time. Wait. No. That can't be it. Mom wouldn't be having a normal dinner tonight if she and Grandma'd had a flare-up.*

A honk behind him let him know the light had changed. As he wasn't in a turn lane, he had to drive on. It took him a few minutes to get turned around and return to the strip mall, but he made it.

He pulled into a parking place, climbed out of his truck, and headed for the nail salon. He'd just reached the sidewalk when someone called out, "Hello, stranger!"

He turned around and there, pulling her huge purse from the back seat of her car, was Ella. She was dressed in a purple flowered dress that hugged all the right places and a blue-jean jacket, her blond hair in a thick braid over one shoulder, with a red ribbon tying it off.

What was she doing here? He sent her a confused look until the truth dawned on him. "*You* drove my grandmother here."

"She had an appointment."

"Good Lord. When I saw her, I thought I was hallucinating."

"Oh, she's here. I didn't want to bring her, but . . ." Ella shrugged. "I'm her Uber now."

What? This was getting interesting. "You're her ride?"

"Well, not by choice. Your grandma can be very, very persuasive."

Oh, Grandma, what are you doing now? "How long have you been driving her?"

"For too long. She gets bored at home since . . ." Ella caught herself, slanting him a cautious look.

There was power in being in the know. He crossed his arms and slanted her a smile. "She's told you about her convoluted and extremely unethical situation."

Ella's eyes widened. "You know about that? I thought she'd fooled the whole family."

"She told me, but Mark and Mom are still in the dark. I don't think this will end well."

"I've told her as much, but she won't listen to me. To be honest, I sort of wonder if now she's not in too deep to quit. Of course, so long as she has me to take her places and run her errands, she has even less of a reason to bring this charade to an end."

He grinned at Ella. "She was having me bring her snacks, but then she stopped. I thought she was just eating healthier, but you must be delivering her daily sugar fix now."

Ella nodded sadly. "The checkout girl at the Piggly Wiggly thinks I'm a raging diabetic. I don't know how your grandma can eat so many sweets and stay so thin."

"That's no secret. She has the metabolism and ethics of a coked-up monkey."

Ella laughed, which made him even more aware of her. Darn, but she looked good in her sundress and jacket and would look even better out of them. He had to clear his throat before he asked, "What are you going to do while Grandma gets her claws filed down?"

She nodded to the coffee shop at the other end of the strip mall. "I was thinking about getting a macchiato and then coming back to my car for a cupcake. I made some for your grandma, but she'll never know if a few are missing. Want to join me?"

Did he ever. *Play it cool*, he warned himself, wondering if she could hear his heart thundering. To let her know he wasn't excited at all, in any way, he glanced at his watch and then shrugged. "I have a few minutes. Coffee would be fine."

There. Calm. Cool. Unimpressed. *You have to keep it up*, he reminded himself. *Don't slip for even a second.*

"Good, because I need some caffeine." She linked her arm with his and smiled up at him. "Shall we?"

She smelled like warm vanilla cake, which made his mouth water. He wondered how he could disengage her arm without letting her know how affected he was by her closeness. As they went inside the coffee shop, he held back, and gestured toward the counter. "After you." There. That seemed natural. *I hope.*

She stepped up to the counter and put in a thoroughly complicated drink order that had more instructions than his grandma's hummingbird cake recipe. When she was done, he asked for coffee with cream.

She sent him a measuring look and he shrugged. "I'm not into that swanky stuff."

"You never were." Her eyes crinkled with her smile. "Do you remember when you said you hated coffee and would never drink it?"

"Tenth grade." The barista called his name and he collected his cup. "I just said it to make you mad. You thought coffee was so fancy."

"It was fancy after I got through with it. Remember how I'd use Grandma Dove's old china cups and saucers? And Aunt Jo bought me those boxes of sugar cubes, too."

"You were a pretentious child back in the day."

"You liked it," she said smugly.

She was wrong about that. He'd liked her, not the overly dramatic coffee time.

The barista called Ella's name. She collected her drink, and they went back to her car, chatting the whole way. He knew he should have just taken his coffee, made an excuse, and left, but that would mean leaving her alone and he wasn't quite up to that yet. *I'll just stay long enough to drink half of this.* Soon enough, they were sitting in her car.

She twisted around and lifted a cake box from the back seat. She opened it and handed him a cupcake. "Chocolate with cream cheese frosting."

It wasn't his favorite combination, but he took it. He watched as she took one and then returned the box to the back seat. "So how did Grandma get you to drive her around? I'd enlist in the Foreign Legion before I signed up for that."

"We have a deal, the two of us. I do this for her, and in return she gives me the one thing she's never given me before—the benefit of the doubt." Ella settled back into her seat, her cupcake in one hand as she took a sip from her macchiato, her gray-green eyes roving over him. "You've changed a lot since I last saw you."

"People do that."

"Yes, but you're a lot more . . ." She hesitated, as if searching for the right word. Finally, she laughed and said, "You're just more, that's all there is to it."

"And here I was thinking you hadn't changed one bit." He took a bite of the cupcake, the flavor and texture surprising him. Darn, but she knew how to make the common uncommon. "There are chocolate chips in here."

She twinkled at him. "Lots and lots of tiny dark chocolate chips. I call these my Chocolate Secret cupcakes."

"Grandma is going to love these." He took another bite and then followed it with a sip of coffee. "Mmm. These two together are something—coffee and chocolate."

"I know, right?" She beamed at him over her almost-gone cupcake, her eyes sparkling.

She had the most beautiful eyes he'd ever seen, her lashes thick and dark. He was instantly hit with a memory of the first time she'd ever smiled directly at him. He'd thought she was the prettiest thing he'd ever seen. "Do you remember biology class? You were a horrible lab partner."

"I was lucky you were in advanced placement, too." Her smile exploded. "I would never have passed without your help."

And he would have never made it through high school without having her smile to look forward to every day. He vividly remembered how happy he'd been to see her in the hallway at her locker each morning. "No one could understand why the most popular girl in school would even talk to a nerd like me."

Her gaze flickered over him, lingering here and there. "Nerds can be hot."

His body heated with the touch of her gaze and, fighting the urge to lean over and kiss her, he instead took a sip of his almost-too-hot coffee. The heat jolted him back to sanity. *What was I thinking, getting into a car with her like this?*

Regaining control over himself, he managed a shrug. "That was a long time ago."

"Not that long ago," she protested with an uncertain laugh. "You make it sound as if we're ancient."

"Not ancient, but certainly more grown-up."

"I suppose so, although my sisters would disagree with that. They think I don't know what I really want and keep trying to talk me into moving back to Dove Pond permanently."

"You'd never do that. You've called this place 'suffocating' and 'dismal.' I've heard you."

A faint flush warmed her cheeks. "It's not that bad. It's just that whenever I'm in Dove Pond, people don't see me as Ella, but as 'one of the Dove sisters,' and they start expecting me to be that—a Dove sister, and not me."

"And you hate that, people expecting things from you." *Like staying with someone after all the new has worn off. Like making a commitment to be there, through the good and the bad. Like love, forever and ever.*

Her gaze dropped to her cup, and she absently toyed with the straw. "I just want to be myself. Happiness requires fluidity and freedom. Otherwise, you're just . . ." She shrugged. "Trapped."

Oh, Ella, love isn't being trapped. It's letting your emotions run free, without check. He knew that was as true as the sky was blue, and yet he wasn't sure how to say it without revealing more of himself than he wanted. More than she wanted, too.

"That probably sounds silly, although . . ." She tilted her head to one side and gave him a curious look, the sunshine slanting in from the car window touching the freckles on her nose. "I was surprised you'd moved back. You swore you'd never live here."

"I used to think this place was too small, but then I lived in Atlanta."

"And?"

"It was too big." He made a face. "And noisy. I wish I— Ah. Here comes Grandma." Both irked and relieved at her appearance, he got out of the car and went to meet her.

Grandma was trying to slide a small bag into her purse without messing up her freshly done nails. On seeing him, she stopped dead in her tracks. "Gray." She didn't sound the least happy to see him.

He sent her a knowing smirk over his cup of coffee. "Taking a spa day, are you?"

Ella climbed out of the car, sipping her macchiato as she watched him and his grandma.

Grandma wiggled her fingers. "I just got my nails done. There's nothing wrong with that."

"There's nothing wrong with it at all," Gray said. "But if you show up at home with a manicure, won't Mom get suspicious?"

Grandma sniffed loftily, tilting her chin in the air. "I'm going to tell Jules I painted my nails myself. I only got a simple French manicure. And look"—she waved her small bag in Gray's direction—"I bought some polish in case she asks questions."

Ella piped up, "Your grandma's pretty good at figuring out things like that. When she got her hair cut, she brought home some of her hair clippings in a Ziploc and put them all over her bathroom floor."

"I'm no fool." Grandma's gaze narrowed on Gray. "How did you figure out we'd be here?"

"I didn't. I was on my way to the hardware store and saw you heading into the shop. Ella's been keeping me company while I waited to say hi."

"Ah. Well, hi. Now, if you'll excuse us, Ella and I have some errands to run and we have scant time, thank you very much."

Gray opened the car door and helped his grandma into the seat he'd just vacated. "I hope you have a lovely day not dying."

She shot him a sour look. "Don't you have something to do?"

"Plenty." He shut the door and looked over the car at Ella, who was grinning ear to ear. "She's all yours."

Ella wrinkled her nose. "Thanks." Her gaze traveled over his face. "I guess I'll see you around?"

He caught the hopeful note in her voice. She wanted him to ask her out. He knew it, and yet he also knew it was the last thing he should do. To calm his galloping nerves, he took another sip of his coffee before he gave her a calm, noncommittal smile. "I'm sure we'll run into each other again. It's a small town."

And with that, despite his whole being screaming that he was being a fool, that a date with Ella would be the most amazing, fun night of his life, he turned and headed for his truck.

He'd just put his hand on the door handle when Ella called out, "Gray?"

Yessss! He kept his face calm as he turned. "Yeah?"

"I'm not doing anything Friday."

"That's nice."

She waited, and when he didn't say anything else, rolled her eyes. "We should do something," she said impatiently.

Despite his agony, he found himself amused at her frustration. He could relate to it so, so well. "Do something like . . . ?"

"Dinner."

Act calm. Don't look excited. He shrugged. "Sure."

"At seven. Pick me up." Without waiting for an answer, she got into her car and left.

Gray climbed into his truck and forced himself not to watch her go, even pretending to check his phone for messages until she was out of sight.

The second she was gone, he dropped his phone on the seat and happy-slapped his steering wheel. It might be their first date, but he was going to make sure it wasn't their last. He'd show up without flowers, without dressing up, without acting as if he were doing anything but a pleasant, friendly-but-not-too-friendly chore. He'd take her somewhere for pizza and, even though it would take every ounce of control he had, he'd keep his distance.

If he wanted Ella around long enough for her to feel something more for him than mere quick-to-evaporate passion, he'd have to work his darnedest to keep some distance between them.

Dating Ella was a delicate, difficult line to walk, but if things worked out the way he hoped, then, boy oh boy, it would be worth it.

CHAPTER 10

ELLA

*In every recipe, there is always the opportunity to add more—
more stirring, more sugar, more time in the oven. That cannot
be said about subtractions. Plan accordingly....*

The Book of Cakes, p. 99
Written: 1792–2019

Ella awoke to the delicious smell of buttermilk biscuits. Yawning, she stretched, listening to the sound of laughter floating up from the kitchen. Ava and Sarah were obviously having a good time making breakfast, which made Ella smile. It was a lovely sound to wake up to.

She pulled her pillow close as she rolled onto her side and saw the morning sun slanting through her window. Outside, huge oak trees swayed in the chilly morning breeze as they cast a moving pattern on the wood floor, the dust motes shimmering like golden sparkles. In the past few weeks, she'd had two coffee meetups and three genuine dates with Gray. They'd all been wonderful, welcome, and laughter-filled. And yet, as much fun as she'd had, they'd left her bemused, unsatisfied, and—oddly enough—intrigued.

She wasn't used to being the person who did the pursuing, and yet that was exactly what was happening. Most of the time, she was the one who called, who texted, who asked if he was free. Sometimes he said no, although he always seemed happy to hear from her, which encouraged her to continue.

She'd forgotten how much she'd liked talking to him. Still, although this time felt different from the last, she knew it wasn't going anywhere. It couldn't, really. They were in two different places in their lives. She had one foot out the door, while he was putting down deep and permanent roots. She sometimes wondered why she was even bothering to see him.

But she knew why.

More than once, she'd caught him looking at her as if she were the last crème patisserie in the bakery case. Those moments never came with a follow-through of any sort, which was as baffling as the man himself.

She thought she'd broken through to him last night. They'd gone to dinner and on a walk through the park on their way home. She'd decided that, once they reached the Dove house, she would kiss him. Once they stepped onto the porch, she'd realized that he'd been thinking about it, too. His gaze rested on her mouth, and before he could think twice and retreat, she'd risen up on her toes and kissed him.

The second her lips met his, the kiss had exploded. It had been a simply astounding kiss, deep and sensual, and had lasted a deliciously long time. When it was over, they were both breathless and shaking. She could feel the beat of his heart against her chest, wild and in sync with her own.

Still fighting to catch her breath, she'd broken the embrace, opened the door, and beckoned him in, sending him a saucy "why not?" smile that had never failed her before.

It worked this time, just not in the way she had intended it to. Gray had pulled her from the threshold, back onto the porch, placed his warm hands on either side of her face and tilted it up. She'd closed her eyes, ready for another passionate kiss, when he leaned forward and instead gently pressed his lips to her forehead.

As odd as it was, the kiss had been sensually intimate. Her body had melted against his, and for a long moment he'd held her there.

But then he'd slowly let her go. Stepped away. And left, leaving her on the porch, wanting him so badly she could have wept.

What on earth was he doing to her? *I'm a fool*, she told herself. Restless, she climbed from her bed and went to open the window. Chilly morning air breezed in, tossing the lace curtains, tugging at her sleep shirt, and making her shiver. She took a deep breath, catching the sound of the wind rustling through the trees, sending a leaf here and there tumbling to the ground. Other than that, it was blissfully quiet. For the moment, Dove Pond was an idyllic, peaceful place. Still, for all the beauty surrounding her, the warm bed she'd just rolled out of, and the challenge Gray presented, Ella's restlessness was growing.

She should leave.

She *wanted* to leave. Sort of.

Now would be better, she decided, brushing her hair back from her shoulder, where the wind had tousled it, only to find a fat swipe of strawberry frosting. *Ugh!*

Scowling, she turned away from the window, grabbed her towel from the hook beside the door, and headed for the shower. *Stupid frosting. I swear I'd leave if it weren't for that frosting and that stupid dream. I'm stuck here until that's resolved.*

As soon as she showered and dressed, she dropped her phone in her pocket and headed downstairs. She'd just reached the landing when she heard Sarah say, "Aunt Jo says Ella will never stay in town for it no matter how much we ask."

Ella paused. Maybe she should make a noise? Or just return to her room for a few minutes?

Ava sighed. "It's too bad we can't convince her to be a judge for the bake-off. She knows more about baking than anyone, and she'd bring a crowd to the event, too."

"I know, but you know how Ella hates this town."

That was unfair. Ella didn't hate Dove Pond. Not exactly. She just didn't like small towns. She bent down a little. By leaning to one side, she could just see into the kitchen through the railing.

Sarah had a steaming cup of tea in front of her. She picked up a small silver spoon and scooped some sugar into her cup, her face creased in a frown. "Do you think she's happy, moving around all the time? She never stays long enough to make friends or get a serious boyfriend or anything. I hate that for her. She has to be lonely."

Ella scowled. Of course she wasn't lonely! Not usually. She'd made friends. Well . . . *good acquaintances* was a more accurate term, but that was enough for her.

Ava spread some butter on a biscuit. "It's as if she's searching for something but isn't sure what."

That's ridiculous. I'm not searching for anything. It was time to put an end to her sisters' deep and unwelcome dive into her life, so she straightened up and made plenty of noise as she came down the rest of the stairs. "Good morning!" she called out as if she hadn't heard a word of their conversation. "I hope you saved me a biscuit."

"They're in the warmer," Ava said.

"We made honey butter," Sarah added.

Ella went to pour herself some coffee and put a biscuit on a plate. "What were you two chatting about?" Ha. No sense in making it easy for them.

Ava and Sarah exchanged looks, and to Ella's surprise, Sarah admitted, "You."

Wow. That was bold. Ella sat beside Sarah at the counter and opened her biscuit, steam rolling out. "What about me?"

Ava rested her elbows on the counter, her breakfast momentarily forgotten as she eyed Ella with a worried frown. "We were just wondering if you were happy."

"Of course I'm happy. I have a great life." Except for those ridiculous dreams and the strawberry frosting and the restless longing she felt every time she saw Gray, she was as happy as could be.

Ella put a healthy dab of honey butter on her biscuit. The butter melted and soaked in, so delicious-looking that some of her irritation melted with it.

Sarah sighed, her breath blowing the steam across her teacup. "I'm sure you've been content, but have you ever been *really* happy? The kind that is so perfect, you never want it to end?"

"That kind of happy doesn't exist."

Ava and Sarah exchanged a look. Then Ava said carefully, "It doesn't last forever, of course. But surely you've had that feeling where you looked around and knew that, for that one moment, everything was just the way it should be?"

Ella finished her biscuit and licked her fingers. "No, and don't tell me you two have had moments like that, because I won't believe it."

Sarah lowered her teacup. "I have them all the time. Especially when I'm at the library and it's just me and the books, and I know you and Ava and the others are safe and sound, and our town is healthy and thriving, and I know I'll see Blake soon—that's when I'm the happiest. I love those moments."

Ava added, "I feel that way here sometimes, especially when it's quiet. I look around and I know I'm right where I belong. But you . . . you've never felt that way?"

Not once. Does everyone feel that way? Surely not. I can't imagine Angela's ever had a peaceful "I'm where I need to be" moment in her life. "Maybe one day. If I do, I'll let you guys know. I—" Her phone chimed. "That's probably Tiff." Ella grabbed a napkin and, wiping her hands, pulled out her phone. "Oh. Tiff scheduled a Zoom meeting for this morning. I forgot about it." Ella stifled a yawn, dropped her phone back into her pocket, and then reached for her coffee cup. "I'm going to need extra caffeine today. I'm sleepy this morning."

Sarah sent her a smug look. "You got home late last night. I heard you come in."

"It was late, and I was exhausted, but I still had one of those annoying dreams." Ella wasn't ready to talk about Gray, as much as her sisters might want her to.

Ava looked up, concern on her face. "Have you had any luck with Angela?"

"I've been driving her all over the place, and while we've gotten a lot friendlier, she shuts me down whenever I bring up that cookbook. I'm going to have to be more direct." Ella took another drink of her coffee and then carried her empty plate to the dishwasher.

"Good luck with that." Sarah got up and pulled her sweater from where it hung over the back of her chair. "I don't think 'direct' and Angela have much in common."

"Truth." Ella looked with regret at her mug of coffee. "Do we have any to-go cups? It'll help me stay warm in the car."

Ava fished a paper cup and lid out from under the counter and handed them to Ella. "Where are you off to?"

"I need to look at some of the video edits before our meeting, and I don't feel like hanging out here. I might just head to your tearoom and set up camp there."

"If you need Wi-Fi, you'll have to go to the Moonlight. Ours went out two days ago and the earliest the company can come to fix it is tomorrow."

"Same for the library," Sarah said. "Erma said hers was off at the boutique, too. Looks like everyone on our block got hit."

"Good to know. I'll be at the Moonlight, then, if you guys need me."

Ava nodded. "Sarah, I almost forgot. Kat called last night, and she wanted me to ask if you could recommend some fun reading once she gets home from Brazil. She said she'd been working crazy hours and is going to need something relaxing."

Kat Carter and Ava were good friends and had been since high school. Ella wondered what it would be like to keep a friendship that long. *It's probably a lot of work.*

"I'll see what I can find," Sarah said. "Maybe the new one from Colleen Hoover. It's riveting."

Ella put down the dish towel she'd been drying her hands on. "What's Kat doing in Brazil?"

Ava pulled another to-go cup from under the counter and fixed herself a coffee. "She's been helping her dad secure a turpentine factory. She says it'll make his fortune a fortune."

"Like he needs that." Sarah cleared her dishes off the counter and placed them in the dishwasher before glancing at Ava. "Do you need a ride to the tearoom?"

"No, thanks. I have to stop by the greenhouses today, so I'll just drive myself. But if you're leaving now, I'll walk you out."

"Okay. See you later, Ella." Sarah headed for the front hall.

"Bye." With a quick wave, Ava followed Sarah.

Ella listened to their friendly talk as they stopped to put on their coats. Soon, the front door closed behind them. She waited until both their vehicles had pulled out of the driveway before she found her cardigan and computer bag. Then, coffee cup in hand, she headed to her car.

A chilly breeze met her, and she was glad of her sweater. It was cool for mid-September. As she drove downtown, she enjoyed the sight of the mountains, where the trees were just beginning to hint at their fall colors.

It would be nice to see the leaves in their full glory. It had been years since she'd been home when that happened, as she usually got here at Thanksgiving, when the trees were already bare. The town was especially beautiful in the fall, almost like a painting, and the air was the perfect temperature—fresh and cool, but not too cold. *I've missed that. Maybe I should stay a few more w—*

She blinked. *What in the world am I thinking?* Of course she couldn't stay here! She had things to do, a life to live. She was getting closer to Angela one day at a time. Lately, Ella thought she could detect the older woman's attitude softening toward her. *Soon I'll be done with these dreams and that will be that.*

But what if Gray and I— She stiffened at the unexpectedness of the thought. *There is no Gray and I.* Sure, he was a challenge, but that was all. It was just that she was enjoying their little get-togethers far more than she'd expected. He took the time to tell her what he was doing with his farm and shared the most amusing stories about the many animals he'd inherited with the purchase, while also asking her tons of questions about her patisserie and the sale and—well, a lot of things. *He listens. Really listens. I like that.*

Which was ridiculous. *He's just being polite.* Muttering to herself at her own foolishness, she parked the car on Main Street.

She left her now nearly empty to-go cup in the car, collected her things, and made her way to the Moonlight Café. Before long, she was seated in a booth with a fresh cup of coffee, her laptop obscuring the adorable street view as she tried to weed through her unread emails. Ella opened the latest email Tiff had sent and found an overly thorough agenda for the morning meeting, which made Ella promptly close it. *Tldr, Tiff.*

Ella loved her assistant, but she tended to overprepare. Instead, Ella opened the email she'd gotten from her lawyer outlining the trouble spots he'd found in a proposed sponsor contract. She responded to the email and then checked the stats on her accounts. Tiff had been right about the "PM to CC" content drawing a lot of attention, far more than expected. They hadn't had interaction numbers this high for a while. *Nice. Very nice.*

She picked up her coffee cup to take a sip and realized its contents had cooled, so she looked around for Marian. Instead, she found Zoe sitting a few tables away, surrounded by folders and a big binder.

Ella called out, "Hello!"

Zoe looked up from where she was marking a spreadsheet with a red pen. "Good morning! I saw you when I came in, but you were busy."

Ella nodded toward Zoe's binder. "That looks intimidating."

"It's the town budget proposal. I promised Grace I'd give it a look."

"Is that part of your job at the bank?"

"Sort of. I'm the bank's representative on various town committees. I help with budgetary questions when I can."

"That's kind of you." Ella wished her sisters could see her now. *I have friends. They just don't give me credit for it.* A thought occurred and she smiled at Zoe. "Want to join me? This booth is big enough for both of us. I promise I won't interrupt you."

Zoe looked surprised, but she immediately began collecting her things. "Sure! It's nice to work beside someone, even if you're not doing the same thing."

Ella glanced at her watch. "Fair warning—I'm scheduled for a short Zoom meeting here in half an hour, although I have earphones, so it shouldn't be too much of an issue."

"No problem." Zoe set her stuff on the table, then slid into the seat across from Ella. "Look at us doing the study-partner thing. It's like college, only we have real jobs."

Ella smiled. She'd always liked Zoe, but then who didn't? She was pretty, smart, and fashionable. More than that, from what Ella had heard from others in town, Zoe wasn't a one-man-all-the-time sort of woman either, so they had a lot in common. "I bet those committees take up a lot of your time."

"More than you can imagine, although I really love the festival committee. They do a lot for this town and, through that, my bank. Your sisters are on it, too."

"Sarah loves the festivals. She says the library benefits hugely from them."

"They're good advertisements for the whole town. We only have two a year, and they take up a lot of our resources, but they're worth it. If you're still here the first weekend of October, you'll get to see the Apple Festival firsthand. It's my favorite."

"We'll see," Ella said smoothly. With any luck, before that two-week mark struck, she'd have won Angela over, banished her bad dreams, and lured Gray into something more than a good-night kiss. *Total success on all sides.*

She smiled at Zoe. "Were you escaping anyone in particular in your office?"

"No particular person so much as a litany of interruptions. The phone rings every few minutes, people pop their heads in the door, and you can forget getting any work done if it's someone's birthday—it's chaos. One time, I put a sign on my door asking not to be disturbed, but my coworkers took it as a challenge. You'd think they couldn't run that place without me."

Ella was pretty sure they couldn't. Marian brought Zoe some coffee and a piece of pie, and refilled Ella's coffee. Once the waitress was gone, Zoe and Ella delved into their work. For a half hour, they were silent. Zoe was quiet as she marked up the report she was perusing. She was much more efficient than Ella, who discovered she couldn't keep her mind on her work at all. Instead, she kept thinking about Gray. *He's just taking things slow. That's all. There's no reason to make this a bigger deal than it is.* She wondered why it bothered her so much. Why *he* bothered her so much.

Ella bit back a sigh and tried to focus on the list of suggested content Tiff had sent. It didn't work, and before long she found herself absently staring at the kitchen. Through the large pass-through window, she caught a glimpse of Jules but didn't see any sign of Mark. *It's too bad I'm not friends with Mark. He's close to Gray and would have some good advice.*

"Are you done?"

Ella realized Zoe was watching her, smiling. Disconcerted to have been caught daydreaming, Ella laughed. "I have a lot on my mind today. How are you doing?"

"I'm sinking under these numbers." Zoe dropped her pen on the spreadsheet and rolled her shoulders. "Why didn't I get a degree in poetry or English or something fun?"

"Because you're ambitious about taking your dad's place at the bank. You were dreaming of doing that even in high school."

"Ah, high school." A dreamy look warmed Zoe's hazel eyes. "Those were good times, weren't they? Almost as good as college. You went to that cooking school in New York, didn't you? I bet that was fun."

"Le Cordon Bleu is many things, but it's pretty intense. Lots of hard work."

"No fun parties or late-night panty raids for you guys, eh?"

Ella grinned. "No panty raids, but plenty of pantry raids. We used to sneak into the kitchen whenever we got the chance to try to perfect something we knew we'd have to do in class while the teacher tore us apart. Most of the teachers were great, but a few thought they were Gordon Ramsay—and I'm not talking about the sweetheart version you see on *MasterChef Junior*."

"Fun times!" Zoe returned Ella's grin. "I—" Her phone beeped, and she grimaced when she checked it. "It's Grace. Do you mind if she joins us? She's in the office and says if she doesn't get a cup of coffee soon, she's going to turn into a zombie and quit her job. We can't let that happen, at least not before the Apple Festival."

"Sure. She seems really nice. She's certainly done a lot of amazing things for this town."

"She saved us," Zoe said simply. "You should get to know her. She's no-nonsense but has a wicked sense of humor." Zoe picked up her phone. "I'll tell her to meet us here."

That was fine with Ella. It wasn't as if she were getting any work done, anyway. She moved her things closer together in anticipation of Grace's arrival.

Ella didn't have to wait long. The mayor walked into the café just a moment later, a brunette whirlwind of energy contained in a fashionable navy blue power suit. No wonder the town was waking up: Grace looked like she wasn't the type to allow anyone to sleep.

"Finally!" Grace sat beside Zoe and waved at Marian. "I'm way undercaffeinated. If they offered a coffee IV drip, I'd order two."

Marian brought a coffee to the table and then eyed Zoe's and Ella's cups. "I'll bring the pot for refills. I'm about to go on break, so let me know if you need anything else."

"Thanks, Marian. I think we're good for now." Grace pulled her cup closer as Marian left. "So . . . what are you two working on?"

"You know what I'm doing," Zoe said. "Ella's just sitting there, staring into space."

Grace's eyebrows rose. "Man trouble, eh?"

Ella flushed. She didn't know Zoe or Grace well enough to talk to them about Gray. In fact, she didn't know anyone well enough to have a conversation like that, which was a little troubling, considering her sisters' accusations this morning. "I'm not having man trouble, just . . . I'd call it anticipation."

"Ooooh, anticipation." Zoe propped her chin in her hand. "Do tell."

Ella gave a prim sniff. "I never kiss and tell."

"Smart move, and classy, too." Grace added some cream to her coffee. "By the way, Ella, on the advice of my niece Daisy, I checked out your Insta account. That post you put up of the pastry case in Ava's tearoom got over two hundred and fifty thousand likes."

Zoe's eyes widened.

Ella shrugged. "Pastries are kind of my thing."

"Dove Pond is kind of my thing," Grace said. "The next time you post, would you mind using a Dove Pond hashtag? We rely on tourist traffic, especially in the fall."

"As soon as the leaves start to change, we get swamped with leaf peepers," Zoe added. "It's good for the town, although I wish they knew how to drive."

Ella shrugged. "Sure. I'll let my team know to add that hashtag, too."

Grace flashed a bright smile. "You're a peach! Zoe, did you finish looking over the festival budget?" Grace opened her laptop, and she and Zoe went to work.

Ella pulled her computer closer. She needed to get back to work as well, but couldn't help watching Zoe and Grace. It was obvious they were close, as they sometimes finished one another's sentences, and had the same sense of humor, which had them both laughing over the antics of the last mayor, who'd become a successful fishing guide in his retirement. Although he was no longer in politics, he apparently made it part of his day to come into Grace's office and offer suggestions on how to avoid work.

Grace, still laughing, said, "He's a piece of work, that one. By the way, did you have time to run the numbers on the Apple Festival?"

"Did it this morning." Zoe dug through her things and then handed Grace a paper. "Our operating costs are up. I know you'll hate to hear this but we need to charge the vendors a flat fee this year or we'll fall short."

"We can't do that." Grace opened a bright red file folder and pulled out a list. "We'll lose some of the smaller, local businesses, and they count on the festival to pump up their sales before winter hits."

Zoe looked at the list. "So what do we do?"

Grace frowned and absently tapped her fingers on the table. "If we could spur our attendance numbers, then the vendors would make more money, and our cut would be higher. Everyone would win."

"Cut?" Ella hadn't meant to say anything, but her curiosity got the better of her.

Zoe answered. "Instead of a flat fee, we charge vendors a tiny cut of their profit over and above their costs. It encourages small businesses to participate." She handed the list back to Grace. "If we can find a way to drive up attendance, then we won't have to— Oh!" Zoe pointed out the window. "There's Aunt Jo."

Sure enough, Aunt Jo stood outside on the sidewalk. She was dressed in a bright pink coat, which contrasted with her purple shoes, and was talking in an animated way to Preacher Thompson. On seeing Ella, she stopped long enough to wave.

"Now, that's what I call a preacher," Grace said. "Aunt Jo says he's an angel come to torment the single women of town."

"I'm not tormented," Zoe said. "I don't date preachers."

Ella would make an exception for this one. She suddenly realized she hadn't answered Aunt Jo's wave, so she waved back.

Aunt Jo beamed and then said something to the preacher while jerking her thumb toward the three of them where they sat in the window, staring.

He turned to look, flashing a smile that made Zoe sigh.

"That smile," Ella said in a reverent whisper. "I saw him give a sermon a few weeks back, but he didn't smile like that. Not once. I would have remembered."

"I know, right?" Zoe shook her head. "Pity he's a preacher." She shifted so her shoulder was toward the window as if to protect herself from him. "Grace, about the festival shortfall? Any ideas on how to drive attendance over what we already do?"

"One." Grace slid the vendor list back into her folder and pulled out another sheaf of papers. "When you look at other festivals in our area, most of them have something we don't: a headliner."

"Like a concert?"

"Exactly, although we can't afford a band or a singer. Production costs for that type of entertainment would wipe out any benefit. A speaker would work if we can get someone big enough. If they were local, we could save on transportation costs as well."

Zoe mulled this over. "A few famous actors have summer homes in this area, and some famous race car drivers, too. I'll put together a list. My only worry is that it's really late to be doing this sort of thing. We're only two weeks out from our event."

"We'll do the best we can. We'll brainstorm with the committee at our next meeting. Maybe someone has a connection we can use. I'll have Sarah put it on the agenda."

Ella's phone buzzed. Tiff texted, *Will be online in five. Zoom call invite in your box.* "I'm sorry, but I have to take this Zoom meeting, if you don't mind."

"Sure," Zoe said. "We need to go over these numbers, anyway."

"Thanks. It'll only take a few minutes." She started collecting her things. "I'll just go outside and—"

"Nonsense," Grace said. "Go ahead and take it here. We won't bother you."

Ella paused. It would be a pain to try to do the call somewhere else. "Would you mind? I promise it won't take lo—"

"There you are!" Aunt Jo stood beside the table with the preacher at her side. Now that he was closer, Ella realized he had the most beautiful eyes she'd ever seen, a mesmerizing golden brown. She wondered if the attendance at the Baptist church had gone up since he'd arrived and instantly realized that was a silly thing to wonder. Of course it had.

"Mind if we join you?" Without waiting for an answer, Aunt Jo shrugged out of her coat and dropped heavily onto the bench beside Ella while the preacher pulled a chair from a nearby table and placed it at the end of their booth.

He helped Aunt Jo hang her cane over the hook at the end. "Aunt Jo, would you like a beverage?"

"Why yes, please. A Diet Coke. While you're at it, I'll take a piece of pie, too." She leaned toward Ella and said in a low voice, "I'm doing some research on the opposition. Jules sometimes lets other bakers put their wares on display. I think she does it just to keep me sharp."

"Glad you're keeping an eye on it," Ella said.

"Does anyone else want anything?" the preacher asked. When everyone murmured, "No, thank you," he left to place Aunt Jo's order at the counter. Then he returned, sliding into his chair with a gracious smile.

Ella's laptop buzzed. "Sorry, guys. I have a meeting. I should probably take this somewhere else and—"

"Go ahead," the preacher said. "We'll be quiet as church mice. Won't we, Aunt Jo?"

"Is that a Zoom meeting?" Aunt Jo leaned closer. "I'd like to see how those work. How many people will be there? Are they in other countries?"

Ella fought the urge to demand to be let out of her corner of the booth, but she was trapped now. "I'll explain in a minute," she told Aunt Jo as she pulled her purse closer and started digging for her earphones. After a moment, she dropped her purse back beside her. "I can't find my earphones. I must have left them at home."

Grace shrugged, while Zoe didn't even look up from her spreadsheet. The preacher and Aunt Jo both mimed locking their lips with a key, which was about as reassuring as it was cute.

Left with no choice, Ella angled her computer away from the others and toward her own corner of the booth. *I'll just check in, say hi. I won't stay long.* She clicked on the meeting link and Tiff popped up, as did three other trendy-looking marketing representatives.

Oh no. Tiff invited the new sponsors. I should have read that email all the way through. Ella managed a weak smile as she waved. "Hi, everyone."

A chorus of hellos followed. Ella waited for them to die down before she said, "Tiff, I'm sorry, but I'm only going to be able to stay for a few minutes."

Tiff's smile slipped, but with her usual positive energy she found it again and dove right in. "You're busy. Sure. The real purpose of this meeting is just to introduce everyone, which won't take long." She quickly made introductions. As Tiff mentioned the names of the brands, Ella caught Zoe and Grace exchanging glances. *Uh-oh. What's going on there?*

Aunt Jo leaned over to whisper loudly to the preacher, "Did you hear that Nike might be her sponsor? I wear those myself." She stuck one foot out from under the table.

"Mighty fine shoes," he agreed.

Tiff blinked.

Ella hurried to say, "Sorry. I'm sitting in the Moonlight Café with some friends."

"The Moonlight?" one of the marketing people, a young lady with stylish short hair and a large, round pair of glasses, said with enthusiasm. "Is that where you had that amazing meatloaf? We've been watching your social media posts these past few weeks."

Ella nodded, and Grace leaned across the table and said to the back of Ella's computer, "For a small town, Dove Pond possesses a unique level of culinary richness."

"That was the mayor," Ella said.

Aunt Jo leaned over so she could see the screen, the top of her head partially covering Ella's face. "I made the blueberry cheesecake Ella had on her Gram last week. And the pink elephant cupcakes."

A chorus of "Who is that?" and "I loved those cupcakes!" broke out.

Tiff piped up, "Ella? Would you like to introduce us to your friend?"

As if she could say no. Giving a weak nod, Ella turned her computer toward Aunt Jo. "This is Mrs. Jolean Hamilton, known to everyone in town as Aunt Jo. She's an amazing baker."

"That's something, coming from you, Ella," Tiff said.

Everyone said hello to Aunt Jo.

Aunt Jo beamed and slipped an arm around Ella. "You all are smart to want to sponsor this one. She's gold, both in the kitchen and out."

Tiff laughed. "Yes, she is. Her followers love her. Aunt Jo—do you mind if I call you that?—Ella's talked about you so much, I feel like I know you."

"Lord, no. I don't answer to much else."

"It's nice to meet you. Your cupcakes generated a lot of comments. People were asking where they could get some."

"I'd be happy to make them for whoever wants them," Aunt Jo said proudly. She settled back in her seat and told the preacher, "Everyone loves a cupcake."

Ella turned the computer back her way.

"See?" Tiff was saying to the marketers. "This is just a sample of the exclusive, engaging content Ella posts on her accounts. Her fans are loving her 'Paris Metro to Country Cute' vibe, and I know you'll be as excited as we are that she'll be continuing the series for another week and perhaps more!"

That brought out a chorus of "We love it!" that would have been gratifying if Ella hadn't been frozen in place at Tiff's saying "and perhaps more." Ella had no wish to make plans beyond that. She wanted to say that to Tiff but knew now was not the time. It would be a grave error for their team to appear out of sync.

Unaware she'd said anything amiss, Tiff continued, "In fact, we've been looking for an anchor event Ella could do to cap off her 'PM to CC' posts. Something significant but rich with country life. Ella and I were thinking she might do a booth at a local event or festival showcasing some of her signature desserts. She could do that in conjunction with an Ella Dove cooking demonstration, followed by a meet and greet. As you guys saw in my email, there are a lot of events coming up in the area, so we just need to pick one." Tiff picked up a sheet of paper. "I was thinking the Sourwood Festival might work— Oh, wait. It was in August. How about—"

"The Apple Festival," Grace said loudly.

Tiff blinked. "Who's talking?"

Grace rose up on her elbows and said to the back of Ella's laptop, "Hi! Grace Parker here! I'm the mayor of Dove Pond and we have a lovely, Southern-themed festival the first weekend in October, just two weeks away. We'd *love* to have Ella as the Apple Festival's headliner."

Ella had to fight to keep her happy social media expression in place as the dreaded Dove Pond expectation net began to tighten around her. *Why, oh why, didn't I go outside to take this call?* "Grace, that's very kind of you, but—"

"Hold on," Tiff said. "An Apple Festival in October. That's perfect."

"Yes, but—"

"Think of all the apple desserts you could make!" Tiff's voice rose with enthusiasm. "Ella, your ancestors founded Dove Pond, too. It's a match made in heaven!"

Ella nodded, trying desperately to hang on to her smile. "Yes, but I won't be here—"

"Ella." Aunt Jo leaned over and said in a low voice, "You'll be here. You've got things to get done, remember?"

Tiff's smile faltered. "What—"

"Just a minute." Ella put her computer on mute and then turned to Aunt Jo. "I'm hoping those things will be done by then."

"I don't know about that. Some things, and some people too, can be stubborn."

Zoe rested her elbows on the table and leaned forward. "What things and what people are being stubborn?"

Ella's face heated as she realized everyone at the table was listening. She waved her hand. "It's nothing. Aunt Jo and I have been working on a tiny project. That's all."

"Excuse me!" Tiff piped up. "Ella, since there's an apple theme, maybe you could make your caramel apple cake at the festival as a demo-type event. It always trends well on your sites, and I know it's excellent, as I had it at your patisserie."

Ella unmuted her computer. "I could do that, but—"

"No buts," the preacher said, his voice rich and deep. "It's a great idea." He nodded at the computer. "May I?"

Great. Just great. Ella turned the computer screen his way.

"Hi, I'm Preacher Thompson of the First Baptist Church. This year, for the first time ever, our bake-off, a famous local cake competition, will be a part of the Apple Festival. I'd like to offer Ella the opportunity to judge for us."

No, no, no! Ella looked at Aunt Jo, who beamed as if she'd thought of it first. And maybe she had.

Tiff clapped her hands. "This just keeps getting better and better!"

One of the reps chimed in, "If Ella's judging, we'd love to sponsor a booth for her."

"Hold on!" said another. "If you sponsor the booth, then we'll sponsor the contest itself."

Hidden from the camera, Zoe jumped in her seat and fist-pumped the air while Grace grinned, looking like the cat who got the cream.

Tiff chuckled. "There's room for everyone. We can sort out the details in a bit."

"Yes," Ella said, trying not to sound as irked as she felt. "I hate to end this, but I really, *really* need to go."

"Sure!" Tiff waved her hand. "I'll call later and we'll confirm the details. Oh, and can you ask—was it Grace who is the mayor?"

Grace said loudly, "I'll call you before the day is out, Tiff. I'll get your contact info from Ella."

"Perfect! This is going to be epic! Bye!"

Ella waved weakly and hit the end-call button.

"The bake-off will be Insta-famous now." Preacher Thompson took a satisfied sip of his coffee. "God has answered our prayers, and you, Ella Dove, will be a stellar judge."

"No one would try to bribe a Dove," Aunt Jo said. "It's a foolproof plan. Plus, now I'm off the hook for judging."

Ella didn't know whether to laugh or cry. The worst part was that she was now chained to Dove Pond for another two weeks.

That was bad. Two more weeks of her sisters hoping she'd find "happiness" and two more weeks of her trying to convince Angela she hadn't stolen her family recipe book. Still, she had to admit it was starting to seem that perhaps—just perhaps—she was making a little progress with Angela. *A very little, but still . . .*

Plus, staying also meant two more weeks of Gray.

She dropped her gaze to where her hands rested on the tabletop. Maybe . . . maybe, this delay wasn't so bad after all. Maybe she could use it to her advantage.

Aunt Jo bumped her shoulder against Ella's. "Look who's the new judge of the bake-off."

Ella gave the older woman a sharp look. "You planned this."

"You're the one who kept announcing you couldn't stay, and then kept doing just that." Smiling, Aunt Jo took a sip of her Diet Coke. "Besides, the bake-off deserves a celebrity judge."

"It's a good move for our little contest," Preacher Thompson said. His golden eyes were bright with amusement. "Ella, you have my undying gratitude."

Aunt Jo added, "You've saved me from temptation, too. It was easy enough to pass on the oranges, but the bribes have gotten better, and you know I have a weak soul."

Grace looked shocked. "What bribes?"

"So far, I've gotten a case of oranges, a ficus plant, a subscription to *Old House Journal* magazine, some chocolate-covered strawberries, and even an espresso machine."

"Don't worry," the preacher told everyone at the table. "I took them all off her hands. The espresso machine fits perfectly on the credenza in the deacon's meeting room, so the entire congregation can enjoy it. I take the purity of our bake-off to heart." He lifted a brow Ella's way. "Now that you'll be judging it, I hope I can count on you eschewing those same bribes."

"I've never taken a bribe in my life. I—sheesh, I can't believe I'm doing this." She pressed her hands to the sides of her head and sank a little farther into her seat. *How had this happened?*

She was still trying to figure it out when the door opened and Gray walked in.

He was wearing his running clothes, his shirt and hair damp from his efforts. Focused as ever, he didn't look around, but went right to the counter, where he spoke to Marian, who was just taking her own lunch from the pass-through window. The waitress was all smiles as she talked to him. He said something that made her laugh and, still shaking her head, she went to fetch him a bottled water from the refrigerator case.

He waited, leaning against the counter.

His mother, still working back in the kitchen, must have spotted him through the window, because she leaned out and waved at him.

Ella watched them, noticing how Jules's expression brightened when she saw Gray. It was at times like this, seeing other people with their moms, that Ella missed her own mother the most.

Marian handed Gray his water. He waved goodbye and left. He'd just reached the door when he caught sight of Ella.

Instantly, his gaze sharpened.

She smiled and lifted her hand in greeting.

A flash of warmth brightened his eyes.

For a breathless second, she thought he would come over, but instead, he suddenly frowned as if he'd just remembered he had something more important to do. With a careless wave, he left.

She might have been hurt by the casualness of his actions, but she'd just caught sight of his water bottle and had seen the way it had begun to bubble softly, steam curling from the open top.

She smiled, delight racing through her from her head to the soles of her feet. She'd seen that reaction before. She'd caused it in other men. And now, she'd caused it in Gray.

Her heart danced. He was just as spun up as she was. *Ah, Gray. We've unfinished business, the two of us.* He was such a challenge, this new version of Gray. He possessed all the things she'd liked about the old Gray—his willingness to listen without judging, his bold intelligence, his intense approach to life, and his sharp wit. But added to the mix now was a supreme sort of confidence and a calm control that intrigued her like nothing else had.

I wonder if he'd like to meet tonight. She shifted a bit so she could see him through the window as he passed by Ava's tearoom. He waved to someone sitting inside, and then disappeared around the corner.

She suddenly realized Jules was standing beside their booth, holding a pot of coffee. Her gaze met Ella's and turned cold. Her mouth held tightly, she refilled the coffee cups closest to her. "Marian went on break. Does anyone else need more coffee?"

"Just the bill for me," Zoe said. "I have to get back to the office."

"You got it." Jules looked at Ella. "I'll get yours, too."

Ella hadn't asked for hers, but she just nodded, hoping Jules hadn't seen her staring after Gray.

"May I have some more coffee?" Grace slid her coffee cup within Jules's reach and then grinned at Ella across the table. "This is going to be the best bake-off ever. Having you as the judge is the best news yet for our little festival."

Jules's frown deepened. "Ella's going to judge?"

"She'll be perfect," Aunt Jo said.

Jules leaned one arm against the high back of their booth, the coffeepot held to one side, her sharp gaze back on Ella. "So you'll be staying until the Apple Festival."

Ella shrugged. "You know how persuasive Aunt Jo can be."

Zoe added, "Ella's social media contacts will boost promotion, too."

"Great," Jules said, bitterness in her voice. "That's how you pick your judge, is it? Instagram numbers and connections?"

"Excuse me," Preacher Thompson said in a gentle tone. "I wasn't going to say anything right now, because it didn't seem the time for it, but to be honest, I think Ella here should be *a* judge, not the *only* judge."

Aunt Jo's smile faded. "She knows what she's doing. She doesn't need any help."

"It's not a question of her abilities. I've been thinking for a while now that a panel of judges instead of just one might protect the reputation of our bake-off. Miss Ella would still be our celebrity judge, of course, but a panel would be harder to bribe."

Ella couldn't find fault with that. "I like that idea," she said. It sounded like a lot less work for her.

Aunt Jo frowned. "Does this mean I'm back to judging?"

"Yes." The preacher looked at Grace. "What do you think?"

"It's your event, so it's not my decision, but I have to say, I think a panel is a great idea."

"I like it too." Zoe tilted her head. "But I'd add at least one more judge. An odd number will prevent ties."

The preacher arched a brow at her. "Are you volunteering?"

Zoe threw up a hand. "No, thank you."

"That's a pity." Preacher Thompson looked around the table. "Any ideas for a third judge?"

Ella shrugged. "Not right off the—"

"I know who," Aunt Jo announced.

Everyone looked her way. She nodded at Jules.

Jules blinked. "Me?"

Aunt Jo nodded.

"Oh no." Jules took a step back. "I'm going to be busy that whole weekend. The Moonlight is doing a barbecue tent for the festival."

"You'd get dibs on your tent site," Zoe offered. "*First* dibs. That might mean the difference between being at the back of the lot or the front."

Grace added, "Which could increase your revenue substantially."

Jules still frowned, but she looked less stern. "That's true." She bit her lip. "Let me get this straight. *If* I agree to judge, then you'll guarantee that the Moonlight's tent will be on the main center aisle."

Zoe's smile faltered. "I don't know if we have room left on the main aisle. We've already assigned those—"

"We'll work it out," Grace interrupted. "Well, Jules? Can we count on you to judge?"

"I suppose Mark can run the tent during the hours the bake-off is happening. We've hired a new cook, and Marian said she could help some that weekend, too." Jules thought a moment, then shrugged. "Fine. Count me in."

Grace couldn't have looked happier. "There, Preacher. You have your judges' panel."

His smile was just as wide as hers. "Praise be!"

Jules held up the coffeepot. "Any more refills?" When no one asked for more, she left, but not before she cast a cool, smug look Ella's way.

Great. Just great. If Jules thought Ella cared who else was judging the bake-off, she was sorely mistaken.

Grace rubbed her hands together. "Three excellent judges, and one of them a celeb. The local media will eat this up. Zoe, add 'update press release' to 'new business.' Ella, you'll be doing more posts from Dove Pond leading up to the event, right?"

"Of course. And yes, I'll hashtag Dove Pond."

"And when it's appropriate, add a hashtag for the bake-off, too. We need all the press we can muster."

Ella nodded. "Sure."

"What a blessing!" Preacher Thompson held up his cup of coffee. "I think this calls for a toast."

"Here, here," said Zoe.

Everyone lifted their mug.

The preacher cleared his throat and said in his deep voice, "To Ella, who is helping her old hometown make bank."

Ella joined in the toast, though she couldn't stop feeling she'd been manipulated. She wasn't quite sure who had done it—Aunt Jo, who was so determined that Ella stay in town; Grace, the ambitious mayor; or the too-charming reverend—but one or all of them had laid a trap and she'd stumbled right into it.

Oh well. She couldn't see her way to undoing it now, not without becoming the town villain. *In for a penny, in for a pound.* Besides, what did she have to lose?

ANGELA

Angela looked out the car window, watching the trees blur as the road wound through the mountains. The windy weather had brought a cold spell to Dove Pond. The leaves wouldn't change without a few freezes, but she could already smell the fresh chill in the air.

She couldn't wait for fall to arrive. She loved the colors, the faint smell of smoke that drifted on the breeze, and the crunch of leaves under her feet. John used to say that fall was that delicious time between iced tea and hot chocolate. Her chest tightened and she had to blink back tears as she tugged her cardigan closer. *I miss you.*

"It's chilly today," Ella said into the quiet. "A cup of tea would be nice."

Angela glanced at her driver, who was bringing them back from a day at the outlet malls in Asheville. Tea *would* be nice. "Earl Grey."

Ella shot her an approving look. "Is there any other?"

"Good answer. Jules only has green tea and some sort of decaffeinated, tastes-like-hot-water herbal stuff, which is crap however you look at it." Angela suspected that Jules had hidden the good, caffeinated tea, but she hadn't found it. *Yet.*

"Let's swing by Ava's tearoom and get some. I've got another bake-off meeting later today, and I could use the energy."

"They meet a lot, don't they?"

Ella rolled her eyes. "Too much."

Angela glanced at her watch and wondered if stopping for tea was a good idea. She'd managed to keep her outings secret from everyone but Gray by staying out of Dove Pond and always—*always*—being home before three, which was an entire hour before Jules was due to arrive home.

As if she knew what Angela was thinking, Ella added, "We'll call ahead so our tea is waiting, and I'll avoid Main Street. You can just stay in the car so no one sees you. We'll have you home well before four."

That could work. "Fine. I need some tea. My stomach is a little upset at your crazy driving."

"Yeah, well, my stomach is upset by the way you yell out the windows at big, angry-looking truckers. That's not cool."

Angela sniffed. "They aren't supposed to be in the left lane for a reason."

Ella shot her an amused look, unlocked her phone, and handed it to Angela. "Want to call in our order?"

"An Earl Grey for you, too?"

"Yes, please, and some coffee cake for us both. Ava said she's been making it from the recipe I sent her, and I'm keen to see how it turned out."

"So long as you didn't make it. I don't have time to get lost in my memories today, thank you." Still, a piece of coffee cake sounded just right. Angela called in the order and left it with a spunky teenager. The call done, she set the phone in a cup holder. "I should have asked before I ordered, but is Ava a good cook?"

"Yes, when she has the time."

"We'll see, won't we?" Angela cast a curious glance at Ella. There was something different about Ella these last few weeks. Early on, she'd been snippy about being forced into driving, which Angela had enjoyed. Who didn't like being the tormentor of one's tormentor? Yet, as the weeks passed, Ella had grown less snippy and more quippy, and was showing her sense of humor, which had made their little outings fun. But during the past few days, she'd been noticeably quieter, lost in her own thoughts as if she were having a conversation with herself.

Angela turned in her seat so she could see Ella better. *What's going on?*

Ella didn't take her eyes from the road. "Stop staring at me."

"I wasn't staring, I was looking." Angela pursed her lips. "No, that's not true. I was staring. You seem different. Has something happened?"

Ella shrugged but didn't say anything.

"Something I don't know about, perhaps?"

Ella's hands tightened on the wheel, her gaze seemingly locked on the road ahead.

Angela decided it was time to take the bit in her own teeth. "Just say it already. You're dating Gray, aren't you?"

Ella's gaze flew to Angela's face.

"Keep your eyes on the road," Angela ordered.

Ella flushed but did as she was told. "Did he tell you?"

"Lord, no. But you two have been seen together. There are no secrets in this town."

"I guess I should have thought of that."

"If you didn't, then you're a fool. Small towns make big gossips." Angela had been unhappy to hear that the two were seeing each other, but she wasn't surprised. Mark had brought the news home just a few days ago. He'd been furious about it, too. Jules hadn't said much, but Angela could tell from the way her daughter's mouth thinned that she hadn't been happy to hear it, either.

But what Angela saw as an inevitable outcome of Gray and Ella's being in the same town, Jules saw as "Ella's fault." *Sorry, but she's wrong about that. Gray isn't an innocent bystander in that relationship. He knows full well what he's getting himself into.* He'd been warned by everyone in the family, and yet apparently he'd decided to press on.

Ella let out a frustrated sigh. "It's not a secret. I just didn't feel like giving you or anyone else a report on my dating life."

"Then don't. It's your business. Not mine." Angela turned a little in her seat and stared out the window, nose stuck in the air and her arms crossed over her chest.

It only took two minutes before Ella smacked her steering wheel. "Fine! Yes, I'm dating Gray and it's complicated."

There you go. Angela turned back around. "*Goodbye* isn't complicated, and that's where you're headed, right?"

"I suppose so. I hadn't—"

"So the day will come and you'll pack up and leave, and Gray will stay here and live a wonderful, full life. Seriously, Ella, there's nothing complicated about this. We already know how this will end. *You* know how this will end."

Ella shot her a quick look, her gaze searching. "Has Gray said something?"

"Of course not, but if there's one thing you are, it's predictable."

Ella didn't look happy at that, but she didn't argue, either. They came to a stop sign. "We're getting close to town."

Angela put on her sunglasses and slid down a little in her seat.

They turned onto Peach Tree Lane, a short, narrow street that ran perpendicular to Main. Ella parked beside Rose's Bookstore and grabbed her jacket and purse from the back seat. "I'll pick up our orders and be right back."

Angela stayed slumped down. "Don't linger."

"We'll get you home with time to spare." Ella climbed out, and Angela was left alone with the hum of the heater.

With nothing to do, she scooted up in her seat just a little so she could see the front window of the bookstore. She knew Rose Day, although not well. Rose was much older and was the matriarch of the Days, a family known for their storytelling. It was said that if a Day told you a story about a flood, it would be so real, the words so vivid, that if you didn't hang on to a piece of furniture, you might get swept away and drown.

Rose had taken the Day family art of storytelling in a new direction: she bought books with wonderful, amazing, rich stories. The books weren't all new, nor were they all bestsellers or classics, but each and every one was guaranteed by Rose herself to be a delightful, wonderful story. They said you could never go wrong with a book from Rose's Bookstore, and Angela was keen to test that rumor.

She wondered if she dared slip into the store and get a book or two, but then decided not to risk it. Peach Tree Lane wasn't as busy as Main Street, but in Dove Pond, you never knew whom you might run into, and it would take only one pair of curious eyes to blow her cover.

Sighing heavily, she let her gaze wander down the street. If she leaned toward the driver's seat, she could see the Moonlight's parking lot. The back door to the café was there, and she could just catch sight of Jules's car near the load-in ramp.

I can't believe I've been here for two months. The time has flown by and Jules and I have never been closer. Still, she was aware of the weight of her own guilt, which seemed to grow by the day. *I have so much to lose. Oh, John, I wish you were here. You'd know what I should do. And you'd give me the courage to do it, too.*

The back door to the Moonlight swung open, and Jules stepped out, carrying a box. She glanced around the almost empty parking lot, and then, apparently assured that no one was within sight, carried the box to a car parked under a shade tree at the very back of the lot.

A man climbed from the car. He was tall and slender, and had salt-and-pepper hair that reminded Angela of John's. She'd seen this man once before and knew he was her daughter's secret now-ex boyfriend, Joe Kavanaugh.

Angela watched as Jules handed Joe the box. The two spoke and it was obvious he wasn't happy with whatever Jules had to say. After a moment, Jules shook her head vehemently and then turned away and hurried back to the café. As she grabbed the door handle, Angela caught a glimpse of the tears streaming down Jules's face. *Oh dear, so much pain.*

Joe stayed where he was, staring in obvious anguish at the door Jules had disappeared through. Finally, sighing, he put the box into his car and left.

Why, oh why, won't my daughter share things with me, or with anyone else, for that matter? Gray has said often enough that she's a closed book to both him and Mark, which neither deserves. We all love you, Jules. I just wish you understood that and would let us in. You're not alone.

A movement across the street announced Ella's return. She was carrying two cups of tea, a paper bag hanging off one wrist.

Angela reached over to open the driver's-side door and Ella climbed in. She set the cups into the holders in the center console and then handed Angela the bag.

She noticed that the sturdy white paper bag had the words *The Pink Magnolia Tearoom* written in cursive over an adorable teacup. "Nice design." She opened the bag. "Let's see what we have."

"The bigger box is our pieces of cake. The smaller one holds two white chocolate and cranberry scones. I thought you might want to take those home with you for later. They should keep in your nightstand for a few days, at least."

Angela narrowed her eyes. "You made these scones."

"I did, so don't eat them unless you have time for a stroll down memory lane. Ava's charging double for my pastries and making a killing." Ella looked smug as she said that. "It's nice to be able to help her out, although to be honest, she doesn't need it."

Angela balanced the larger box on the console, stashed the box of scones in her big purse, and then dropped the empty bag at her feet. She picked up her tea and took a sip. "You added honey." She'd forgotten to ask for it, and it was nice that Ella had remembered.

Ella took a sip of her own tea and sighed happily. "The perfect temperature. My sister is a pro."

Angela opened the larger box, the smell of coffee cake rising through the air and making her mouth water. She dug out a napkin and handed a piece of cake to Ella.

"Thank you." Ella lifted the cake as if to take a bite, but then hesitated. "Do we have time to eat this here or should we get on our way?"

"Five minutes won't hurt."

"Thank goodness." Ella tasted the cake, her eyebrows rising. "Mmmm. Ava followed the recipe."

"Is she the non-recipe type?"

"Not usually, but she's really busy right now, so I thought she might take a shortcut here and there."

They were quiet a moment, enjoying the cake and hot tea. Angela had to reluctantly admit that she and Ella had a lot in common: a love of desserts, a sharp sense of humor, and a rather startling, sometimes not-always-acceptable-to-others free way of seeing life. It would be nice if Angela could do this very thing—spend the day shopping, talking, laughing, and yes, having a cup of tea and a piece of cake—with Jules instead of Ella. There was something about sharing cake with someone. It was a simple celebration of everyday life.

Angela cast a considering look at Ella. It was at times like these that Angela found herself wondering about Ella and the lost Book of Cakes. The more she thought about it, the more she wondered what, exactly, Ella would do with an old, rather worn-out recipe book. *But if she didn't take it, then who did?* There could be no other answer.

"Oh, look at the time." Ella popped the last bit of her coffee cake into her mouth and dropped her napkin into the empty paper bag at Angela's feet. "We should get going."

"That was an excellent cake." Angela wiped some crumbs from her lap as the car moved into the street. "Sour cream, cake flour, cinnamon, brown and white sugar, a hint of salt, toasted pecans, a nice dash of vanilla, and . . . nutmeg?"

Ella sent her an appreciative look. "You've always had amazing taste buds."

Angela smiled and sipped her tea.

A few moments later, they were back home. Ella turned her car into the driveway and parked near the walk. She'd just turned off the car when she looked at the top of the drive and flushed, a smile twinkling in her eyes. "Oh, look. Gray's here."

What? Angela had twisted in her seat to gather the shopping bags from the back seat, but now she looked over her shoulder. Gray's truck was parked beside the carriage house. *Darn it. Ella will want to say hi and—* To her dismay, she realized that Ella had already gotten out of the car. *Great! If Jules shows up, she'll think I've been facilitating—* Her gaze locked on the corner of a car peeking out from behind the large truck. *Oh dear! Mark is here too.*

Angela scrambled out of the car. "Ella, don't—" But she was talking to empty air, as Ella was already halfway up the walkway, carrying their shopping bags.

"Ella! Wait!"

Unaware of the danger she was walking into, Ella called over her shoulder, "It's no problem. These aren't heavy."

Angela grabbed her purse and bags and hurried after Ella. "Stop!" She had to hiss rather than yell. Heaven forbid she make enough noise that someone inside the house might hear her. "Ella, stop! Mark is here!"

Ella finally heard her. Her steps slowed to a stop and she looked over at the driveway. "Oh, sheesh. I didn't see his car."

"I almost missed it, too." Angela cast a hasty glance at the house, relieved no one was peering out the windows. "Give me the bags. You need to go."

Ella handed the bags to Angela. "He has to know you haven't been home. What will you tell him?"

"I have no idea. Just go." Angela whirled around and managed a total of two steps before an especially full bag ripped open, a pink silk negligee and matching robe pouring out.

"Oh no!" Ella scrambled to collect the lost garments.

"Ella, just g—"

"Grandma?" Mark stood in the open door dressed in jeans and a faded red T-shirt, his eyes wide.

Great. Just great. Angela forced a smile. "Hi!"

His gaze went from her to her shopping bags and then to Ella, who stood holding the negligee and robe. "*Ella?* What are you doing here?"

Angela shrugged as if getting caught with the family's nemesis was an everyday occurrence. "Never mind her. Can you help with these bags?"

He came to take some of the bags from her hands. "I don't understand. You were shopping? Gray said you were in your room taking a nap."

Think! Angela instructed herself. After a second, she blurted out in a strangled voice, "Doctor's appointment." Yes. A doctor's appointment. That was the ticket.

Mark's startled gaze flickered over her face.

Angela faked a tired smile. "In Asheville. A specialist."

Ella took a few steps closer. "I drove her because—" She gulped and looked at Angela.

"No Uber," Angela said hastily. "Not a one. Can you believe that?"

Mark didn't look convinced. "So you asked *Ella* to take you?"

"Oh, it wasn't any trouble," Ella said brightly. She handed the negligee and robe to Angela. "I didn't mind."

"But I'm home now, so—" Head high, Angela clutched the clothing and walked past Mark. "Let's go inside. It's getting cold." Without waiting to see if he was following, she went inside and hastily piled the clothes she carried onto the entryway table.

She was relieved when she heard his footsteps behind her.

He came into the foyer and piled the shopping bags beside the umbrella stand. "Grandma, why didn't you call m—"

"Mark, please. It's obvious why I asked Ella. Gray was off somewhere, and I couldn't bother you as you and your mother were at work. As they say in the restaurant business, the dinner special must go on." Angela was a little irked to see that Ella had followed Mark and now stood just outside the door.

Mark's gaze dropped to the shopping bags he'd just carried inside. "You went shopping *and* to the doctor's? I didn't think you'd have the energy to—"

"Of course I didn't go shopping," Angela said sharply, moving to stand beside the door, which effectively placed her between Mark and Ella. "She shopped while I took a nap in the car. Didn't I, Ella?"

Ella nodded faithfully. "Those bags are all mine."

He frowned. "Then why did you bring them in here?"

Angela and Ella stared at him.

"We—" Ella cast a wild look at Angela. "We didn't want them stolen. Right?"

Whew. Yes! "Right. Not while—" Angela gripped the door handle, trying to think. "I—I invited her inside for a cup of hot tea to thank her for helping me get to the doctor, and we didn't want her purchases to get stolen from the car while she was here." There. Surely that would end this torture.

Mark ran a hand through his hair. "That you'd ask Ella of all people—" He clamped his mouth over the rest of his words and shot a self-conscious look at Ella. "Sorry. It was nice of you to help Grandma."

"She would have asked someone else, but I came by to—to ask her about a recipe I was working on. That's when she got the call from her doctor, reminding her about the appointment, and so I thought, 'Why not?'"

Oh my, thought Angela with admiration. That was rather clever of Ella. If it hadn't been so close to the time Jules came home, Angela might have encouraged Ella to actually join them for tea, just to give her story a little more authenticity. But there wasn't enough time; Jules could come home anytime now.

Angela leaned against the front door and pressed her hand to her forehead as if taking her own temperature. "I don't feel so well. Is it hot in here to you all?"

Mark was instantly attentive. "You did too much. You should sit down."

"I should." She gave Ella a weak smile. "We'll have to have that cup of tea another time."

Ella nodded as she backed onto the porch. "Sure. I'm glad your doctor's visit went well."

"Wait." Mark collected all the shopping bags. "You forgot these."

"Oh. Right." Ella took them, her hands instantly full.

Great, Angela thought. *Just great.*

He picked up the negligee and robe from where Angela had left them. "I guess we can put these—" He looked at the full bags and her overly full hands. He gave a helpless shrug and then carefully draped them over Ella's shoulders.

Her face red, she mumbled, "Thanks." She started to turn when her gaze locked on something over Angela's shoulder. "Hi, Gray."

Darn it. Angela stayed where she was, holding the front door half-closed. They didn't have time for this!

Mark cut Gray a hard look. "You said Grandma was in her room taking a nap."

"Wasn't she? Huh." He smiled at Ella. "What's all this?" He gestured to the shopping bags and the negligee and robe hanging from her shoulders.

"We—I mean, I went shopping while your grandma was at her doctor's appointment in Asheville."

"Ah. I see. Grandma, you should find out what store Ella got that sleepwear from. It's in your favorite color."

Angela fixed him with a stern gaze. "I'll do that."

He nodded. "I wish I had a day to go shopping. I spent the whole morning fixing a fence after Pickles decided to see which was stronger, the rails or his head."

Pickles? Angela cast a questioning look at Mark, who looked just as confused as she was.

But Ella knew. "You said he was a stubborn bull."

"You should come and meet him one day." Gray leaned one shoulder against the wall and crossed his arms. "Grandma, you're holding on to that door as if you're trying to keep the wolves out. Why don't you let Ella come on in?"

Angela realized she was still holding the door half-shut. She gave him a meaningful look but didn't move. "I'm tired. We should have this little get-together some other time."

Gray shrugged. "You can take a nap right now if you'd like." His gaze returned to Ella, and he nodded toward the shopping bags in her hands. "What else did you buy?"

Ella smiled jauntily. "Shoes. Three pairs."

He laughed softly. "With those tiny heels you like so much?"

"All three."

"I knew it."

Angela had known they were dating, but the low, quiet way they were talking seemed personal, even intimate. They were closer than she'd realized. And any minute now, Jules would walk through this very door and see exactly what Angela was seeing—that Gray was already well on his way to being back in love with Ella.

Oh dear. Angela rubbed her suddenly aching eyes, aware of Mark's horrified look as he stared first at Gray and then Ella. As much as Angela hated giving up her free chauffeur, there was no way she could appear to condone this.

Angela gripped the door and pasted a smile on her stiff lips. "Thanks for stopping by, Ella. It was kind of you to take me today." As Angela spoke, she slowly shuffled forward, pushing the door closed.

Ella backed away, stepping out onto the porch. "Sure. Just call if you need—"

"I will!" Angela shut the door.

"Grandma!" Gray had pushed himself from the wall and now glowered at her. "That was rude!"

"She said she couldn't stay."

He scowled as he passed her and opened the door, but Ella was already walking back to her car. He turned back to Angela. "There was no call for that."

"I said goodbye first. Besides, I'm tired, and I'm sure she has somewhere to be."

"Gray," Mark said before his brother could reply, "don't be hard on Grandma. You know what Mom would say about Ella being here. She's not happy you're seeing her."

Gray's jaw tightened. "What I do and don't do is none of your business, or hers."

Mark flushed. "Come on, Gray. You know Ella Dove is bad news. The last time you—"

"Don't."

"Gray, I—"

Gray turned on his heel and left.

Angela and Mark followed him to the porch. "Gray, don't leave," Angela ordered.

"We just don't want you to make the same mistakes as before!" Mark said sharply. "Remember how she—"

"I remember everything." Gray stopped on the bottom step and glared up at his brother. "You have no idea what really happened. None of you do. So back off."

"Gray, don't—" Mark started.

"No. You're a great brother, but you're not my dad."

Mark stiffened. "I just don't want to see you get hurt."

"Then don't look." With that, Gray left, calling to Ella, who was just now climbing into her car.

Mark started after him, but Angela grabbed his arm. "Let him go. You'll just make him mad, and he'll do something stupid."

"It's too late for that." Mark scowled. "This isn't going to end well. She's toxic."

To her surprise, Angela realized she didn't agree with that. But now was not the time for an argument. "However it ends, he's right. It's his decision and not ours. He—"

Gray's truck growled to life.

Mark cursed under his breath and went to the far edge of the porch so he could see the driveway. "He's leaving. She's following him in her car."

"Then there's nothing more we can do. Not now." Angela felt as if all the stiffness had leaked out of her bones. She left Mark outside and made her way to the living room, where she sank onto the chaise.

Mark arrived a moment later, looking far more upset than he should have.

"Mark, leave it be. Gray can handle whatever happens."

"You don't know how he gets when—"

"Pah. I know. I might not have lived here long, but I've seen how he can get. Look, you might be right and they're not good for each other. I don't know. But it's not our choice to make. It's his."

"Not good for each other?" Mark shot her an incredulous look. "Why would you think Gray wasn't good for Ella? He's everything she's not—stable, reliable, kind."

"Oh, please. She's not a horrible person. She's just not the right person for Gray."

"We can agree on that, at least." Mark blew out a sigh and dropped into the chair opposite the chaise. "Mom's going to have a cow when she hears about this."

Of course she will. Jules had blamed Angela for Gray's encounter with Ella in the Hamptons. *Will she blame me for this, too? Probably.*

Angela glanced under her lashes at Mark. "I suppose you'll tell your mother Ella was here."

"She's going to be furious."

"She would be . . . if she knew about it."

Mark's startled gaze met hers. "You think we shouldn't tell her."

Angela nodded. "It won't change anything, and it'll upset her."

"But—"

"Think about it, Mark. Your mom already knows Ella's been see-ing Gray." Angela shrugged. "Mentioning that Ella was here, at the house, serves no purpose. None."

He considered this for a moment and then gave a frustrated sigh. "You're right; it won't change a thing."

Relieved, Angela rubbed her forehead where an ache was begin-ning to form.

Instantly, worry darkened Mark's gaze. "What did the doctor say?"

"What doc— Oh. Him. He said I should rest, eat better . . ." She waved her hand. "That sort of thing." She leaned her aching head against the high back of the chaise. "Why are you home so early? Is everything okay at the café?"

"It's fine. We were slow this afternoon, so I left early. I was going to see if you'd like to take a drive and get some ice cream, but when I arrived, Gray was already here and said you were asleep. I was waiting for you to wake up to ask you."

Angela would bet her bottom dollar that if she looked at her phone, she'd find texts and missed calls from Gray where he'd tried to let her know what was going on.

Mark dropped back in his chair, looking as wrung out as she felt. "I didn't mean to make him mad."

"He's touchy where Ella's concerned."

Mark was quiet a minute but then sighed. "I understand what he sees in her. She's funny and super confident, and she has a great laugh—there are a lot of good things about her. But he knows how she is. There is no happily-ever-after where Ella is concerned."

"He's intelligent. He'll figure things out." Angela pulled her cardigan closer.

"You're cold." He stood. "I'll light a fire. Mom had me fill the firewood racks last week, so everything we need is right here."

"Is it cold enough for a fire?"

He grinned, his eyes crinkling. "If we have to, we can turn the air-conditioning back on." He went to the fireplace and in an amazingly short time had everything arranged. "There. That should do it."

Angela came to stand beside him as he clicked a long lighter that had been resting in a box on the mantel. A small curl of smoke lifted from the paper he'd stuffed under some thin split wood. Sure enough, after a moment, the smoke thickened and then, with a *pop*, a blaze sparked to life. "The first fire of the fall," she said.

"But not the last." Mark replaced the lighter in the box. "We'll let that grow for a minute and then add more wood."

"You're very talented at this."

"Dad taught me. He was good at handyman stuff. You know, build-ing fires, splitting wood, fixing broken lamps. That sort of thing."

"And you take after him." The kindling popped and a few more flames appeared. "I never knew your dad as well as I wish I had, but he seemed very trustworthy. You knew he was the kind of man who would do what he said he would."

Mark cut her a grateful look. "He was the best. I miss him every day."

She slipped an arm through his and gave him a hug. "I'm sure he's watching over all of you. You've been such a help to your mom. I don't know what she'd do without you."

Mark gave a rueful chuckle. "She'd hire another line cook."

"And an assistant manager, and a stock manager, and a— You do a lot more than cook at the café."

"I try." His gaze returned to the flames, which were now crack-ling merrily. Mark used the poker to move the wood so the fire could breathe. When he finished, he replaced the poker and dusted off his hands. "There."

There, indeed. She moved closer and held out her hands to the warmth. "Thank you."

He pulled a large ottoman closer to the fire. "Sit here. You can put your feet toward the heat."

She did so while he leaned with his elbow on the mantel, star-ing down into the flames. After a minute, he sent her a rueful smile. "Grandpa doesn't like fires, does he? He says they are messy and aren't worth the trouble. The second he left for Florida, Mom had the chimneys cleaned and put in a standing order for a cord of wood."

"She's pretty good at getting her way, even when she has to wait for it. It's her greatest strength." *And probably her greatest weakness, too*, Angela decided. She sent Mark a curious look. "What about you?"

He looked at her, surprised. "What about me?"

"All this talk about how Gray and Ella will never make it as a couple, and you haven't once mentioned your own love life. You and Gray are both handsome and smart enough to attract high-quality partners, thanks to your excellent genes. Surely there's at least one girl you're interested in around here."

Mark gave an awkward shrug. "I date some."

"Some what?"

He burst out laughing. "Women. I just . . . I don't know. Right now, Mom needs me. Once things settle for her and Gray, maybe I'll get serious about that."

Jules had been right when she'd said Mark felt too responsible for his brother and mother. Angela could see and hear it in everything he said and did. "Mark, you know I'm not one to criticize—"

He laughed and then looked self-conscious. "Sorry."

"That's fine. I have opinions. I'm not ashamed of that. But I worry about you. You're living for your mother and brother, but it's time to live for yourself. Go out, meet some people, have some fun."

"You make it sound as if I'm just hanging around, twiddling my thumbs. I'm busy, you know that. If I met the right woman, I'd ask her out. I just haven't met her yet."

"The only way you could meet a woman is if she came into the café, climbed over the counter, and peeked around that huge order wheel your mom had installed."

"Ha! I could meet someone from one of the farms we get produce from. Or downtown when I'm at the grocery store. I'm there about twenty times a week."

"If you were looking, maybe. But you're not. You're waiting for your mom and Gray to get settled first. That's not right for someone your age. You deserve someone of your own."

"I deserve a grandmother who doesn't hound me about my lack of dates." When she opened her mouth again, he stopped her with an amused look. "I appreciate what you're saying, but it's not me. Mom and Gray both need me. I don't mind that."

"Gray does. If he heard you say that, he'd tell you to jump off a cliff."

Mark reluctantly broke into a grin. "He would say exactly that. But only after he made fun of how I comb my hair or something equally lame. He—"

His phone rang and he dug it out of his pocket. "Hi, Mom. I just started a fire for Grandma. Yes, it's nice. I—" He listened a moment. "Right now? Yes. Sure. I'll call you when it's done." He hung up and made a face. "Mom's laptop crashed. She needs me to do the payroll before five."

"See? You're the manager whether you have the title or not."

He shrugged. "Do you need anything before I go upstairs and fire up my computer? It will take a while to get the payroll done."

"No. I'm good here. Thank you."

He headed upstairs, leaving Angela sitting on the ottoman in front of the crackling flames. She soaked in the warmth and realized that her headache had disappeared. Was it the heat or Mark's reassurance that he wouldn't tell his mother that Ella had been at the house? *I shouldn't encourage her children to lie to her.* Good grandmothers didn't do that. But good grandmothers and mothers never let their kids think they were dying, either.

Angela sighed, watching a green flame flicker among the orange and yellow ones. The day was coming when she would have to tell Jules the truth. *I just need to find the courage. Oh, John, I hope you're keeping an eye on me. I'm going to need all the help I can get.*

CHAPTER 12

ELLA

*The worst dish in the world is the one that's been left
unmade, untried, and untasted.*

The Book of Cakes, p. 101
Written: 1792–2019

In her dream, Ella ran as hard as she could, her feet slapping the pavement, crunching through the dead leaves and small twigs that had fallen from the stark trees that loomed overhead. Oddly, this time she was wearing a ball gown of sorts, something white and gauzy, the long skirt catching at her running shoes as she tried to escape the horror that chased her.

Panting wildly, she looked over her shoulder. The huge cupcake thudded after her, the scent of strawberry thick in the air.

Her chest aching from the effort, she ran straight up Hill Street toward the Stewart house—only this time, she somehow knew that if she got there, she would be safe. Just ahead, a high line of shrubs towered, blocking the house from her view. If she could push through those bushes and make it inside, the cupcake couldn't get her. Nothing could.

She struggled to reach the line of shrubs. The cupcake's hot strawberry breath burned her as she sprinted. As she leapt over the curb toward the shrubs, her foot caught a stump and she tripped, catapulted forward with her hands outstretched. She was going to hit the ground in an ugly way, but at the last moment, strong arms caught her—

Gasping, she woke up, her blankets kicked off, a thick streak of strawberry icing across her forehead. It took a few minutes for her heart to slow down enough for her to breathe. That was the first time she'd sensed another person in one of her cupcake dreams. Before now, all she'd known was that when she reached the Stewart house, the cupcake would disappear. But to feel *safe*? What did that mean? Aunt Jo seemed to think Ella's dreams would eventually tell her what she needed to do, but darned if Ella could figure them out.

Pressing a hand to her aching chest, she sat up and swung her feet to the floor. Would she ever have a normal night of sleep again? She leaned over and glanced at her phone where it sat on the nightstand. It wasn't quite seven yet. Outside, the sky was just starting to glow, but the room was still dark. Ella picked up the damp washcloth she now kept beside her bed and wiped off the frosting. It was all so discouraging. She was doing everything she could to work her way through this. Angela seemed to be softening some, that was true. But Ella was still having her dreams, and they were getting more real, the swipes of strawberry frosting thicker and bigger.

"Stupid dreams," she muttered. "Nothing seems to be enough."

She heard the bathroom door across the hallway open and Kristen's unmistakable footsteps clumped down the hallway before thundering down the stairs. Teenagers, Ella thought. Not a quiet bone in their bodies. Not a one.

Ella stood and stretched. In the distance, she heard a deep male laugh and realized Dylan was here, too. She made a face. She wasn't in the mood to watch Dylan flirting with Ava this early in the morning. *Not until I've had some coffee.* At least the bathroom was now free, which was good, as she had yet another meeting about the bake-off later this morning, this one at the library. *Meetings, and more meetings. Yay.*

Yawning, she slipped on her housecoat, grabbed her towel from the hook behind the door, and had just reached for her doorknob when she heard the bathroom door across the hallway close. *Darn it, Sarah!*

Mumbling under her breath, Ella dropped her housecoat and towel at the foot of her bed and climbed back under the covers. She'd forgotten how chilly this old house could get. Although it was better now with the updated heating system, there was still an unmistakable chill in the air this morning.

She pulled the covers up to her chin and turned onto her side so she could look out the window. The sky was turning more golden with each passing minute. Dad used to love the morning hours, getting up way before the sun rose and heading to the kitchen so breakfast would be ready when everyone got up. Ella had always hated mornings, but sometimes, as he tiptoed down the hallway, the floorboards right outside her bedroom door would creak and wake her. She'd quietly slip out of bed, dress, and follow him to the kitchen. He was always glad to see her and would set her on a stool he kept just for her, where she'd sit and watch him cook. It made her sad to remember those times. *This house isn't the same without him or Momma. It feels hollow.*

Irked at the sadness of her own thoughts, she kicked off her covers and was relieved to hear Sarah coming out of the bathroom and heading downstairs. *Finally!*

Of the many things Ava had updated in their old house, Ella was the most grateful for the plumbing. When they were growing up, the showers had been finicky—that was what happened when seven sisters shared a bathroom—but now there was a far more plentiful supply of hot water. Ella had never been so glad of that amenity as she was this morning.

She turned on the hot water and stood in the shower for a long time before she washed her hair, the steam thick around her. To her irritation, the scent of strawberry still hung in the air despite the water pouring over her.

Grimacing, she closed her eyes and rested her forehead against the cool tile. Mere months ago, the idea of staying in Dove Pond longer than a few days had made her groan at the thought of the boredom she was about to face. But strangely enough, she wasn't bored at all. *I'm too busy to be bored.* She'd gotten sucked into the bake-off drama and still had to send Tiff content for their accounts. Plus, she'd been spending time with her sisters and Aunt Jo, too. And then there was Angela and her many shopping ventures, and the time she spent with Gray.

Gray. She wished she could see him more often. He was fun. Fun was good, wasn't it? With her eyes still closed, she blindly reached for the hot water handle and turned it up, sighing happily as the steam around her thickened.

For the life of her, she couldn't figure him out. Their last few dates had lasted long into the night, but not for the usual reason. Instead of ripping off each other's clothes and tumbling into the nearest bed, which was normally how she liked to spend her late hours, they'd instead done something far more unlikely—they'd talked.

Really talked. For hours and hours, too.

Up until now, she'd thought she knew all there was to know about Gray, but she'd been wrong. She'd discovered he'd changed quite a bit since their high school days, a fact she'd overlooked during their summer fling a few years ago. He now loved the peacefulness of the countryside, had become an excellent farmer and "Cow Dad," as he called it, and was passionate about developing faster and more efficient food sources. He was super enthusiastic about hydroponic farming, something he felt was crucial to the success of their planet. He called himself a "scientific environmentalist," which she found sort of adorable. It fascinated her how much he cared.

So much passion. But none of it's for me. Well . . . that wasn't exactly true. Their conversations had been punctuated with plenty of heated kisses, although he always stopped things right there. She might have been insulted except for times she'd caught him watching her with a hungry, longing gaze that probably matched her own.

She cracked open an eye and noticed that the sun was now streaming through the bathroom window. *Darn it.* She reluctantly turned off the water with fingers that had gone pruney and got out. She threw on her robe and, with her hair wrapped in her towel, returned to her room, shivering in the sudden cold of the hallway.

She got dressed in a pair of leggings with a bright purple tunic top and, her hair dried and braided over one shoulder, went downstairs. When she got to the landing, she could hear Ava and Dylan talking in the sitting room. She rolled her eyes. She couldn't face Dylan's sappy longing for Ava without at least two cups of coffee, and maybe three.

She glanced at the hall clock as she passed. *Phew.* Despite her overly long shower, she still had time to grab some coffee and breakfast from the Moonlight to take to the meeting with her.

Ella had Jules to thank for the new bake-off meeting time. It had been her suggestion that they move the meetings from the afternoons to early, early morning. She'd said something about it being the best time for her because of her tight restaurant schedule, but Ella couldn't shake the feeling that the only reason Jules had made that suggestion was because she knew how Ella felt about mornings.

"Fine, have your stupid meeting before I'm even awake," Ella muttered under her breath. "I'll come caffeinated and ready to rumble." She put on her coat and slung her purse over her shoulder, glancing inside it to make sure her meeting folder was there. Reassured, she headed for the front door, trying to hurry past the sitting room so no one would notice her.

"Hey!" Ava called.

Darn it. Ella pasted a smile on her face and came back to the door. Dylan was sprawled on the couch, his arm along the back, probably in hopes that Ava might sit beside him and lean against it. Instead, she was curled on the overstuffed chair across from him.

"Good morning," Ava said. She was dressed in her usual work overalls, her hair tied back. "If you'd gotten up earlier, I'd have made you breakfast."

"I'm going to grab something on my way to my meeting. Morning, Dylan. Did you come to have breakfast with your daughter?"

"I did. You just missed her. She left for school."

"I hate to hear that," Ella said drily. "Kristen is a delight in the mornings."

Ava snorted.

Ella smiled. "I bet she loved having breakfast early in the morning with her super cheerful father before a hearty day of fun high school hijinks."

"She ignored me completely," Dylan admitted. "Fortunately, I speak grumpy morning teenager and realized that her lack of communication was in fact a compliment on my superior parenting skills."

Ava grinned. "Don't let him fool you. He's devastated. He barely touched the chicken and waffles I made."

"I beg to differ, madam! I ate everything on my plate the first time and only balked when I had my second helping. You have to understand that I have a poor, shrunken bachelor stomach and can't handle such blissfully good food. It was—" He kissed his fingers to the air.

Ella had to laugh. "Ava's a great cook."

"Hardly," Ava said, although she looked pleased. "But I'm good enough. Plus, I know how to cheer up cranky teenagers and it's *not* by telling annoying dad jokes."

Dylan gave her a mock-outraged glare. "Don't critique my daddying skills. They're finely honed in ways you couldn't possibly understand."

Ava gave an exasperated sigh. "Right now, I'm more interested in your contracting skills." She looked at Ella. "Some of the tiles around the dining room fireplace are loose. They need fixing."

Dylan sighed sadly. "Your sister has called me at least a dozen times about those."

"And you still haven't fixed them," Ava said impatiently.

Ella thought that Dylan would be more likely to fix the tiles if Ava stopped calling him, but she wasn't about to say a word. "I'd love to stay and see if the tiles get fixed, but I've got to get to the judges' meeting. We're to confirm the bake-off judging criteria today. Sarah's letting us use the conference room in the library." It would be lovely to have a meeting that wasn't about tight budgets, security, fire exits, and the million and one things that needed to happen in order to properly stage a public event. *I'm so glad Tiff stepped in to handle the details. I couldn't begin to do it myself.*

Ava held up a finger. "A word of warning. Sarah will probably invite you to get some coffee from the break room, but don't fall for it. It's so weak, you can read through it."

"I have just enough time to stop by the Moonlight, so I should be able to avoid the library coffee."

"Smart. I heard Jules Stewart volunteered to judge."

"I think she's there to keep an eye on me."

Ava's mouth thinned. "I don't like how she treats you."

One of the things Ella had learned about Jules was that the lady knew how to smile politely while at the same time skewering one with an icy look. "I'll admit that she's been a bit cold toward me."

"'Bitter cold with heavy snow and sleet' is more like it."

"Don't worry; I'll wear a hat and scarf. That'll help." Ella checked the clock in the hallway again. "I'd better get on my way. Enjoy your morning, guys." She waved and left, catching a glimpse of Dylan smiling up at Ava.

A twinge of jealousy hit Ella, surprising her. *That's ridiculous. I don't want that. I want . . .* She didn't know what she wanted. But it wasn't that. *Heavens, no!*

She backed the car out of the driveway and then drove down Elm Street. She'd never wanted a deeper, nondisposable relationship. She'd enjoyed her breezy, uncomplicated dating life, happy in the knowledge that when the seasons changed, she'd get a new coat and a new boyfriend, too. That kept things light, which she liked, and prevented any sort of potential heartbreak.

As she turned off Elm Street onto Main, she wondered why she worked so hard to avoid heartbreak. Maybe it was because she'd watched her mother suffer so profoundly at the death of her father. That had been brutal, and it seemed that Momma had never gotten over it. Years later, when Momma died, the doctors said that she'd had a weak heart, but Ella had always thought Momma's heart was not "weak" at all, but simply "broken." Heaven knew Ella's heart had been damaged when Dad died.

That was probably the reason she avoided long-term relationships. But maybe it was something else. Maybe it was also because she'd never met anyone who'd made her feel safe or cherished enough to experience the type of blissful, effortless comfort Momma and Dad had shared. Ella wondered if she and Gray could ever be that close. *That would be something, wouldn't it? I—*

She blinked. *Whoa! What in the heck am I thinking?* Gray had sunk roots in Dove Pond, which made him a no-no right off the bat. She couldn't envision a future here. *I'd never have a life again.* She hadn't even been here two months and she'd already been trapped into judging the bake-off, lulled into providing tons of free endorsements for the businesses in town, tricked into becoming an unpaid Uber driver, and forced to sacrifice her beloved sleep to serve on cranky committees at godless hours of the morning.

Heaven knew what the people in this town would expect if she moved here permanently. *Who needed that?*

Still, she had to admit that it was just short of adorable how much Gray loved this town and his farm. Last week, when they were on their way to catch a movie in Asheville, he'd had to stop by his place to pay the mason who'd finished repointing his old chimney. Halfway up the long drive, Gray had pulled his truck up to the fence where his Highland cows were grazing. Ella had never seen a Highland cow up close, so she'd been happy to get out with him. To her delight, Gray had introduced her to the whole herd. With endearing seriousness, he'd told her the name of each cow and given a brief summary of their individual personalities. She'd never been more charmed by him than she was when a too-cute-for-words calf had come running up when it saw Gray standing at the fence. Her heart had melted even more when Gray had sheepishly admitted he'd named the calf Adorbs for "obvious reasons."

He loved his farm, his animals, and his life. *And if I wanted it to happen, I think he might love me, too.* But . . . did she want that? Did she want to invest in a relationship that could only come to its completion here, in a town where she didn't want to live? Besides, all relationships were destined to end in some way—through disappointment, bitterness, betrayal, or death. Sure, that seemed grim, but Ella had watched it happen over and over. And she knew the cost of such a loss.

She made a face. All relationships were finite. And she, for one, didn't want to live with that future devastation hanging over her head. Not now, not ever.

Muttering to herself about her own ridiculousness in even considering anything else, she parked in front of the Moonlight, grabbed her purse, and got out of her car. The morning chill combined with a brisk autumnal breeze made her glad she had her coat. Tugging the collar closer, she hurried inside and saw Marian working behind the counter.

Ella slid onto a stool and hung her purse on a hook under the counter. *Another fabulous touch from Jules.* "Good morning, Marian. I'd like a coffee and a breakfast sandwich to go."

"Coffee coming right up." Marian handed Ella a menu and then nodded to the chalkboard. "Those are the day's specials."

Ella read the list and had to laugh. "Who's been watching *Our Flag Means Death*?" Every sandwich was named for a character from the show, which she loved.

Marian grinned over her shoulder as she poured Ella's coffee. "That was Mark's idea. I don't think Ms. Jules has ever seen a single episode."

"He has good taste in television."

"I haven't watched it yet, but he swears by it." Marian set the paper coffee cup in front of Ella with a lid, some sugars, and a small pitcher of cream. She slid her order pad and a pen from her apron pocket. "What'll you have?"

"A Stede Bonnet, please. Hold the Pepper Jack."

"You got it." Marian scribbled it down, marked it as "to go," and slid it on the order wheel.

Ella added cream to her coffee and cast a careful look at the pass-through window, where she saw a cook she'd never seen before working the line. Behind him, Mark cracked eggs onto the hot grill.

He looks tired. I should ask Gray what's going on with him.

Mark looked up and their gazes locked. After an awkward second, he flushed and then turned back to the grill.

Her face heated and she glanced around, hoping no one had noticed. *I guess I deserved that for staring at him.* Sighing, she took a sip of her coffee. The brew was rich and slightly bitter, the cream soothing the edges. She had to admit, it was pretty good coffee. *Maybe I should take a picture for Tiff to—*

"Ella?"

She turned.

Mark stood at her elbow, still wearing his Moonlight Café apron. He managed an awkward, perfunctory smile. "Hi."

Well. This was surprising. "Hi," she returned politely.

He grimaced. "I don't mean to bother you, but I wanted to thank you for taking Grandma to her doctor's appointment."

Which Ella hadn't done. *Oh, Angela, you owe me for this.* "It was nothing."

He flashed a wry grimace. "I don't know that I'd call anything having to do with Grandma 'nothing.'"

Ella had to smile at that. "She has a big personality."

His gaze flickered over Ella's face. "She's a lot like you. I don't think I realized that until now."

"Thank you. I've always liked your grandmother. She's one in a million." *Thank goodness.*

Marian returned to her place behind the counter. She slid two more orders onto the wheel and then stopped to pour some coffees.

Mark eyed the orders hanging from the wheel. "I'd better get back on the grill. I just wanted to come out here because I—" He stopped as if struggling to find the words. Finally, he said, "I probably should have said this sooner, but I'm sorry."

"Sorry? For what?"

He shook his head. "I . . . For everything. My family's always thought the worst of you, but what you did for Grandma the other day, taking her to the doctor and not making a big deal of it, made me—"

"Mark!" The line cook used his spatula to point at the last two orders Marian had slipped into the wheel. "This says a number twelve with sausage. Which do I use? The pepper sausage or the turkey?"

"I've got to go." Mark gave her a wry smile as he backed away. "Just . . . thank you." With that, he turned on his heel and headed for the kitchen door.

She watched him resume his place at the grill and felt a flicker of guilt for misleading him about Angela's whereabouts the other day. *When he and Jules find out how much I've helped Angela cover up her big lie, they're going to hate me even more.*

That was a depressing thought.

"Here you go!" Marian set a white paper bag on the counter in front of Ella. "Ketchup for your hash browns?"

"No, thank you." Ella paid and hurried to leave, careful not to look in Mark's direction.

She arrived at her meeting with minutes to spare. Preacher Thompson was already there with Aunt Jo, who'd brought Moon Pie with her, as she always did. Ella was glad when the cute pug curled up under Aunt Jo's chair and almost immediately started to snore.

Grace and Zoe showed up next, both dressed in suits more appropriate for a power lunch in Manhattan than a meeting in the Dove Pond Library, followed shortly after by Sarah, who immediately offered everyone coffee from the library break room.

Ella murmured a thanks and pointed to the to-go cup she'd brought from the Moonlight. *Spared again.*

Jules arrived last, wearing her usual blue jeans and T-shirt. Once everyone had taken their places at the table, Ella turned on her computer and linked in Tiff.

"I think that's everyone," Ella said as she turned her laptop so that everyone could see Tiff.

"Good morning!" Tiff said brightly. "First of all, I want to thank Grace and Preacher Thompson for putting me and the team in charge of the logistics for the bake-off. It's given us a huge amount of leverage with the sponsors."

"You're quite welcome." Preacher Thompson dipped his head.

Grace said earnestly, "We knew you'd do great. I wouldn't have agreed to it otherwise."

Ella knew Grace had been more than happy to hand the planning of the bake-off to Tiff. There were limits to what Grace and her mostly volunteer committee could accomplish on their own. Meanwhile, Tiff was a natural event planner.

Tiff beamed from the screen. "Thank you for your trust." She rubbed her hands together and grinned. "Okay, then. Let's get this meeting started. We've spent most of the last few meetings talking about advertising, contest setup, and awards. So today's meeting will cover judging and logistics. I emailed each of you an agenda, along with diagrams of the various potential setups for the tent. We got the biggest one we could find, and will have room for one thousand forty-five attendees—"

Aunt Jo gasped. "Butter my butt and call me a biscuit! We've never had a turnout like that."

Grace smiled smugly. "We had a great response from the online ticket sales, so Tiff and I decided to expand the audience size as much as possible."

"Money in the bank," Zoe said.

"We've already sold out at the higher number, too," Tiff added. "We'll have room for the audience, the stage with display tables for the cakes, and of course we'll have a sound system for the judging. We plan on miking the judges during the event, although the mics should be turned off during deliberations. Grace has graciously allowed us to turn the town hall waiting room into a greenroom for the judges. Sarah has promised to get some of her library volunteers to stand guard and only allow judges and necessary others inside."

Sarah beamed. "They are super excited to do it, too."

"We're so fancy," Aunt Jo said approvingly.

"Oh, it'll be fancy," Grace said. "Tiff hasn't mentioned yet that she's ordered a refreshment table for the greenroom, with sandwiches and such, plus coffee and teas. She's also arranged to have some makeup artists *and* hairdressers available."

Aunt Jo leaned toward the preacher. "Forget what I said on the way over—I'll be happy to judge again next year."

Tiff looked pleased, which made Ella grin. "Tiff, do you want to tell everyone about the sponsors and what you've got them doing to support the event?"

"Of course." Tiff shared her screen, pulling up a PowerPoint as she launched into an explanation of the free giveaways, paid media placements, and monetary contributions donated by each sponsor. Even Ella thought it an impressive list.

As Tiff spoke, Ella cut a glance at Jules, and realized that, for all her noninvolvement, the café owner was listening intently, and even nodding now and then. *I wish I knew where that silly cookbook was. If I could find it, maybe Jules would lighten up some.*

Ella wasn't sure why she cared, but she did. And it had nothing to do with her frosting episodes, either. In getting to know Gray and in spending so much time with Angela, Ella had realized that no matter how much Jules annoyed them, they respected and loved her, too. *I wish I knew her better.*

"I think that's it as far as logistics," Tiff announced, pulling Ella from her musings. "Ella, do you want to take it from here?"

"Sure." Ella pulled the folder from her purse and handed packets to the committee. "This is the agreed-upon scoring method along with some sample score sheets. Tiff, I emailed yours."

"Got it."

Grace and Zoe pored over the document together while Jules read quietly.

Aunt Jo pulled out her glasses, perched them on her nose, and then held the paper at arm's length. "There are numbers on here. You're going to have to explain those to me."

Ella smiled. "It's simple. Judges will score the cakes using the rubric on the next page—" She caught Aunt Jo's confused look and added, "It's the chart on page two."

Aunt Jo flipped to the chart and read through it. "This looks simple enough."

Ella nodded. "Once you've scored the cakes, you'll hand in your sheets. Zoe will tally the results."

Zoe waved from where she sat next to Grace. "I've already got a spreadsheet set up to do it for us."

Grace added, "That way, we'll have a record of the results."

Aunt Jo dropped her judging packet back on the table. "So long as I don't have to do it, I'm happy."

Ella could understand that. "Once we have the results, we'll announce the top twelve cakes in no particular order. We'll start the final round with clean score sheets. From there, we'll start the process again, only this time we'll be judging just the final twelve cakes."

The preacher nodded. "It'll be a heck of a lot easier choosing a winner from just twelve cakes."

"No kidding." Aunt Jo took off her glasses and put them back into her purse. "I like this. Things are much more organized this year."

"How many entrants are there?" Sarah asked.

"Forty," Aunt Jo said. "I do believe that's the first time we've filled every spot, and there's still a week to go."

Grace tapped her finger on the sample score sheet Ella had handed out. "I like the categories—presentation, texture, difficulty of bake, and flavor. Makes sense."

"It's a lot fairer than our old standard," Aunt Jo admitted. "Which was 'Better than I can make' or 'Good Lord, who made this mess?'"

"It's good we'll have written score sheets this year, too," Zoe added, "In case there are any complaints."

Preacher Thompson looked up from his packet. "We've never had a challenge. With the exception of the bribery scandal, no one has ever complained about a bake-off outcome."

"Wellllll . . ." Aunt Jo said.

Everyone looked at her.

"I'm not saying I participated in this, because I wouldn't. But there's always a lot of smack talk from the losers after the bake-off."

Preacher Thompson's mouth dropped open. "Smack talk? I never heard any."

"That's because people don't say those types of things in front of a preacher. They say it to one another, usually in the women's restroom on the second floor of the church." She waved her hand. "Or so I've heard."

He looked crestfallen. "I had no idea."

"Welcome to the real world," Zoe said.

"Oh yes," Aunt Jo said. "It can get ugly. People will claim their entry was overlooked, or that their cake got hot in their car and was unfairly judged due to the icing looking a little melty, or that someone had a predilection for this or that flavor, or that so-and-so was related to the judge, or . . . Honestly, I can't remember them all." She shrugged. "You know how people are."

Grace narrowed her gaze. "Aunt Jo, last year, when your pecan coconut cake didn't place, didn't you say that—"

"The past is in the past," Aunt Jo said firmly. "As Zoe pointed out, it's a good thing we have this brand-new scoring matrix to keep us on the straight and narrow from here on out."

"Amen!" Preacher Thompson agreed.

"Thank you, Preacher. Ella, I hate to move on from the scoring topic, but I have a question about this tent." Aunt Jo kicked off her shoe and used her foot to scratch Moon Pie's back. "It's getting cold out. Will there be any heat? These bones don't handle the cold the way they used to, and it's been uncommonly chilly lately."

"That's a good question," Grace admitted. "I'll ask the rental company about that. They should have some heating options."

"Great." Ella checked her agenda. "If that's it for scoring, we're down to new business. Does anyone have anything to add?"

"I had an idea!" Tiff said in her bubbly voice through the laptop. "I don't know if you want to do this, but if you have broadcast capability, you could add an overflow area."

"Overflow area?" Zoe asked.

Tiff nodded. "People can watch the event on TV via livestream. That way, when we exceed the tent capacity, people attending the festival can still watch. We'll also provide a live link so anyone with an internet connection can watch from wherever they are."

Grace sighed. "That's a great idea, but we'd have to rent a space and there's no money in the budget for it."

"Well, darn," Sarah said. "I like the idea of an overflow room. If we had a larger meeting space in the library, we could do it here."

Aunt Jo turned to the preacher. "What about the church? Could we have it in the meeting hall?"

"We could, but the ladies' circle is using it to hold the crafts they intend on selling during the Apple Festival. It'll be full."

Well, darn. Where else could they have it? Ella mentally walked through town, thinking of each building and its space. Ava's new tearoom was too small and much too narrow for a viewing. The same could be said for the Peek-A-Boo Boutique and the—

Jules cleared her throat. "What about the Moonlight?"

Ella blinked. "You wouldn't mind?"

Jules lifted one shoulder. "Not at all. I'll just ask the new line cook to work, as we'll be a little short-handed between that and doing the barbecue booth."

"You have both Wi-Fi and TVs, right?" Tiff asked.

"We have Wi-Fi, but no TVs. Mark wants to put some in, but I've resisted, as I like that our customers can talk to one another without a TV blaring in the background."

"I can help with that," Grace said. "The town has two smart TVs that we use for our business outreach events. We can set those up in the Moonlight and hook them to your Wi-Fi. I'll get them preprogrammed so that when the time comes to watch the livestream, all you'll need to do is turn them on."

"Perfect!" Tiff said brightly. "People, I'm getting excited!"

When was Tiff anything else? Ella wondered. "When do you fly in?"

"The team and I will be there Friday morning, bright and early. We want to get a time-lapse vid of the setup Friday afternoon, and then wander around Friday evening and Saturday and capture the different booths and food options. We'll finish up Sunday afternoon with a dramatic look at the First Baptist Bake-Off. I know there are fireworks and a bonfire afterward, but we wanted to make it feel like the bake-off is the festival's grand finale."

The preacher chuckled. "There's nothing wrong with some creative storytelling."

"Not at all," said Grace.

Ella put down her pen. "Any other new business?" She cast a careful look around the table, but no one said anything else. "I guess we're done, then. Unless there is an issue, we won't be meeting again until an hour before the bake-off, in the greenroom. I'll—"

Jules raised her hand.

Wow. Two engagements in one meeting. "Yes, Jules?"

"I'm just curious. How did we get so many people to buy tickets for the bake-off? There aren't a thousand people in this town."

"The internet," Grace said. "Mainly via Ella's social media platforms. To be honest, most of the audience is coming to see her."

Ella wished everyone would stop looking at her. It made her feel like an animal in a zoo.

Tiff jumped in. "And remember, it's more than just the ticket holders who will get to watch the bake-off. The biggest audience will be online, as we're live streaming it. We expect a minimum of five hundred thousand people to tune in, and probably more."

"Five hundred thousand?" Jules gave a surprised, disbelieving laugh. "To see a cake contest?"

Tiff shrugged. "If the demo or the bake-off goes viral, the number will be higher than that. Ella's fans love seeing her bake, so it could happen. That reminds me: Ella, did you decide what you're going to make for the demo?"

Tiff had brought up the cooking demonstration at their last meeting. It would be a separate event from the bake-off and would be its own fundraiser. Grace had suggested that the money from the baking-demo ticket sales could be given to the library for new book purchases, which had thrilled Sarah.

Ella pulled a piece of paper from the back of her folder. "Tiff thought I should make another caramel apple cake—"

"I taught you that," Aunt Jo said proudly.

Ella smiled. "Yes, you did."

Preacher Thompson patted Aunt Jo's arm. "I've had your caramel apple cake and it's divine. If Ella's is anything like yours, people will be happy as punch to learn how to make it."

"Let's do that one," Tiff said. "This is an Apple Festival, after all. And Aunt Jo, maybe Ella can have you on as a guest or a special assistant of sorts. Ella, what do you think?"

"Sure!" It would be lovely to be back in the kitchen with Aunt Jo.

Tiff wrote a new to-do on her list. "Send me your ingredient and equipment needs and I'll make sure everything is in the demo tent when the time comes." Tiff looked up and down her list. "That's it for me. I can't wait to see this little town of yours, Ella. It seems like a movie set: too good to be true. It'll be crazy to see the real thing."

"I'm sure you'll love it." Ella looked around the table. "Last chance. Are there any more questions?"

Everyone looked at each other, and for a moment the only noise came from Moon Pie's not-so-gentle snores.

"Terrific," Ella said. "Adjourned!"

"That was quick." Grace capped her pen and stood as she slid her notebook into her satchel. "I've got my to-do list. Tiff, I'll text if I need anything else."

"Sounds good," Tiff said. "See you all on the big day!" With a wave, she signed off.

Zoe closed her notebook. "This year's bake-off is going to make this the biggest Apple Festival we've ever had. Thank goodness for Tiff."

"We're lucky to have her," Ella admitted. She smiled around the table. "Thanks for coming, y'all. It's going to be a fun event."

Everyone started collecting their stuff. Sarah said her goodbyes before she hurried back to the front desk to help the new assistant librarian. A few minutes later, Grace left with Zoe, both of them talking about the "golden ratio" and Tiff's "amazing omnichannel marketing."

The preacher waited as Aunt Jo collected her cane and purse, then he helped her into her coat. Afterward, he bent down and gently woke Moon Pie.

The dog came awake with a snort and a weird little hop. "Easy there, Goliath," the preacher said. "We've got to get you and your momma home."

Aunt Jo leaned on her cane. "Come on, Moon Pie. Ella, I look forward to doing that demo with you."

"Me too. I can't think of anyone I'd rather bake with."

Aunt Jo's brown eyes twinkled, and she said with a broad grin, "It'll be just like old times, won't it?"

"Exactly like old times." Ella gave Aunt Jo a hug before the preacher herded the older woman and her sleepy dog from the room.

Ella slid her notebook back into her purse, her mind already composing the ingredient list she'd send to Tiff. As she turned to pick up her purse, she realized Jules was still sitting in her chair. "Oh! I thought you'd left with the others. Did you have a question about the scoring system? It looks complicated, but it's not, really."

"I understood it." Jules's expression grew troubled, her dark brown eyes carrying a hint of worry. "I wanted to ask you something."

Ella sat back down. "Should I get my notes out? I can—"

"It has nothing to do with the contest." Jules's voice was sharp. "This is about Gray."

Oh, wow. We're doing this today, are we? Ella sent a wistful look toward the door. She felt a little ambushed, and realized now that she'd taken Jules's involvement in the meeting, along with Mark's kindness earlier this morning, as signs that Jules might be softening toward her. *Apparently not.* "What's up?"

"What's going on with you and Gray?"

That was direct. Ella supposed she could be, too. "We've been seeing each other." Well, they were also laughing and holding hands and talking about life and its foibles . . . stuff like that. And yes, there'd also been some kissing, but not as much as Ella would have liked. But Jules didn't need those details. "Gray and I haven't hidden anything."

"You're still planning on leaving, though."

"Yes." The word was harder to say than she'd expected. "I can't see myself living here. I've told him that too. Many times, in fact."

"I see. What will you do once you're done here?"

Ella shifted uneasily in her chair. "At one point, I'd thought I'd go back to New York, but . . . now I don't know." It was odd, but the thought of going back to New York was less appealing by the day. She didn't know where she'd go. All she knew was that the second her horrible strawberry dreams ended and the bake-off was over, she would be free to leave.

"Look, I don't care where you go or what you do. That's up to you." Jules hesitated and then added with a sour grimace, "I don't even care that much about the Book of Cakes—not like I used to, anyway. Just keep it. But Gray?" Her brown eyes searched Ella's face. "Please, just let him be."

Let him be? Good Lord, what did this woman think Ella was doing? It wasn't as if the man was a prisoner. "Jules, I promise you that I haven't tricked or misled Gray into anything. He's an adult. He's in charge of himself and the decisions he makes."

As Ella spoke, Jules's mouth thinned. "I know that. But whether you or Gray want to admit it or not, you have some sort of hold over him. One he can't shake."

"That's not—" Ella threw up her hands. "No. I'm not going to argue with you. Gray knows what's what. But if it'll make you feel better, I'll remind him that I'm leaving."

"You need to. He's—" Jules's mouth folded in a straight line, and it took her a moment to regain control. When she did speak, her lips trembled the slightest bit. "He feels things deeply. He always has.

And even though I don't understand it, you are his weakness. He's going to be torn apart when you leave, just like the last time."

Jules looked so bleak that Ella didn't know what to say. "I can't do more than tell—"

"You can do a lot more! Every minute you spend with him is pulling him deeper into your world. And when you're done, then what? You'll leave. You'll leave even if it crushes him."

"Jules, I don't want to hurt Gray. And he knows that. I'm not that callous."

"According to your millions of fans on social media, you're the perfect Ella Dove, the best baker ever, and the nicest person in the world. But I know better than that. I've seen how you operate, how you sweep into a place, charm people into short and easy relationships, capture their hearts, and then stomp on them on your way out the door."

"That's not true. I truly care about Gray's feelings—"

"Then prove it." Jules stood abruptly, raking her chair across the floor, the noise jarring. "If you care for him, even a little, you'll stop seeing him now, and not when it's convenient for you."

Ella frowned. "You're assuming things are far more serious than they are."

"Am I?" Jules picked up her things, her movements jerky. "I can't wait for the bake-off to be over, because then things will get back to normal around here. I just hope that when you're done, there will be enough of Gray left for me to put back together." With a final glare, she walked out, leaving Ella sitting alone.

Whew. That had been difficult. Drained, Ella sank back into her chair, her thoughts swirling, her heart beating a sickly beat. *I'm not going to hurt Gray. He knows I'm leaving. I've told him repeatedly.*

And yet, he never seemed to respond when she said it. He merely shrugged and changed the subject. Maybe . . . maybe being honest wasn't enough.

Jules was right. The best thing Ella could do was to end it now. For some reason, the realization made her heart sink to the bottom of her soul. *I'll miss him.*

That shocked her. She would miss him deeply. He'd been the best part of her visit.

Oh no. Oh no, no, no! She pressed her hands to her eyes, a sick feeling in her stomach. *I need to*—have *to*—*end this right now.* She'd tell Gray that she never allowed her relationships to get to the "it's going to hurt to end this" stage, and how she usually had a firm idea of where the line was. But how, in this relationship, for reasons she couldn't fathom, she was no longer sure. Which left her—them—with a dilemma.

Did they continue on their current path until they faced a certain heart-shredding ending, or did they protect themselves and end things now when they still had enough of their good sense left to move on and enjoy life?

Oh yes, she and Gray needed to have a talk, and soon.

CHAPTER 13

GRAY

"Just the guy I wanted to see."

Gray closed his truck door and saw his brother crossing the driveway, the morning sun giving him a fifteen-foot shadow. "What's up?"

Mark's gaze landed on the shoebox Gray was carrying. "Did you get another pair of running shoes? You bought a new pair last week."

Gray shrugged. "They were on sale. I'm going to give them a try right now. You're welcome to come along."

"I don't run. I keep in shape lifting boxes of lettuce." Mark showed off his biceps. "Impressive, huh?"

"You don't want me to answer that, do you?"

Mark grinned. "Probably not. Did you just get back from the farm? It's barely seven in the morning."

"I had a lot of cow stuff to do, so I've been up since five."

"'Cow stuff'? Is that technical farm-speak or did you just make it up?"

"It means I did a lot of cow-related things and I'm too uncaffeinated to explain them all to you." Truthfully, he'd spent an extra hour there stacking the new bales of hay. The work had burned off some of his pent-up energy, which he'd sorely needed. "Did you want something? I just came here to take a shower. I don't have hot water at my place yet, but that's about to change."

"I guess you'll be moving in soon."

"This week, I hope. My home is coming along nicely." Gray couldn't keep a smile from his face as he spoke. *Home.* It was such a short word, and yet it meant so much.

"That's great." Mark shoved his hands into his pockets. "Mom sent me to ask if you think you'll be eating dinner with us this evening."

"I'd like to, but I can't."

The jovial light in Mark's eyes faded. "You're seeing Ella."

He was. He would pick her up around six and take her out to eat, where she'd charm him once again and make him forget, at least for a while, that she was doing her best to be more mirage than woman.

The bake-off was a mere week away, and whenever he'd asked about her plans after that, she'd been vague. Too vague. His jaw tightened. *Don't go there. Just take things one day at a time. Slow and steady wins the race.*

"Blast it, Gray," Mark said in a tight voice. "I wish you'd stop being so darn stupid."

Gray shrugged. "I like her. That's all that matters."

Mark opened his mouth, but Gray cut him short. "Don't." There was nothing Mark could tell him that Gray didn't already know. Ella was as honest as they came. She was also the sexiest, funniest, most spirited woman he'd ever met. And yes, her pastries could make a guy remember the first time he went fishing with his dad in a way that was so real that it was almost as if he'd gotten to relive it. But for Gray, that wasn't what made her special. It was her wit, her style, her sense of humor. The whole package.

Sadly, Ella's real superpower had nothing to do with baking. It had to do with keeping people—namely him—at arm's length. Whenever a conversation or moment got personal, she retreated as if chased by demons. Gray rubbed his neck, trying to ease the tension that had gathered there.

Mark's eyebrows lowered. "Can't you see what she does to you? It's not healthy."

"Stop it. I swear, but if you pitched your voice just a hint higher when you said that, I'd think it was Mom standing here talking, not you."

Anger flashed in Mark's eyes, but after a moment, his shoulders slumped, and he gave a rueful grimace. "I did sound like Mom, didn't I? I hate that."

"Not as much as I do. Just leave it be, Mark. I've got everything under control." *Sort of.*

Mark sighed and leaned against Gray's truck. "Grandma says I should butt out of your life and stop trying to replace Dad."

"She's right. And for the record, you're horrible at it. Dad never said things like 'Be careful' and 'Don't take chances.' That was Mom. Dad was the one who always told us, 'Live large,' 'Follow your dreams,' and 'Don't shy away from challenges.'"

Mark was shocked into silence. "Good Lord, he did say things like that, didn't he? I should have remembered that. It's funny, but every year, I feel as if he's slipping away a little more. Do you ever wonder if you'll forget him?"

"Not completely. He was way too much a part of our lives for that to happen."

Mark sighed. "I guess so."

"Look, it's tough losing a parent. I had a counselor once who said it's like being fast asleep in a warm bed on the coldest night of the year, and then, when you're least prepared, someone rips off the blankets and leaves you shocked, frozen, and vulnerable. All at once."

"Yeah, it's exactly like that. One day, we should go down to Po Dunks and lift a glass in his name. I think he'd have liked that."

Gray had to smile. "You're buying. I'm spending all my money on an old farm. Meanwhile, you're making a killing at the Moonlight *and* living with Mom for free."

"You think it's free?" Mark's smile had disappeared. "You know how she is."

Gray nodded toward the apartment. "This place will be empty once I move to the farm."

"It's too close. But I've been thinking about moving out. I haven't told Mom that, though. Not yet, anyway." Mark hesitated and then said, "I love her, but it's a lot, to work with her all day and then face her across the dinner table every night, too."

"She can be imposing."

Mark frowned. "She never opens up, does she? I don't blame Grandma for not telling Mom she'd let Ella take her to the doctor. Mom would have had a cow over that."

"Or two."

"And she's gotten worse since she broke up with Joe. I'd like to sympathize with her about that, but since that was a secret relationship, there's not much I can say about it." He raked his hand through his hair. "God, but she's a tough one. I'll never understand why she didn't just tell us she was dating. He seemed nice enough."

"She didn't tell us because she still thinks we're in middle school."

Mark nodded morosely. "Speaking of which, I'd better get back inside or she'll be out here thinking one of us died." He headed toward the walkway, calling over his shoulder, "See you later?"

"You know it." Gray tucked the shoebox under his arm and climbed the stairs to the apartment. He entered and was immediately engulfed in the quiet. He used to treasure quiet times like this, but lately it had seemed flat. Lonely, even.

He went to take a quick shower to rinse off the thick layer of barn dust before he ran. He'd made the mistake of running without getting the dust off before, and he'd chafed in places he hadn't thought possible.

He undressed, threw his clothes into the waiting basket, turned on the hot water, and waited for the steam to curl over the top of the shower before he got in. It felt heavenly. Gray closed his eyes and leaned against the wall, letting the water sluice over him. He'd lied to Mark when he'd said he had things under control. He didn't, of course. Gray couldn't be with Ella without paying the ultimate price. He knew it by the way his heart ached whenever she was near, almost as much as his body yearned for her. It was as if he were balanced on a razor-edged mountain peak, and no matter which direction he tumbled, he was doomed to land directly at her feet.

Every time he saw her, every time he thought about her—every time he smelled vanilla or caramel or chocolate—she was the food that fed his desires. Her kisses tasted of pralines, her thick blond hair smelled of coconut cake, and her shoulders made him think of white chocolate macarons. He couldn't eat without thinking of her and couldn't sleep without dreaming of her. And every day, he thought about her more. When he remembered the softness of her lips under his, the generous curve of her waist, the—

"No." He slammed the water from hot to cold and let the icy sharp droplets shock him out of his line of thought. It only took a minute, and he was ready to get out. Shivering a little, he dried off and got dressed.

Why was he seeing her so much? Why was he tormenting himself by spending time with her? That was the question he'd read in Mark's face. And Gray didn't have an answer. If she was nearby, and he could see her, he would. That was just how it was. He couldn't stop her from running away. That was her choice, not his. But he could prolong her stay by letting her feel safe, unthreatened by him or his expectations.

He'd vowed that this time would be different, and so far he'd managed to keep that vow. And he had to admit that there was one huge benefit to the path he was now pursuing. He would lose his heart to Ella all over again, but this time, if he couldn't convince her to stay long enough to give them a chance—a real chance—then he would say his goodbye and let her go. *That's it. Let. Her. Go. I can do that.*

Right?

Gray raked his hand through his damp hair, and then pulled on some running shorts and a long-sleeved T-shirt. Dressed, he stuffed his feet into some old, worn running shoes, grabbed the box holding his new ones, and headed out. He usually ran on the trail through town, which circled the park, and then went along Sweet Creek a short distance before looping back. Today would be no exception.

He got out of the truck and, after stretching, ran toward the trail. He tried to focus on his run and not think too much about Ella or anything else as he went. *Focus on the present. One foot in front of the other. The slap of my feet on the pavement. The breeze rustling through the fall trees. The sound of the creek tumbling over the rocks. Run faster. Faster. Her lips. Her eyes. No! Run. Don't think. Run!*

And yet, no matter how much or fast he ran, little flashes of her broke through, like sun reflecting off water.

Five miles later, he finished, out of breath but his imagination undeterred. As he left the trail near his truck, he smelled burning rubber. *Not again.*

With a groan, he dropped to the grass and yanked off his shoes, wincing when he saw the partially melted soles, burned by his thoughts rather than his efforts. Sighing, he tossed the shoes into the bed of his truck, where they joined several other ruined pairs of shoes. He was glad he'd bought the new pair with him. The burning desire he had for Ella was killing him—and his shoe supply—but he had no idea how to stop it.

He put the new shoes on and realized he was thirsty. So he left his truck where he'd parked it and headed to the Moonlight.

He went inside and swept a glance at the customers, both relieved and deeply disappointed that Ella wasn't there. He made his way to the counter and nodded to Marian, who was busy moving clean water glasses to a tray on the counter. "Hi, Marian."

She looked up and, seeing him, beamed. "Well, well, well. If it isn't the prodigal son. How are you doing?"

He shrugged. "I can't complain."

"Oh Lord, I could, but I won't." She grinned. "What'll you have?"

He slid onto a stool. "An iced tea."

"No food?" When he shook his head, she looked disappointed, but left to get his drink. When she returned, she set his iced tea in front of him. "No sugar, right?"

He nodded, pleased she'd remembered. "Thank you."

"You're welcome." She leaned on her elbows and regarded him with a curious gaze. "Been running? Your face is red."

He nodded and took a grateful gulp of his tea.

"Haven't seen you much these past few months. Two, maybe three times now. Been avoiding your momma?"

He smiled at the censure in her voice. Marian had worked at the café for decades. Gray wasn't sure how long exactly, only that even she was impressed by how long it had been. "Sorry, I've been working a lot."

"I heard your new place is something. Redoing that old farmhouse, aren't you?"

He explained his plans for both the house and the farm. Marian listened, nodding now and then, and asking questions.

A bell rang and she straightened up. "Just a moment." She went to the pass-through window, picked up a basket of fries, and set them on the counter in front of him.

He smiled. "How many free orders of French fries have you given me over the years?"

"I can't count that high, and neither can you. But you're welcome." Her blue gaze softened. "It's good to see you, Gray."

"You too."

She flashed a broad smile and then left him to eat his fries in peace as she went off to seat some new customers.

French fries made life better, he decided. He'd just reached for one when his phone beeped. He almost dropped it in his haste to get his phone out of his pocket.

We still on for dinner tonight?

That was all she wrote, but it made him grin from ear to ear. His thumb flew over the keyboard: *Six still good?*

Perfect, she wrote back. *Where are we going?*

He was going to suggest an Italian restaurant in Asheville, but as he went to type it, he hesitated. He'd taken Ella by his farm a few times, but he'd purposefully kept the visits short. The farm was his baby. He loved the place and he worried that, as a result, she might feel the need to not like it, which would hurt. But maybe the time had come. Maybe he should share his future with her. Why not?

He typed in, *It's a surprise. I'll pick you up at your house.*

She sent him a smiley face.

Sighing, Gray set his phone on the counter and pushed it away and then pulled his tea closer. He'd take Ella to the farm and show her the new hydroponic system and the updates he'd made on the house. He hoped she'd like them. He—

"Whoa, what's that?"

Gray looked up to find Trav standing at the counter, his helmet tucked under one arm. Trav nodded to the glass of tea in Gray's hand.

Gray looked at it. The tea was gently steaming, the ice long gone, the glass growing hotter by the second. Gray muttered a curse and set the glass on the counter so firmly, tea sloshed over the rim and hit his hand. "Ouch! That's hot."

"It's like that, is it?" Looking concerned, Trav slid onto the stool beside Gray. "I thought you were taking things slow."

"I have been." Gray eyed the now-hot tea. He kept telling himself that he had his emotions under control, but then stuff like this happened. *I need to admit it. I have zero control over my emotions when it comes to Ella.* He sighed. "I just invited Ella to see the farm. We've stopped by a few times, but I haven't shown her around. I thought maybe the time had come."

Trav eyed Gray's still-bubbling glass of tea. "Maybe it's past due."

Gray moved the glass farther away. "What are you doing here?"

"I called in a breakfast order for Grace. She's got meeting after meeting this week because of the festival, so I thought I'd surprise her."

"That's nice." Gray looked at Trav. "Can I ask you something?"

"Sure."

"I like Ella. No, that's not—I think I love her. I might as well say it out loud."

Trav nodded to the steaming tea. "That's not really a secret, is it?"

"No. I guess not. I'm pretty sure she's starting to warm up to me. I just don't know when I should tell her how I feel. She's so gun-shy about things like that."

"Tell me about it. Grace was the same way."

"Really?" At Trav's nod, Gray asked, "How did you know when to tell her, then?"

"I waited for her to let me know she was ready."

Gray nodded, feeling worse. If only he had that luxury. He absently watched Marian going down the counter, refilling coffees.

Trav sighed. "Ella's not there yet?"

"She may never be. She avoids relationships. Flings, she'll have. But nothing too serious. I was trying to do that, you know. Just pretend we're casually dating while maintaining enough distance that she really got to know me. It's been going well, but she still gets nervous when I say something personal."

"You want more."

"I've wanted more from the day she first smiled at me in tenth grade. I can't tell her that, though."

Trav clapped his hand on Gray's shoulder. "It sounds like she needs more time."

"Probably. But I'm afraid she'll leave before we get there. In fact, I know she will. She's already got one foot out the door. And if I tell her how I feel, she'll bolt."

A bell rang and Marian took the container from the window and put it in a bag. "Trav, this is yours."

Trav stood up, took the bag, and handed her a folded bill. "Keep the change."

She beamed. "Thank you!" She headed for the cash register.

After she left, Trav looked at Gray. "I don't know Ella like you do, but you have to be honest with her. In some ways, you've been playing a game—one of her own making, but still a game. Maybe it's time to just put it out there. Tell her the truth."

"And if she doesn't like that?"

Trav shrugged. "Then it wasn't meant to be."

That was hard to hear. But Gray couldn't argue. "Thank you. I needed to hear that."

Trav clapped Gray on the shoulder once more. "I'd better get this to Grace before it gets cold. But if you need to talk, give me a call."

"Thanks. I may take you up on that."

Trav smiled. "I hope so." With a nod, he left.

Gray sighed and slid a ten-dollar bill under a napkin, placed his too-hot tea on top of it, and then left the café, the chilly air making him shiver as he hunched his shoulders and made a beeline for his truck.

It was time to stop playing games and just be honest. Tonight, Ella Dove would be introduced to the real Gray. He only hoped it didn't scare her into running for the hills.

CHAPTER 14

ANGELA

Across town, Angela picked up her plate and took a deep breath. "There you are, my little beauty." She'd just used the toaster oven to heat the final white chocolate and cranberry scone she'd talked Mark into bringing her from the Pink Magnolia Tearoom yesterday, and it smelled divine. She'd eaten the other one last night, and not only had it been delicious, but Ella's baking had done its usual magic and left Angela with some thoroughly delightful and bittersweet memories of her first anniversary with John.

What a time that had been. They'd been wildly in love, unable to keep their hands off each other. On that day, it had been raining cats and dogs and she'd come down with a sniffle. To her surprise, John had canceled their fancy dinner reservations and had instead ordered a feast delivered to their New York apartment. He'd spread a blanket on the floor, opened the doors to the balcony wide so they were enveloped in the sound of pouring rain, and had what John called "a romantic urban picnic."

The memory had been as sweet as the white chocolate icing on the scone and had left her with both tears and a smile. It was lovely to remember him in such a vivid, real way, like visiting another time and place.

Angela closed her eyes and held the plate closer, savoring the scone deliciousness that rose to meet her. *I hope I have a Christmas memory this time. John always loved Christmas. He—*

The front door opened, and Jules called out, "Mom?"

Uh-oh! Heavens, didn't anyone stick to their work schedule in this town? Angela looked around wildly for a place to safely store her scone. Her gaze fell on the toaster oven, but it was still hot and might overheat it. *I'll hide it in the real oven.*

That would work. She opened the oven door and bent down to slide the plate inside. No one would look for it in here. After Jules went back to work, Angela could retrieve her scone and eat it in peace and qui—

"*Mom!* What are you *doing*?" Jules's hand closed around Angela's arm and yanked her away from the oven.

It took all of Angela's skill to keep her scone on its small plate. As soon as she was sure it was safe, she pulled her arm free from Jules's viselike grip. "Look what you almost made me do! I could have dropped it!"

Jules's gaze fell on the plate now cupped between Angela's hands. Relief spread across her face. "You were getting something out of the oven. I thought—" She couldn't seem to finish the sentence.

But Angela had noticed that Jules's eyes were now shiny. *Oh dear, she thought I was trying to—* "No, no, no. I was just trying to keep this scone safe."

"Safe from what?"

Angela gave a weak shrug. "Mice?"

Jules's eyes narrowed. "Wait a minute. You were going to eat it."

Sighing, Angela nodded.

"You're not supposed to have sugar. Where did you get it?"

"Oh. Somebody brought it to me. Gray or Mark or . . . I can't remember who."

"They know better than that." Jules reached over to take the plate from Angela's hands.

Angela didn't let go.

Jules frowned and tugged again.

Angela held tighter, watching anxiously as the scone slid toward the edge of the plate.

"Mom!"

Darn it! Angela reluctantly tore her gaze from the plate. "It's just a scone."

Jules's mouth thinned. She released the plate. "Fine. Go ahead. No one is listening to me today anyway." She turned on her heel and went to drop her purse on the kitchen table. She yanked out a chair and sank into it, her face turned toward the window as if she were just now seeing the mums that had sprung up last week. Angela noticed the faint shadows under Jules's eyes, the tightness around her mouth. As much as it pained her, it was clear that Jules needed the scone more than she did.

"Here." Angela carried the plate to the table and placed it in front of Jules. "You eat it."

Jules raised a startled gaze to Angela and then flushed. "No, no. It's yours. I'm being silly. Here." She slid the plate in front of the empty chair beside her. "Please. Go ahead. It's—I don't know why I was making such a big deal over it."

Angela sat down and slid the plate in between then. "Why don't we share?" She picked up the butter knife and cut the scone in two. "There. One for each of us."

"Mom, that's nice, but you don't have to." And yet the lines around Jules's mouth had eased.

"Just think of all the harm you'd be preventing by keeping me from eating this by myself. And look, since I cut it in half, the calories have drained out of it."

A reluctant smile touched Jules's mouth. "It does smell good."

Angela slathered butter on both pieces of the scone. "It's white chocolate and cranberry. It might be lethally delicious."

Jules gave a wry grin. "I guess we'll just take our chances, won't we?"

Angela smiled and scooted the plate a little closer to Jules. "So . . . tell me about this very bad day you're having."

"Oh, Mom." Jules looked as if she were a half inch from crying. "I think I made a mistake."

Things at the café must have been stressful today. "Did you order too much hamburger meat? Your dad did that once. Put an entire extra zero on an order. That's why the Moonlight now has the meatloaf special. We did that so we could sell at least some of that meat before it went bad. To our surprise, it was so popular, it became a regular thing."

Jules sent her a surprised look. "I worked with Dad at the Moonlight from the time I was fifteen and he never once told me about that."

"Your dad never remembers that sort of thing. But ask him about a time you messed something up instead of him, and you can't get him to stop talking."

Jules shook her head, laughing. "I love Dad, but he is a bit stuffy."

Oh, the things Angela could say to that. "What was this mistake you think you made?"

"It's not about work. And it didn't even happen today, but I keep thinking about it and . . . I shouldn't have done it. It's about Gray."

Uh-oh. "You said something to Ella."

Jules gave an embarrassed wince. "I told her to leave Gray alone. Actually, I ordered her to do it."

"Rookie mistake. That'll just encourage her." Angela knew that because she knew she'd react the exact same way.

"I know, I know." Jules sighed and pulled the scone plate closer. "I shouldn't have done it. I knew it even while I was saying it, but I was already too far gone to stop. He'll be furious when he finds out."

"Has he said anything to you about it?"

"Not yet. But he will the second she tells him."

Angela thought about it for a minute. "I know Ella pretty well. If she hasn't told him yet, I'll wager she's not going to."

Hope flickered across Jules's face. "You really think so?"

"I do."

"That would be great." Jules absently touched the edge of the plate. "I wish she'd just go ahead and leave. If I thought it would get her to go sooner, I'd even tell her she can keep the Book of Cakes. It would be worth it."

"Wow. You really want her gone, don't you?"

"Desperately. I can see he's falling for her." Jules shook her head. "I know you said to let them be and that Gray will figure things out, but . . . Mom, what if he doesn't?"

"Then we'll have to be there for him when that happens. That's all we can do."

Jules's shoulders slumped. "I'm not good at the whole 'let them find out they're making a mistake' portion of parenting. I want to get in there and fix everything." She grimaced. "Liam used to make fun of me for it."

"You're a mother. Mothers want to protect their children. It's a fact as old as time."

"I guess so." She absently picked up the scone and took a bite. The second her lips closed around it, she closed her eyes. "Oh my gosh. *So. Good.*"

Yes, it was. Angela picked up her half and tasted it, chewing slowly so the melty deliciousness would stay in her mouth for as long as possible. *Oh, Ella, no one understands a scone the way you do.*

"These are amazing," Jules said, taking another bite. "Aunt Jo is a terrific baker. I should order some for the Moonlight. I—" She laughed, having to cover her mouth and swallow before she could continue. "I have a confession to make."

"Oh?" Here it came, an Ella memory.

"Do you remember when Aunt Jo first started baking desserts for the Moonlight? You and Dad ordered pies, cakes, cookies, brownies—just about everything from her." Jules's gaze softened and Angela knew she was seeing all of those desserts as if she'd gone back in time. "Mom, I lived for those. I loved them so much that I stole one once in a while. You and Dad never knew."

Angela smiled. "You hid under the desk in the office and ate them when we were busy during the lunch rush."

Jules's eyes widened. "You knew?"

"There was always an order form with those desserts. Aunt Jo was really good about that." Angela remembered all the times she and Don had hidden around the corner, trying not to laugh as they waited for Jules to finish whatever cookie or brownie she'd snuck off with. "Your dad and I thought it was a fair payment for spending all that time at the café with us. You helped a lot, even back then."

Jules gave a wry smile, popping another bite of scone into her mouth. "All this time, I thought I was so smart."

"You were young. We never realize how much we don't know until we're too old to admit it."

Jules laughed and licked some butter off one finger. "I loved those times in the café kitchen when it was just you, Dad, and me. It felt like our own private world, and no one else belonged there but us."

Angela had to smile. "Do you remember when the pipe broke in that big sink in the back?"

"I do! Dad jammed a broom handle into the pipe to stop the water until the plumber came. It worked for about three minutes and then the pressure shot that broom like a water cannon into the ceiling." She laughed. "Oh, the language Dad used. And you wouldn't stop laughing either, which just made him madder."

"I couldn't help it. His face was so red! Those were good times." Angela finished her scone and pushed her plate away, memories flitting across her mind like clouds being chased through the sky by a storm. *Oh, Ella, your desserts always remind me how much I've forgotten.*

Jules sighed and looked at the empty plate. "That was delicious. Aunt Jo is talented."

Angela nodded, unwilling to ruin the moment by admitting the scones had been made by Ella. "Your dad and I were always glad Aunt Jo never opened her own restaurant. She's the only person who could have run the Moonlight out of business."

"You loved the Moonlight, didn't you?"

"I did, but not as much as I love you."

"Thank you. That's nice to hear." Jules pulled a napkin from the holder in the middle of the table and wiped her fingers. "Mom, how am I supposed to handle watching Gray head off the Ella cliff? I can't seem to keep my mouth shut. I worry about him so, what with his anxiety and the way he feels things so deeply."

"He has his life under control. He has for a long, long time. You just don't see it. But maybe it's time you did."

"I know. But I can't stop remembering how difficult life used to be for him. I just want to protect him."

"So does Mark. You both need to give Gray some room."

Jules sighed. "They were so young when Liam died. Losing their father changed them both, but in different ways. Gray came away quiet and anxious, but Mark went in an entirely different direction. I can tell he feels responsible for both me and Gray."

"Your stepfather noticed that very thing," Angela said. "John used to say that Mark was trying to fill his dad's shoes but they were too big for a boy his age."

"John was right." Jules sent Angela a regretful look. "I should have spent more time with him. With both of you."

Oh my gosh. John, did you hear that? You always said she'd come around. To keep her tears at bay, Angela dusted imaginary crumbs off the table in front of her. "I can't promise you much, Jules, but I can promise you one thing—Gray's going to be just fine, whatever happens with Ella."

"I hope you're right." Jules sank a little in her chair. "Have you seen how many fans Ella has on social media? All day, every day, thousands of people are telling her how awesome she is and how her baking is the best they've ever had and how she's so this and so that. . . ." Jules made a face. "It's hard to see that and know how she's treated Gray and probably others, too."

"Social media is a waste of time. That stuff is all fake."

"Yeah, well, the bake-off has already sold out and the committee needed an overflow area. So I offered up the café."

"I suppose that'll be good publicity for us."

Jules nodded. "Which is why I also volunteered to judge. If the festival is successful, it'll be due to Ella's influence, which I hate. Still, it could bump up our fall revenue to new levels. I just wish Gray weren't here."

"He'll be fine." Angela reached over and captured Jules's hand and held it tightly. "Stop worrying so much about Gray and Ella and spend more time worrying about yourself. You have important things to do without wasting your time thinking about her."

Jules gave a reluctant smile. "You're right, of course." She put her other hand over Angela's. "I don't know if I've said this enough, but I'm glad you're here."

"So am I. I can't thank you enough for letting me stay here. It . . . it was more than I expected." Or deserved. Angela cut Jules a side glance. "Jules, it's been a long time since Liam passed. Have you ever thought about dating?" She waited, holding her breath. *Come on, Jules. Share your feelings. You aren't alone. I'm right here.*

Jules flushed, but she didn't answer.

"You deserve a second chance to—"

"I should get back to work." Jules went to stand.

Angela gently tightened her hold on Jules's hand. "I know you were dating someone, and it ended."

Jules's eyes widened. But after a second she sank back into her seat. "I don't want to talk about it."

"Why not?"

Jules's mouth thinned and she shook her head.

"At least tell me why you broke up with him."

A stubborn, angry look settled on Jules's face, but a hint of sadness lurked in her eyes.

Angela knew that look. *Oh no.* "Jules . . . did *he* break up with *you*?"

Jules yanked her hand from Angela's. "I said I don't want to talk about it!"

"That *dog*! How dare he?"

Jules's eyes widened. After a shocked moment, she gave a surprised, shaky laugh, the tension leaving as quickly as it had appeared. "He wasn't a dog. It was my fault."

"As if!"

"Mom, seriously. I don't blame him. I expected too much." Jules leaned back in her chair, looking suddenly tired. "Joe and I started dating a long time ago. In the beginning, I didn't tell anyone because I didn't want the boys to think I was trying to replace their dad. Joe agreed and said the boys had to come first. He was great about it. Or he was back then."

"And now?"

"Now he wants our relationship to be public. The trouble is, he may want that, but I don't. I've gotten used to the way things are and I like it, having my privacy and no one asking questions. Which is what I told Joe. He said that was all he needed to know, and he ended it."

"Jules, I'm so sorry."

"No, it's fine. I'm fine." Jules grabbed a napkin from the holder on the table and swiped at her eyes. "I just have to get used to being alone again. That'll take time."

"I'm sure you'll figure everything out. You always do."

A smile flickered across Jules's face. "Thanks, Mom. It's nice to be able to share that with someone."

"You're not the only one weighted down with secrets. There are some things I need to tell you, too." Angela took a deep breath. "When I divorced your dad—"

"No! Mom, please. I don't want to rehash history."

"We need to. There are things you don't understand. Jules, when I divorced your dad, I expected you to live with me. When you convinced the judge to let you stay here in Dove Pond, it"—Angela's voice trembled—"it broke my heart. I cried for months about it. But I never gave up hope. Even after the divorce, I thought you'd eventually come to your senses and come live with me."

"I belonged here, in Dove Pond, with Dad."

Angela found it hard to swallow. "Maybe. It was a painful time for all of us. But you had a home with me. I decorated a room for you, and bought you a bike, and invited you to stay with us over and over and over. John did the same. I saw the letters he wrote you."

"What you did, leaving Dad and me—it was devastating for both of us. It *hurt* us, Mom."

"I know it was hard for you. I saw that. But your dad? Honey, your dad and I weren't happy together. Just think of how he is with Lisa now. He laughs and teases and makes jokes. He was never like that when he was married to me. In fact, he's since told me that he's glad I left when I did. He said it freed him and that he was able to find true happiness because of it."

"He did not say that."

Angela shrugged. "Ask him. Have you ever tried talking to him about it?"

"It makes him sad. Or it did." Jules seemed to realize she'd twisted her napkin into a knot, and now she tried to smooth it out on her knee. "I hate always talking about that time. I still do."

"You see what happened, don't you? You never asked your dad about our relationship and why it failed, because you didn't want to make him sad, and you wouldn't ask me about it because you were angry with me."

"I suppose so, yes. But I was just so mad you left us like that."

"I didn't leave you and your dad, Jules. I just left him."

"But . . . I never once heard you fight."

"People who don't talk don't have fights. And the few fights we did have, we hid from you. You, of all people, know how it is. You never want your children to see the struggles, do you? Didn't you and Liam sometimes fight and keep it from the boys?"

"We—I suppose so." Jules frowned. "It wasn't the same."

"Wasn't it?" Angela smiled wryly. "Your father and I were too different, even from the beginning. He had a loving family and lived in this big house." She looked around the beautiful room. "You know how I've always loved this place, especially after growing up in a rusty single-wide down by the river. But it wasn't just this house; I loved his parents, too. They were wonderful, both of them, and so kind to me. Meanwhile, my parents didn't care one whit about me, and they made it clear that the sooner I moved out of the trailer, the better."

"They couldn't have been so mean."

"You don't remember them, as they were gone by the time you could walk, but that's exactly how they were." Angela gave a short laugh. "Their desire to push me out made me eager to push myself— sometimes past my own limits. By the time your dad and I met in high school, I was wilder than a loose hair on a porcupine."

Jules smiled. "Dad said he used to love your free spirit."

"That's one way to put it. For every ounce of me that was a rule breaker, there were a hundred ounces of him that were determined to follow those same rules. His parents never had to put pressure on him to do things, because he put it on himself. He became what everyone expected him to be: an honors student, the president of his class, the star quarterback. He was doing it all. But I think it made him feel a little trapped."

Jules was quiet a moment, absorbing this. "You must have represented freedom to him."

"I think so, at least at first. And if I represented freedom to him, he represented safety to me. Then you happened."

"And you had to get married."

"Your father always had to do what was expected. The marriage was quick, hasty, and it was immediately obvious to us both that it was a mistake. But after you were born, we made you our focus. You and, eventually, the café."

"But then you left. Dad would have never divorced you. He said as much."

"Jules, when I left, your dad and I hadn't slept in the same bed for over two years. The marriage wasn't working. We both knew it, but your dad kept hanging on because he hates change more than he hates unhappiness. If I hadn't found the courage to leave, we might still be together, every bit as miserable, and probably more so."

Jules's gaze dropped to the floor. After a minute, she said reluctantly, "It took Lisa almost two years to convince him to move to Florida, and it was his idea to begin with."

"And how long did it take to get him to change the menu at the Moonlight? He'd had the exact same one for over twenty years. Every time there was a price change, he'd just put a little sticker over it. It was ridiculous. Some items had ten or more stickers."

Jules chuckled. "I had the menus reprinted the second he handed me the keys to the Moonlight."

Angela gently took the now-shredded napkin from Jules's hands and placed it on the table. "Now do you see why I divorced your dad?"

Jules nodded slowly. "I guess, on some level, I knew things were bad. But for some reason, I got mad at you and not at him."

"That's because you have a big heart and felt sorry for him. You've always felt way too responsible for the people around you, just like Mark. Your dad hated the divorce, and I have no doubt he was a little lost after I left."

"He was miserable for a while. He never told me not to visit you, but I always felt guilty leaving him here alone. You had John, but Dad just had the Moonlight. I felt like I couldn't leave him."

Angela had to swallow her own tears. "You didn't deserve to go through that. None of us did."

Emotion darkened Jules's brown eyes. "I really hated you. I'm sorry for that."

"It's understandable. But Jules, it's time we left all of that in the past. I've enjoyed staying with you so much. I can't thank you enough for letting me be here."

Jules smiled. "It's been nice having someone to talk to. I can't share everything with the boys."

"Of course not, although I'm sure Mark would think he could handle it." Angela sighed. "I wish he were a bit more independent."

"Mark? He *is* independent. I don't force him to live here."

"No, but you certainly haven't made it easy for him to leave, which can be the same thing. I worry about him. He needs more of a life than this house and the Moonlight."

"Mom, no one is stopping him."

"Then maybe he needs encouraging. I asked him the other day why he's not dating anyone."

Jules stiffened. "Why would you ask him that?"

"Because I'm a manipulative grandma, that's why. Don't you want him to find a nice girl and settle down and have a few kids of his own?"

"I suppose." Jules stifled a sigh. "That sounds bad. Of course I do. He's just never said anything about it, so I've assumed he's been happy with the way things are. Maybe there isn't anyone he likes here in town?"

"There are plenty of young women around here. One day, he'll make someone a terrific husband and, in a few years, a top-notch dad. But he won't do either if you don't let him know it's okay. He feels too responsible for you and Gray, just as you feel too responsible for them. Frankly, it seems as if Gray's the only one with some balance here."

"I'm balanced." Jules's tone had sharpened again.

"Then prove it! Be happy yourself. Have a life and let your kids see you do it! Our children measure their lives against ours, and if they see us denying ourselves all the time for their sakes, they believe that's how they should live, too."

Jules didn't say anything for a long moment, and then she lifted her shoulders with a sigh. "Maybe you're right. Maybe—darn it, parenting is hard!"

"Oh, honey. It's a maze on top of a trap, wrapped in a torture chamber, and slathered with guilt. That's what parenting is."

Jules laughed and, to Angela's everlasting happiness, leaned over and enveloped her in a huge hug. "Oh, Mom. I'm so glad you came."

Angela melted into the hug, wrapping her arms around her daughter. *This is what I came here to do. The only thing left is to confess my latest sin and admit that I've been staying here under false pretenses. There isn't a better time than now.*

Jules released Angela and smiled. "I'm glad we talked. I needed this."

Angela realized she was clasping her hands together so tightly, they ached. She eased her grip and placed her hands flat on her knees. "I needed it, too. Jules, I always want to tell you the truth, not just about the past, but about the present." Angela took a deep breath. "When I came here after John's death, I wasn't entirely tru—"

Jules's phone rang.

"That's Mark." Jules got up, brought her purse to the table, and pulled out her phone. "Hello? Hi. No, I just stopped by the house to see Mom. I'll be in soon, I just—" She listened a moment more and then frowned. "Can't you send Missy to the Piggly Wiggly to get some? Oh. That's right. She doesn't come in until four today. I'd forgotten that."

Jules nodded as Mark talked, and then said, "Sure. I'll just pick some up on my way in. No problem. Bye." She hung up and dropped her phone back into her purse. "The grocer messed up our order and didn't deliver a single leaf of lettuce. You can keep going without a lot of ingredients, but lettuce isn't one of them. No salads, no hamburger toppings, no garnishes—it's a long list of nos."

"I suppose you need to get going, then." Apparently now wasn't the right time for a confession, after all. More relieved than she cared to admit, Angela decided that tomorrow would be a better day for truth-telling. Or the day after, even. *At least I tried.*

Jules smiled, looking almost shy. "Thanks for the talk. Maybe later tonight, if you're not too tired, we can take a ride into town and have some frozen yogurt from that cart in the park? It's not too cool at night yet, and it's not bad for yogurt. I—" Jules's phone rang again. "Sheesh, it's Mark again. All right already! I have to go. Bye, Mom." She answered her phone as she headed out, the sound of her voice fading as the door closed behind her.

Angela was left alone in the kitchen with two empty plates and a few remaining crumbs of an Ella Dove scone. In one conversation, she'd accomplished everything she needed to except for one small thing. Her confession.

Tomorrow, she told herself. *I'll do it first thing tomorrow.* For now, she'd enjoy the feeling of having finally, *finally*, connected with her one and only child. She glanced out the window and smiled. *John, as usual, you were right.*

CHAPTER 15

GRAY

At six that night, Gray walked up the steps to the Dove house porch. But before he reached the top step, Ella came dashing out, wearing a short and flirty dress and a long cardigan. "See you all later!" she called over her shoulder as she went.

She sailed down the steps, grabbing Gray's hand as she passed him, and pulled him along with her. "Hurry," she said under her breath. "Ava and Sarah are hoping they can talk us into a Scrabble night."

"Scrabble, huh? Maybe we should stay. Chemists are really, really good at that game. We'd slay."

She laughed. "We would, wouldn't we? Maybe next time."

Gray helped her into the truck and then climbed into the driver's seat.

She looked at him expectantly. "Where are we going? That new Italian place in Glory? If you're tired of pizza, Grace told me about a new Asian-fusion restaurant in Asheville."

"Instead of going out, I thought you might like to visit Adorbs."

"We're going to your farm?"

He nodded. "I know you've dropped by a few times, but I've never shown you the house. Would you like to see it?"

She looked surprised, but shrugged. "Sure, why not? It'll be nice to see your Highland cows, too. If I'd known they were even cuter in real life than they are in pictures, I'd have gotten one years ago."

"Terrific." He jerked his head toward his back seat, where a large brown paper bag sat. "I brought takeout. I'd cook for you, but the kitchen hasn't been redone yet. I'm sad to say that it's still in its original, primitive form."

"No worries. Adorbs and takeout sound pretty good."

He started the truck and they headed to his place, Ella chatting effortlessly, telling him about her day and the sold-out bake-off and cooking demonstration. He asked the occasional question, but mostly he just savored the feel of being with her.

When they got to the farm, he parked in the gravel drive near the house. "Want to eat now? Or see the cows?"

"I'm pretty hungry. Do you think Adorbs would feel slighted if we ate first?"

"Not at all, especially since I got us the meatloaf special from the café." He grabbed the bag from the back seat and led the way up to the house.

She stopped on the wide porch and looked around with appreciation. "This is much bigger than it looks from the driveway."

"When I first came to look at this place, the real estate agent told me it had 'a spacious porch.' She didn't mention there were huge holes in it, where the wood had rotted out. But it's been fixed now."

She squinted at the ceiling of the porch. "Haint blue! I love that shade."

He opened the door and stood to one side. "I need some rocking chairs."

"Yes, you do." She walked past him into the foyer. It was partially done. The floors had been newly repaired and refinished but were covered with Ram Board to protect them. The walls had been painted a creamy white to offset the original dark wood trim. A small, simple brass-and-milk-glass chandelier sat on a crate in the corner, ready to be hung from the waiting blue electric box visible in the ceiling.

"It's not finished." He could have kicked himself for stating the obvious.

She wandered around, running her fingers over the newel post at the bottom of the stairs. "You're leaving the original woodwork intact. I like that."

"Look what we found when we started working." He walked to the wide, framed opening that led to the living room and slid a pocket door into sight. "Every entry doorway had these. They were still here, still on their tracks, too, but someone had covered them up."

"Ridiculous." She followed him into the living room and stood in the middle of it, looking around. "So much light. That's a huge fireplace."

"There are four of them this size, two on this floor and two upstairs. Every tile surround is different. I'm trying to restore those, but it's been a chore finding matching tile."

Her gaze moved up to the high ceilings. "Uncomplicated and yet strong. I like your style."

"This house was built in the same era as your family home; it's just not as ornate."

"Whatever the age, it has a great vibe." She turned in a slow circle, and then said simply, "I love it."

He couldn't have been prouder. She saw past the unfinished windows, the covered wood floors, and the half-completed masonry. Smiling, he held up the paper bag containing their dinner. "We can eat in the kitchen. It's not finished, but the workers made it a break room, so there are folding chairs and a few sawhorses with boards over them we can use for a table."

"That's all we need. I'm ravenous."

They went into the kitchen, but Ella stopped at the door. "I'm surprised this room isn't further along. Having trouble making decisions?"

"Something like that." He looked at the blank area where the cabinets and appliances were supposed to go. "My contractor is about to go crazy, but I don't know a lot about kitchens, and I can't figure out what I want." He shrugged and went to the so-called table and set the bag on the edge of it.

Ella shot him a curious look. "Why don't you just go online and find a picture of a kitchen you like?"

"I like everything. To be honest, I'm not really picky about kitchens. All I need is a microwave and a mini-fridge, and I'm good."

She shuddered. "Not me."

"Maybe you could help me pick out some appliances and stuff while you're here."

Her gaze flickered away. "Maybe."

And there it was, that nervous, no-way look she saved for whenever he made any suggestion that might move them from point A in this almost-relationship to point B. Usually, that look challenged him to remain in control and maintain his distance, but today it just hurt.

His throat tightened and he turned back to the makeshift table and unpacked the paper bag. "Here we go. Two meatloaf specials from the Moonlight with garlic mashed potatoes and green beans, two bottles of sparkling water, and . . . the piece of resistance, two pieces of coconut cake."

She chuckled. "It's *pièce de résistance*. But you had me at 'coconut cake.'" She wandered to the table and eyed the food and plastic utensils. "You went gourmand on me."

"I aim to please." He gestured to the folding chair next to his, which was the less rusted and bent of the two.

She sat down and picked up her plastic fork.

He joined her and searched for an innocuous topic of conversation. "What are your sisters up to? I see Sarah and Ava all the time, but never hear about the other four."

"Alex and Madison are still in Raleigh. Alex works as a veterinarian and Madison is a doctor and has her own practice." Ella waved her fork. "They live just a few houses from each other, but they haven't spoken in years."

"Wow. What happened?"

"Some sort of argument. They won't give us more details, although we're all pretty sure it was over a guy."

That figured. "And Taylor?"

"She's still working in academia, but not teaching as much. She's doing research in London right now, but she's due back in the States in a few weeks."

"So she's doing well too, then."

"I think so." Ella frowned. "She's not a great communicator, that one. Tay lived in Paris for almost six months back when she was finishing up her graduate degree. When I first moved there and was looking for an apartment, I reached out to her to see which areas she'd liked and which she hadn't. But all she would say was 'All of it was beautiful.' Which, as advice went, was pretty bad."

Gray unwrapped the silver foil from a pat of butter and put it on his mashed potatoes. "Tay was a few years ahead of us in school. Smart as a whip, that one."

"She's a total research nerd, so she travels most summers. Reads all the time and never takes a break. She's worse than Cara, our computer guru."

"Your sisters are all so different. Now that I think about it, I'm glad I have only one sibling, even if he's an overly bossy brother."

"It's a drain during the holidays. But when we're all together . . ." Ella's smile softened. "I do love seeing them. Or I do for a few days and then . . ." She made a face. "I don't know. It's just time to go."

Time to go. That's what she'll be saying to me in a few days. He stabbed a green bean with more force than was necessary. "Are you ready for the bake-off?"

"Sunday can't come fast enough. Way too many people in this town take this event far too seriously. Honestly, the only thing I'm looking forward to is the caramel apple cake demonstration with Aunt Jo. We're doing it early in the day Sunday, and she's super excited about it. I had to convince her that we didn't need to wear matching outfits."

"I would pay to see that. Aunt Jo is an event all by herself."

Ella pretended to shiver. "Imagine her with a mic."

"I'm afraid to. Mom said your assistant has been a big help with the bake-off."

"Grace is over the moon about that, too, as it lets her and the committee focus on some of the other events."

"I bet so."

"Tiff and the crew are coming in Friday morning. They've reserved a block of rooms at the Last Chance Motel. Ava's disappointed I didn't invite them to stay with us, but I don't think she realizes how young and loud Tiff and her crew can be. They need a place where they can socialize without keeping me up until all hours of the morning." She winced. "I sound old, don't I?"

"You sound normal. I'd hate that, too." He watched her take the final bite of her meatloaf and smiled when she closed her eyes.

"Mm." Ella pointed with her fork to where her meatloaf had been. "Amazing."

"Mark's a pretty good chef." And a darned good brother, too, despite his overbearing ways. It was funny, but since Grandma had come to town, Gray had started appreciating his brother more.

When they finished eating, Ella put down her fork and leaned back in her folding chair. "That was delicious."

"I hope you saved some room for dessert." Gray set out the boxes that held their pieces of cake.

She opened the box. "There's always room for coconut cake." She took a bite and closed her eyes. "Oh my."

He tried not to watch her lick her fork, and failed miserably. To regain enough of his ability to think to maintain the conversation, he feigned a huge amount of interest in his own piece of cake.

Ella looked around as she took another bite. "When are you moving in?"

"Soon, if things go okay. The hot water heater is being delivered tomorrow."

"You have furniture here, then?"

"I've already set up my bedroom upstairs. My living room and dining room furniture is in a stall in the barn, under a tarp. I'll bring it all in when they're finished—"

She'd placed her hand on his knee. His jeans didn't stop the wave of heat that instantly crashed through him.

Startled, he met her gaze.

She pointed to his hand. He still held his plastic fork. Curls of smoke were coming from it, and it was sagging, melting in his too-hot touch. He dropped the fork and pushed himself from the table. "Ella, no. We can't do this."

"Why not?" she asked impatiently. When he didn't answer, she tilted her head to one side and frowned. "I can't figure you out. Sometimes I'm sure you want me, but then you stop. Why?"

Tell the truth, Trav had said. *It's time*. Gray raked a hand through his hair. "It's like this. When we started talking again, I wanted it to be different. I wanted this—us—to matter."

"Matter?"

He nodded, wishing he knew what was going on behind her gray-green eyes. "I wanted to take things slow and for us to get to know each other without the distraction of the chemistry we have."

"Can't we do both?"

"I wish. But no, I don't think we can. What we've been doing has been working, at least for me. We've been talking, Ella. *Really* talking. And it's been wonderful."

"Wonderful . . . *and* frustrating."

He had to smile. "That too."

Her gaze moved across his face as if searching for something. "I'm going to miss you when I leave. I didn't expect that."

That was promising, and it was far more than he'd hoped for. He slid his hands into his pockets and took the plunge. "There's a solution to that. You could stay here. In Dove Pond." *With me*. It was hard, but he managed to keep that last bit to himself.

"Gray, that's . . . I don't know what to say."

"Then don't say anything. Just think about it. But I know you don't have plans after this, so why not stay here? Why not give us a chance, Ella? A chance for something that will last longer than a couple of too-short months?"

Her gaze moved past him to the window. "It's beautiful here, but I . . . I don't know, Gray. I want something bigger. Something more. Do you know what I mean?"

He did. Trying not to let her see how much those words hurt, he gave her a brief nod. "I guess that's that, then." He collected their trash and put it in the paper bag. "Would you like to see Adorbs now? I hear him calling."

Ella's gaze stayed locked on him. "There's no rush, is there? We could go see Adorbs later."

He was tempted. God, how he was tempted. *She's not going to make this easy, is she?* "We should go now. He won't stay near the fence for long." Gray went to the door, opened it, and waited.

She crossed her arms and leaned back in her chair. "Maybe I want to stay here, with you."

"I can't do that, Ella. I'm not interested in one-night stands. Not with you. I want more than that. I want dates, and kisses, and intimate conversations, and anniversaries, and family dinners, and . . . hell, I want it all."

"Gray, don't." She placed her hands on her knees and leaned toward him. "Look, I feel something for you. I do. But I can't promise you more than this moment. I just can't."

"Why not? We're good together. We always have been. You've enjoyed this past month, haven't you?"

"I have. A lot, to be honest. But I don't 'settle down,' and I don't make promises I can't keep." She took a deep breath. "Once the bake-off is over and I've settled a few things, I'm leaving."

Every word felt as if she were shooting arrows through him. He had his answer. There was precious little left to say. It took every ounce of effort he possessed not to argue with her, to try to change her mind, but he bit his tongue. "Do you want to see Adorbs before I take you home?"

Ella's eyes looked shiny, but she didn't offer another word of hope. "If you don't mind, I'd like to say goodbye." With a tremulous smile, she got up and walked past Gray, leaving the door open behind her.

He followed, wishing with all his heart he could find the words that might change things. She headed for where the cows had gathered by the fence under an apple tree. He matched her step for step, pausing only to take a deep, steadying breath, catching the scent of strawberries and coconut. He'd told her the truth, and now he had his answer.

"Hi, Adorbs." Ella picked up an apple from the ground and held it over the fence. "I love these shaggy critters."

Adorbs pushed his way forward and took the apple from her, eating it in a sloppy way that made Ella chuckle. When he was done, he stuck his head through the fence rails, looking for more.

Ella patted the Highland calf, scratching his fluffy head between his ears.

Gray watched morosely. *Great, I've been rejected and now I'm jealous of my own cow. This day can't get worse.*

She tilted her head. "Can I ask you something?"

"About Adorbs? Sure."

"No. About you." Her eyes, darker than usual, regarded him with curiosity. "You're happy here. Why?"

He looked past her to the field around them. It was getting dark already, but final rays of sun lingered, brightening the red of the barn until it glowed, and making the grass even greener than usual. "There's something calm and right about this place. I felt it the second I came here."

"Is that why you bought it? Because it made you feel calm?"

"Partially. I was ready for something bigger, too. Something just mine. And this was it."

She nodded, still scratching Adorbs through the fence. "I've never felt that way about a place."

"Neither did I. And I never thought I'd end up farming either, but here I am."

She looked beyond him to the pasture that stretched out toward the mountain. "It's peaceful here. I get good vibes, and I've been to a lot of different places."

He leaned against the fence. "Do you miss Paris?"

"No. I mean, I loved it there, but it was time to go. Do you ever feel that way? As if you were just done with a place and it was time to leave?"

"My old job."

"You've only felt that way once?"

He nodded.

"I feel it all the time. Maybe I shouldn't. I—" Adorbs sniffed Ella's dress pocket. She chuckled. "Easy, buddy. I don't have any snacks in there."

Adorbs sniffed again, nudging her as he did so.

"Seriously, there's nothing in there. Here. I'll show you." She rammed her hand into her pocket. She froze the second her fingers disappeared. "Oh no."

"What's wrong?"

Ella slowly pulled her hand out. It was covered in pink frosting.

Gray tried not to laugh but couldn't stop. "Looks like you've been pranked."

"It wasn't a prank, it—" She closed her lips over the rest of her sentence. "I need to wash my hands."

"Sure. There's a spigot on the side of the barn." He walked with her, their shoes crunching on the gravel. When they got to the spigot, he said, "Hang on. I'll get you a rag."

He went to the tack room, where he kept his supplies, and pulled out two rags from the bag he kept there. He returned and handed her a rag and watched as she scooped out the frosting from her pocket. Once she'd gotten out as much as possible, she wet the rag and cleaned her pocket as well as she could. That done, she rinsed the cloth and handed it back to him. He tossed it onto a bale of hay while she washed her hands.

"Looks like one or both of your sisters are out to get you," Gray said. "Maybe we should have stayed and played Scrabble after all."

"Or not." She turned off the spigot and shook her hands to dry them.

Gray pulled out the other rag and draped it over his arm. "Your towel, madam."

She took it, drying her hands silently.

He could see she was thinking. "Trying to figure out who did this to you?"

"No." She shot him a searching look. "I think . . . I think I need to go home."

That was disappointing, but he wasn't surprised. He'd played his hand, and she'd been clear in her answer. He forced himself to smile. "Sure."

He followed her to his truck and opened the door for her, and soon they were on their way, driving past the herd where it still gathered under the apple tree.

Ella was quiet for most of the ride, her eyebrows lowered as if she were mulling over a problem.

As they turned onto her street, she broke the silence. "Thank you."

"What for?"

"For being so patient. Not just with this, but with life, and me, too."

"I'm patient when I know the outcome will be worth it. And you, Ella, are worth it." He turned his truck into her driveway and switched it off. "You deserve to be happy."

"So do you. I don't know what I'm supposed to do, but . . . Gray, I—" She bit her lip. After an agonizing moment, she splayed her hands over her knees. "I hate this. I wish things were different, but they're not. *I'm* not."

She opened her door.

He reached for his own so he could walk her to the porch, but she didn't give him a chance. With a quick wave and a mumbled goodbye, she hurried up the sidewalk, moving so fast she was almost at a run.

He watched as she disappeared into her house. The last time he'd watched her walk away like this, he'd felt miserable, wondering what he could have done differently, what things he could have said to persuade her to stay. But this time, all he felt was an infinitely deep sorrow, as if his soul had been irrevocably and permanently cut in half.

His heart heavy, he turned his truck back on and went home.

CHAPTER 16

ANGELA

"It looks like someone kicked over an anthill."

Angela straightened from where she'd been collecting her purse from the floorboard of Gray's pickup. Throngs of people filled the park.

Before Angela moved to New York, the Apple Festival had been an important annual event, but it had faded as the years passed. Every leaf season, it seemed to be smaller and thinner. But no more.

Jules had said that Grace had successfully revived the festival, but Angela hadn't expected this. Rows and rows of tents featuring local businesses and craftspeople filled both the town park and Main Street, which had been blocked off from one end to the other. In the middle of this madness, near the town fountain, sat a huge tent surrounded by a long line of people, which snaked twice around it and then down the sidewalk.

Angela was glad she'd put her foot down with Jules about attending. It hadn't been a fight, exactly, but Angela had had to threaten to walk to town on her own to get here before Jules finally caved. Of course, Jules had then tried to ruin that moment of triumph by coming up with an endless list of "things you should do" and "things you shouldn't do." Angela had just nodded and smiled, knowing full well she was going to do pretty much whatever she wanted. "I don't think I've ever seen this many people in Dove Pond."

"Hurrah," Gray said dully.

She shot him a sharp look. "That's about the tenth negative comment you've made today. What's going on?"

He shrugged. "I'll just be glad when this day is over."

"I think we all feel that way." Angela turned so that she faced him on the truck seat. "The word on the street is that Ella will be flying out with her assistant and the crew when they leave."

His mouth tightened. "I didn't know that, but I'm not surprised." He stared out at the crowd with an unseeing gaze, his expression as dark as a summer storm over the ocean.

Angela sighed. "It might help if you talk about it."

Gray didn't say anything else; he just stared into the distance, his jaw tight.

Quiet and secretive, that's what he was. But perhaps he'd gotten that from her. Unbeknownst to Jules or Mark, Gray had taken Angela to Ella's cooking demonstration earlier today.

Aunt Jo had stolen the show, as she'd spoken way too loudly, as though a mic were the same thing as a bullhorn. Still, she had provided fun, running commentary, a perfect complement to Ella's charming and accomplished presentation. But the moment that had caught Angela's attention the most was when Ella and Gray had seen one another across the room. *There is something there. I wish she could see it. I know Gray does.*

It was sad, but people never ran as hard from those they hated as those they loved. She could see that Ella had feelings for Gray; Angela just wasn't sure if they were strong enough to give Ella the strength she'd need to break her bad habit of avoidance. Angela winced. *Of course, I'm a great one to talk about avoidance.*

Gray sighed. "Are you ready? I'm to drop you off at town hall."

"Then what will you do?"

"Go home."

Angela swatted his arm.

He'd turned a startled gaze on her. "What was that for?"

"For not talking. This"—she waved her hand his way—"is not working. When you have a problem, you talk it through. You don't bottle it up where it'll turn into poison."

Reluctant amusement softened his expression. "So I should talk through my feelings the same way you've talked through your imminent death with Mom?"

Angela sniffed. "That's a different situation. Besides, I've tried."

"You've *tried*? What happened? Your tongue got tied?"

"It's worse than that. Apparently, I'm a total chicken. A weakling. A marshmallow."

His eyebrows rose. "I was expecting an excuse of some sort, not the truth."

"Yeah, well, I'm out of excuses. I keep waiting for the right moment, but there's no such thing. The truth is that I'm scared. I can't stand the thought of her being disappointed in me. I don't want her to cut me off again."

"She's changed a lot these past few months." Gray shrugged. "So have you. But she'll forgive you quicker if she finds out from an honest confession than in another way."

"Maybe." But there were no maybes. He was right and she knew it. "I'll tell her today."

"Good." He looked at his watch. "We'd better go. Mom will be looking for you."

She slanted him a glance and frowned at the shadows she saw

under his eyes. He wasn't sleeping well; that was obvious. Even with all her own problems looming in front of her, Angela's heart ached for the sadness that rested under Gray's stony expression. "I don't know where things stand with you and Ella, but if you love her, then . . ." Goodness, she never thought she'd say this to Gray, but she just couldn't stand to see him looking so miserable. "If you love her, then go after her. Throw your heart over the wall."

"I told her how I feel. It didn't help."

"So you said some words. Maybe what she needs are deeds."

He frowned. "You think a grand gesture would change her mind?"

"No, but it might show her how serious you are."

"That's an interesting idea. I'll think about it." He managed a faint smile before he climbed out and came around to the passenger side to help her out.

She leaned on his arm and climbed out of the truck, stopping to adjust her duster-length cardigan. She'd dressed up a bit, wearing navy slacks and a silky gray shirt, and had even put on a touch of makeup. She really didn't have a choice, seeing as how her daughter would be one of the stars of today's show.

Gray escorted her to the door. "Here you are."

"Aren't you coming inside? Jules said she put you on the list."

"Maybe later. I think I'll head over to the hardware tent and pick up some pet-friendly salt for my porch. Mom and Mark should be waiting for you inside."

Angela realized he wasn't ready to see Ella yet. "Fine. I'll be here when you get back."

Gray nodded and she went inside, stopping to check in with a serious-faced volunteer who, clipboard in hand, was guarding the door.

Angela hadn't taken more than two steps inside when Mark spotted her. "There you are." He led her to two chairs beside the large window overlooking the street, away from the noise coming from the park. "Have a seat and I'll fetch you some hot tea. There's a concession area and everything." He pointed to the other side of the room, where long tables held a catered meal of sandwiches, salads, and snacks. A coffee and tea station had been set up at the very end. "Earl Grey, right?"

"Yes, please." She looked around the room, amazed that it was as busy inside as it had been outside.

Across the space, Jules was getting her hair blown out by a beautician. Meanwhile, Aunt Jo and Ella were at two other stations, getting their makeup done. Over in the corner, a number of Tiff's team were gathered around a table crammed with laptops and a few larger screens as they edited several videos. Angela realized that what she was seeing wasn't just the bake-off, but the business known as Ella Dove. *She's a brand now, and it goes beyond her baking. Funny, but I hadn't really thought of her that way.*

"Here." Mark reappeared and handed her a cup of gently steaming tea. "It should steep for another two minutes. I didn't add honey, but if you'd like—"

"Pardon me!" A tall and slender bald man dressed in black rushed past, waving a curling iron like a wand and yelling for cucumber water.

Mark watched the man disappear in the crowd. "They're all so thin. Do you think they eat anything?"

"An oyster cracker, maybe. But just one."

Mark chuckled, his gaze sweeping the room as he sank into the chair next to hers. "This is crazy."

"Bizarre." She captured the tag on her tea bag and bobbed it up and down in the hot water, soaking in the scent of bergamot. "Thank you for this. I needed it."

Mark suddenly frowned. "Where's Gray?"

"He went to check out the hardware tent."

"How is he?"

Struggling. She started to say as much, but just then a young lady whizzed past pushing a cart filled with ice and bottled water, which made Angela slide her feet back under her chair to protect them. "Maybe we should go sit in the tent. We're just in the way here."

"And miss the excitement of the greenroom?" He smiled at her. "Mom asked me to keep an eye on you. It can be pretty hectic in here, to say the least."

"She doesn't even know I'm here. I— Oh. She's waving." Angela waved back.

"Hi, Mrs. Harrington!"

Angela blinked as Missy from the Moonlight rushed by with two cups of coffee from the snack bar. "Good afternoon. Are you working here today and not at the Moonlight?"

Missy nodded, beaming. "Kristen and I are key grips, but just for the contest. We run errands. I've got to get this coffee to the main tent, but it was nice seeing you!" The teenager sent a quick smile to Mark. "And don't worry, I won't miss my shift. As soon as the contest is over, I'm going straight to the Moonlight."

"Good." He watched her leave and then sighed. "There is no such thing as employee loyalty anymore."

"Is everything ready at the Moonlight for the livestream?"

He nodded. "Marian just called and they're already at capacity. We made some sheet cakes to serve in honor of the bake-off. Marian's already got them sliced and ready to serve."

"What kind of cakes did you make?"

"Two coconut sheet cakes, two chocolate cakes with chocolate fudge frosting, and two vanilla cakes with white frosting."

"Gray's going to be sad you didn't make his favorite."

Mark smiled. "I'll make him one before the week's out. I promise."

It was nice seeing Mark so relaxed. Happy, even. "You're enjoying this."

"The festivals are great for the Moonlight. Zoe says Ella's social media has more than doubled the turnout. She'd know. No one in this town gets Dove Pond the way Zoe does."

I detect a hint of admiration in that tone. Hmm. Angela cast a cautious glance at Mark and then said with studied indifference, "She's an amazing woman, Zoe is." Angela waited, but Mark didn't say anything. She tried again. "She's beautiful. Like a model."

Again nothing.

Angela surged ahead. "She's smart, too. Can't run a bank without having a decent brain, and I hear she owns a darn nice house right on the lake, so—"

"Stop it!" he said through clenched teeth as he glanced around to make sure no one had heard his grandmother. "Not another word."

"Why haven't you asked her out?" Angela elbowed him. "Imagine being the kept man of the owner of a bank. You'd become a town legend."

He flushed, a sheepish look on his face. "She's something," he admitted.

"So ask her out!" Good Lord, what was wrong with her grandsons? *Jules, I'm blaming this one on you. Ella's history and her fear of commitment would make any man hesitate, but Mark doesn't have that excuse.* "You won't know until you try."

"But I do know. I have about as much chance of getting Zoe to agree to go out on a date with me as I do of winning the bake-off, and I didn't even enter."

"There's your problem. You never try." She shook her head. "Between you and Gray, I'm about done advocating for your love lives. If you two don't get off your rumps, you're both lost causes."

Mark's half smile disappeared. "Did Ella—"

"No, no, no," Angela said hastily. "Gray is fine. I was just talking in general." She took a sip of her tea, trying to think of a safer topic, and was relieved when, from across the room, Aunt Jo drew their attention by letting out a large guffaw.

Her voice carried across the room as she told her hairstylist, "That's when my little Moon Pie leapt right over the porch railing and ran out into the road to confront that bear!"

"Oh no!" The hairstylist, a young woman with dyed black hair that was shaved on one side and left long on the other, leaned forward. "What happened to poor Moon Pie?"

"Moon Pie jumped that bear, that's what."

"He did not!"

"Jumped him and grabbed him and shook him as if he weren't forty times his size." As Aunt Jo spoke, she mimed out her words, shaking an invisible bear like a dishrag.

"Yeet!" the girl exclaimed. "Pugs aren't that big. A bear would swallow him whole."

"He would have if he'd been a real bear. Turned out it was just an old rug that had fallen off a truck and crumpled up to look sort of like a bear. Still, Moon Pie didn't know that. He thought that was a real bear and was fearless."

"Whew. I'm just glad he was okay. I'd have died if Magpie, my Pomeranian, had gone after a bear, fake or not."

Mark said in a low voice to Angela, "I don't believe a word of that, but it makes Moon Pie sound like a warrior."

"I've never seen that dog awake, much less fierce," Angela admitted, taking a sip of tea. "He—"

"Mom?" Jules beckoned from across the room.

Angela smiled. "I'd better see what she wants. I'll be right back."

"Take your time. I'm going to the concessions table to see if there are any donuts left."

Angela collected her purse and, careful not to spill her tea, made her way to where Jules sat in front of a makeshift vanity. She was wearing a black satin makeup cape to protect her blue suit while a tall, angular young lady with impressive dragon tattoos worked diligently on her eye shadow.

Angela had to admire the cosmetologist's deft work. "Jules, you look fabulous."

The girl beamed. "Ms. Jules is a natural."

"Thank you." Jules frowned at Angela. "Find a chair. You agreed not to stand too much today."

"Jules, I'm fine. I—"

"Mom."

Angela sighed and looked around.

The cosmetologist pointed to a chair that was partially hidden in the corner behind a cart. "You can use that one if you'd like."

"Thank you." Careful of her tea, Angela dragged the seat so that it was near Jules, settled her purse to one side, and sat down. "This is ridiculous. I'm not an invalid, Jules."

Jules closed her eyes while her eyeliner was being applied. "How's it going out there? Did you get a look inside the tent?"

"No, but there's a line of people waiting to get in."

The makeup artist piped up. "You can see inside the tent if you look from the window beside the double doors."

Angela put her hot tea on the corner of the dressing table. "I'll go look."

"Mom, don't— Just wait. I'll ask Mark."

"He's at the snack table. Be right back!" Angela left before Jules could say anything else. When she reached the window, she peered out. The side of the tent was open, roped stanchions keeping people in line as they got their tickets checked.

At the far end of the tent, past rows and rows of people, was a red-carpeted stage. On it stood two lines of tables, weighted down by dozens of cakes, each covered by a delicate-looking glass dome and ready for judging. Beside the stage stood several large box lights and cameras angled into place, while a rather antiquated sound system stack sat off to one side. Some very-tech-savvy-looking youths swarmed around the equipment, checking and rechecking.

Angela knew from Jules that Tiff had decorated the stage and tables with flowers from Ava's greenhouses. Large battery-powered candles borrowed from Ava and Sarah's house flickered between the cakes, too, and reflected off the glass domes. Tiff had said the decorations would draw attention to the stage and add "light and texture" to the photos and cake close-ups. Angela didn't know about that, but she had to admit it looked beautiful from here.

But despite the cool-looking stage area, it was the excited buzz in the air that really held Angela's attention. Everyone was laughing and talking in ways that did her tired heart good. *This is a special town. I don't know why I didn't realize that when I lived here.*

She attempted to do a head count but finally gave up and returned to her seat. "The whole tent looks full, but there are still a ton of people in line."

Jules had her head tilted back so the cosmetologist could apply powder, but she managed to say, without moving her face too much, "I hope the Moonlight is busy, too."

"I'm sure it is. You're a terrific businesswoman, Jules. Your dad must be so proud. I know I am."

"There," said the cosmetologist, spinning Jules in her chair so she could see herself in the mirror. "What do you think?"

Jules turned her face this way and that. "I look ten years younger!"

She slid forward to allow the young lady to remove the cape from her shoulders and then reached into her pocket and handed her a tip. "Thank you. You did a terrific job."

The girl pocketed the money, her smile warm and genuine. "You're welcome."

Jules collected her things.

Angela shot Jules a side look. "Are you nervous? That crowd's pretty big."

"They're not here to see me." Her gaze moved past Angela to where Ella sat across the way, wearing the same black makeup cape as Jules had. Where Jules and Aunt Jo had had one makeup person and one hairdresser, Ella had three people working on her at once. One was curling her hair, another was working on her eyebrows, and the third was painting her nails. Nearby, one of Ella's many assistants read something aloud from her phone.

"She's a production all by herself," Angela muttered under her breath, rather admiring that fact.

Jules opened her mouth to reply, when a tiny girl burst into the room. She looked almost elvish, with a gamine face and short yellow hair that stuck out in odd ways. "Five minutes until we go live, people!" She waved her clipboard in the air. "Where are my judges?"

"Coming, Tiff!" Aunt Jo handed her bright pink hat to the hairdresser to pin it in place.

"I'll be right there," Ella called from her station.

"I've got to go," Jules said.

"Go, then. I'll be waiting over here." Angela retreated to the corner she and Mark had originally occupied, and was glad when he joined her a moment later.

Aunt Jo, cane in hand, strolled to where Tiff waited. "Here I am, ready to judge." She turned to Jules. "I haven't eaten a bite of lunch today, knowing I'd have to be ready to taste-test. Did you eat?"

"Nope. I'm hungry enough to eat a horse."

"That's good," Aunt Jo said approvingly.

"Jen, come mic our judges!" Tiff called out. "Jen is our sound guru."

A tall, round girl appeared. She had red hair and freckles and was wearing a pair of too-large overalls over a bulky sweater. She set down the box she carried, which was filled with cords and wires, and gave the group an awkward wave. "Hi. I'm Jen, the sound tech."

Aunt Jo beamed. "Jen miked me up for the baking demonstration just like on *The Voice*."

Tiff sent her an amused look. "Just remember that you don't have to yell. We're using that same sound system in the tent we used for the baking demo, and while it's not exactly state-of-the-art, the audience will be able to hear you just fine if you talk in a normal voice."

Jen was already busy untangling wires. She mumbled under her breath, "Not a state-of-the-art system—ha! That's what happens when you rent your equipment from a cow auction house."

"I beg your pardon?" Jules said, looking surprised.

Jen made a face. "This area is wedding central right now because of leaf season, so sound systems of any kind were scarce. This system will do, but it's a bit old."

Ella joined them. "Hi, everyone."

"Jen, you can start the brief now," Tiff said.

Jen pulled out a mic attached to a clunky box by a thin black cord and showed it to Ella, Jules, and Aunt Jo. "The mic is on this clip, which should be attached to a lapel or collar. It connects to this box, which can either be clipped to your waistband, or you can put the whole thing in a pocket, so long as it's secure and won't fall out. Either way, we'll snake the wire under your clothes so it's not obvious."

"Are they hard to operate?" Jules asked.

"Easy-peasy." Jen pointed to a button on the center front of the small box. "Just hit this button when you're ready to speak. Hit it again when you want to turn it off. When it's working, this green light will be on. If there's no light, it's off."

Jules frowned. "You can't control these from the booth?"

"There's no external control for these mics. Just turn them on before you want to speak, and then turn them off when you're done."

"It's simple," Aunt Jo said. "I like that."

Tiff choked out a laugh. "You say that now, but we had to chase you down after the cooking demonstration because you'd left yours on and everyone heard you talking about the reverend in a very colorful way."

Aunt Jo grinned. "He knows he has a fine pair of legs. I've told him that before."

Jen set about fitting the judges with their mics. She hooked up Aunt Jo first. "Let's do a mic check. Can someone open the window so we can hear the speakers in the tent?"

"I'll do it," Mark called out. He went to the window closest to the tent and opened it.

"All right," Jen said. With a click, she flipped on the mic. "Say something."

"*CHECK!*" Aunt Jo yelled. The sound blared through the tent outside, setting off a wave of gasps and murmurs.

Jen took her hands off her ears. "Aunt Jo, just talk in a normal voice. The mic will do the rest."

"Oh. Sorry." Aunt Jo cleared her throat, then said very softly, "Check, check, check."

"Sounds good," Mark said from the window.

Jen did the same for Ella and Jules before asking Mark to close the window. She gave the "okay" sign to Tiff.

"Perfect." Tiff glanced at her watch. "It's time. The preacher is going to do the welcome and intros. But first, let me remind you guys how this will go down. While the preacher is speaking, all three of you should be waiting off stage left. When he's done, he'll call you up one at a time and introduce you, bringing up Ella last."

Jules looked relieved. "I'm glad we don't have to introduce ourselves."

"Ella thought that would be easier. As you go onstage, you'll see three clipboards like this one." Tiff held up hers. "Each has the judging sheets and two pens. The cakes are numbered, and one slice from each cake will already be cut and sitting on a plate, with three forks. You'll go to each cake, check the number against the scoring sheet, and then taste, judge, and move on. Drop your used forks into the empty cups behind the cakes. They'll be collected later."

Jules raised her hand. "Should our mics be on during judging?"

"No, keep them off. Jen is going to broadcast some music during the judging. That will let you discuss the cakes without being overheard by the audience. After you've filled in your scores, Ella will hand your judging sheets to Zoe, who is ready to enter them into her spreadsheet and tally the scores. Once she's done, Grace will check them, and together they'll hand the results to Ella, who will announce the finalists while the losing cakes are removed. The remaining, finalist cakes will then be arranged on the front table; a fresh slice from each will be plated and clean forks set out for each of you."

"That's when things get hard," Aunt Jo said. "It's always more difficult to judge once the riffraff is gone."

"It always is," Tiff agreed. "Which is why, after you re-taste the finalist cakes, you'll bring your notes and return here to figure out the winners. You'll have thirty minutes to confer and debate. Preacher Thompson arranged for the choir to sing as entertainment while the crowd waits."

Aunt Jo beamed. "They're going to sing a Britney Spears medley. I heard them practicing last night."

"Any questions?" Tiff asked. When no one said anything, she gave them a bright smile. "All right, then. We're ready. This way, people!" She held her clipboard over her head and led the way out, the judges falling into step behind her.

Angela went to follow, but Mark caught her arm. "Did Gray say how long he'd be?" he asked. "He hasn't shown up yet."

"I don't think he's coming."

"Why not?"

Angela glanced to where Ella was walking out the door.

Mark frowned. "I knew it! She dumped him again, didn't she?"

"He wouldn't say, but he looked upset."

Mark's mouth tightened. "You know what happened, and so do I. I tried to warn him."

And she'd tried to convince him to make a grand gesture, advice she was sure he'd ignore.

"Grandma?"

She realized Mark was staring at her with narrowed eyes. "What?"

"You look guilty. What did you do?"

"It's none of your business, but—" Heck, she might as well tell Mark what was going on with Gray. It wasn't as if it could be kept secret. "If you must know, I told him that if he was really serious about Ella, then he'd find a way to show her."

"Grandma, no! He should let her go and get on with his life."

"I don't think he listened to me, so you can relax."

"Good. That's the worst advice you could give him. He'll—"

A roar rose outside, indicating that the judges had stepped into the tent and Ella's fans had spotted her. Angela had to raise her voice to be heard. "Gray will figure things out. Let's go. I want to watch the judging."

Mark looked as if he might say more, but the noise prevented it. They made their way to the tent. There were no more seats, so they stood with the production crew along the side of a fabric wall.

The preacher, looking handsome in his black suit, invited Grace up on the stage to read a proclamation announcing the beginning of the Baptist Bake-Off. With that, they were officially underway. The next half hour passed in a blur as Aunt Jo, Jules, and Ella tasted, tested, marked, and wrote comments on cake after cake while Jen played some sort of music through the sound system. It had thumping beats and no lyrics, but the younger crowd seemed to love it.

Once the tasting was over, Zoe took the score sheets and went to a side table where her laptop and a small printer sat. In a remarkably short time, she pulled a page from the printer and showed it to Grace. After a whispered conversation, they handed the sheet to Ella. With a "Thank you," Ella turned on her mic and announced the finalists. Both cheers and unhappy murmurs rippled through the crowd.

Angela leaned closer to Mark. "Why do these people care who the finalists are? They can't possibly know the contestants."

"Before they started, Zoe asked Tiff to put up pictures of each cake along with their baker so people could get to know the contestants. Then someone on Tiff's team had the brilliant idea of adding a voting button so people could pick their favorites. Ella's sponsors are holding a drawing for a special prize pack that they'll give to one of the fans who picked the winning cake."

"A prize? I wish I'd known. I would have voted." She watched as Missy and Kristen moved the finalist cakes to the front table.

Grace stepped up to the mic and made announcements about parking and the location of an ATM while the judges went to work on the final round of cakes, tasting each one and making notes. Grace finished her announcements by inviting everyone to the final Apple Festival event, a bonfire at the high school football field, which was just behind the park. That done, she introduced the First Baptist choir. As they filed onto the stage, all wearing Britney Army T-shirts, the judges headed back to the greenroom for their final discussion.

"Let's go," Mark said. "I want to know who has the winning cake. I've got twenty bucks on Erma Tingle's coconut cream."

Angela thought that the deliberations would be better than hearing a Britney melody, so she agreed.

They'd just caught up to the others at the greenroom door when Aunt Jo's voice boomed over the speaker system. "That hummingbird cake was—"

Ella grabbed Aunt Jo's arm and pointed to her mic.

Aunt Jo muttered something under her breath, pulled her headset control from her pocket, and punched the button. The green dot faded. "I don't know how that happened. It turned itself on while it was in my pocket."

"The button isn't secure. You have to be more careful." Ella opened the door and let everyone inside. As the door closed, Ella collected three chairs and put them in a circle. "Let's do this."

She, Aunt Jo, and Jules sat down and began sorting their notes.

Angela inched closer, wanting to hear the final discussion.

Mark moved with her. "Now that it's quiet," he said in a low voice so the others wouldn't hear, "I wish you'd find Gray and tell him you didn't mean what you said earlier."

Angela waved her hand, her gaze locked on the judges. "He doesn't listen to me. Not usually."

"But if he does? Grandma, if he makes this grand gesture you suggested, it could be really embarrassing for both him and Ella. That was a—"

Jules turned to look over her shoulder at the two of them. "What are you guys talking about?"

Ella and Aunt Jo turned to see who Jules was talking to, curiosity on both of their faces.

Oh no. Angela cut Mark a warning look. "Don't—"

"We're talking about Gray," Mark said without sparing her a look.

"Grandma told him that if he really wanted to get back with you-know-who, then he should make some sort of a grand gesture."

"*What?*" Jules stood, her face set in angry lines. "Mom, why would you tell him something like that? Ella is not for him, and he knows it. She's going to leave the same way she did last time." Jules turned to glare at Ella, who sat stiffly, refusing to acknowledge Jules or anyone else.

That made Jules even angrier. In that moment, her pent-up frustration melded with her fury and it all spilled out. "Don't just sit there and pretend you don't have any say in this, Ella Dove. You've been flirting with my son like crazy this past month, without a care in the world as to how that'll affect him. And now you're going to pack up and leave, which surprises no one. That's who you are, isn't it? A heartless flirt."

Ella's face reddened. "Jules, this isn't the time or place to—"

"Oh, this won't take long. You've known how I feel about you ever since the day two years ago when you callously broke my son's heart *and* stole our family cookbook. Worse, you've used that very cookbook to further your own career. On stolen recipes, no less!"

Ella jumped to her feet and dropped her notes in her seat. "That's it. I'm tired of all these ridiculous accusations. That's not true, not a word of it! What happened between me and Gray is a private matter. And for the millionth time, I never took your recipe book!"

"You did! You're a thief and a liar, and if those people out there knew what you'd done, they'd leave you like the—"

The door flew open, and Gray stood there, glowering, Tiff peeking around him. "*Stop it!*" he thundered.

Jules flushed. "I'm sorry, but it's the truth and you know it. Ella—"

Tiff pushed her way past Gray. "*One of your mics is on!*"

What? Angela turned to look out the window. A crowd of young girls was on the other side of the glass, their phones held up. "Are they filming us?"

"Oh no," Jules said, looking stricken. "I didn't—"

"Close the blinds!" Tiff waved her hands. "Close the blinds *now*!"

Angela and Mark hurried to the windows and soon the blinds were all drawn.

"Whose mic is on?" Tiff asked frantically.

Ella turned to Aunt Jo. "Check your mic."

"It's not me!" Aunt Jo fumbled as she struggled to pull her mic box out of her pocket. "I turned it off twice now and— Oh. It was me." She clicked it off, sending Ella a regretful look. "Sorry. It must have come back on when I sat down."

"No, no, no!" Tiff pressed her hands over her face. "Ella, everyone heard that and there will be video, too. I—I have to get back out there and make an announcement. We have to do some damage control or— Oh Lord, this could be bad."

"I should be the one to speak, not you," Ella said, her face as pale as it had been flushed just a few moments earlier. "Those accusations were about me."

"What will you say?"

"The truth. That's all I have."

Tiff swallowed and then nodded. "Right. I'll buy us some time and ask the choir to do another round while you work out what you're going to say. I— Yes. The show must go on." She cast a disappointed look at Jules before leaving, with a regretful shake of her head.

Ella watched her go, her gaze stopping on Gray, who stood beside the door. Ella managed a weak smile. "I guess I'll have to leave town now."

He took a step forward, but then caught himself. Instead, he spread his hands wide. "I'm so sorry. Mom shouldn't have said that."

"He's right," Jules said, looking deflated. "Ella, I didn't mean for our conversation to be public like that. I lost my temper and . . . I'm sorry."

Ella threw up a hand. "Don't. We'll talk about that later. But right now we need to judge those cakes."

Looking miserable, Jules nodded and returned to her seat.

Angela's heart ached for her daughter. Jules was stubborn and proud, but she loved her sons with all her heart and was a lioness where they were concerned. Angela wished she could explain that to Ella, but there were too many people standing around. *I'll talk to her later. She needs to understand why Jules is so passionate about protecting her family.*

"Great day in the mornin'," Aunt Jo muttered. "This event is going to hell in a handbasket. Now the whole world thinks Ella is a thief, which is the most ridiculous thing I've ever heard, and I've heard *a lot* of dumb things in my life."

"You're right," Ella said wearily. "I didn't take that book. I wish I knew who did, though." She sat back in her chair. "But we need to focus on the contest right now. If you'll get out your notes, everyone, we can start."

The three judges went to work. Jules didn't speak much, and Angela noticed that although Ella was polite, she didn't once look directly at Jules.

Mark had been watching Gray, who still stood by the door. "He looks beaten."

Angela agreed. "It wasn't Ella who did that to him. It was your mom and her suspicions and you and your refusal to let him make up his own mind about his life."

Mark bit his lip. "It's not Mom's fault, Grandma. It's mine."

It was nice to see Mark admit his duplicity in this. "Neither of you has been fair to Ella."

"It's worse than that. I—" He closed his eyes and raked his hands through his hair. "I have to fix this."

Fix it? That would be nice. But Angela couldn't think of a single thing he could do that would smooth over the giant rip his mother had just made in Ella's life. "I wish you could—"

He walked with a suddenly purposeful stride to where the judges sat. "Ella?"

Gray took a threatening step forward. "Don't!"

"Good Lord!" Aunt Jo hopped to her feet, grabbed her cane, and stepped between Ella and Mark. "You Stewarts need to leave poor Ella alone!"

"Mark!" Angela hurried to catch his arm. "Leave Ella be! You've done enough as it is."

"I can't. I—I need to say this. And if I don't do it now, when will I?" Mark fisted his hands at his sides and clenched his eyes closed. "Ella, I need to tell you something. I know you didn't steal the Book of Cakes. It was me. I stole it."

CHAPTER 17

ANGELA

Angela poured two cups of tea and set them on the kitchen table. Gray sat at the chair at the end, his expression a mixture of fury and hurt.

"What a mess." Angela sat down across from Gray.

He sent her a hard, fuming look.

"Your brother—wow. I had no idea. And that after your mother just let it all out, as if she were a water hose with a crimp in it that suddenly released." Angela had hated leaving Jules behind, but she still had her bake-off duties to attend to. After Mark's confession, which had left Ella pale and shaking, she'd ordered everyone out of the room except the judges. *What a mess.*

Angela's phone beeped. "Mark and Jules are on their way home." She put her phone down. "That isn't going to be an easy ride for him."

Gray shook his head slowly. "I never thought Mark would do something like that."

"Me neither." She sighed and toyed absently with the tea tag. It was clear their little family needed to work on themselves and their relationships with each other, which made it all the more imperative that Angela stay. *I can't leave them now. They need me.* And, to be honest, she needed them.

Gray pushed his tea away. "Do you have anything stronger?"

She looked at her own cup and realized Gray was right. Tea was too weak for a moment like this. "Single malt whiskey?"

A faint of glimmer of humor softened the lines around his mouth. "I knew I could count on you."

"Of course." She got up and opened the door under the kitchen sink, bent down, and dug around a bit before she came out with a bottle of twelve-year-old Macallan. She pulled out two water glasses and poured them both generous measures and added some ice. "When your mom gets here, this is iced tea."

"Iced tea. Got it."

She hid the bottle once more and carried the glasses to the table.

He took an appreciative drink.

She sank back into her seat and watched him. They were silent for a long while until he sighed. "I guess it's a good thing Ella isn't staying in Dove Pond. I don't think anyone could survive the onslaught of gossip she'd have to face. She must hate me now."

"You didn't do anything. But the rest of our family? We need to work on a few things." That should have been hard to say, but it wasn't. Which was depressing. Angela took a small sip of her whiskey, the soft burn welcome after such an exhausting day.

"This family," Gray said with disgust. He sank back into his silence, but this time he took the whiskey with him.

She watched him over her glass. What a day. Jules's broadcasted accusations had shocked the crowd of Ella's followers. Worse, apparently several people—maybe even hundreds (Angela wasn't quite sure of the exact number)—had posted Jules's ugly accusations online.

Tiff had gotten her wind back and had gone into damage control mode, but even Angela could see she was worried it wouldn't be enough. From what Angela had overheard before she'd left, one of Ella's sponsors had already signaled their intention to pull their support.

Angela stared into her glass. *If only Aunt Jo had kept her mic on a moment longer so everyone could hear Mark's confession. All the crowd heard were Jules's horrible accusations.* After the winner was announced, from what Angela knew from the texts Jules had sent her, Preacher Thompson had tried to set the record straight by telling the crowd that, yes, there was a missing recipe book, or had been, but that Ella was innocent and the real culprit had confessed. But it was too late. The accusation was out there.

When they'd gotten home, Gray had checked Ella's social media accounts and had groaned on seeing that #recipethief and #EllaDoveFAKE were trending.

Angela sighed. "I never knew a video could go viral that quickly. Over a million views."

"And counting," Gray said grimly. "Tiff said people are already dropping off Ella's platforms like flies. People are calling her a pretender and a fake. It's bad, Grandma. So bad."

Angela nodded sadly.

The sound of a car door slamming came from the driveway. Angela leaned back so she could see out the window. "Your mom is walking as if she's got stick legs that don't bend, and Mark looks like he just swallowed a whole lemon."

Gray's jaw tightened, but he didn't say a word.

The front door opened and a moment later Jules and Mark came into the kitchen. Mark immediately came to stand near Gray while Jules put the two bags she was carrying on the table.

Angela instantly perked up. "Meatloaf specials?"

"I certainly didn't feel like cooking. Not now, anyway." Jules took off her coat and tossed it over a chair, then sat down. She pulled the containers from the bag and handed them out, putting Mark's in front of his chair. "Sit and eat, all of you."

Angela could tell from the way Mark was looking at Gray that he was torn between leaving and begging his brother for forgiveness, but after a stiff moment he sank into his chair.

"Is that whiskey?" Jules pointed to Angela's glass.

"This? Of course n—"

"I'll have one too, please."

Oh, wow. Two surprises today. "Sure." Angela got up and fixed Jules a glass of whiskey. "Mark?"

He shook his head.

Angela set Jules's glass in front of her and then sat back down. She forced a smile. "Well! Here we all are."

Gray ignored his food, his hand tightly closed around his glass.

Jules frowned. "You should eat."

"I'm not hungry."

Mark leaned back in his chair, looking exhausted. "Me neither."

Angela discovered she wasn't hungry either. What she really wanted was another sip of her whiskey, which she took.

Mark scooted even farther down in his chair. "We might as well get this over with. I need to tell you guys what happened that day."

Gray didn't even look at him.

Mark's hands, which lay in his lap, curled into fists. "Gray, I was an idiot. I know that now—but back then, I felt like I had to do something. Since I was little, I used to love the time we spent in the Hamptons. It was always the best of times for us. For the most part, no one argued, and things felt . . . I don't know, *right* in some way. But then Ella showed up. And after a while, it seemed as if she was destroying us."

Angela had just taken a sip of her whiskey, but at that, she looked up. "*Us?*"

"After Ella started visiting, the arguing began. Mom wasn't happy about her and Gray. And she blamed you for bringing her around, so you two were arguing. And Gray . . ." Mark gritted his teeth and leaned forward, resting his elbows on the table as he clasped his hands in front of him. "To me, it seemed that Ella was the problem, and I worried that the longer she stayed, the worse things would get."

"That was all in your head," Gray said.

"Maybe. But I knew what would happen to you after she left. I just wanted her gone. I didn't plan on taking the Book of Cakes, but one morning, as I was walking through the kitchen, I saw it on the counter and realized that was my chance. I just had to hide it. I knew Mom would blame Ella and make Grandma send her away."

Jules sent him a flat look. "Ella would have left on her own, without you doing that."

"Not as quickly. The longer she stayed, the worse it would be for Gray."

"Baloney." Gray's expression darkened. "If you all had spent more time getting to know Ella instead of plotting against her, none of this would have happened."

Mark sank deeper into his seat. "It was a stupid thing to do. I admit it. But I felt *someone* had to do *something*."

Jules shook her head, her disappointment obvious. "For the past two years, whenever we talked about our lost recipe book, you just stood there and let me think the worst of her. I can't believe you did that."

Gray took a swig of his whiskey. "All of you owe her an apology."

"I apologized to her," Jules said. "More than once, in fact. But it doesn't seem like enough."

Mark nodded. "I did the same, but—" He lifted his shoulders. "She said it was okay, but it was obvious she was still upset."

Angela watched how the light sparkled in her whiskey, a thought suddenly occurring. "Mark, where is the Book of Cakes?"

Mark looked at Jules.

She picked up her purse, pulled out the book, and placed it on the table. It was an old, old book, the cover threadbare in places, the binding loose, and the corners rubbed raw. Pages and pages of hand-written recipes on various pieces of paper stuck out at odd angles, scribbled writing visible here and there. "It was in the safe at the Moonlight this whole time, hidden in a box of old tax records."

Gray raised an eyebrow at his mother. "And you never saw it?"

"I thought it was in Europe with Ella," Jules said impatiently. "It never dawned on me to look for it at the café."

"Sheesh." Gray shot his brother a hard glare. "You're an idiot."

Mark slumped in his seat. "I know. After I took that stupid book, I didn't know what to do with it. You can't just throw out a family heirloom, and you sure as heck can't sell it, not that anyone would want it. So I put it in a plain envelope and hid it. Mom leaves the accounting to me now, so I knew it would be safe there."

"At least you took care of it," Angela said, trying to find the silver lining in this dark cloud.

Jules pushed her food away. "Gray, I'm so, so sorry. I shouldn't have blamed Ella, but I thought she was the only person who stood to benefit from stealing that cookbook."

Mark shot her a thoughtful glance. "That, and you were jealous of how well she and Grandma got along."

Everyone looked at Mark.

He shrugged. "I'm right, aren't I?"

Jules flushed. "That's not true. Although . . ." She slipped a glance at Angela. "It did seem a little unfair that you treated her as if she were a member of the family and you barely knew her."

"She likes a lot of the same things I do. She likes cooking and shopping and stuff like that."

"So do I!" Jules said. "You took her shopping and you two cooked together and were always laughing and—" She clamped her mouth shut and gave a tight shrug. "You like her."

Oh, wow. It was funny how you could believe with all your heart that you knew how someone you loved thought and felt, and yet you could be so absolutely and incredibly wrong. *What other things did I miss over the years?* She shook her head. "Jules, all this time, I've been wishing you were the one I could shop and cook with. Maybe . . . maybe I used Ella as a replacement because I missed having those times with you."

Jules winced. "I've been such a fool. I just—" She reached over and took Angela's hand in her own. "That's all behind us now. Mom, I'm glad you're here."

"Grandma?"

Without looking, Angela could feel the weight of Gray's hard gaze. He thought it was time she admitted her sins to Jules. He was right. She should do that very thing. She opened her mouth, but instead of a confession, she heard herself repeat, "We all owe Ella an apology."

"Good Lord," Gray muttered.

"Of course," Jules said. "She's probably packing up right now. I saw Sarah before I left and she said there was no way Ella could stay in town now."

"Sarah was sort of rude about it," Mark added.

Jules shrugged. "She was angry. She has a right to be. We weren't fair to her sister."

That was all well and good, but Angela could see no way to deal with the Ella situation other than giving her time. They all needed to sit back and let the chips fall where they might before they could pick them up again.

Which is a pity, but it is what it is. Angela wondered if it would look bad if she got up and refilled her empty glass. "This has been a very liberating and truth-telling day, but this whiskey is making me a bit sleepy and I need a nap, so . . ." She stood, taking her glass with her.

"Hold on," Gray said in a frosty voice. "This little family gathering has been special. We've been honest with each other, told secrets we've kept hidden, that sort of thing." His blue gaze bored into her. "Do you have anything to add, Grandma?"

Angela avoided looking directly at him. "No. I mean, everyone has secrets, right? I'm so tired—"

"Gray, let her go," Jules intervened. "She's not well, and this excitement can't be good for her. I daresay that whiskey wasn't a terrific idea, either."

Angela held her glass a little closer.

Gray crossed his arms and leaned back in his chair, his eyebrows raised. "Now."

That was all he said, but Angela knew she'd missed her chance to escape. *I have no choice. I have to face the music.* Angela sighed and sat back down, wishing she'd gotten more whiskey while she was up.

Confused, Mark looked from Gray to Angela and then back. "What's going on here?"

Angela took a deep breath. *Sheesh, this is hard.* "Jules, I need to tell you something."

Jules had her glass halfway to her mouth, but at this, she lowered it. "Yes?"

She's going to be so, so, so mad at me. I just know it. Still, it was time. Past time. "It's about my health. Or the seeming lack thereof." Angela took a deep breath and then jumped right in. "When I arrived that first day, I told you that death was a complicated thing, or that it was hard to face, or— Honestly, I don't remember exactly what was said, because I'd taken a sleeping pill for the plane. But whatever I said, you took it to mean that I was dying. Like soon. But I'm not."

Jules's eyes widened. "Mom. You're . . . *not* dying?"

"No. Well, we're *all* dying, in a general sense. But I don't have a due date on me or anything or— To be honest, I'm fine. There's no reason I shouldn't live to be a hundred, maybe more. I shouldn't have let you think I was on the brink of death, but you were so sweet after that, and we were getting closer, and having all the conversations we should have had before but couldn't, and I . . ." Tears threatened to close Angela's throat. She held her glass tightly with both hands and managed to get out one last sentence. "I couldn't give that up."

Oh God, that sounded so bad, even to me. Angela closed her eyes and waited for the eruption she knew would happen. *Which I deserve.*

"Oh, *Mom*!" Jules gave a muffled sob.

Angela was engulfed in a hug so tight that she couldn't breathe.

A hug. Not a rant or a fuming scream or anything else.

Just a hug. *She loves me. She really, really loves me.*

Her eyes suddenly wet, Angela slipped her arms around Jules and hugged her back. Gosh, how she loved this prickly, proud, stubborn child of hers. *Because she's just like me.*

After a moment, Jules pulled back. She grabbed a napkin from the holder on the table and dried her eyes. "I— That's the best news I've had all day." She gave a watery, shaky laugh. "Heck, the best news I've had all year. Maybe more."

Mark looked stunned. "I— That's— Wow. Grandma, I was pretty sure I had a lock on it, but I think you won the Biggest Secret Award of the day."

"Yay," Gray said in a biting tone. "Look at us, admitting all our lies. What a terrific, healthy family we have."

Angela ignored him and accepted a napkin from Jules. "I'm just glad that your mother isn't mad at me."

"Oh, I'm furious," Jules said, dabbing at her eyes. "Once this glow wears off, we're going to have a talk, you and me. But right now I'm just glad you're okay."

That was far more than Angela had expected. *Or deserved.* "I didn't plan any of it. I was higher than a bluebird when I got here and could barely speak. But I should have told you the next day."

"Yes, you should have."

The faint hint of disappointment in Jules's eyes made Angela's heart ache. "I came back to town hoping you and I could work through some of the damage caused by the divorce and our past. John always encouraged me to reach out to you more, but you never seemed to want that."

"I was hurt. But having you here these past couple of months has let me see that I've let it go on for too long. I've always loved you, Mom. I just hated how much our life changed because of the divorce, and I blamed you." She gave a small, bitter laugh. "I guess I'm like Dad and don't handle change well. It just made me so mad, and I had to blame someone."

"Oh, honey, I never wanted you to feel abandoned or unloved. Your dad and I both loved you. More than anything. But you made it so hard. I couldn't figure out how to get over the wall you built between us."

"Well, you did it. I just wish you hadn't done it through a lie."

"It was more of an omission than a—" Angela caught Jules's expression and flushed. "Sorry! It was a lie. I was wrong. And I'm deeply sorry."

Gray pushed his empty whiskey glass away and stood. "I hope you guys will excuse me. I need some fresh non-family air right now."

Angela looked at him, noticing with concern how white he was around his mouth. "Are you going to see Ella?"

"Why bother? After today, Ella Dove's had enough of our family to last her a lifetime."

Mark leaned forward. "You didn't do anything wrong. She knows that. Look, if it'll help, I'll tell her that myself."

"No," Gray said shortly. "It's over."

"Are you sure?" Angela asked. "Go talk to her."

Gray shook his head and headed for the door.

He'd almost reached it when Jules called out, "Gray?"

He stopped and looked back.

"Don't let this ruin things for you," she said softly. "Give her another chance, even if you don't give us one."

Without another word, Gray left.

CHAPTER 18

ELLA

There are dozens of ways to do every part of the baking process. It is up to the baker to decide which way works best for them and their recipe, whatever it may be.

The Book of Cakes, p. 130
Written: 1792–2019

Golden with a hint of pink, the morning sun gleamed through the windows of the Dove house kitchen. Ella emptied the measuring spoon into the mixing bowl and then stopped to take a long, deep breath of the cinnamon-scented air. There were health benefits to this spice, like antioxidants and anti-inflammatory properties. That was all well and good, but for her, it was the aroma that she loved best. The smell of good cinnamon soothed her when nothing else could. And right now, she could use some soothing.

She couldn't seem to free her mind from a slew of emotions so tangled, she didn't know where to begin unknotting them. Her thoughts jumped from Mark's agonized expression when he'd confessed stealing the Book of Cakes, to Jules's disbelief and then hurt, to Gray's growing anger as the events unfolded.

There was a lot of hurt in that family, and she wasn't sure why. But she was hurting, too, and it had been her own restless feelings that had sent her here, to the kitchen, well before the sun rose. She didn't know what exactly she was feeling. All she knew was that it was a lot, and in some ways, painful. *Think about cooking instead. You can't think about two things at the same time.*

She'd just reached for the measuring cup holding the confectioners' sugar when Kristen appeared, looking sleep-tousled in pink pajamas, her purple-streaked hair falling in her face.

"Good morning," Ella said. "I didn't wake you, did I? I've been trying to be quiet. I even mixed the dough by hand instead of with the mixer."

"Nah." Kristen yawned and stretched. "I usually get up about this time on school days. I guess it's sort of a habit now."

"That's right. It's a holiday for you today, isn't it?"

"Fall break. We have two days off." Kristen slid into a seat. "What are you making?"

"Cinnamon buns. They're proofing right now, but I should be able to put them in the oven in a few minutes."

"Oh, wow. I'm glad I woke up."

"They're better warm. And since you got up so early, you'll get the first one."

Kristen looked pleased. "Can I have extra icing?"

Ella nodded her approval. "You can always, *always*, have extra icing." She continued her work, the movements calming and clarifying, as they always were. She'd had a horrible night, tossing and turning this way and that. And when she'd finally fallen asleep, she'd had her dream again. This time, though, the cupcake hadn't chased her to the Stewart house, but instead had taken her by the hand and calmly walked her there. When they'd arrived, the entire house seemed to be lit from inside, glowing and warm. Ella had left the cupcake on the walkway and headed up the porch stairs. Just as she got to the top step, the door had opened, a brilliant light blinding her, so bright it had woken her up.

She'd lain in her bed, staring at the ceiling. It took her a long minute to realize that along one of her arms sat a tiny row of perfectly made pink-frosting rosettes. *Still? You have to be kidding me.*

And yet, she hadn't been as irritated as she usually was, which made no sense. Whatever answer she'd hoped to find in Dove Pond, she hadn't found it. And now it was time for her to go. *I guess I'll just have to get used to strawberry frosting.*

But that wasn't the worst of it. She would also have to get used to not seeing Gray. Her heart ached at the thought.

She sighed and pushed the finished icing to one side, forcing herself to smile at Kristen. "Do you drink coffee? I made some."

"Not plain coffee. Just lattes and stuff like that."

"Ah. I can't help you there."

"That's okay. Ava can make me one when she gets up. She's good at it." Kristen plopped her elbows on the counter and rested her chin in her hands. "I'm surprised you're up this early. Yesterday was a pretty big day for you."

"Too big. I didn't sleep well." Which was sad, as she'd come home late after the bake-off so exhausted she could barely stand. The scene with the Stewart family had been emotionally draining, but thankfully Tiff had kept the event on its feet. After Mark's big reveal, Tiff had gotten them all back on track. They'd rated the finalists and announced the winning dessert, a truly delicious brown butter cake. *I need to get that recipe from Rose Day.*

Ella gave a reluctant smile. Rose might be in her eighties, but when Ella had handed her the trophy, she'd acted as if she'd been crowned queen. She'd queen-waved to the crowd and then proceeded to pull out a set of note cards from her pocket and demanded she be given the time to deliver an Oscar-like acceptance speech.

A timer went off and Ella went to pull the pan of proofed rolls from their resting spot. She slid them into the preheated oven and closed it. "There. Now we wait. If you won't have coffee, how about some hot chocolate?"

Kristen's eyes lit up. "Yes, please."

Ella set about making some as Ava came downstairs in her PJs, tugging on a fluffy robe. "You guys are up early."

"Ella's making cinnamon rolls."

"Oh, wow! I love those." Ava perched on a stool beside Kristen. She watched as Ella pulled out the hot chocolate mix and some milk. "I suppose you'll be leaving soon."

"This evening. I'm going to follow Tiff and the group to the airport. We're taking the red-eye back to New York."

Ava's disappointment was palpable. "I wish you'd stay, but you know that."

"I do." She reached across the counter and clasped Ava's hand. "And I love you for it."

The doorbell rang. Ava frowned. "Who in the world would come by this early?"

"It's not Dad," Kristen said. "He's supposed to meet me at the tearoom before my shift for lunch."

Ava slid off her stool, tugged her robe together, and went to answer the door. Ella finished the icing while Ava spoke to their early-morning visitor.

Ava came back to the kitchen, frowning. "It's Mark and Angela."

"Tell them to go away."

"I did, but they said they've come to apologize. I invited them in, but they thought it might be better if they just spoke to you on the porch."

Those were the last two people Ella wanted to see, but she supposed she was going to have to do so at some point. It said a lot that Gray wasn't with them. *Don't think about him.* To be honest, she couldn't because every time she did, her eyes filled with tears.

She untied her apron and dropped it on the counter. "I won't be long, but if the timer goes off, can you take the rolls out of the oven?"

"Sure." Ava took over making the hot chocolate for Kristen without a word.

Ella grabbed her cardigan on her way outside, pulling it on as she stepped onto the porch.

"There you are," Angela said briskly. She was dressed in a trench coat, a scarf over her hair, making her look remarkably similar to Queen Elizabeth II. She jerked her head toward Mark, who stood beside her, hunched in his coat. "He has something he wants to say."

He shot his grandmother a frustrated look. "You make it sound as if I didn't want to come. I'm the one who said I needed to do this." He turned to Ella. He looked as tired as she felt, and she realized she wasn't the only one who'd been awake for most of the night. "I know we talked briefly yesterday, but I wanted to apologize again. Ella, I'm really and truly sorry for what happened. I shouldn't have done it. I just . . . I let my worry for Gray overcome my good sense all of those years ago. It was a stupid thing to do, and once I did it, I didn't know how to undo it."

Angela muttered something under her breath that sounded like "So stupid!"

Mark cut her a hard look. "At least I didn't pretend I was dying."

Angela's face reddened, but before she could retaliate, Ella said hastily, "Mark, thank you for coming. I appreciate the apology. And hey, I have sisters, and if one of them needed me, I'd do whatever I could to help them too."

He brightened, looking relieved. "Thank you. I was afraid you'd be too mad to talk to me. I wouldn't have blamed you if you were."

Ella shrugged. "I've got a lot going on. To be honest, I'm just relieved the book has been returned. Your mother was pretty certain I'd taken it."

"My mom is going apologize, too, but she's working right now. She'll be over later."

"There's no need."

"There is. She wasn't very fair to you. None of us were."

Ella eyed Angela. "And you? Are you going to apologize, too?"

Angela adjusted her purse where it hung over her arm. "Mark, you can go to the car now."

He frowned. "Why would I—"

"I'll be there in a minute. I need to speak with Ella." When he didn't move, Angela added, "Alone."

He sighed and sent Ella a frustrated look. "You see what I have to deal with?"

"Oh, I know. Trust me."

Her instant reply made him smile. "I'll be seeing you at the Moonlight before you leave town, I hope."

"I might make it this afternoon. I have to say goodbye to Aunt Jo. Besides, do you think I'd let something like this keep me from your meatloaf special one last time?"

He flushed. "Thanks. That's . . . I don't know what to say."

"Your grandmother's right about you. You make the best meatloaf in the South."

"She said that? Grandma, that's quite a compliment."

Angela sniffed. "You can bask in your glory in the car. I need a minute with Ella and I'm getting cold."

He closed his eyes a moment as if silently counting to ten and then said, "Fine! I'll wait in the car. Ella, see you around."

Angela waited until the car door closed and then she turned to Ella. "Has Gray been by?"

Ella's heart stuttered. "No."

Angela looked disappointed. "I'd hoped . . ." She pressed her lips together. "I guess it's not meant to be, then."

Ella could have told Angela that, but she couldn't get the words out. "I don't want to talk about him."

"Of course. I'm going to apologize, because that's what I came to do, but I have to say, I feel as if this little episode has been good for us. It's made things even."

"Even? You made me drive you all over town and—"

"I know what I did. And yes, I'm sorry that happened. But apologies don't fix things, do they?"

Ella frowned. "They can help."

Angela made an impatient gesture. "When we first spoke, you wanted something. I think you called it an absolution?"

"For something I didn't do!"

"I know that now. I think, in a way, I knew it then, too. When the Book of Cakes went missing, Jules was certain you were the one who took it. I was trying to regain her trust—heck, I've been trying to do that since she was eleven—and so I took her side." Angela's clear blue eyes, so like Gray's, searched Ella's face. "I shouldn't have done that. I knew you well enough to know you'd never do something like that. And I let that moment ruin one of the best friendships I've ever had. I regret that."

Wow. "Thank you. I missed our friendship, too."

"We should focus on that. I didn't come today to hear Mark apologize. You know he's sorry for what he did, and that as stupid as his actions were, he was acting with good intentions. I knew you'd forgive him." Angela's gaze narrowed. "But I also knew you'd be thinking about how heavy everything in Dove Pond seems right

now, and how you are itching to escape it and start fresh somewhere else."

Ella tugged her cardigan closer and crossed her arms against the
morning chill. "I like starting fresh."

"It can be nice to start over now and then. But you've made a habit
of it. I came this morning to tell you I'd like us to be friends again, to
bake together and go shopping together. I enjoyed that. But we can't
do that if you leave."

"Look, I hear what you're saying, but—"

"No buts. You need to stay here, in Dove Pond. It's time you
stopped leaving, Ella, and started arriving."

What did that even mean? "Angela, I can't—"

"Pssht. Don't 'can't' me. I'm the Queen of Can't. I can't admit when
I'm wrong, I can't face my own bad decisions. Heck, until recently, I
couldn't get my own daughter to love me—" She stopped and pursed
her lips. "Well, that's going better, but still . . . You know what I mean.
Ella, I've seen Gray look at you, and it cuts me every time."

Ella's face heated. "That's between me and him."

"Yes, it is. But do you want to know why it hurts so bad when I see
how Gray looks at you? It's because that's how John used to look at
me. And I'd give my right leg—heck, I'd give *both* of my legs—to see
that look just one more time. Just for a second. If Gray isn't in love
with you yet, he's well on his way. But if you leave, you'll never find
out what that's like. What the two of you are like."

Ella had always thought John and Angela's love was special. "I
always envied you and John."

"We were lucky to have found each other. Stay in Dove Pond,
Ella. Stay with Gray. Give him, and yourself, the time to see what
you have."

"Angela, that's— I don't know if I can do that."

"You should at least try. He's been defending you, you know. He told us all off, and even got Mark to promise he'd video his confession and send it to your assistant."

Ella didn't know what to say. Her heart ached, and for some reason, knowing Gray was trying to help made it worse. "Mark doesn't have to do that."

"Tell that to Gray." Angela tilted her head to one side. "It's scary, isn't it? Taking a chance on someone. You always run before things get painful. I'm in pain right now because John is gone. And it's a deep, deep pain, Ella. I live with it every day. But I wouldn't have given up five minutes of the time I spent with him, even knowing I'd have to live with this pain for years after. That's how big of a joy he was, how wonderful our time together felt." A tear slid down Angela's cheek. "It was so, so worth it."

Ella's eyes were far from dry when she stepped forward and hugged her friend.

Angela hugged her back, hard. "Give him a chance, Ella," Angela whispered. "Give us all one."

They stood there a long, long minute, and then Angela gently released Ella and wiped her eyes. "I'd better go. Mark is due at the Moonlight for the breakfast shift. Jules will have my hide if I don't have him there in time."

"Thank you for coming, Angela. I can't promise I'll stay, but I'll think about it."

"You'll do what's right for you. When the time comes to make that decision, you'll know the answer."

Ella managed a smile. "I'm not sure I have what it takes to make a relationship work long-term, never mind calling a place home indefinitely. I get restless and afraid and then—" She lifted her shoulder. "That's me. Who I've always been."

"It would be sad if we never changed, wouldn't it? I don't know your path, Ella. Only you get to choose that. But give it some thought.

See if, maybe, it's time to find a new way to deal with your emotions rather than trying to leave them behind." Angela put her hands on Ella's shoulders. "You're capable of so much more than you know." She gave Ella a slight shake and then released her. "Now go. I don't know what deliciousness you're baking this morning, but I can smell it from here, and you'd better get it out of the oven before it burns." Angela gave Ella a final, tremulous smile and then turned and headed for the car, where Mark waited.

Ella pulled her cardigan tighter around herself and watched them leave. As Mark's car turned out of the driveway, a faint breeze shook the trees and sent a welter of leaves raining down on her like confetti. Ella turned her face to the sky and closed her eyes, letting the leaves fall where they might. *Is Angela right? Is it possible to find a love deep enough to soften the pain that same relationship can cause? It would be nice to believe that. But I don't know if I can.*

Being with John might have been the right thing for Angela, but there were no guarantees that Ella and Gray's relationship would be just as wonderful. *I need something, a sign or a feeling of security or . . . Sheesh, I don't know what I need. Whatever it is, I haven't found it yet.*

Sighing, she brushed a leaf from where it clung to her shoulder, and then went back inside.

CHAPTER 19

ELLA

*Reminder: Never underestimate how much love
can be found in a perfect piece of cake.*

The Book of Cakes, p. 147
Written: 1792–2019

Later that night, Ella reveled in the quiet as she sat on the front porch, her suitcases already in the trunk of her car. In a while, Tiff and the crew would arrive in their rental van, and she would follow them to the airport.

Inside, she could hear Sarah and Ava talking as they did their laundry. Ten minutes ago, she'd come downstairs with her luggage and said her goodbyes, promising to return at Thanksgiving. She wouldn't, though. She'd spent enough time here. Her heart couldn't handle her spending any more.

Her phone pinged, and she looked at it. Tiff was on her way, so Ella stood and collected her tote bag. Tiff had been a whirlwind since the bake-off fiasco and had done an amazing job shifting the online commentary. She'd called every influencer she knew, promising all sorts of future assists if they put out messages of support for Ella. It was an old trick, but it had worked. Mark's confession had helped, too. Tiff had widely distributed the video and it was one of the most watched on TikTok.

That was sweet of him, especially since he knew he'd be in for some online abuse, which has been harsh and immediate. Ella grimaced. *Some people can be so brutal.*

Tiff seemed relieved that both the sponsors and followers were back on "Team Ella," as she'd called it, but Ella didn't care. They were what they were, and she knew all too well that public attention was fickle and shallow. She was a free spirit, she told herself, and this weekend had only reaffirmed her long-held belief in the joy and simplicity of being alone.

And yet . . . she couldn't forget Gray, his smile, or that he'd defended her. She hadn't needed him to, but it was nice he'd cared enough to try. *I'm going to miss him.*

It was an odd feeling, missing someone before she'd even left. In her whole life, she'd never felt this way. *But then, I'm tired and it's been a difficult few days.*

Sighing, she tugged her coat closer as the chilly evening breeze sent dead leaves rustling across the driveway. Maybe . . . maybe she was being too hasty. Maybe Angela was right and she should stay a little longer. "Nonsense," Ella muttered to herself. "I can't. I'm finished here. I thought I'd find answers and maybe end those annoying dreams, but instead I was publicly embarrassed and—"

Lights approached. *Ah, the van.* She headed down the walk, the van lights blinding. "Hi, Tiff. I—"

The lights turned off and she realized it was Gray's truck sitting in the driveway. He climbed out and faced her, the wind mussing his hair and tugging at the corner of his flannel shirt. "Hi, Ella."

Suddenly, all the desolation she'd felt earlier crashed into her heart and her vision grew blurry. "Gray, I—"

"Don't." He came down the pathway. "Just stay there. I have something to say, and then I'll leave you alone."

But despite what she'd just been telling herself, she suddenly realized that she didn't want him to leave her alone. She opened her mouth to say so, but the words wouldn't come. Her emotions were so raw, so strong, that she almost crumpled under them. *What the heck is wrong with me?*

He stood in front of her. "I've been trying to figure this out. Us out. And I can't. But I've realized one thing." He took a deep breath, his gaze locking with hers. "Ella, I love you."

She blinked. She normally avoided those words like the plague. She never said them, and she hated hearing them. Usually, a sentence like that would set her feet flying and her desire to leave would grow tenfold.

But this time, something odd happened.

She found herself standing still, her heart pounding, but not in a restless, "better run" way. Instead, the steady beat warmed her, even in the evening chill.

"I love you and I'm not going to just walk away from that. So . . ." Gray took a deep breath. "I've made a decision. If you'll have me, wherever you go, I'll go."

What? "You'll go with me? To New York?"

"Wherever you want. New York, Spain, Australia—I don't care."

She didn't know what to say to that. "Gray, I— You can't do that. You love your new place. You just bought it, and the house isn't even done yet."

"I know," he said simply. "I'll figure it out."

"And what about Adorbs and the other animals, and your hydroponic system, and—"

"Don't worry. Mark can watch the animals for now. He owes me. But that's not what's important. What's important is us and our future and—" He gave a broken laugh. "You just have to say the word, and I'll be there. I know you like your freedom, your space. I'll give you as much of that as I can. But, Ella, I'm not finished with this. No matter what it takes, I want to at least try. Over the years, I've met a lot of women, but they were all wrong. They were wrong because they weren't you."

Ella could only stare up at him, unable to think past the most important words he'd uttered. He loved her. She'd heard those words before, but she'd never felt them. And this time, oh, how sweet they were. It was as if every word were a macadamia wrapped in velvety chocolate.

He gave an odd, awkward laugh. "It's been a weird, horrible twenty-four hours. I'm sorry about my family, what they did. I can't promise they'll behave themselves. I can't control them, or myself, apparently. I— Geez. I'm rambling. I'll just . . ." He grimaced and raked an impatient hand through his dark hair. "Damn it, I had this speech all planned and I can't get it out."

She understood exactly how he felt, because a raft of words had collided in her throat too, and she couldn't speak either.

"I guess I've said everything I should, but . . . Ella, I love you and I accept you for who you are, a wanderer, a never-stay-anywhere person. If that's what makes you happy, then fine. I'll find a manager for my place and go with you. Because as much as I love my house and the farm, it'll never be a home without you."

She closed her eyes. She loved him, too. She always had. But was it enough? What *was* enough? *We have so much going against us—our history, his family, my wanderlust. So many things.*

"Oh, geez, you look upset. Ella, don't—I'll leave. You know where to find me if—"

"Wait." That one word seemed to unjam all the others that had been stuck in her throat. "I've never had a serious relationship, not a real one. I've told myself I hated them for so long that . . . I guess that's who I think I am. Or thought I was. But maybe I've been lying to myself. Well, obviously I was, or I wouldn't feel like this—"

He flashed her a look so full of hope that she took a deep breath, letting the fresh air fill her lungs. It helped to clear her thoughts. "Sometimes the thing we say we hate the most is really just the thing we're the most afraid to fail at. I'm afraid of staying somewhere, of making a home, of loving someone and then losing it all."

"Oh, Ella. We're all afraid of that."

Ella nodded slowly. "If this doesn't work, we'll both be wrecked."

"Completely." He gave her a lopsided smile. "But I'm not some soft little daffodil, and neither are you. Whatever happens, we'll figure it out and we'll survive it."

"But doesn't love mean that you do your best not to hurt the other person?"

"Love isn't painless. Sometimes it hurts just because it's raw and real and vulnerable. But never loving . . . Ella, I'm telling you right now, that's worse than a broken heart."

The evening breeze tugged at her coat and made her shiver. As she crossed her arms, her fingers brushed something sticky.

Startled, she stopped and looked down. There, on her fingertips, was a faint slash of strawberry frosting drawn into a tiny heart.

"What's that?" Gray captured her hand and lifted it so the porch light shone on her fingers. "That's strawberry frosting."

She nodded.

"That's my favorite. Every year, for my birthday, Mom bakes me a cake with strawberry frosting."

She looked down at the frosting, her eyes widening. *Oh my gosh. It wasn't Angela at all. It was Gray.* She closed her hand over the small heart, and her fingers tingled. When she opened her hand, the frosting was gone.

Unbidden, tears filled her eyes.

"Ella?" His fingers brushed her cheek. "Please don't cry. I—"

She threw her arms around him and held him tight, her heart beating against his.

She knew what she wanted.

Over the past few months, each step she'd taken had been a step toward Gray and a step away from the life she'd once lived. It had been a step toward the house she'd grown up in and the little town that had always welcomed her, even when she'd ignored it. Each step had been a step toward where she was meant to be, toward her future, where she was free to be herself.

This was where she wanted and needed to be, now and forever. Here, in Gray's arms.

In that instant, Ella Dove knew she had come home.

EPILOGUE

ELLA

It isn't about perfection, but about richness. It isn't about sweetness, but about love. It isn't about the prettiness of the decorations, but about sharing something you made with your own hands with those you love the most. Those are the qualities of a truly memorable dessert.

Written by Jules Stewart in 2023
The Book of Cakes, p. 203
Written: 1792–2023

Ella shoved her Santa hat back from her eyes and pulled the pan of blueberry scones out of the oven. "Careful!" she told Kristen and Missy, who were hovering nearby, both wearing the exact same striped leggings that made them look like Christmas elves.

"Can I have one now?" Missy asked, her eyes locked on the pan.

"Only if I get your assigned portion of ribs." Ella did love ribs, but so did just about everyone at their winter cookout today. Her phone buzzed, and she looked at it, smiling when she saw it was from Tiff. *Have a merry Christmas!* she'd written.

Ella texted back a string of Christmas emojis. Tiff was still doing her usual magic, Ella's media numbers were growing once again, and the flap from the bake-off was long forgotten.

"Hmm. This would make some good content." She scanned the pear torts, rhubarb crumble, and warm scones now sitting on the counter beside Aunt Jo's massive hummingbird cake. "Would you guys mind getting some good shots for my accounts?"

"Us?" Kristen couldn't have smiled any wider. "We'd love to!"

Missy nodded eagerly. "You take pictures of the food already on the table. I'll get some of the decorations."

Ella watched them head to the dining room, smiling when she saw Dylan kneeling beside the fireplace, examining the tiles on each side, Ava pointing out which were loose. Ava had jokingly threatened to never again speak to him if he didn't fix the surround, which meant he'd shown up with his toolbox and a grin.

"They're so cute," Sarah said, coming with Zoe to sit at the counter.

"Adorable," Ella agreed.

Zoe fiddled with one of her reindeer earrings as she eyed the desserts. "I wonder how long it'll be before there's a wedding here at Dove House." She cut a measuring look at Sarah. "Someone has to be first, right?"

Sarah blushed. "Maybe."

Ohhh, that wasn't a very strong "maybe." "I, for one, already have a cake planned, for whoever it is," Ella said. The funny thing was, she wasn't kidding. In the weeks since Ella had decided to move to Dove Pond permanently, she'd found herself involved in so much more than her own life and romance, which were both going well. Really, really well, if she were honest.

Her gaze moved past Sarah and Zoe to where Gray stood outside by the grill in his Carhartt coat, his Santa hat a match to the one she wore. He was laughing with Blake, Mark, and Preacher Thompson, who were all huddled around the grill for warmth. Gray must have felt her gaze, because he looked up, and his eyes brightened when he saw her, a sexy half smile curling his mouth.

She smiled back. She loved him. Loved his laughter and his teasing. Loved how tender he was with the border collie puppy he'd brought to the farm just a few weeks ago, and how gentle he could be when he caught her crying over a movie in the middle of the night.

If she closed her eyes now, she'd remember this morning when they'd stayed in bed, talking and laughing and loving. So far, life with Gray had turned out to be far, far different from her expectations. It was fun, exciting, and rewarding—everything she'd never thought a dedicated long-term relationship could be.

She was enjoying every minute, although Gray was still holding firm about "going slow." They hadn't moved in together yet, even though (surprisingly) she'd suggested it more than once.

It helped that he understood her better than she understood herself and had gone out of his way to make life on the farm wonderful, even letting her design her dream kitchen. But the best part was that whenever he suspected she was beginning to feel restless, he planned a trip out of town, sometimes just a long weekend in Asheville or Savannah, but it was enough. Those brief but romantic trips eased her wanderlust and made her enjoy coming home. *Home, where I belong.*

She'd learned a lot since she'd returned to Dove Pond. She'd learned that love didn't always arrive neatly wrapped and labeled. She'd learned that family, as messy as it could be, could keep you warmer on a cold winter day than any fireplace. But most of all, she'd learned that real magic didn't come from exciting adventures, social media clicks, or a fat bank account. Real magic came from finding just the right type of chocolate to make your favorite cookies with. It came from that ease and comfort you got when you walked down a street you really, really knew. It came from eating hot biscuits with honey butter with your sisters at the same kitchen table you'd sat at when you were five. And it came from waking up with the man who made you smile.

"No one makes a cake like Ella," Zoe sighed. "Sarah, you're so lucky. You're going to have the best wedding cake ever. All you need now is a dress and a preacher."

"And a groom. Blake and I are doing well, but he hasn't asked me yet."

But he would. They all knew it, too. Ella picked up a tray of cookies and carried them to the buffet beside the Christmas tree, glancing into the sitting room as she passed. Aunt Jo sat in front of a crackling fire, talking to Angela and Jules, who seemed closer than ever. Meanwhile, Kristen's grandma stood nearby, laughing at something Angela had just said.

Smiling, Ella returned to the kitchen and focused on the vanilla bean icing she was making to drizzle over the scones. *One day at a time. That's the best way to live. No more fear of the future or lingering in the past. There's just today, and that's enough.*

"Hey!" Mark came inside. "Blake sent me for the sauce."

Ella nodded toward the blender.

He loosened the plastic jar and started to go, but then paused. "Gray said your numbers were back up on your social media sites, thanks to your little trips here and there."

"And Adorbs," Sarah added. "Ella, you need to set that calf up with his own page. He's gold."

"He's photogenic, that's for sure." Ella noticed that Mark was staring at Zoe.

He lifted his hand. "Hi, Zoe."

Ella and Sarah exchanged amused glances.

"Hi," Zoe said without looking up from where she was searching for fallen crumbs under the rack where the scones were cooling.

"Listen, this might sound abrupt, but . . ." He took a deep breath and then said quickly, "The theater in Asheville is having a play this Saturday. I mentioned it to Aunt Jo, and she said you might want to go."

Zoe reluctantly gave up her search for crumbs. "What's the play?"

"*A Tree Grows in Brooklyn.*"

Sarah squealed. "Oh my gosh! Zoe, you've read that book. You loved it."

"Hmm." Zoe eyed Mark for a moment. "You're paying?"

"Of course." He waited, looking eager and uncertain.

"And driving?"

"I'll have my car detailed, too."

"Zoe!" Sarah rolled her eyes. "Say yes already. You read that book for a reason. This must be it."

Mark flushed. "Hey, if she doesn't want to go, that's fi—"

"I'll go," Zoe said. "Saturday. Pick a good restaurant. I like steak."

"Great. I'll pick you up at five." He looked so happy that Ella had to smile. Over the past few months, she'd gotten to know Gray's family better and she was on the verge of liking every one of them—even Jules. *Who would have thought that would happen?*

Beaming and looking a little dazed, Mark carried the sauce back to the patio. He must have told Gray and Blake his good news, because they started congratulating him, pounding him on his shoulder until he protested.

A crash from the dining room made Ella turn around.

"Oh no!" Sarah and Zoe hurried toward the sound.

Ella joined them in the dining room. Dylan was still crouched beside the fireplace, a large tile shattered at his feet.

Ava had her hands on her cheeks, her mouth a perfect O.

"What happened?" Zoe asked.

Kristen and Missy, who were on the other side of the big table, were on their tiptoes, trying to see. Kristen pointed to the fireplace. "Dad was trying to see which tiles were loose when one gave way."

"But look what's under it," Missy said, her eyes wide.

There, under the tile, was a small black iron door.

Aunt Jo had just come into the dining room, her cane in hand. "What the heck is going on?"

Angela leaned forward. "It looks like a tile fell out of the fireplace surround. And look, there's a little iron door."

"Is it a bread warmer?" Ava asked.

"It's smaller than any bread warmer I've seen," Dylan said. He dusted off some of the crumbled mortar and then hooked his finger in the iron ring that was on the front of the door. He tugged once. Twice. The third time, it opened.

Ava leaned over his shoulder to see what was inside.

"Move!" Aunt Jo said. "We can't see anything."

"There's a box in here." Dylan pulled it out and handed it to Ava.

"Oh, wow." She dusted it off and then carried it to the table.

Everyone crowded around. It was an old cigar box, the faded mustard-colored cover featuring a man fishing in a stream while a girl in a red dress hid behind a tree, watching him.

Ava opened the box.

Ella had to lean to one side to see around Sarah. Inside the box was a bundle of old letters tied with frayed ribbons, and some very old photos. An old necklace with a silver key hanging on it was curled in one corner.

Ava fished out the necklace and held it up, the old gold shining where the sunlight streamed in from the windows.

"Who could have put that there?" Zoe asked, obviously awed.

"I have no idea." Ava returned the necklace to the box and then reached for the letters. She opened one, and then another. "There's no names here. Just initials."

"Which initials?" Kristen asked.

Ava set the letters back on the table. "*R* and *T*."

Sarah made a frustrated noise. "The two most common letters in the alphabet."

Ava picked up the photos. "Oh my gosh. I don't recognize the man, but the woman . . . That's Sarafina Dove."

Sarah's eyes widened. "No way!"

"Who's that?" Missy asked.

Sarah took one of the photos from Ava. "Sarafina was a journalist back when most women didn't have jobs. She did some amazing reporting, uncovering all sorts of corruption and— She's mentioned in a book in the library. I'll get it for you."

"Wow." Kristen peered at the photos. "Who's the man?"

"I don't know," Ava said. "It could be her husband, but . . . she didn't meet him until later in her life. I—geez, I have no idea who that is." She gave a knowing smile. "I guess I'm going to have to make a phone call."

Ella knew instantly what Ava was thinking. "Tay."

"There's no better researcher. She's always been fascinated with Sarafina, and you know how she loves a mystery."

Sarah had to agree. "It'll take her a day, maybe less, to figure it out. But then we'll know and—"

The doors from the patio swung open and Blake and Mark entered, each carrying a platter piled with ribs. "Dinner's ready," Blake said, as he and Mark placed their platters on the table in between the waiting sweet potato dish and baskets of rolls.

"I'll put these away." Ava scooped up the contents of the little box. "We should eat while the food is hot."

Sarah looked around the table. "I'll bring in the iced tea." She headed to the refrigerator. "I'll get the green bean casserole from the warmer, too."

While she did that, Ava set the box out of the way on the fireplace mantel before sitting at the table.

Ella took her seat, Gray swiftly claiming the one beside hers. She watched with a smile as everyone gathered around the table, all of them talking at once, the hum of their voices as comforting as a warm quilt on a cold winter morning.

This was home. And although Ella didn't know exactly what the future held, she couldn't be happier.

THE MOONLIGHT CAFÉ'S COCONUT CAKE

clee

Cake

- 1½ cups (3 sticks) salted butter plus 2 teaspoons (to grease the pans), room temperature
- 3 cups plus 2 tablespoons of cake flour
- 2 cups granulated sugar
- 5 large eggs, room temperature
- 2 teaspoons vanilla extract
- 1½ teaspoons coconut extract
- 1 teaspoon baking powder
- ½ teaspoon baking soda
- ½ teaspoon salt
- 1 cup whole milk
- ⅔ cup sweetened shredded coconut

Frosting

- 1 cup sweetened shredded coconut
- 2 (8-ounce) packages cream cheese, room temperature
- 1 cup unsalted butter, room temperature
- ¾ teaspoon vanilla extract
- ¼ teaspoon coconut extract
- 2 cups confectioners' sugar, sifted

Make the Cake

Preheat the oven to 350°F. Grease two 9-inch round cake pans and line the bottoms of each pan with parchment paper. Grease the paper and sides of the pans, then dust each pan with a tablespoon of flour.

Using an electric mixer on low speed, mix together the butter and sugar until light and fluffy.

Add the eggs one at a time, mixing well after each addition.

Add the vanilla and coconut extracts and mix. The mixture will look slightly lumpy.

Sift together the remaining flour, baking powder, baking soda, and salt. Add the dry mixture to the wet mixture on low speed, alternating with the milk. Mix just until combined. Fold in the coconut.

Divide the batter evenly between the prepared pans and use a spatula to smooth the top of each.

Bake for 45–55 minutes, or until a toothpick inserted in the center of each comes out clean. Cool in the pans for 30 minutes, then remove the cake layers from the pans and finish cooling on wire racks.

Make the Frosting

Line a baking sheet with parchment paper and spread the sweetened shredded coconut in a thin layer. Bake at 325°F for 6–8 minutes, or until the coconut just starts to brown at the edges. Remove from the oven. Allow to cool completely.

In a clean bowl, with the mixer on low speed, combine the cream cheese, butter, and vanilla and coconut extracts. Add the confectioners' sugar and mix just until smooth.

To assemble the cake, spread a ½-inch-thick layer of frosting on the top of one cake layer. Top with the other layer and frost the top and sides of the cake. Sprinkle the top and sides with the toasted coconut.

ANGELA STEWART'S
HUMMINGBIRD CAKE

Cake

3 cups plus 2 tablespoons of
  all-purpose flour

1½ cups granulated sugar

1 teaspoon baking soda

1 teaspoon salt

2 cups very ripe mashed bananas

1½ cups canola oil

1 cup chopped walnuts

1 (8 ounce) can crushed pineapple,
  drained

3 large eggs, room temperature

Cream Cheese Frosting

2 cups confectioners' sugar

1 (8 ounce) package cream cheese,
  room temperature

2 cups butter, room temperature

1 teaspoon vanilla extract

Make the Cake

Preheat the oven to 350°F. Grease and flour two 9-inch round cake pans.

In a large bowl, sift together the flour, sugar, baking soda, and salt.

In a separate large bowl, mix together the mashed bananas, oil, walnuts, pineapple, and eggs until completely combined.

Stir the flour mixture into the banana mixture until combined. Divide the batter evenly between the prepared pans. Gently tap the edge of the pan against your palm to settle the mixture until it's smooth on the surface.

Bake for about 1 hour, or until a toothpick inserted into the centers comes out clean. Allow to cool for 10 minutes on a wire rack before loosening the sides of the cake from the pan with a dinner knife. Place a cooling rack on top of the pan and swiftly flip the cake onto it. Repeat with the other cake. Allow cakes to cool completely before icing.

Make the Frosting

In a medium bowl, use an electric mixer to beat together the confectioners' sugar, cream cheese, butter, and vanilla extract until smooth.

To assemble, when the cakes are completely cool, spread a ½-inch-thick layer of frosting on the top of one cake layer. Top with the other cake layer and then frost the top and sides.

AUNT JO'S
CARAMEL APPLE CAKE

Caramel Sauce

Note: Before you begin making the caramel sauce, make sure you have everything ready to go, and that the cream and butter are right next to the pan. Making caramel is a fast process that cannot wait for hunting around for ingredients. If you don't work fast, the sugar will burn.

½ cup heavy cream	½ cup water
1 teaspoon vanilla extract	1 cup granulated sugar
¼ teaspoon ground cardamom	6 tablespoons salted butter

In a large measuring cup, thoroughly mix the cream, vanilla extract, and cardamom. Set to one side.

Put the water in a heavy-bottomed 2- or 3-quart saucepan and add the sugar. Place over moderately high heat.

As the water begins to heat, stir gently but constantly with a whisk or wooden spoon. Do not allow the mixture to splash up the sides of the pan as you stir or it might crystallize. (Hint: You can brush water up the sides of the pan before heating it to reduce the tendency of the sugar to crystallize if it comes into contact with the cooler sides of the pan.)

As the sugar melts, reduce the heat a bit to keep it from burning. Continue stirring until all of the mixture has thickened and the temperature reaches 350°F on a candy thermometer. (The mixture should be a medium amber color.) Immediately add the butter and whisk until melted.

Remove the pan from the heat. Slowly count to three to allow the caramel to cool enough to keep it from foaming, then carefully add the cream mixture, and whisk until smooth.

Let the caramel sauce cool in the pan for a couple of minutes, then pour it into a glass mason jar and let cool to room temperature. (Remember to use pot holders when handling the jar filled with hot caramel sauce.) If not using immediately, place the lid on the jar and store in the refrigerator for up to 2 weeks.

To reheat the caramel sauce, microwave in 30-second intervals just until warm and pourable. Alternatively, heat in a double boiler or a heatproof bowl set over a pot containing a small amount of simmering water.

Cake

Apple Topping
1 cup caramel sauce
1 teaspoon ground cinnamon

2 large (or 3 medium) apples, diced into approximately ½-inch pieces

Cake
½ cup plain yogurt or Greek yogurt
1 cup granulated sugar
3 large eggs
1 teaspoon vanilla extract
2 teaspoons baking powder
½ teaspoon salt

1½ cups all-purpose flour
½ cup canola oil
1 cup caramel sauce

Whipped cream or ice cream, for serving (optional)
Caramel sauce, for serving (optional)

Preheat the oven to 350°F. Line a 9-inch round cake pan with parchment paper. Grease the paper and the sides of the pan.

Make the Apple Topping

Pour ⅔ cup of the caramel sauce into the prepared pan and tilt the pan to coat the entire bottom. Sprinkle with the cinnamon, then add the diced apples in an even layer; the apples should cover the caramel sauce.

Make the Cake

In a large bowl, whisk together the yogurt, sugar, eggs, and vanilla until smooth. Add the baking powder, salt, and flour. Whisk to combine. The mixture will look lumpy.

Add the oil and stir well until the mixture is smooth.

Pour the batter into the prepared pan. Bake for 35–40 minutes, or until the top of the cake feels springy to the touch and a toothpick inserted into the center comes out clean.

Cool the cake in the pan for 10 minutes, then use a dinner knife to loosen the sides of the cake. When you're done, cover the pan with a plate and quickly invert the pan to allow the cake to drop onto the plate. Slowly and carefully, lift the pan off the cake.

Pour the remaining caramel sauce over the cake. Serve warm or at room temperature, with a dollop of whipped cream or ice cream, if desired.

THE
SECRET RECIPE
of
ELLA DOVE

KAREN HAWKINS

This reading group guide for **The Secret Recipe of Ella Dove** *includes an introduction, discussion questions, and ideas for enhancing your book club. The suggested questions are intended to help your reading group find new and interesting angles and topics for your discussion. We hope that these ideas will enrich your conversation and increase your enjoyment of the book.*

INTRODUCTION

Three lives converge as a wildly talented baker returns to Dove Pond to face her past in this entry in the charming series that proves that sometimes miracles really do happen. . . .

Ella Dove is an acclaimed baker whose desserts spark cherished memories in those who taste them. A restless soul, Ella goes wherever the wind takes her—but this time, she's coming home to Dove Pond. Years ago, her mentor, Angela Stewart Harrington, falsely accused her of stealing her beloved family recipe book. Now, driven by a haunting dream, Ella believes it's time for them to reconcile.

Angela has her own share of amends to make. Her daughter, Jules, has never forgiven her for divorcing her father, and they've been estranged ever since. But just as Angela begins to hope that she and Jules might fix their tattered relationship, a miscommunication turns into a lie that could destroy everything.

Meanwhile, Jules's son, Gray, is shocked to learn that Ella, his first love and first heartbreak, has returned to Dove Pond. But even though he knows Ella is a wanderer and will soon leave, he's unable to stop himself from falling for her a second time. Can Gray find a way to convince Ella to give him, and their magical town, a serious chance? Or is he once again on the road to a broken heart?

With so much at stake, Ella, Angela, and Gray must learn to accept one another—flaws and all—forgive the many mistakes of their pasts, and trust that love can, and will, always find a way. For fans of Alice Hoffman and Sarah Addison Allen, *The Secret Recipe of Ella Dove* is a delicious read that will warm your heart and charm your senses.

TOPICS & QUESTIONS FOR DISCUSSION

1. When we're introduced to Ella Dove, she is grieving the loss of her father—a loss that left "a void in her heart that was so big, she feared she might fall into it and be lost forever" (page 2). Years later, we meet Angela when she is experiencing similar feelings of loss following the death of her husband, John. Hawkins writes that Angela "used to think death was the worst thing that could happen to a person, but now she thought it was being left behind. She was deeply lonely, and had she stayed in New York, she was certain that loneliness would have killed her" (page 38). How do Ella and Angela grapple with loss and subsequent loneliness? Discuss the similarities and differences between their responses to grief, and feel free to bring other characters from Dove Pond into the conversation.

2. Ella and Gray are described as "polar opposites." In high school, Ella "was outgoing and had tons of friends and lots of dates, while [Gray had] been a quiet, silent sort who watched the world through a dark lens" (page 59). Besides physical attraction, what do you think draws Ella and Gray together? Do you agree with the Stewart family—is Ella an incompatible match for Gray and inconsiderate of his feelings?

3. Angela and Jules have an obviously complicated relationship, which we mainly view through Angela's perspective. Angela believes the divorce from her first husband should have been simple, but Jules's distrust of change and refusal to accept John continues to be a wedge in their relationship. Do you think this is a fair assessment on Angela's part? Put yourself in Jules's shoes and try to understand this story line from her vantage point. What do you think Angela and Jules must do to mend their past wounds?

4. As one of her many attempts to clear her name with the Stewart family, Ella bakes a cake for Angela. It's difficult for Angela to resist Ella's bribery because the beauty of an Ella Dove cake "wasn't just the flawlessness of the bake, or the richness of the flavors, although they were something to behold themselves. It was the unexpected memories those perfect combinations of flavor and texture stirred. The glimpses of special, exquisite moments from one's past were astoundingly real and, oh, so precious" (page 118). In the book and real life, what roles do food and scent play in the invocation of memory? Have you ever tasted something that you felt had magical qualities? Something that reminded you of a specific moment in time?

5. Ella's intended short stay in Dove Pond keeps getting prolonged. Her unresolved feud with the Stewart family is one contributing factor, but there is also a push from her assistant/social media manager to capitalize on Dove Pond's small-town charm. How do you feel about Tiff's character? Does she have Ella's best interest at heart? Hawkins creates a world of magical fantasy that simultaneously mirrors many aspects of our own reality. Do you know any Tiffs in your life? Feel free to open these questions up to a broader discussion about the power of social media in Dove Pond and within your own communities.

6. Ella returns home in search of answers to an unusual, reoccurring dream: a giant cupcake with strawberry frosting chasing her through the streets of Dove Pond. The dream is always followed by the appearance of annoying and inconvenient dollops of strawberry frosting in her actual life. Ella's dreams become more unsettling when she starts driving Angela around town and is startled one night to find "a long streak of beautifully piped pink frosting swirling from her ring finger all the way up to her shoulder" (page 137). What do you think are the meanings of Ella's wherever you go'" (page 18). Do you agree with this sentiment? By the end of the novel, do you think Ella agrees? Discuss how Ella's decision to stay with Gray in Dove Pond reflects not only character growth but a deeper understanding of Aunt Jo's earlier words of wisdom.

12. The epilogue begins with an entry from Jules in the Book of Cakes. Jules writes, "It isn't about perfection, but about richness. It isn't about sweetness, but about love. It isn't about the prettiness of the decorations, but about sharing something you made with your own hands with those you love the most. Those are the qualities of a truly memorable dessert" (page 325). Given that Jules captures a central message of the story, what examples can you recall of characters bonding through a shared meal? What examples of this can you recall in your own life? How and why do you think food brings people together?

ENHANCE YOUR BOOK CLUB

1. Bake one of the desserts mentioned in the book. A few ideas include Aunt Jo's Caramel Apple Cake (page 337) and Ella's strawberry shortcake with homemade whipped cream (page 117), but there are a lot of other recipe options woven throughout Ella's story.

2. Create your own Book of Cakes with either family members or friends by collecting everyone's favorite recipes and baking tips. Print multiple copies of everything and host a scrapbooking night, or (for a more easily shareable, eco-friendly option) use an online recipe organizer. Try not to lose anything!

3. Consider hosting your own Bake-Off. It doesn't have to be as big as the event in Dove Pond. Gather some eager participants for an afternoon of baking and tasting. If you think you can get a sizable turnout, perhaps charge each attendee a small fee and contribute the proceeds to a worthy cause.

dreams and corresponding appearances of strawberry frosting? Why do you think the appearance of the frosting gets worse after her arrangement with Angela?

7. In a rare moment of vulnerability, Ella shares with Gray that she doesn't find Dove Pond as "suffocating" and "dismal" as she has previously expressed. But she's tired of people seeing her as "a Dove sister" (page 164) rather than as an individual. How would you describe Ella's relationship with her sisters? Do they share any of Ella's noncommittal, adventurous personality? If not, what do you think is the root of Ella's restless nature?

8. Angela comes round to admit that she and Ella have "a lot in common: a love of desserts, a sharp sense of humor, and a rather startling, sometimes-not-always-acceptable free way of seeing life" (page 201). She wishes that she and Jules could share similar interests and qualities. Compare and contrast Angela's relationship with Jules to her relationship with Ella. Do you think Angela has a healthier relationship with Ella than with her own daughter? Why or why not?

9. With the Bake-Off drawing near, Jules has a difficult conversation with Ella about Ella's ending things with Gray. Chapter 12 concludes with a question about Ella and Gray's relationship: "Did they continue on their current path until they faced a certain heart-shredding ending, or did they protect themselves and end things now when they still had enough of their good sense left to move on and enjoy life?" (page 237). How have Ella's feelings toward Gray and Dove Pond changed throughout the novel? With this in mind, do you think Ella will take Jules's advice?

10. Mark reveals at the end of chapter 16 that he's the one who stole the Book of Cakes. Did you expect this, and do you feel that his reasoning is justifiable? How does Mark's honesty serve as a catalyst for forgiveness between other characters?

11. When Ella first arrives home, Aunt Jo tells her, "'You can't move to happiness. You have to find it where you're at so you can take it with you